"What begins as a deceptively cutesy urban fantasy soon ups the ante with the gathering darkness and sharp details of the ongoing price of magical servitude. This is a fireball of a start to Nelson's Grimm Agency series." —*Publishers Weekly*

"Nelson is no one-hit wonder, as this new tale is as dark and wondrously twisted as the first. If you like your fairy tales a bit grim (yes, pun obviously intended), then this is the series for you!" —*RT Book Reviews*

"J. C. Nelson's twisted, quirky take on fairy tales is pure fun! . . . Prepare to be entertained!" —*Fresh Fiction*

"Nonstop action, an awesome cast of characters . . . an excellent opening to a new series!" —All Things Urban Fantasy

"The plot moved quickly and the pacing was steady, keeping me well entertained, and the characters, specifically Marissa, were fantastic . . . A good read." —A Book Obsession

"The twist on our world, on fairy tales, on society in general, is great fodder for some fantastic escapism . . . [Nelson] has obvious talent." —Bookworm Blues

"An exciting, action-packed debut that will have you up till the early morning and laughing out loud till your inside[s] hurt." —Short & Sweet Reviews

the
REBURIALISTS

J. C. Nelson

ACE BOOKS, NEW YORK

ACE

An imprint of Penguin Random House LLC
375 Hudson Street, New York, New York 10014

Library of Congress Cataloging-in-Publication Data

Names: Nelson, J. C., 1973–
Title: The reburialists / J. C. Nelson.
Description: New York, New York : Ace Books, 2016.
Identifiers: LCCN 2015026951 | ISBN 9780425278192 (paperback)
Subjects: | BISAC: FICTION / Fantasy / Urban Life. | FICTION /
Fantasy / Paranormal. | FICTION / Fairy Tales, Folk Tales, Legends &
Mythology. | GSAFD: Paranormal fiction | Fantasy fiction
Classification: LCC PS3614.E44564 R43 2016 | DDC 813/.6—dc23
LC record available at https://lccn.loc.gov/2015026951

PUBLISHING HISTORY
Ace trade paperback edition / March 2016

PRINTED IN THE UNITED STATES OF AMERICA

10 9 8 7 6 5 4 3 2 1

Cover art by Tony Mauro.
Cover design by Daniellè Mazzella Di Bosco.
Interior text design by Tiffany Estreicher.

Penguin
Random
House

For Isaac

Acknowledgments

This book would not exist without the aid of a number of people who listened as I bounced my ideas off them, read drafts so raw they contained splinters, or helped me revise and polish until this became something I'm proud of. Thanks to the gang at CC. Laurel, Andy, John, Lexi, and Chris, I really appreciate your time. My agent, Pam Howell, remains a bundle of awesome. My editor, Leis Pederson, gave me great insights into how to make the story even better. And my family, who put up with me getting up early and going to bed late as I told yet another story. Thanks to you all.

the
REBURIALISTS

I

BRYNNER

Putting the dead in their graves was easy; keeping them there gave me a full-time job. A job that came with hazard pay, full medical coverage, and a life insurance policy that covered every form of death from being buried in a lost tomb to getting stung to death by scorpions. It didn't cover getting stabbed on a fire escape by a jealous woman. So I climbed the fire escape of a hotel in Greece like the building was on fire (it wasn't) and like my life depended on making it to the top (it probably did).

Beneath me, my date from last night's champagne ball cursed in Greek. The only part I understood for certain was my name, Brynner, and that her name was most definitely *not* Athena. Athena would be her sister, my date from two nights before.

I patted the knives sheathed on my hips and checked my messenger bag. Wallet? Check. Passport? Good. Cell phone? Thank God. Fresh pine branch, sharpened to a point? All the essentials.

Not that any of those would help me against an angry woman or her sister.

On the rooftop, I crouched behind two air conditioners. They rattled and labored against the summer night.

"Brynner?" She insisted on mispronouncing my name. Briner is what you soak a ham in before you cook it. Brynner, like the grin I'd turned on her the night before, was mine. She looked over the edge of the far side. All I had to do was wait for her to climb down, and I could make a dash for the roof access door.

My cell phone rang from inside my bag, like the worst-timed game of Marco Polo ever.

She spun, zeroing in on the noise. "Brynner." She circled the air conditioner to where I crouched, my shirt unbuttoned, the white bandages across my chest barely concealing fresh stitches.

"Hi . . . Elena."

She pointed the knife at me, trembling with rage. We'd enjoyed a wonderful room-service breakfast until she answered the hotel door and had an awkward conversation with her sister. "What is my name?"

My cell rang again, the emergency tone. I flipped it out with one hand and kept my eyes on Dimitra. Dina? Now that I thought about it, it wasn't clear which of the two lovely embassy representatives had chased me out the window. "Can you give me a moment?" I asked her, holding both hands up as I backed away. Jealous women and angry badgers deserved their space. "Brynner Carson speaking."

A computerized voice on the other end barked out, "We have a situation, asshole. Get a move on to the shipping district. Car's out front." That would be Dale Hogman, field team commander of the Bureau of Special Investigations.

"Call someone else. We just had a situation, and I'm in a bit of a situation myself right now."

Elinda? Athena? She yelled at me in Greek, something about a goat and my mother.

"Is that the native you had draped over you last night? Saw her on the telecast." Dale didn't bother hiding his amusement. Or his familiarity with the scenario.

"Could be her twin from the night before." I'd consumed more than my share of wine even before moving to a more private celebration.

"Love her and leave her. We've got a moldy-oldy on its feet. Trust me, no one else is going to be able to handle this one." Dale cut the call off, right as Etria came for me.

She swung the knife at me in a high overhand arc, not bad for killing a mummy, but not the best way to carve out a man's heart.

I stepped to the side and caught her wrist, spinning her around.

A younger me would have leaned in to kiss her before dashing away. A younger me once got kicked in the family jewels for doing exactly that, so I let her land rump first and ran for the stairwell. Two nights ago I was a celebrated hero. Last night I was an honored guest, and by tomorrow morning I wouldn't be able to smile at a waitress in the city without getting spit on.

Women talk.

And that is exactly why I preferred my day job, my night job, my going-to-get-me-killed job. I sprinted down the stairs, met the driver at the front door of the hotel, picked up my bag of equipment from the passenger seat, and called back in to headquarters on my phone. "Brynner Carson. Give me the details."

"Now you're in a rush? Sure you don't want some more time

to work things out?" The strangled gasp from the other end sounded like a man's throat being crushed, but I knew better. I'd seen Dale in person enough times to know he was just taking a cigar puff through his tracheal tube.

"I don't think couples counseling will help. I'm on my way." I strapped on my Kevlar and titanium body armor while the driver careened down cobblestone streets. "Situation report?"

"Like I said: Corpse woke up a few hours ago. Took apart three guards and half a cargo crew."

We continued downhill into the port, veering past cranes and loading trucks. "Near the water?"

"Better. On a *boat*."

"Bullshit." Even on my first day working for the Bureau of Special Investigations, even on my first assignment, I knew better than to think you'd find a meat-skin going for a swim, or even a stroll on the beach.

Dale waited so long I thought he might've dropped the call. "No. And that ain't the freakiest part. It knows you."

My hands froze, leaving one boot untied. Freakiest part in this particular conversation was a series of contests. Freaky that a three-week-old corpse had reanimated and gone on a rampage? A little. Well, not really. More like just about every day working for the BSI.

Freaky that one had done so on a *boat*? Completely. Contact with living water could drive the Re-Animus straight out of the shell. That scored an eight on the scale of batshit crazies, where one would be the homeless guy at the grocery store, and at about five we hit dead things. "How can you be sure?"

"This one's talking."

I yanked my boots tight and shook my head. "Bullshit."

"And writing hieroglyphics in blood."

"Bullshittier."

Dale laughed, a rumbling cough that sounded like he'd need to tweeze a piece of his lung out of his breathing tube. "And if you believe the cargo guys who got away, this one's asking for you by name."

That killed the friendly banter deader than the corpse had been a few hours earlier. Because meat-skins, or the Re-Animus running them, *never* spoke. Though I wanted to sleep in the sun for a month, I couldn't let this one get away.

"Happy hunting. Don't get dead." Dale clicked out.

I rode the rest of the way in silence, wondering where my life went wrong. Probably around eighteen, when I walked into a BSI field office, signed my name, and asked where the nearest dead thing was.

The car pulled to a stop and I got out, a walking armory of wood and religious symbols from damn near every religion on earth, including a few that sane folks didn't practice anymore.

The police stepped out of my way. Sure, the cops might handle normal criminals, but they left the dead to us. Donuts didn't have a habit of ripping your insides out and playing with them. As I passed, they made the sign of the cross, which was fantastic, assuming the meat-skin I was up against had been Christian. Not a bad guess for Greece, where Orthodox Catholics made up the majority.

I tore the cordon out of my way and walked up the cargo ramp alone.

I hated cargo ships, and not just because they housed warrens of steel boxes with narrow pathways, perfect for a meat-skin to hide in. I hated them because I could get seasick just *standing* on a boat. Hell, I puked in a canoe at summer camp.

At least it let me tell a lie, that my stomach was roiling because of the waves, not because I was hunting something that killed six men less than an hour ago. Something that might well be hunting me in turn.

Closing my eyes for one moment, I listened, threading my way through a forest of sounds to find the one that didn't fit. Dale hadn't lied. Beneath the undercurrent of traffic and the splash of waves, a voice like gravel and coffins echoed in the hull of the ship.

Which meant I wasn't dealing with your garden-variety walking corpse. Dale had been right to call me. It was a Re-Animus. An unholy spirit known for animating the dead and tearing apart the living. Again.

It whispered into the shadows, mumbling at times and moaning at others.

Dad said Re-Animus never spoke, for fear of what secrets might slip out. That the act of stealing a body was so heinous that their very souls cried out to be imprisoned the way they imprisoned others. Controlled the way the Re-Animus did the dead.

Someone never mentioned that to this one.

Stake in hand, I jogged along the deck till I came to a cavernous hole leading to the cargo bay. Imagine a football field inside a boat. Now turn off the stadium lights, and turn loose one recently live corpse run by something so foul we had to invent a word for it.

That, right there, is why I looked forward to vacation.

I hopped down stacks of cargo containers, well aware each hop sent a booming echo through the hold. The meat-skin might be dead. The Re-Animus in the driver's seat would have had to be to miss my coming.

And things grew weirder still.

In the distance, at the far end of the hold, a torch flickered. Not a flashlight. The Re-Animus had lit an honest-to-God torch, like a tiki torch. It illuminated a dim circle on the vast hull of the ship, and in the flickering light, the meat-skin shambled back and forth.

Dale called it a moldy-oldy. Meaning someone dead a few weeks. Plenty strong but not exactly a threat so long as people did the sane thing and *ran*. Away, not toward it like I did. Fresh corpses could be downright deadly.

The ones everyone feared, the mummies, could barely move, let alone threaten someone. The worst they might do is get dust all over you when they disintegrated. This body had all the signs of a grave robbery gone wrong. The grave cuffs still hung from one wrist.

It turned toward my light, one eye sagging and the other wild. And began to laugh. "Carson. Finally." So the Re-Animus was still on board this corpse. Fully present. Fully capable. Odds were, it was the same one I'd dealt with two nights before, though it hadn't been so talkative then.

"That is one ugly ride you picked. It's an island. Couldn't you find someone who'd spent at least an hour in the sun?" I stayed just beyond the torchlight, hopefully farther than it could leap.

It took a step forward, staggering to the left. "I had a great body. I had a whole collection of them, before you showed up to ruin things. We'll settle that some other time. I've come to speak with you, Carson."

"I'm not really in a mood to talk, but I could arrange for a therapist to call you, if you want."

The corpse turned away, slouching back toward the hull,

where it resumed painting by gnawing a finger and dabbling with the blood that oozed out.

Score: Dale, 3. The thing wasn't writing. It was drawing. Technically, it was writing as well, since the pictures were hiero-glyphics.

While it had its back turned, I crept up on it as stealthily as I could, my stake drawn. Green pine could suck the power right out of the meat-skin, killing a chunk of the Re-Animus. The key? Getting in the first blow. I leaped forward, driving the stake down in an arc meant to strike just above the shoulder and continue down into the rib cage.

The Re-Animus caught my hand without looking. "Carson, you killed one of my favorite bodies that way not three days ago."

I was in trouble.

The last body was fresh and fast, designed to ambush the unwary, but this one had been chosen for a different purpose. After I'd destroyed its last host, the Re-Animus must have spent the last three days pouring itself into this body, building it up for pure strength. Under the force of its grasp, the armor on my wrist crackled and shifted.

It swung another hand around, gnarled fingers grasping at my throat. I didn't wear a titanium neck brace for style, but neither could I keep my feet on the floor as it lifted me higher, then twisted my head so I couldn't look away.

"I came to deliver a message." Its foul breath washed over me, the stench of rotten fish and clogged toilets. "The old man's body molders, and now she stirs. Give back the heart, Carson. Carson's blood took it, she whispers in dreams. Carson's blood will pay if it isn't returned."

He liked to talk, so while I could still breathe, I wanted to set a trap, luring information from it that might lead me to its true home. "Let's say I had it, and I wanted to give it to you? Who would I send the heart to?"

"The darkness follower. The edge walker. The eater who lives in sin and walks the new temple. You know only what I am commanded to tell you, lesser Carson."

And that right there, that pissed me off. With my free hand, I drove a stubby silver blade into the arm holding me, and when my feet hit the floor, I hurled myself at the meat-skin. Four years of high school football taught me how to lead with my shoulder, drive with my feet.

Using my momentum to drive a stake through an animated corpse when we hit the hull wasn't covered in physical education, though. Thank God my dad had homeschooled me in corpse killing.

The stake sizzled and popped as it drove the Re-Animus out. Black clouds of smoke billowed out into the night. To me, dying Re-Animus smelled like burning hair. Three breaths later, I stood alone. Me, a once-again dead body, and the lap of the waves.

I snapped a picture of its finger painting with my cell phone and called Dale. "I put our walker back to bed. You've got to see what it was drawing. I'm sending a picture now."

After a moment Dale swore. He'd tweaked the inflections on his voice module to get the curses just right. "You didn't repeat any of that out loud, did you?"

"According to you, I can barely read the instructions on a condom wrapper. Pretty safe bet I didn't read the glyphs. That what I think it is?"

When Dale spoke, his voice trembled, as much as it could, being mostly mechanical. "Wipe it off the walls, get the hell out of Dodge. I'm booking you a flight back to the U. S. of A. We need to talk to the director."

I rolled the corpse over, making sure it was dead for good. "The Re-Animus threatened me. It might just be some sort of curse."

I waited for what seemed like an eternity for Dale to answer. "No. I've seen that pattern before. I think it's a spell."

2

GRACE

I didn't do evenings, weekends, or fieldwork. Not because I had a six o'clock bedtime, a social calendar, or a problem handling guns. Working for the Bureau of Special Investigations didn't pay well enough to justify staying past five, missing the evening news, or getting torn to pieces by an animated corpse.

So a phone call at three in the morning on a Saturday from the BSI headquarters in Seattle started my day off wrong. Having to travel from Portland to Seattle before seven o'clock on a weekend didn't fit my idea of an auspicious beginning. If I had my way, starting the workday during single-digit hours would be illegal.

I made good time, catching the train in Portland, and then a cab to BSI headquarters at the south end of the lake. Like every day in Seattle, the clouds hung overhead, obliterating vitamin D and drizzling depression on every inch of the city. No wonder those folks worshipped coffee.

Unlike our Portland branch, BSI headquarters in Seattle never closed. I walked through the door at a quarter to six, waving to the security guard in the lobby.

He looked me over, letting his gaze linger in all the wrong places, and gave me a cheesy smile. "Receptionist training doesn't start until eight, miss. But if you wait, I'll show you around the cafeteria when it opens for breakfast."

I let the friendly demeanor I preferred to use drain away. I could be a bitch if I had to. "That's *Senior* Analyst Grace Roberts. I'm here for an emergency meeting, so you can sign me in now and show yourself the cafeteria." Men tended to look at my hair and think, "Blonde, and dumb." They'd look at my face and say, "Barbie got a college degree." God only knew what they thought about my figure, but regardless of what my first supervisor thought, the only assets I used to advance my career were between my ears, not my legs.

He kept his mouth shut while I signed the logbook and scanned my badge. When I stepped out of the elevator on the twentieth floor, I found a shriveled, ancient man in a lab coat waiting. His white skin had more liver spots than a leopard and enough spider veins for an army of tarantulas. I read the tag on his coat and froze.

Dr. Alvin Thomas, BSI head of Analysis. Meeting Dr. Thomas was like meeting Elvis, the president, and Albert Einstein all at once. Dr. Thomas turned out to be depressingly short, making my six feet feel like eight.

He peered up at me through thick glasses, and the wiry white mustache on his face spread as he smiled. "Grace Roberts. So good to finally meet you, after reading so many of your papers."

I froze.

My papers? I'd jotted down theories on the BSI contributor net, more rambling rants than proper papers. "Which rants—I mean, what subjects did you find—"

"Your theory on viral susceptibility for Re-Animus control. Your field protocol for proper assessment of control violation." He nodded. "And of course, your rebuttal to Operative Kingman's protocol for dispersal of evil. While I could have requested almost any translator, I would prefer the assistance of another skeptic."

The field teams carried iron crucifixes and wooden crosses, garlic and a million other herbs. Relics, they called them. Yet behind every one of these, a principle surely lurked. Herbs, for instance, might interfere with communication pathways in hosts. Iron impurities might disrupt communication. Wood could (and did) cause allergic reactions.

Even the Re-Animus, or controlling mind, was more likely a composite organism than an evil entity. Such opinions did not earn me many drinks from my coworkers. My aversion to mixing business and pleasure earned me fewer invitations to drink at all.

"I'm definitely skeptical." I reached out, and he shook my hand in a weak grip.

With that, Dr. Thomas turned and opened the door, leading me into the lion's den. Inside, the mauling had already begun, delivered by the BSI director herself, Margret Bismuth. Meeting Dr. Thomas fulfilled one check box on my bucket list. I'd imagined meeting Ms. Bismuth, but in my mind, it involved power lunch at "Women of BSI" and trading stories, not getting glared at on entry.

An average-height African American woman with mottled brown skin, she radiated power. From her crossed arms to the way she looked over her bifocals, everything about her gave off an essence of pure authority. Her silver hair and sharp features made it easy for men to distort her into a caricature, judging from the notes I'd seen posted on Analysis message boards. I stood, smiling, as she roasted the older man across the table, her tone a blast of napalm. "Dale, I believe it's time for you to explain why you'd wake me up at midnight for something like this."

Her victim stammered, then sat up. When he spoke, his voice was a machine, mechanical, but broken in gasps. "We found another spell, ma'am, in Greece."

Dr. Thomas and I snorted in unison. A spell? Hardly. The field teams labeled anything that disrupted a Re-Animus a "holy relic," even the most disjointed vocalizations became "a curse," and in the rare occasion that a corpse so much as stumbled into a wall, the resulting marks got called "a spell."

Director Bismuth clicked a key on the presentation screen, bringing up a picture.

Taken by a drunk on a cheap cell phone by the light of the moon, the image was less writing and more a jumble of incoherent glyphs. My training kicked in. Like any writing, the key was to pull out distinct terms and break them from pictures to concepts. The tension that had built up in my shoulders drained out as I fell into a comfortable pattern.

I walked around the table, entranced by the images.

Before I ever became interested in pathology or radio waves, before I developed my first composite theories, I'd had a solid job reading hieroglyphics. But this writing looked like the scrawlings of a syphilitic maniac.

I pointed to one image, the sign of a pintail duck. "What made this? What was the writing implement?"

Blank faces stared back at me, until Director Bismuth cleared her throat. "Ms.—"

"Roberts." Dr. Thomas answered before I could. "Grace Roberts, senior analyst. Her theories on co-organisms . . ." He trailed off under her withering gaze.

"Ms. Roberts, did I invite you to speak?" Her eyes shifted to Dr. Thomas. "Or to this meeting at all?"

I took a seat across from the field team, beside Dr. Thomas. He waved a hand, as if it were an explanation. "Ms. Roberts is here at my request. Our normal translator came down with an unfortunate case of maternity leave."

Director Bismuth scanned the field team. The man with the mechanical voice had to be their field commander. The one on his left, their equipment manager. Her eyes stopped on the last man. His silver pin identified him as a field operative, but that wasn't what caught my attention.

From the close-cropped black hair to the prominent nose, his face resembled a renaissance sculpture more than a man. Not a model but a man of action, and probably little thought. Wide shoulders and an easy stance said he wasn't afraid at all of meeting the director.

Which meant he'd probably never met her before.

She nodded to him. "Go ahead."

With flowing ease, he rose from the chair, easily my equal in height, if not experience, and strode to the screen. "These parts were here when I arrived. This over here, the meat-skin wrote with its finger. Well, what was left of it."

His voice, rich like coffee with caramel, brought a smile to my lips.

One I squelched.

"That explains the sloppy penmanship." I pointed to the vast smudge in the middle of the picture. "But not that."

He laughed, a deep baritone. "That's where I tackled and staked it."

How could he be so cavalier? Such artifacts gave us our best insight into the Re-Animus consciousness. From them we'd pieced together theories that actually made sense, compared to "evil spirits" and "demonic possession."

I risked the director's wrath to drive my point home. "Do you have any idea what you did? What the value of these scenes are?" I couldn't help myself. The clearest sample of co-org writing in one place I'd seen in six years, and not only did he kill the co-organism, he destroyed the evidence.

He put his hands together and bowed his head. "I'm sorry." His tone said differently. "I was more concerned about the fact it was trying to crush my windpipe than about taking a picture for the fridge."

What kind of rookie with dreams of "monster hunting" would engage up close and personal with a co-organism? "Why didn't you use standard tactics? Back off, trap it? Pin and hold? We could have had firsthand samples."

I hadn't made it six years in the BSI without learning to pay attention. The stares, the hidden smiles suggested I'd made an embarrassing mistake.

Director Bismuth cut in before he could answer. "His field team is currently short three members; Operative Carson took appropriate measures. What can you make of the remnants?"

Carson. As in Heinrich Carson? BSI operative number one? He'd been hunting co-organisms long before the government got involved. No. Heinrich Carson would have been at least sixty if he were still alive, ready to stake out a desk instead of a co-org.

Which meant the cocky man in front of me had to be—

"Brynner Carson." I didn't mean to speak his name out loud. A name associated with as many disasters as perfect operations. A man I'd heard stories about more than once.

He grinned back at me and winked. "Guilty as charged."

No wonder people told stories about him, though the Brynner Carson before me didn't quite live up to the legend. No woman on his arm; no smell of alcohol on his breath. In fact, a seeping bloodstain over his right pec told me the man could and did bleed.

I looked back to the director. "It's interpretive. Neither completely phonetic or symbolic, these glyphs indicate host exposure to late Egypt. If memory serves, it's a passage from *The Book of the Dead*. At least, it was."

I ignored the laser pointer, choosing to move closer to the screen and point things out myself. "This would have been interesting. This"—I pointed out the smudged area—"is repeating the same set of ideas over and over. Unique content was in the destroyed area; this represents degeneration of the pattern, where it simply repeats."

Director Bismuth nodded, her eyes flicking over and passing on, in what I took as a form of approval. "And what is it repeating?"

I broke them down again, trying to keep my gaze on the screen instead of the man it wanted to wander to. He watched me, his eyes locked on my face. I'd probably missed the whole-body-scan most men couldn't or wouldn't avoid. Instead I focused on the table, going over the symbols. *Organ center. Spirit center.* "It says, 'The heart.'"

BRYNNER

No one told me there'd be special company. I'd been called up before Director Bismuth more times than I could count. I'd own more medals than any other operative if it weren't for a fifty/fifty split between commendations and criminal charges.

Meeting in person with Dale always left me creeped out, because his dedication to making sure he died of lung cancer made him a walking monument to the tobacco trade. No one said anything about *her*.

Grace. Grace Roberts, according to Dr. Egghead. When she focused on the screen, I focused on her. Must remember her name. Couldn't forget her face. The smooth sweep of her nose, the way she kept her golden hair pulled back, and enough curves to tell me I sat across from a woman, not a girl.

Must not stare, I reminded myself. Last time I let my eyes wander, I wound up climbing a fire escape. I couldn't look away, but I could keep my eyes off her rear. Okay, I looked once. Twice, just to be sure I saw right. If I had any prayer of not getting chewed out, I'd have to look at my laptop or her chin, ignoring all points in between.

Work women. Completely off-limits. Absolutely forbidden, and in this case, totally unforgettable. She looked to the director over and over. Probably hoping for approval, recognition that Grace had done a good job.

And my reputation must have preceded me, because no matter how I moved my head or tapped my pen, she kept her eyes off me. Smart woman. Of course, she was upset about the smudges on that spell.

It sounded like she'd drunk Dr. Egghead's Kool-Aid and gone back for seconds. The name "corpse-organism" didn't do a meat-skin justice. In fact, it implied exactly the wrong thing, in my opinion. That it was alive.

The good doctor and the director argued over the significance of "the heart," while I turned over its words in my head. Dale raised a shaky hand and waited for our attention before wheezing out, "It asked for Brynner by name. Carson." Dale's arms trembled as he slapped another nicotine patch on. By my watch, he'd made it almost eleven minutes without a cigar, which was an improvement.

The director's eyes swiped to me like a sword blade through a meat-skin. "Mr. Carson? Confirm?"

I nodded. "And it asked if I brought the heart. Said my blood took it, and my blood would pay if it wasn't returned." When I said "heart," Grace leaned in, listening. I locked my gaze on the laptop rather than let it coast down her cleavage.

Director Bismuth nodded. "Indeed. The same Re-Animus you dispatched two nights before. Angry about losing a host?"

I shook my head, wishing I could ask everyone to leave before I answered. "It said it was delivering a message. And it was talking about my dad."

3

GRACE

The co-org spoke? About Brynner's dad, Heinrich Carson? The original field operative, killing co-orgs before there *was* a BSI. Author of most of the field procedures. Also, distributor of countless superstitions and other bunk. I knew the name. Knew the legend of the man that even the Re-Animus feared.

I couldn't contain the question. "What did it say about him?"

Brynner turned toward me, his face suddenly tense. Worried. Then he looked back to Director Bismuth. "Could we discuss this in private?"

She nodded, her gaze never leaving me. "Ms. Roberts, I'd like a report on the spell by eleven o'clock. Both a literal translation and your best interpretation of what remains."

"It's not a spell." I enunciated each word and met her gaze. Challenging the director of the BSI might not be a good career move, but letting professional people bandy around words like "magic" was even worse. "There's no such thing."

"Get her out of here." Brynner glared at me, his chest puffed out like a rooster.

Dr. Thomas beamed at me. "A woman after my own heart. The number of times they've thrown me out of—" He cut off as the director's gaze swept toward him.

And on to me. The director kept her tone completely neutral. "I'll be waiting for that report. The good doctor will find you a temporary office while you work to translate that . . . passage."

"Spell." The man with the oxygen mask took three tries to spit out that one word over his ragged cough. "Call it what it is."

My BSI badge didn't have a black diamond in the corner for nothing. I'd registered myself as a confirmed atheist and absolute skeptic days after taking the job. With the minuscule pay hike came a duty, an obligation to be the voice of reason. "I'll call it what it is. An artifact. An engraving. A text." I looked to each of them in turn. "You don't need terms like 'magic' for such things to be fascinating. You don't need mystical forces to want to understand. There's no need to make up—"

Brynner shot to his feet, then winced and held his arm across his chest. "Get the hell out."

I should have left. Swallowed my pride and walked away. But after so many years of listening to crosses, crucifixes, ditch witches, and *crap*, I'd had it. "People look up to you. When you say things like 'spell,' you perpetuate myths." I looked to the director, making my case straight to her. "Have you ever seen a spell performed?"

She shook her head.

"You know anyone who has?"

I didn't think she was going to answer. I'd already gathered a handout with the pictures and a transcript of the event, ready to leave, when she spoke. She looked at Brynner, and her eyes glistened. "There have been reliable witnesses."

And his gaze, full of anger moments before, now fell. He closed his eyes and sat down, still holding his arm across his chest.

To quell my frustration, I nearly ran from the conference room, pacing the halls until I found a kitchenette where I could curse in peace. Why did I have to challenge the director? I needed this job. Needed the steady pay, the reliable hours. All I had to do was keep my mouth shut, black diamond or not.

"You did well in there." Dr. Thomas walked in after me and poured himself a cup of coffee so stale it smelled like burnt paper. "I'm sure Portland misses your services."

"That was well? I challenged the director and pissed off the BSI golden boy and whoever cancer man is."

"That would be Dale Hogman. Field team commander for all of BSI, and the only one allowed to give direction to Mr. Carson."

Great. I clutched my printout until the paper crinkled. "You said a lot of nice things before the meeting, but I could have used backup in there."

Dr. Thomas nodded. "You chose to argue existence, not nature. In that battle, you are on your own. Debate the driving force behind a corpse organism, and I'll back you up. Discuss space folds and gravity distortion, and again, I will be your ally."

"So you are saying there are such things as spells? Magic?"

"I'm saying, Ms. Roberts, that many phenomena were labeled magic before being understood. The proper role of a skeptic is to probe for the truth. Given a credible witness and evidence that some form of event occurred, I don't waste time on 'if.' I do spend a great deal of thought on 'how.'"

All this talk of spells and spirits had me ready to spend time alone with the hieroglyphics. I let the fight drain out of my voice. "I have a report due in a few hours and a lot of work to do." Was it *possible* that magic existed? Yes. There also might be a man in a red suit delivering gifts at Christmas and a giant rabbit crapping chocolate eggs at Easter.

Dr. Thomas nodded and waved for me to follow him to a beige broom closet with barely enough room for a computer, and a whiteboard the size of a pizza platter. "I trust you can make yourself at home here. Perhaps we could have lunch later. I'll be in the labs this morning, once you are done with your presentation."

He wandered off without waiting for an answer. My BSI login worked, giving me access to *Thule's Encyclopedia Hieroglyphica*, the definitive guide to both human- and co-org-influenced hieroglyphics, and my own notes, developed over years of learning what combinations of glyphs might indicate different concepts.

And with that, I forced my mind to work on the text. More important, away from Brynner Carson, and the spell he seemed to cast on me without even trying.

BRYNNER

Once that infernal woman left, the tension in the room dropped a thousand percent. I'd grown up around Director Bismuth. Heard Mom and Dad call her "Maggie." Even tried it myself. Once. Still, I didn't want to have the discussion I knew was coming.

"Mr. Carson. Brynner." She waited for me to look at her. "What did it want?"

"I can't be sure." I floated my best lie. One that was part true, because with the meat-skin once again dead, I couldn't question it about which particular heart it wanted.

"Hazard a guess."

She'd known me too long to be fooled. I probably read like an open playboy to her. "The heart."

"I grasp that. Ms. Roberts's translation makes that clear. Which heart? What heart?"

I bit my lip, trying to speak, not finding the words. At last, like chewing broken glass, I found something I could say. "The one Dad had."

Dale whistled, the air coming through his tracheal tube whining. He'd worked with Dad, before the emphysema reduced Dale to a shadow of a man. "Was it the one . . ."

He wouldn't dare say it.

"Dad kept a lot of crap."

"Brynner, was it in the one in the Canopic jar?" Director Bismuth had no qualms about asking hard questions. Even about subjects she knew I didn't talk about.

I stood, ignoring the shooting pain in my chest where cracked ribs and stitched wounds hadn't even begun to heal. "I don't know. I'll think about it. I've got to get my gear to the armory and file a suitcase's worth of receipts. May I be excused?"

Director Bismuth stood, appraising me over her bifocals. Probably thinking how much she wished Dad were still around. "I expect you at the eleven o'clock translation briefing. Young man, how are you holding up?"

"Three cracked ribs. Twenty-seven stiches. I'll heal."

"Your father would be proud." She took off her glasses and rubbed her eyes.

"If you really think that, you didn't know my old man. I need to get my armor done, and then I can go pick up another assignment."

She tilted her head, eyeing me. "I'm concerned about your psychological report. While your performance is unquestioned, your equipment manager and dispatcher both report that you behaved erratically in Greece. You won't be going out on assignment until after I sign off on it."

"You can't take me off active duty. I'll chase the meat-skins by myself if I have to." I expected her to yell at me about the embassy staff, not threaten the one good part of my life: the chance to slaughter dead things.

"You'd arrive ten minutes too late every time. We're connected with all first emergency responders. They call us directly, not you."

Like that mattered. "Dad always got there first. Dad was doing this before you were around to coax and guide. Dad put more of those things back in their graves before there was a BSI than after."

"You aren't your father." Her words stung like a whip. "My decision stands."

I grabbed my duffel bag from the floor beside me and marched out of the room, holding on to the anger inside me. Anger could be a shield. Could protect me from myself, from everything around me.

I stomped down the hallways until I arrived at the armory, where the tech dumped my entire duffel bag onto the table. The tall East African man smiled at me with perfect white teeth and brown eyes. "So nice to have a visitor. What did you bring me?"

"Didn't have time for an equipment check between my last two operations." I read the name stitched into his uniform: Lavel.

"Two? You had six months and you went out in *this*?" He held up a piece of my Kevlar, white stress lines creasing it.

I shook my head. "Three days. Two operations."

His forehead creased, like he thought I was joking. Then he picked up the scanner and ran it over my armor. The RFID tag beeped, and his eyes went wide. "Mr. Carson. Such an honor to see you here. I met your father once."

Of course he had. Everyone met my father, or knew my father, or wanted to know my father. Lavel dumped my crumpled underwear and clothes into the same bin as the Kevlar plates. "Most of these should have been replaced ages ago. Going out in this, you're going to get killed."

"One way or another. You can swap anything but the chest plate."

Lavel turned the chest plate over and whistled. The Kevlar inserts had seen better days. The plate itself wasn't laminate plastic, but pure silver, tarnished to a purple black. On the surface I'd engraved every religious symbol on earth, including the McDonald's logo.

"You need a full refit. Where are your weapons?"

I opened a box in the bottom of my duffel and drew out two silver daggers, their edges inlaid with amber on one side and alabaster on the other. Dad's weapons. The amber drained a meat-skin's strength; the alabaster acted as a poison. One nick and even if the meat-skin got away, the breakdown process was irreversible.

Lavel covered them reverently. "I'll check these in under your name. You gonna stay with us for a while?"

"No. I work Western Europe these days." What I needed

more than anything was to leave Seattle, leave the U.S., and get back to work.

"A shame. I'll replace what I can, but it will take me weeks to make a full set for you."

I gave him a pat on the back, ready to find a temp office and catch up on my sleep. Instead, the overhead intercom cut in. "Brynner Carson, please report to Medical."

I swore. "I don't have time for this."

Lavel laughed. "Heard that from field operatives more times than I can count. How long has it been since your last med eval?"

"Longer than my last refit."

"Med's on the fourth floor. You'll get a lollipop and a Band-Aid." As I left, he chuckled to himself.

I found my way through the halls up to Medical. An Indian nurse there met me at the door, her hair tucked back in a head-band, her accent faintly English. "Mr. Carson, my name is Saiay Sanjay. I'll be performing your tests this morning. Right this way."

"I don't need this. I had an X-ray just the other day. Ouch—"

She pinned my arm down, drawing blood from it without so much as a warning. "Well, we'll take our own, just to be sure. And we'll check white blood count, cholesterol"—she eyed me with a knowing look—"*diseases*."

"I'm clean."

"I'm sure all the ladies in the city will rest easier when the test results come back." She drew out the needle and stuck a bandage, yellow with hearts on it, on my arm.

From there I suffered the usual indignities. X-rays. Dental checkup, blood pressure, which was definitely higher than nor-mal. After three hours, she finally came back in. "I have good news, Mr. Carson. All your tests that should be positive are pos-itive. All of the others are negative."

"So I can go?"

"After your appointment, yes."

I quashed the annoyance, turning it into desire, or as close to it as I could come. "What do you say *you* interview me? We could go grab some food. I'd be happy to answer any question you have. I bet you work long hours. What do you say we go give each other a checkup?"

She giggled. "You are so funny. They don't say that about you. Dashing, yes. Charm, well, I can tell that's no exaggeration. But your sense of humor. Dr. Nagashindra will see you now." She pointed down the hall.

I walked past the rows of exam rooms, to a large office. The nameplate read "Chandresh Nagashindra." Below it, the words "Doctor of Psychiatry."

And I was done. I spun on my heel . . . to find the hallway blocked. Sanjay stood there, hands on her hips.

Behind me, a deep voice boomed in an Indian accent, "Mr. Carson, this is the right office."

From the dimly lit room emerged a short Indian man, with wispy black hair where he wasn't bald. He offered a firm hand and nearly dragged me into his lair. Four hours of sleep I could have had, four hours.

He started with easy questions, meant to make me smile. Make me relax. What was my last assignment? What about the one before? What about Athena? What about Irena? It didn't matter what I said, he must have written several pages for every answer.

I could have said "Orange" and he'd have turned it into *War and Peace*. Worse yet, I couldn't sense a pattern to his questions. A driving desire, or goal. Dad always said to ask, so I did. "What exactly are we doing here? When did the third degree become standard operating procedure?" I didn't mean to let the hostility inside creep so far into my voice.

After scrawling another phone book, he clicked his pen closed. "Two years ago. Three years *after* your last mandatory yearly interview."

"So you haul every field op in here once a year and drag them through this? No truth serum? No waterboarding?"

He switched to a fresh pad and wasted another tree. "No. I'm concerned about you, Brynner. The Greek embassy mentioned demands for absolute silence in your hotel rooms. Your vital monitor reports that you haven't been sleeping more than forty-five minutes at a time. You are showing classic signs of severe burnout, mental and physical exhaustion, and possible post-traumatic stress disorder."

I willed my fingers to stop running along the blade sheaths on my belt. "I do a damn good job."

"You are more than a piece of equipment, a machine with a function. Mr. Carson, how are *you*?"

"Fine." I offered my only answer. Ever.

He scribbled again, surprisingly short. "And if you could not answer 'fine'? If your ability to continue this work rested on delivering an honest, complete answer?"

I froze. While I might not play office politics, I grasped his threat. "I'd have to think about it." My cell phone chirped, my fifteen-minute warning for the briefing. "I have to go."

He nodded. "I'll wait to deliver my report until after you answer. Take your time, but you won't be choosing any new assignments until after we're done."

4

BRYNNER

By that point, I didn't care about the translation. I was pissed at the director over my psychiatric mugging. So when I slammed open the briefing room door and she wasn't there, I admit to being slightly confused.

Grace Roberts sat at the head of the table. A laptop's glow lit her face, making her complexion bluish white. Again, I drank in her features, the petite nose and thin lips, her angular chin that lead to a tantalizing neckline, and from there, the shadow of her cleavage.

She cleared her throat.

Grace had used the remote to turn the lights on while I was otherwise occupied.

I turned away, focusing on the cold, gray day outside rather than the woman who radiated such warmth. "Where is everyone else?" After a moment, I glanced back, now that I could keep myself in line.

Grace crossed her arms over her chest. "You're early. According to Dr. Thomas, everyone in this office shows up fourteen minutes late."

"I'm sorry." What exactly I apologized for, I couldn't quite say. My stare. My late colleagues. My total inability to conduct a normal conversation with her.

She gave a bitter laugh. "Don't be. I get paid by the hour, and I need all the hours I can get. Driving a desk does not pay well."

I nodded. "That's because a desk won't try to tear your arm off, and all you have to do is save the spreadsheet, not save someone from it."

Grace narrowed her eyes; her bottom lip curled under. "No one gets paid enough to go hand to hand against co-orgs." She paused and then frowned, her fierce expression softening a degree or two. "Standard operating procedure is to drop them with incendiary rounds. You could get killed."

As far as I was concerned, using a gun was cheating. "Guns aren't my style, and rules don't account for when there's a meat-skin loose in an oil refinery, like last Christmas. Or a school. Like a week ago. If the meat-skin's on a ship, the fuel will *burn*. Stick to your desk job; you'd do more harm than good in the real world."

She sat back in her chair, her eyes narrowed, lips pressed together, looking like steam would come out her ears any minute now.

The quiet hiss of Dale's oxygen tank broke the silence as he rolled in to take a seat. A moment later, Dr. Thomas joined him, and after that, Director Bismuth.

I waited until Director Bismuth sat down, and took the seat across from her. "Ma'am, we need to talk about that doctor—"

"If you don't mind," Grace cut in, her eyes tired, her voice strained, "this is my meeting. Let me deliver my report, get out of here, and you can talk all you want when I'm not around to hear it. I've got plenty of drama without borrowing yours."

Director Bismuth's eyes narrowed at me. "If you don't mind, Ms. Roberts, a quick question. Did my favorite field operative ask you to dinner?"

Oh, please. I wasn't that stupid, most days. I did have a couple of tattoos I'd love to let Grace interpret, but the director would kill me. Or even worse, fire me.

The look of horror on Grace's face hurt worse than any tongue lashing the director could hand out. "He most definitely did *not*. And if he knows what's good for him, he won't."

Director Bismuth gave her a weak smile. "My sentiments exactly. Proceed."

GRACE

Ask me out to dinner? Not hardly. The things his eyes said he wanted to do with me didn't include dinner or conversation. Not that he wasn't attractive. If I was into the sort of man who spread himself thinner than butter, Brynner Carson would be quite the catch. Given his easy smile, the way he relaxed in front of the triad of BSI leaders, and spoke with confidence, no wonder women smiled back.

I derailed that train of thought, focusing on the ideographs before me. "My translation is complete. Everything I can still make sense of doesn't support it being any sort of spell." I waited, shoulders hunched, for someone to challenge my statement, and breathed a sigh of relief when they let me continue.

"The artifact is divided into phases, each of which seems to convey a thought pattern. The top two are mostly intact. The bottom two are"—I looked at Brynner—"less intact."

I pointed to the northwest quadrant of the circle. "Here we have a repeating sequence of terms, some of which are well-defined; some required interpretation."

Director Bismuth held up a wrinkled palm. "How can you be sure of the meaning if you had to interpret?"

"I can't." I waited for that to sink in. "Some words have definite meanings. Hieroglyphics are both ideographic and phonetic. Sometimes a symbol set means a word, and sometimes it spells out a word, and sometimes you have to put the two together."

I pointed to a set of figures on the laptop. "Let's say you have this phrase, which means 'diseased,' followed by this bird. What do you think it means?"

"Bird flu." Dale's electronic voice rang out, followed by laughter from everyone but Brynner.

Brynner shook his head. "Shitty."

"Brynner Carson, you will apologize at once." Director Bismuth shook her finger at him.

He didn't back down. "I didn't say, 'It's a shitty translation.' I said it means—"

"He's right." The question, in my mind, was how he knew this. "The disease is clear. To put it together, you have to understand that ducks are nasty, filthy creatures. They smell, they crap everywhere. Think about how you'd feel being around one constantly."

Recognition gleamed in the director's eyes. "So 'duck disease' becomes 'foul.'" She raised her eyebrows to Brynner, probably trying to get him to notice her rephrasing of his choice in words.

He wasn't paying attention to her. No, his eyes never left me. Which made it harder to focus on what I was doing. For some reason, he focused on my face instead of my breasts, unlike most men.

I struggled to regain control of my meeting and keep the swarm of butterflies in my stomach from showing. "So we combine phrases, phonetic meanings, and contexts to interpret. This section I translated for you before. It means 'heart.'"

Their eyes followed the pattern, which circled the artifact. "And this is 'important,' or 'holy.' And this is 'lost.' So I believe that one of the key ideas is the Re-Animus is seeking something lost. Something important to it."

I pointed to the northeast segment. "The section here also contains repetition. 'The way,' 'appear,' 'travel.' It could be an expression of desire to go home, or of the Re-Animus itself being lost."

Absolute silence met me, so I forged ahead. "This segment was destroyed in a careless accident. Which also damaged the other. In it, I can only reliably translate four terms. 'Ra,' 'the god of the sun,' 'pharaoh,' and 'daughter.' If we take this last glyph and assume it was in fact a basket, the phrase would be 'the pharaoh's daughter.'"

Brynner's gaze jerked over to the screen, as did Dale's and the director's. Then they exchanged glances among themselves.

The only phrase I'd ever said that got a reaction like that was years ago, when I told my ex, "I'm pregnant." And thankfully, that wasn't the case now.

The director's eyes narrowed on me, like she could somehow

divine if I told the truth. "Thank you, Ms. Roberts. How likely do you find it that the term 'heart' might be literal?"

"Possible. Anything's possible. We're dealing with nonhuman intelligence trying to communicate with us in a language that isn't precise." I sat down.

Brynner stretched his arms. "Or it could mean 'coffin.' The coffin glyph looks just like this, only missing the tail."

I pointed to the distinct edges. "There's no outer mark to agree with that. See here, here, and here. I do this for a living. Trust me."

He snorted. "Dad wrote in these all the freaking time. Day in, day out. I used to get chore lists in hieroglyphics. He kept a *diary* in them."

Director Bismuth silenced him with a glare. "Mr. Carson's translation skills rank at roughly a kindergartner with a foul mouth, so I greatly appreciate your attention and effort, Ms. Roberts."

She turned to Brynner. "Where is the heart?"

"I don't know." He spoke so softly I could barely hear him over the hiss of Dale's oxygen tank.

"Brynner Carson, tell me where it is." She tapped a pen on the table in frustration while she waited.

"I already said I don't know. I wish I did." He hung his head, his fists clenched. "Dad kept it. He hid it."

The sorrow in his voice hit me like a gut punch. Though the prudent thing to do was take my laptop and leave, I couldn't resist asking. "Where is what, exactly?"

The director and Dr. Thomas exchanged a glance, then Dale nodded in agreement. His computerized voice sang out into the silence. "The heart of Ra-Ame."

I knew that name. Some sort of urban legend among field

teams, like Santa Claus and the tooth fairy. I waited for someone else to speak up. To say something that would make this whole thing make more sense. "Dr. Thomas, could I speak with you in private?"

"Absolutely." He rose, and we exited. "How may I help you, young lady?"

"I'm out of my league here. Why aren't you speaking up? They're talking about Ra-Ame like she's real."

He didn't answer. He just turned and walked down the hall, waving for me to follow. We rode the elevator in silence, then passed a set of double-locking doors and entered a pristine white lab.

The refrigerated lab was at least thirty degrees colder, making goose bumps stand up on my arms. "Shouldn't we be in the meeting?"

"Let them wait. I consider myself a man of science." He pointed to a plexiglass window. Inside, an armless corpse with gray skin stumbled in circles. "So we study. We consider. We analyze. Do you believe the co-orgs exist?"

"Of course. There's one right there."

"And the Re-Animus affecting it?"

I paused. Was this some sort of test? "I believe there's a force at work. Probably viral, possibly some form of collective organism. Not an evil spirit or demon."

"Do you have trouble believing that Julius Caesar existed?"

I grasped his line of reasoning. "Of course not. And I agree it's possible that a woman named Ra-Ame existed. Ra-Ame, the hideous monster, Ra-Ame, the source of all Re-Animus, those sound more like fairy tales to me."

"And to me." He led me to another table, where an electron scan of co-org tissue showed the changes wrought by the Re-

Animus. "But like the co-orgs, there may be rational explanations for the legend of Ra-Ame. Ones the others might not recognize. Belief is easy for them."

Of course it was. "I don't believe in anything."

He smiled, showing crooked yellow teeth. "That's why I like you. Let's go inject some sanity into their discussion, shall we?"

I followed him through the building to the conference room, where voices shouted. Dr. Thomas stepped to one side. "After you, Ms. Roberts." He threw the door open.

Brynner stood inches from Director Bismuth, each of them beet red. He gestured with his hands, coming so close to pushing her I wondered if I should call security. "This isn't any of your business." He looked around at the others, carefully avoiding me. "Any of you."

"I say recovering and securing this heart is what is most important, and therefore, it is what you will do, unless you'd like to pursue a change of career." Director Bismuth's voice boomed out, leaving no room for debate.

I slipped over and grabbed my purse from the chair, doing my best to stay out of their argument. Drama was one thing my life had more than enough of. They could fight it out on their own.

I almost made it to the door.

"Ms. Roberts, I can't help but note your personnel file has a request for working extra hours." The director's steel tone said she might know why I wanted them.

Did we really need to have this discussion now? "Yes."

Director Bismuth walked around the table, leaving Brynner standing alone. Once she wedged herself between the door and me, she continued. "Tell me, have you ever considered field operations? The pay is several times what you make now."

Brynner and I laughed at the same time, then I scowled at

him. "I don't kill things. If I find a spider in my apartment, I throw it outside instead of squashing it."

She nodded. "Field operations are more than pulling triggers or slinging blades. Come with me. Let me explain a few things about Heinrich Carson." She turned to leave, and I followed her.

Brynner leaped over the table, moving that mountain of a body like a gazelle, and wincing as he landed. "Hey. You can't do that. You can't just go discussing my family with a stranger." Brynner's voice shook. Anger? Or Fear?

Director Bismuth nodded slightly. "Well, if you would like to attempt a briefing, be my guest. Make certain Ms. Roberts has the information she needs, and I won't feel the need to amend your tale."

While I couldn't tell for the life of me what they meant, I'd read enough people to know the answer was coming if only I could keep my mouth shut.

Brynner looked away, staring out the window. "Dad kept journals. Lots of them. Every day of his life. He used to write in Latin, or Russian. When he joined the BSI, he switched to hieroglyphics."

"Didn't you say he wrote your chore list in hieroglyphics?"

For a moment, a smile worked its way back onto his face. "I didn't say I *did* my chores."

That was my kind of extra hours. I gave him a courteous nod. "I'll pass on the fieldwork, but the journals I can help with. Have them sent to my branch by secure courier; I'll make it my top priority. Depending on how many and how long they are, full translation with annotation could take days or weeks."

Brynner looked to the director, something passing between them I couldn't decode.

Director Bismuth shook her head. "Heinrich Carson's effects are held by his sister-in-law, in New Mexico. The BSI is not permitted to remove them, or indeed, to access them under normal conditions. I'd like you to go on-site and do the translation there. We're looking for a Canopic jar that was in Heinrich Carson's possession. It seems reasonable to think the location would be recorded in one of them. Probably one of the last ones."

Though the opportunity could change everything about my situation, I had other obligations. "I can't."

Brynner nodded in agreement. "It doesn't matter. Aunt Emelia won't let her in the house, since she's BSI. I'm not even sure she'd let me in."

Director Bismuth smiled, as though he'd just fallen into her trap. "Your aunt will most certainly allow Ms. Roberts access if you bring her home with you to meet them."

"*No!*" We shouted in unison, then looked at each other.

He spoke first. "I'm not going back there. I'd rather quit. What happened to not going out on assignment until the shrink said so?"

The thought of Brynner stretched out on a couch made me laugh, and wonder for an instant what he'd look like relaxed, instead of coiled like a spring.

"You wouldn't quit. Ever." The director gave him a smug smile. "This job is your life. I believe our psychiatrist said you wouldn't be choosing any assignments until he signed off. This one isn't your choice." She looked from him to me. "And you. I'm not asking you to sleep with him. In fact, Mr. Carson is forbidden to enter into relationships with BSI employees. I'm ordering you to travel to New Mexico, read through some dusty books, and phone in your reports. Field operative pay."

She didn't understand. I picked my words carefully. "I have

weekly obligations in Portland. I have to be there every Friday."
I didn't add that I had to pay in cash because I'd bounced so
many checks. "And I don't want to get killed."

Brynner rolled his eyes. "Yeah, because New Mexico is a
real hotbed of meat-skin activity."

Director Bismuth leaned in and whispered, "I grasp your
problem. You need to pay for your daughter's nursing care."

I almost died of embarrassment. My daughter and her condition were my business, not Brynner Carson's or anyone else's.

Director Bismuth ignored my chagrin. "I might point out
that this job would more than pay for your considerable debt,
and wire transfers are a normal method many people use. Never
mind, Ms. Roberts. I'll consult the Northern California office
translator instead."

She turned on her heel, and I reached out, grabbing her elbow.
"Wait."

"Yes, Ms. Roberts?"

"I'll do it." A wave of adrenaline and relief washed over me.

She nodded in satisfaction. "The two of you will leave immediately."

5

GRACE

"Immediately," in my book, meant "right after you get home from Seattle, where you can make arrangements, pack a change of clothes, and generally speaking, get ready for a trip to New Mexico." In the director's mind, immediately meant "on the next flight out of Seattle-Tacoma International Airport."

Brynner tugged on the director's elbow like a preschooler. "I need four hours. Armor's not ready."

"Didn't you just tell Ms. Roberts 'New Mexico is not a hotbed of co-org activity'? Go with her, and let her assist us in finding out what your father did with the heart. I don't know what importance it has, but if a Re-Animus wants it, I want it more." Director Bismuth gathered her papers and left the room.

Brynner waited until the door closed to speak. "You have a daughter. How old?" He tilted his head, a warm smile on his lips.

I knew exactly where giving in to smiles and charms led. "How about we make a deal? I don't ask the director questions about your family, you don't ask me questions about mine."

Dr. Thomas cleared his throat, rose, and beckoned to me. "May I have a word before you leave?"

I followed him out to the hall, where a nervous teen girl waited with a leather messenger bag, a golden field operative star, and a freshly minted badge with my name on it.

Dr. Thomas smiled at her. "Grace, this is our newest intern, Kelly. Kelly, meet Grace Roberts. Senior field analyst. Ms. Roberts is going out on assignment to determine the location of, and recover, an artifact." He took the bag from her and handed it to me.

My stomach dropped to my ankles when he emphasized "field." Then clean through the floor as the girl looked at me with a gaze of awe. She mumbled to me, clearly at a loss for words, and then darted away, as if I might bite her.

"What was that about?" My sense of awe around Dr. Thomas faded with each moment.

"Just giving my intern someone to look up to. I used to go on assignment, and kept that packed. A toothbrush, deodorant, and a spare shirt. All the essentials. I really envy you."

I slung the bag over my shoulder. "Why? I'm going to New Mexico."

"I love my lab work, but I used to collect samples firsthand." He raised his chin and pointed to a swarm of liver spots on one side, which obscured a wide scar. "A co-org almost tore my throat out." A distant smile spread across his face. "It was amazing."

I liked my throat untorn. "We're going to New Mexico. Not Egypt."

He bobbed his head in agreement. "I know, I know. But an old man can dream. Go on, Ms. Roberts. Keep your eyes open and your mind sharp. As they say in the field, don't get dead."

At the entrance to the BSI building, a Bureau driver waited, jingling keys as he leaned up against a black sedan. "Mr. Carson." He nodded to Brynner. "Who's the looker?"

I cut off Brynner before he could answer. "Grace Roberts. *Senior* field analyst. When I want your opinion on how I look, I'll let you know."

"Whoa." The driver's face flushed red, and he held up his hands. "You should learn to take a compliment. I haven't seen you around, and now you're with him—"

"She's not *with* me, and I think the phrase you were looking for was 'I'm sorry, it won't happen again.' Can we get going, Lou?" Brynner dropped his duffel bag in the trunk, and then opened the door for me.

How he could be so polite and yet so irritating, I couldn't begin to say. We were rolling through the tall buildings of downtown Seattle, climbing hilly streets on our way to the freeway, when the scanner blipped to life.

A woman's voice rang out over the radio. "All field teams, we have co-org activity on Pier 77."

"On the water. Again." Brynner's voice came out a whisper. Then he spoke louder. "Take me there."

Without warning, our driver did an illegal U-turn. "Field Team B responding," he said into the radio mic.

Co-orgs? With me in the car? That was not what I signed up for. I tapped the driver on the shoulder. "We have a flight to catch."

He slammed on the brakes, skidding to a halt beside a gaggle of tourists. He looked at me, his gaze darting to the BSI badge on my lapel. His eyes narrowed, and he looked to Brynner. "You two a field team or not?"

"I'm a field team all by myself. Get me there as fast as possible." Brynner looked out the window, avoiding my gaze.

Wrong way down one-way streets, squeezing between parked delivery trucks, our driver broke every traffic law in existence as he forced his way through Seattle morning traffic. Even the flashing purple lights on our roof didn't make the morning crush disappear.

When we reached the waterfront, the police made room, letting us past a line of patrol cars and through a mob of bystanders without the good sense to stay away.

Lou popped the trunk and retrieved Brynner's bag while an officer approached on my side. Brynner exited, and I watched through the back window as he circled the car to show his BSI badge.

"According to witnesses, there's either one or a dozen meat-skins in that restaurant." The officer pointed to a building jutting out over the water on pilings.

That just seemed wrong. Co-orgs avoided water, due to the interference it caused with host control. That a Re-Animus could hold on to a co-org over that much water defied logic.

Brynner retrieved a plain metal box from the bag Lou held, and set it on the trunk right behind my seat. From it, he pulled two silver daggers. The blades glowed with a tint of yellow, where amber coated them.

Heinrich Carson's blades, made famous in half a dozen movies. Where the blades came from and how he'd manufactured them were secrets the elder Carson took with him to his grave.

Brynner finished adjusting his knife sheaths and glanced toward the crowd barrier. "Any civilians?"

The cop shook his head. "Two unaccounted for, but if there's anyone left, they're good as dead. No one's going in there after them. You want to line up and shoot through the windows?"

Brynner opened his mouth in wordless astonishment, then found his voice. "You think there might still be someone in there and you didn't check?" He clenched his hands into fists, his face flushed red. When he spoke, he did so through gritted teeth. "I'm going in." With one arm wrapped across his chest, he jogged toward the building.

"Lady, you're going with him, right? It's against policy to act alone." Our driver, Lou, looked down at me from outside my window.

I rolled down the window to answer. "I don't think he cares about policy." What sort of man would take that kind of risk for people he didn't know? As for me, going into a building full of co-orgs wasn't in my career plan. I shook my head. "I'm not that kind of field operative. I don't even have a weapon." Being a translator, I didn't get a gun at graduation; I received a complete copy of *Thule's Encyclopedia Hieroglyphica*.

Lou cursed and walked to the trunk, pulling out a box. He threw my door open and tossed the box in my lap. "Deliverator, with standard co-org ammo. Every third bullet's a wax pellet loaded with pine, silver, and holy water. I checked the ammo out this morning after the priest blessed our armory."

"I told you, I'm not that kind of field operative. I'm an analyst. I read hieroglyphics." I set the box down and scooted across the seat.

"You've got to be kidding." He didn't bother trying to hide his contempt. His shock.

Lou could get over it. I didn't have years of training on how to waltz into dangerous situations and kill the dead. Now was not the time for a crash course.

Until the screaming started.

BRYNNER

At least Grace Roberts had the good sense to stay in the car. After her arbitrary field promotion back at headquarters, I'd worried she might decide that a pay upgrade meant a responsibility upgrade. If she got killed as part of my team, it would be my fault.

I went in through the doors and ducked behind the front bar.

From across the dining room came shuffling footsteps. I peeked in the mirrored wall of the bar, using it to find out what we were dealing with. A flicker of movement caught my eye. I watched the form in the mirror. The graceless movements. The lurching lack of balance.

A shambler. The disjointed movements made it clear. When a Re-Animus was done with a corpse, it could choose to let it go. Remnants of the Re-Animus would keep it moving, but unintelligent. The result was a co-org, to use Grace Roberts's term, without direction.

It would move aimlessly, until something caught its eye. Then it would attack. Sharpened fingernails, razor-sharp teeth, and inhuman strength made a shambler plenty dangerous.

Nothing I couldn't handle, or didn't handle a dozen times a year. I waited until it dragged past, then vaulted over the bar. My ribs sang out in pain, letting me know I hadn't taken a vacation. Hadn't rested.

Rest was for the dead.

My feet caught a glass as I leaped over, and it crashed to the floor in shards. The shambler jerked around, looking in my direction.

I held still. Without a Re-Animus driving it, the shambler would be attracted to movement and sound. Despite the name, fresh ones could almost run.

This one was fresh. A corpse less than a day old. Dark spots along the fingers where blood pooled, eyes that weren't sunken in. Good and bad, in a way. Given time, the Re-Animus could strengthen a corpse. Give it insane power.

This one hadn't been dead long enough for that. Whatever the Re-Animus did, it did, and let the corpse go. I held still, willing even my breathing to stop. It turned, a wheezing breath escaping it. Its core nervous system still tried to respond, even after Re-Animus exposure.

In the restaurant, someone sobbed.

The shambler veered away, shuffling down the line of tables.

I followed, my blade drawn, freezing as it turned a corner and doing my best to remain silent as I closed in on it. All I needed was for it to stay focused on something else.

The sobbing continued, from under a wide, circular table covered with a red tablecloth. If there'd been a Re-Animus in control, the shambler would have pulled off the cloth and looked under it. Instead, it bumped into the table and shuffled in circles. Each time, it swung loose arms, and each time, came up empty.

When it came around to face me, it stopped. The malfunctioning brain couldn't pick out what I was. Wouldn't know me as a field operative of the BSI. But it could tell I wasn't a piece of furniture. The empty eyes stared out at me, waiting for me to move. It raised a hand with raw fingertips toward me. Buried in a fine suit, this meat-skin would have fit in perfectly during dining hours, if it weren't for the fact that it seemed to prefer its meal on the hoof—or the sneaker.

The meat-skin lunged for me.

I stepped to the side, swinging my knife at its outstretched arm. The amber coating on the blade flashed, black smoke pouring out where I'd scored a hit, and the shambler moaned in pain, almost as loudly as I did from the exertion.

The wounded shambler raged about, flailing arms, lurching back and forth. I backed up, letting the amber do its dirty work. Every second now, Re-Animus remnants spread thinner and thinner, until it could no longer control the corpse and I'd have another dead body.

It stumbled and threw the table to the side, death throes giving it the strength of twenty men. I'd seen them break marble before. Seen them smash their own skulls in blind fury.

Where the table had been, a woman cowered, her arms wrapped like iron around a young girl. She shrieked and kicked her feet, jerking backward.

I ran head-on between them, swinging the knife up as the shambler's gaze locked downward, an empty thought of killing its only driving force.

Arms outstretched, it fell forward, its hands twisted into vicious claws.

I drove my blade into its heart, ignoring the black smoke that poured out like water, ignoring the flailing that smashed me in the chest, tearing my stitches.

I collapsed to the ground on top of it, then pushed my way up. The woman still wouldn't look at me, squirming her way backward, dragging the little girl underneath another booth table.

I gasped, forcing myself to breathe through the pain. "It's all right. I killed it."

My words broke through to her, and her glassy eyes fixed on me. For one moment, she focused. She screamed again. Looking past me.

I took a breath of fire through cracked ribs and looked over my shoulder. Two more shamblers were emerging from the kitchen, faces and hands bloody. They paused for a moment, dead eyes scanning the restaurant. Then locked onto the booth, and the woman wailing like a banshee underneath it.

They came for us all.

6

GRACE

The constant chatter of the scanner disappeared, drowned by the crowd's roar. They crushed each other in a mad attempt to flee. The screaming inside continued, audible even inside the car, along with the sounds of breaking glass and shattering dishes.

"You going to help or not?" Lou's face looked the way I felt. Absolute terror, pure white fear.

I glanced down at the Deliverator, but couldn't keep my hands from trembling just thinking about it. I'd passed the mandatory firearms training course when I joined the BSI. Knew the gun wouldn't bite. Knew it could kill. "Call for help. Get another field team down here."

He shook his head, patting the walkie-talkie clipped to his belt. "Jesus, lady, there's co-orgs showing up everywhere. There's not going to be another team."

I offered him the Deliverator. "I could do more harm than good in there. You do it. I'm a translator."

"That badge says different." He looked at my BSI badge, almost accusing me.

Field pay. Field operative. Didn't the director tell me this would be safe? I didn't sign up for killing co-orgs. I didn't sign up for killing spiders. One look at Lou said he might be the only person in the situation more terrified than I was.

From the safety of my office, taking on the dead seemed so much easier. For one split second, I wished I believed the way the other field operatives did. Wished I had a bag of religious symbols and the confidence someone *wanted* me to win. But as far as I could tell, we made our own decisions.

I took my Deliverator and stepped out onto the pier. I wasn't even dressed for a fight. Sure, I wore the same shade of dark gray all BSI personnel did, long sleeves and pants, but that was the end of my similarity to Brynner. My suit wasn't even one of the normal tailored ones. I bought it on the clearance rack at a thrift store. Not that the police could tell. They backed away, giving me space. Thinking I was somehow ready, or trained. Or fit.

I couldn't ignore the screams of terror inside. With a shaky hand, I pulled open the restaurant door. My heart pounded in my chest like it was trying to make a break for the safety of the car. In that moment, I stepped out of my safe, normal assignment and into a building with a real co-org.

I couldn't see the source of the screaming. Like most of the pier restaurants, the dining room ran parallel to the water, and wide windows from floor to roof showed sparkling waters beyond. The co-orgs stood out, silhouetted by sunlight across the water. I'd seen them in labs before. Stripped of clothing, tattooed with measurement marks so our scientists could detail changes in the body structure. These still wore the clothes they were buried in.

Behind me, the door clicked closed, and one of the co-orgs turned toward me. Once an overweight man, most of its belly was gone, a raw expanse of intestines all that remained. What was the phrase Brynner used for it? Meat-skin? It fit. The thing in front of me sagged on its bones, jaws hanging loose, eyes vacant.

Just behind it, Brynner wrestled with another one, while another corpse lay on the floor.

I set my feet, raising the Deliverator in both hands to keep steady. The .22 I'd used in training barely kicked at all. When I squeezed the trigger on the Deliverator, it just about tore my arm off.

A hole the size of a teacup blossomed in the co-org facing me. It lurched backward, slammed into a table, and staggered forward. I waited this time, putting a bullet directly into its sternum. And still it lumbered toward me.

"Hold your fire, damn it!" Brynner screamed as he fell backward.

Recognition bloomed, making me sick. The bullets had passed right through the co-org in front of me and buried themselves in the co-org he fought. Two inches over and they would have punched a hole right through him.

So I chose the better part of valor, running down the row of tables, throwing chairs down behind me. This one truly seemed mindless, stumbling, falling, and then getting up and sprinting. I outran it, circling the dining room all the way back to where Brynner wrestled.

The co-org lay on top of Brynner, with one arm wrapped around him. With the other arm, it attempted to strangle him.

By attempt, I mean "did a good job." I ran at it, doing my best soccer kick right into its ribs.

I might as well have kicked a boulder. The Deliverator slipped from my hand, and I went flying over both of them, tripping and crashing into a chair. My leg went numb everywhere it wasn't sending bolts of pain through my spine.

Brynner bellowed, "What are you doing here?" He seized a broken chair leg, shoving it into the co-org's mouth. In the same movement, he rolled out of the way of the one chasing me and swiped at its ankle, tripping it.

It fell at my feet, its head crashing into a table corner on the way down.

Brynner whipped out a set of daggers and stabbed both of them into the co-org he'd been fighting with, releasing a cloud of black smoke.

I stared. My first time ever seeing a co-org die. The patterns in the smoke weren't random. They were almost like gnats in flight, or a swarm of bees. The smoke—the smoke might *be* the Re-Animus. The idea left me amazed. Stunned.

The co-org at my feet latched on to my ankle. With a grip like stone, it crawled its way along me, using the foot I'd smashed as leverage. I rammed an overturned chair at it, kicked with my other leg, and used both hands to intercept the claw it forced toward my throat. All I could think of was my daughter, her eyes closed while she slept in bliss. I'd never see her again.

A shot rang out.

The co-org on me stiffened, his claws nicking the skin on my neck.

Black smoke poured from a bullet hole on its side.

Brynner shoved it with his foot, rolling it off me. "First two out of every three rounds are stoppers. We use them in

the legs to keep the meat-skin from going after someone else."
He put the gun carefully to the co-org's chest and pulled the
trigger three more times. "Every third one is pine, silver, holy
water, and iron ore."

I knew that. Somewhere, I remember hearing it repeated
during firearms training, when I shot at monster-shaped paper
targets with red paint bullets. That's what the driver had tried to
tell me as well.

The co-org stopped writhing and fell limp.

Brynner looked at the gun with disgust, and then back to me.
"You almost killed me. *Always* look downrange of your target."
He removed the magazine from the Deliverator and hurled it at
my feet. "You had no business coming in here. There's a reason
we say, 'Don't get dead.'"

"I was trying to help you." My voice sounded distant,
scratchy and high through the haze of adrenaline and fear.

"Do I look like I need your help?" Brynner sat down on a
booth seat. Every breath he drew came with labored effort.
Blood soaked through the front of his shirt, and his skin turned
pale blue as he sagged over.

I snapped open my cell phone, calling BSI emergency services.

"State the nature of your emergency," said the operator.

"This is Grace Roberts, employee ID 44902. We have a
field operative down."

I floated on a cloud of pain killers through the night, and a haze
of guilt and anger the next day. At noon, the doctors released
me, content I had no concussion. They let me go with a handful
of aspirin and a wrap on my foot that made squeezing into my
comfortable tennis shoes near impossible.

I had nowhere to go.

Home was a two-hour drive, and my car was back at BSI headquarters. So when I limped out the door of the hospital and saw Dr. Thomas waiting, I could only feel relief. He didn't ask questions. Just opened the door, let me get in, and drove me back to BSI headquarters.

In the parking garage, he cut the engine and looked over at me. "You could have been killed."

"I know. I almost shot Brynner by accident."

"I doubt you were trained for those situations, Grace. You have a powerful mind, and determination, but those are only part of dealing with field operations. I'm sure next time you'll be less likely to shoot him. Right now, the director would like to speak with you." He opened his door, and we got out. "Just remember that field teams always stick together."

I rode the elevator to the director's office on my own, limped to her receptionist, who, to my dismay, opened the door for me without delay.

She leaned into her phone. "Grace Roberts is out of the hospital." She looked back at me with a look of pity. "The director will see you immediately."

I dragged my foot on the way into Director Bismuth's office, making each step slow and careful.

She sat behind her desk, reading a report. She didn't look up to meet me. "You weren't walking like that when you exited the elevator." With one hand, she pointed to a bank of camera monitors. "Tell me again what it is you do for the BSI?"

I faced her head-on. "I'm a first-rank translator for ideoglyphic languages. Minor in Egyptian culture."

"Did your courses include training in heavy arms?"

"No."

"What is the outfit you are wearing?" The director stopped to rake her gaze over my bloody clothes.

I stuttered, starting to name brands.

She cut me off, her jaw set, her eyes narrow. "Is it laced with Kevlar? Fitted to your body? Designed to withstand two hundred pounds per square inch? Because if it is not, I have to ask *what you were thinking.*"

"The driver said—"

"Our drivers have a license, a GED, and get paid minimum wage." The director stood. "Answer the question."

I grasped at Dr. Thomas's suggestion like a lifeline. "Field teams back each other up. Always."

Without answer, she walked past me, slamming the office door shut. Director Bismuth began to pace around the room, watching me the whole time. After several laps she stopped. "Ms. Roberts, how did you wind up at the restaurant?"

I recounted the story, and how Brynner charged in. How I felt like I *had* to do something. "He was part of my field team."

She nodded, then punched numbers on her desk phone. "Put me through to room 223. This is Margret Bismuth. You'll find me listed under 'Family.'"

The phone clicked, and after a moment, Brynner answered. "Carson speaking."

Director Bismuth's eyes bulged from her head, and she snarled at the phone. "How could you do that? What were you thinking? You were supposed to be on a plane to New Mexico. You foolishly led an analyst into a situation with multiple co-orgs."

"Good to hear from you, too, Aunt Maggie." Brynner coughed. "Did Grace tell you she almost shot me? I'm fine, in case you are wondering."

She glowered at the phone like her gaze could melt it. "You are *not*. Medical didn't clear you to take active assignments. I didn't clear you for this operation. And you should know that I have Grace Roberts in my office right now."

I think the noise from the other end was the sound of Brynner choking.

"You are the closest thing I have to family, Brynner Carson, but you will *never* be your father. Heinrich Carson put other people's safety first."

She spun in her chair, her back to me. "You will escort Ms. Roberts to your aunt and uncle's home and ensure she obtains access to your father's journals. Your only assignment will be to rest and heal. I've read our psychiatrist's report. He wrote enough about you to cover an entire field team."

Only silence answered.

"Your priority is to determine the location of this heart. It is your only priority. If I find that you have led Ms. Roberts into contact with another co-org, I will terminate your association with the BSI. I love you like a son, Brynner, but I can't allow you to endanger others. Now, get ready. You'll leave on the three o'clock flight."

She didn't wait for his answer.

The afternoon sun sparkled on distant ferries moving in and out of the port, and the office building murmured with noonday work. I was lost in my own head, rewinding the conversation to play it over in my head again and again.

"You're his aunt?"

When the director turned back to me, the edges of her lips curled up ever so slightly. "Not in the strictest sense, but some family you don't get to choose. Lara and Heinrich were my best friends. I meant what I said when I dispatched you. You are to translate Heinrich's journals, file the reports, and come home."

"Brynner didn't ask me to go into the restaurant."

"No, but I ordered him to catch a flight, and he ignored me. He should have known you would follow him. Field teams do in fact stick together."

I nodded. "Next time I'll leave the co-orgs to him."

"I meant what I said to you about this being a safe, quiet assignment. There isn't to be a next time. If Brynner does attempt to drag you into another encounter, you are to call me immediately."

She walked around the desk, pressing a business card into my hand. "Do I make myself clear?"

"Yes, ma'am." I rose, sensing a dismissal.

BRYNNER

Hospitals were like a second home to me. By eighteen, I'd spent so much time in them it just seemed natural to visit now and then. The doctors had sewn my wounds back together and wrapped my chest in tape, but the pain stayed with me.

I didn't take pain meds.

I couldn't.

My dad's words came back to me every time I looked at pills. "Drugs will make you vulnerable. Vulnerable will make you dead." Better to embrace the pain and live than let a meat-skin slaughter me while I languished in a drug-induced stupor.

And they had tried to get Dad. Tried every which way they could. Crawling out of the tanks at gas stations. Jumping off overpasses when Dad drove by. Anything to get at the man who hounded and haunted them throughout the world.

They didn't hate me the same way. I'd sent more meat-skins back to the grave than I could count. Only had one call me by name. No. My Dad's name. What I needed was a vacation. To find a sunny spot in the Middle East where I could float out on a raft, a few feet from shore, and rest.

Sleep. Forget.

Instead, Director Bismuth treated me like some errand boy. "Go fetch your father's notes, Brynn. And take Grace Roberts with you. Don't go doing the only thing you've ever done, because she won't stay in the car."

Speaking of Grace, that's who met me at the hospital door. She wore the same tired clothes from yesterday, splattered with meat-skin blood, and even with bags under her eyes, she looked beautiful. Though she favored her right foot, she offered me a hand. "I thought this time I'd drive. Even with my injury, I can get us to the airport without any side trips."

I trudged around the car and opened the door.

"I said I'm driving." She flashed me an angry glare.

I bowed my head. "A gentleman opens the car door for a lady."

She sure didn't open the car door for me. I got in, strapped on my seat belt, and wondered what we'd talk about for twenty-five minutes. Or three hours, on the plane. "Is my gear bag in the trunk?"

Grace hit the open freeway and changed over four lanes in one smooth sweep. "Director Bismuth said you wouldn't be needing your armor."

A wave of panic like an ocean undertow hit me. "We have to go back."

She didn't look away from the road. "We have to make our flight this time. You might not care, but I need my job."

I fought down the nerves. "Please. Please. Ms. Roberts— Grace. We have to go to BSI headquarters. I left something personal there." I tried to keep the desperation out of my voice.

She slowed down so we weren't passing state troopers and glanced over her shoulder. "She sent a box for you. In the backseat."

I almost threw myself over the seat, wincing as my stiches pulled, but my hands brushed cold steel. I slid the box back into my lap and ran my thumb over the lock. With a hiss, the bars retracted.

Inside, black velvet cradled my blades. The only part of my arsenal I couldn't rebuild or replace. Relief made me weak and accented the pain coursing through me.

I waited for her to ask. Ask about the blades. Or why my hands shook when I didn't know where they were.

She waited until we almost reached the airport. "You want to tell me about this place we're going? Some sort of survivalist compound? Do they eat dogs? Train with rattlesnakes and run on broken glass?"

I couldn't help but laugh. "No. Emelia and Bran take after Mom." I'd said the word "Mom." I bit my lip. "Emelia's a doctor. Bran sells insurance. Life, car, whatever."

We pulled up at the airport, where the BSI courier took our car. At the security center, I dropped the bag with my blade box on the conveyor and took out my BSI badge.

The guard waved me on through, but stopped Grace.

"Grace Roberts? I need to see your badge, ma'am."

Grace fumbled around her neck and brought out the placard. "Why?"

He handed her the second metal box in my bag. "Signing your weapon through."

Grace managed to keep her shock hidden until after we'd exited to the concourse. There, she found a seat and snapped the box open. Inside sat a Deliverator and three magazines. She read the scrawled note attached and clamped the lid closed like her gun might try to escape.

While she fussed, looking out the window, I snatched a glimpse at the note. In handwriting like smashed spiders, it read, "Another relic from my days collecting samples. Welcome to the field. Don't get dead."

7

BRYNNER

The first hour in a metal can with Grace left me no doubt how she felt. She'd probably heard stories about me. Most of them were true. Maybe all of them. It wasn't her animosity that bothered me. An angry woman is one step from a passionate woman. It was the way she distanced herself, even crammed into airline seats, flying cargo class. The luggage had more room than we did, but Grace didn't even brush elbows with me.

And I worried about what she'd think when she met Emelia and Bran. They knew secrets I didn't share with anyone.

Then the in-flight service came. The flight attendant checked back with me over and over, each time showing enough ivory in her smile to make a poacher jealous. Certainly enough to make Grace jealous. Of my drink.

"Excuse me," she said as the flight attendant brushed my arm. "Could I get another glass of wine?"

The flight attendant shook her head. "I'm sorry, miss. We're all out." Then she leaned over and whispered in my ear, her lips tickling. "Can I bring you anything from first class?"

"Wine." I winked at her. "Red, please."

"Of course, Mr. Carson. It's an honor to have you on board." She came back a few minutes later with a miniature bottle and a note saying she'd love to put the lay in my layover if I had time. I waited until after the flight attendant retreated to offer Grace the bottle. "Can I buy you a drink?"

She looked out the window, but her gaze kept creeping back to the bottle. "Buy? Just offer that bimbo a smile, and I'm sure she'll give you *anything*."

"Grace. Can I call you Grace?" She didn't answer, and I took that for a yes. "I can't help but notice you forgot to say, 'Thank you for saving me from the meat-skin.' That your first time in close quarters with one?" I pushed the wine toward her.

Grace grudgingly took the bottle. Then she sighed, and pratically whispered, "Thank you for saving me. But I did call an ambulance for you."

"We'll call it even, then. I saw your face while the meat-skin tried to kill you. What were you thinking of?"

Grace stared out the window at the clouds. "People I wouldn't see again."

"Your daughter. You spend a lot of time with her?"

"Not as much as I'd like."

I refilled her glass, and held it up for her. "Please?"

As she took it from me, her fingertips touched my hand, smooth and warm against my palm, sending a spark of static electricity up my arm.

Grace took a long drink. "What do you want from me?"

That was a question I wasn't ready to answer. "Just talk to me. Would it kill you to sit in that chair, relax, and talk to me?"

"I'm not the latest puzzle for you to figure out. How about you pay some attention to someone else? Like your biggest fan in the airline uniform?" Grace looked over the rows to where the flight attendant stood.

I kept my eyes on Grace. "I like puzzles."

Her eyes lit up. "All right. I'll make you a deal. You solve a puzzle of mine, I'll talk with you the rest of the way. I'm sure with another hour, even I couldn't resist your charms."

Now that was my sort of agreement. "Lay it on me. Two trains in opposite directions? How much wood could a wood-chuck chuck?"

Grace giggled. "Oh, please. There's a secret about the relationship between the numbers one, three, seven, and eighteen. You tell me what it is, you solved my puzzle." She flipped open a magazine and began browsing, making an impressive effort to ignore me.

And I spent the rest of the flight doodling. Doing sums, division. Putting them in every conceivable order and algorithm. When the plane touched down, I crumpled up the napkin and grabbed my carry-on. "Fine. You won. What's the secret?"

Grace kept her mouth shut until we hit the concourse. "The secret is I didn't want to have to talk to you. There's no relationship between those numbers. Or us."

I stalked off to rent a car and pretended I couldn't hear her laughing to herself. While I waited for them to pull the car up, my anger cooled, replaced by a cold worry, like a headache and storm cloud over me at the same time.

From the moment we left the airport, I sank into a funk

that I couldn't shake. With each turn and mile, my worry mounted. Finally, we pulled into the long gravel driveway of a sprawling one-story house. A porch swing hung from the wraparound deck, looking out across the cacti.

Without touching it, I remembered the feel of the wood and creak of the chains during hot afternoons. Everything, from the buzz of hummingbirds to the sawing song of grasshoppers reminded me of the last summer I spent here. Of why I left.

And why I hadn't returned.

"Are we going in at some point?" Grace interrupted my reverie, a bead of sweat marring her perfect porcelain skin.

No. Not if I had my way. I'd just stay in the car for the next three weeks.

The front door flew open, and out burst my aunt Emelia. She had Mom's dark black hair down to her shoulders and wore a tan cotton tank top and crucifix necklace. So much for staying in the car. I unlocked my door and swung it open, only to find Aunt Emelia blocking my way.

"Brynner Carson, I'm so glad you're home." She carefully hugged me, avoiding the stiches and my ribs. Then she let me go and walked around the car to grab Grace by the hand. "Maggie gave me a call. Told me you two were coming. Grace, isn't it?"

The momentary look of terror on Grace's face told me she had no more of an idea what to say than I. "That's right. Grace Roberts. It's a pleasure to meet you."

"No need to be so formal," said Aunt Emelia. "I'll take a look at your foot once you're settled in. I'm looking forward to a family dinner. I've been waiting to embarrass him with some of these pictures for years." She looked over to me, a smug smile on her face.

I hadn't panicked so hard since the time six meat-skins ambushed me on the way home from the dentist.

To my absolute relief, Aunt Emelia took Grace's bag and turned back toward the house. "Come on in, young lady. I want to check Brynn's stitching and what kind of mess he's made of himself this time."

"Ma'am," Grace called, "if you don't mind, I'm excited about translating this. I really can't wait to get working."

Emelia stopped short. She turned and crossed her arms until Grace looked away. "I haven't been 'ma'am' in nearly thirty years, and if you call me anything but 'Aunt Emelia' you and I will have cross words. There will be enough time for work later, now get inside and get you some tea."

And more than anything, I wished Grace had been right. That we were going to a survival camp where the worst things were broken glass, rabid dogs, and rattlesnakes. Inside that house, I wasn't Brynner Carson, celebrated BSI hero. Or even Brynner Carson, son of Heinrich Carson. I was just Brynner, or boy.

I'd rather have taken on snakes, dogs, and glass.

We passed through the front door, into Emelia's formal living room. As a child, I never dared set foot in it. The cushions on the couch were always placed just so, the curtains drawn and tied. Even as an adult, I shuddered when Grace stepped onto the carpet in her shoes.

"Shoes by the door," I whispered. I kicked off my boots and set them together, then tiptoed through the living room into the kitchen.

Emelia emerged from it, shoving a tall glass of sun tea at me. "Sit."

Grace stepped on the heels of her shoes to take them off, but otherwise didn't move.

"Sit," said my aunt.

Grace looked at her clothes, covered in bloodstains, and back to the immaculate couches. "I'm sorry, I was called up from Portland and all my—"

Emelia cut her off. "You didn't get time to pack? You poor thing." She waved Grace along after her, and turned down the hall. "Shower is this way. I'll wash your clothes and find you something to wear. Those BSI folks would work you to death. Let's see that foot of yours as well."

I couldn't relax until I left the living room.

In the kitchen, chilled air from the vents made goose bumps ripple across my skin. I opened the fridge and took out a bowl of grapes. Ten years on, and Emelia still kept them in the same place.

"I didn't know if you'd actually come. Maggie said you were on your way." Aunt Emelia's voice startled me, making my adrenaline race.

"I didn't get much choice."

She nodded. "I hoped you'd come home to see us."

"I always meant to. I've just been busy. Meat-skins everywhere. Too many of them, not enough of me."

Aunt Emelia leaned over, looking at my chest. "Grace's foot is bruised, not broken. Now, I hear you got yourself busted up bad in Greece. You want to tell me about it or just show me the wounds?"

I'd seen this routine more times than I could count, growing up. I knew better than to argue.

She pulled out a kitchen chair and turned on the lights. "Come on, boy. Off." Aunt Emelia disappeared, replaced by Dr. Emelia Homer.

I knew, from years of trying, better than to fight with Dr. Homer. I peeled off my shirt, struggling to slide the sleeves down.

With practiced ease, she ripped off the tape, taking half my chest hair with it. "Boy, what did you tangle with?"

"Re-Animus."

She looked at me like I'd tried and failed to lie. "I know that. What was it riding in at the time?"

"An investment banker, I think. At least, as best we could tell. As soon as it knew I was there, it tried to butcher me like a chicken. It was collecting victims, using a brothel as a front."

"And the bullets didn't work?"

Her tone said it was a trap. One I'd heard her try to spring on Dad throughout my youth. "You know me. Bullets aren't really my style."

"Oh, yes. That and 'Emelia, I couldn't get a clean shot.'" She imitated Dad's accent, with long *e* sounds and thick consonants. "Where have I heard that before? Those stitches would look bad on a corpse. We're going to do them right."

She disappeared down the hall and returned with a suture kit and a needle.

"No drugs."

"Brynner Carson—"

I held up my hand the way Dad did. "No drugs. Drugs leave you—"

The sting of a needle on my shoulder bit me like a fly. As fast as it came, she pulled the needle out and shoved it into a sharps container. "Stubborn Carson men."

I rubbed my shoulder. "I don't need stitches on my arm. Or vitamin D. And I had a tetanus shot at both hospitals."

"Fine. Be that way, but get out of my kitchen chair. Lie in the recliner, and I'll stitch you up." She practically yanked the chair out from under me.

The hours of flying, the stress of so many days on the edge wore on me, and I stumbled my way to the recliner. Once I'd relaxed, she snapped on nitrile gloves and opened a new set of syringes.

"I said no drugs—" Somewhere along the way, she'd replaced my hands with iron anvils. Even my eyelids took supreme force to keep open.

"I heard you." She injected me along both sides of the wound, counting off in steady time.

The numb feeling that spread along the wounds should have caused my heart to rattle in my chest, but the adrenaline wouldn't come.

"Is the Valium taking effect?" She looked into my eyes, gauging my pupils. "You look nice and comfy. Let's get that wound sewn up right."

And that right there was why I hated going home.

GRACE

Showering in a strange person's house was exotic by my standards. I lived a quiet life, doing my best to make sure nothing of importance happened around, to, or by me. Still, the rules my mother taught me growing up stayed with me.

Be clean.

Be quiet.

Her third rule, "Be careful," I didn't need. Mom's bad choices in men weren't my bad choices. No, I'd made all new ones of my own. And lived with the consequences every day.

When I cut off the water and toweled dry, I found my clothes missing. Replaced, in fact, by a mishmash of clothes that might have fit when I was thirteen, or might be wearable when I was fifty. Still, it beat wearing co-org blood and smelling like hospital. Once I was dressed, I found my way back to the living room.

There, the woman Brynner called Aunt Emelia leaned over him, working a needle and thread through his skin in a way that made my stomach churn. She glanced up at me. "We're almost done here. Brynner got the bad end of a meat-skin. Maybe next time he'll shoot it instead of shaking hands with it."

Brynner stared off into space, his eyes glassy.

"Is there something wrong with him?" I waved a hand in front of his face.

She nodded. "He's got Heinrich Carson's genes and my sister's stubbornness. I gave him something to help him relax. Boy's still with us. Just moving slow."

It registered to me he wasn't wearing a shirt. His muscles, even at rest, showed clearly, from wide pectorals to an abdomen that said if he ate the fries, he ran the stairs.

Scars covered his tanned skin. From the new one, a slash that started at his abdomen and worked its way up to his collarbone, to dozens of white bars, burns, and scratches.

I didn't mean to stare. Or to admire his body. What sort of strength did he have? Where on earth had he gotten those scars?

"He's always had a fine build." Aunt Emelia nodded to me. "Well, not always. In the fourth grade he had a chest like a pencil and ran around with a squeaky voice like a parrot."

My cheeks heated up, and I stammered a protest.

"So how did you and Brynner meet?"

At those words, his head lolled over in my direction, his eyes pleading with me. The legendary Brynner Carson didn't look so impressive now.

"A briefing. We met at a field briefing. The first time I'd ever seen him up close."

Brynner let out a sigh, relaxing back.

"Not the first time I'd ever *heard* of him, of course."

Brynner's eyes fluttered open, and his gaze locked on me.

Emelia shook her head. "I'll bet not. What do you think now that you know him?"

I wanted to relish this moment, but fear wasn't an emotion I enjoyed, my own or others'. I spoke with care, choosing each word. "I think I don't know the real Brynner Carson. I think I've heard what people think. Maybe what he wants people to think."

Emelia rewarded me with a smile and a nod. "And how's he been sleeping?"

"Sleeping?" I couldn't stop my mouth from falling open. Or the surprise or shock on my face. "I can't really say. We've only been together a short while." Whether I counted it by hours on the plane or days since I took the assignment, it was true.

Aunt Emelia put a hand on her chin and waited for me to say more, but I'd said enough already. "Well, we'll ask him later when he's feeling more talkative. Let me go wash up, and I'll make some dinner. My husband will be home soon and eager to see you both."

By dinnertime, an hour and a half later, I'd grown used to Emelia. Her open and warm nature made it hard for me to distrust her, even though I'd had plenty of practice. The two times I broached the subject of Heinrich's journals, her one-word answers made it clear this was not the time.

So I busied myself in the kitchen, cutting salad, until the sound of a distant garage door opening announced someone arriving.

After a moment, a stout man in his sixties bustled into the kitchen. Tall, with wide shoulders and a protruding belly, he walked right past me to squeeze Emelia in a bear hug. His black polyester suit looked like something from the eighties.

Then he turned and looked at me, tipping his head. "Ma'am."

"Grace Roberts, sir." I dried my hands and offered him a handshake.

He looked me over from head to toe like a horse trader making an appraisal. "You're too pretty for our boy. You come here with him on purpose?"

"Hush," said Emelia, smacking him in the chest. "Go set the table. And check on Brynner; he's been dozing." After he ambled out, she looked at me. "I'm sorry. Bran has a habit of speaking his mind."

"He called me pretty. I think I'll let him live."

Bran called from the living room, his voice dark with worry. "Emmy, the boy's doing it again."

Emelia turned off the stove and ran to the living room with me at her heels. Brynner thrashed back and forth, caught in a nightmare. His lips moved, but no sound came out.

"Aren't you going to wake him up?"

Emelia nudged me. "He might take it better from you."

"I don't get paid—" I clamped my mouth closed, reminding myself that I *did*. Field grade, field operative pay. Kneeling by the recliner, I put one hand on his arm. His skin radiated heat, making my fingertips tingle. "Brynner, wake up. Come on, wake up."

He didn't move.

I shook him, and his head lolled. He was whispering words through gritted teeth.

With my other hand, I reached out, cupping his jawline. "Brynner." His beard stubble scratched my hand, his skin almost fever hot. "Brynner, wake up."

Brynner's eyes shot open, wild, feral. He lunged at me.

8

BRYNNER

The dream unfolded the same as before. Mom, her face slack with horror and realization. The blood running from her chest where a spear protruded. Her gaze locked on the silver jar in her hands as the air before me shimmered.

She tossed it, her blood-flecked lips mouthing words without voice. "Brynner."

I moved to go after her, but in the dream, like my memory, my legs weighed two tons each, and my arms wouldn't move. The monsters looming behind her watched the Canopic jar sail through the air. Into my hands.

"Brynner, wake up." Fueled by guilt, I hurled myself toward the fading image, forcing my arms to reach for her—

And off the couch, onto a hardwood floor. Sweat covered me. My limbs shook.

"Get off me." Grace Roberts's voice squeaked the words.

She lay pinned beneath me, gasping for breath. A few feet away, my aunt and uncle watched, not even trying to hide their amusement. I pushed myself off Grace, ignoring the pain in my chest. The embarrassment hurt more. I wanted to make an impression on Grace, not a belt-buckle-shaped bruise.

Grace struggled to disentangle herself, then scrambled away, a mixture of fear and concern on her face.

What did I say? What did she hear? I rose to my knees, woozy from whatever Aunt Emelia had given me. And afraid. Fear was normal. A constant in my life.

"Son." Bran Homer, the man who raised me from the day I turned nine until I ran away. He offered me a hand up and over to the dinner table.

I'd eaten more relaxing dinners in the morgue, waiting for bodies to get checked in. Still, it wasn't my fault. You try having dinner with a family you haven't seen in ten years and see how much eating you get done. I forked my chicken, pushing it around my plate, until the silence grew so heavy I couldn't stand it anymore.

"Tomorrow, I want to look at some of Dad's things." I glanced to Emelia, knowing it was more her call than Bran's.

Emelia nodded, as though I'd just said I was going fishing. "Of course. Grace tells me she's going to translate them for you."

Grace said what? I bit my lip until it hurt, then forced another tack. "You did good work on the stitches. Feels better."

Bran took another chicken breast and tore into it. "You'll be going down to the clinic tomorrow with your aunt."

"But I need to be here with—"

Aunt Emelia shot me a warning glance, telling me I'd be better off picking a fight with a rattlesnake. The snake would give in sooner.

Grace offered a conciliatory smile to the both of us. "I'll be okay on my own. I'm a big girl." About then, my mind finally registered that Grace had changed clothes. Not that she didn't look stunning in a gray suit with co-org blood spattered on it.

Just that she seemed to be rocking the eighties, with her hair in a ponytail and a button-down blouse she couldn't button all the way up. And no bra? I clamped my eyes on my plate, hoping she hadn't noticed me noticing her.

Grace set down her drink. "Ms. Homer—"

"Girl, what did I say? It's Emelia. Or Aunt Emelia, please, sugar."

Grace nodded. "Aunt Emelia, is there a drugstore in town? I need to stop off for a few things on my way to the motel."

"Motel?" asked my uncle, like she'd just said "Brothel." Which, given what the Big 8 motel was most often used for, made sense. "You don't want to stay there."

Aunt Emelia pushed away from the table. "I'll go make up the bed for you in Brynner's room."

Grace spewed tea back into her cup, letting it dribble down her chin. At least it didn't come out her nose.

I stood up to pat her on the back until she held up a hand. "Thank you, Aunt Emelia, but BSI rules say it's not a business trip if at least one of us doesn't stay in the motel."

"That's right," said Grace. "Rules are rules. I'll be back in the morning before you know it."

Bran didn't bother hiding his distaste, wrinkling up his nose like I'd stepped in something in the yard, but he kept his opinions to himself. "The boy will show you the way out there later.

If you insist." He pointed to the key rack on the bar. "Son, the Black Beast is yours."

Driving Grace around in that would be a lethal blow to my pride. A coat of black house paint, cracked vinyl cushions, and worst of all, no backseat made it definitely not my kind of vehicle. "I'm not taking her anywhere in it."

"Then you'll walk." That same infuriating patience he used every time I blew up at him as a teen came back. "Now, let's pray."

Aunt Emelia brought out the prayer bells, lit the incense, and offered Grace a bell. "Honey, something wrong?"

"No." She squirmed, as if the incense might burn her. "I— I don't do prayer bells."

"It's okay, sugar." Aunt Emelia blew out the incense. "Are you Jewish? We can throw open the door for Elijah, if you want. Bran can say mass in Latin. We're flexible."

"I don't actually do religion."

I counted twenty heartbeats before Bran spoke. "But you're a field op."

Grace folded her hands together, speaking with slow patience. "I'm a translator on field assignment."

"So you don't actually believe in *anything*?" My uncle raised both eyebrows and squinted at Grace.

And like a soldier marching to a massacre, Grace answered. "Yes. I believe in science. In math. In chemistry. I believe in understanding the world rather than making up stories to explain how it works."

Aunt Emelia almost dropped the tea pitcher.

"No," said Grace. "I don't believe in a sky wizard who makes up rules against pork. I don't believe in a devil who wants me to sacrifice goats. And if a Jewish carpenter crawls out of his grave, Brynner will probably put him back in it."

Emelia leaned across the table toward Grace, as if she could force her to understand. "You have to believe in something. You have to."

"I believe I'm hungry," said Grace. "Could you please pass the mashed potatoes?"

Food was practically my aunt's first religion, and every dish she served got baptized in gravy she made from bacon grease. She handed the bowl to Grace, her lips drawn into a frown that said she hadn't given up yet.

After the most awkward meal of my life, I volunteered to do dishes by myself. I polished every plate and cup until it sparkled, in an attempt to give Grace and Aunt Emelia the time they needed to air their differences.

Only when the arguing died down did I grab the key ring for the Black Beast. In the living room, Grace wore a peaceful expression, while Aunt Emelia wrung her hands.

Aunt Emelia fidgeted as I came in, then looked back to Grace. "I just think a little religion might make you feel a lot better."

"I really appreciate the concern, and I know you are trying to help, but I feel fine. I'm fine." Grace looked like I felt every time I said I was fine.

I held up the keys. "It's getting late, and Grace and I have to work tomorrow. We should probably get her settled in at the motel."

Emelia sighed and crossed her arms. "We'll talk tomorrow."

Grace followed me out into the chill New Mexico night. I stopped by the Black Beast, a Ford pickup manufactured sometime before Abraham Lincoln, or possibly before Father Abraham himself. "It's not far to the highway. The Big 8 isn't high-class, but it's low-cost, and last time I was in town, the ice machine still worked."

"I'm good almost anywhere." Grace ran one hand along her hair self-consciously. "About that drugstore." She walked toward the rental car.

"Orting's. It's on Main. We'll drive over to it first." For just a moment, it felt like a normal conversation. The kind I'd have with any woman. If I talked with women. I never remembered the mindless conversations in the evenings, and the morning after was often embarrassing.

By every right, the evening had disaster marked on it. Aunt Emelia drugging me. Grace knowing about the nightmares. Aunt Emelia and Grace arguing about religion.

But what worried me most was how easily I'd returned to this world, this life.

It felt almost normal.

GRACE

I can do this.

I could do anything for field pay, I told myself. Even tolerate Aunt Emelia's attempts to inject gods I neither knew nor needed into my life. When I agreed to come, I'd thought putting up with the legendary Brynner Carson would occupy all my patience. Thing was, I couldn't tell if the legends about Brynner were myth or mistake. Here, he was just Brynner. Or "boy."

And his family, their fierce loyalty and drive to protect one another made me jealous in so many ways. I followed Brynner in our rental car, all the way to the drugstore. I'd forgotten small-town life, where everyone knew everyone. The attendant took one look at me, realized I was a stranger, and gave me a suspicious glare. But then Brynner walked in behind me.

She took one look at him, and her face lit up. Forgetting me, she rushed over to shake his hand, asking to see his BSI badge, wanting his autograph. Wondering if he remembered her. He smiled and nodded. "Tamara, right? You went to Benton, a few classes behind me."

Her eyes widened, and she pulled her mouth into an expression that said she was either happy or hungry. The way her eyes darted back and forth, the nervous tremble in her fingers as she tapped the counter, even I could tell.

He'd done it again. With that easy personality, projecting trust and confidence, I had no doubt the *other* rumors I'd heard about him were equally true. How he never slept alone, regardless of where he was.

Once I'd gathered a few basic toiletries, a cheap T-shirt labeled "Bentonville," and a pair of sweatpants closer to my size, I checked out, while Brynner waited for me by his truck.

"Do you work with him?" asked Tamara.

"Yes."

She looked out the window. I could've handed her my yogurt punch card instead of the BSI credit card. "What's he like?"

I took my bag once she'd rung it up. "You tell me."

Outside, Brynner leaned against the grill, his gray BSI jacket zipped all the way up. "You look tired. We'll have you set up in fifteen minutes."

"Your drugstore sells clothes and power tools."

"And ice cream. Don't forget the souvenirs for people who accidentally get off the interstate. Welcome to small-town life."

"Speaking of not forgetting, you have an amazing memory.

And a fan." I glanced over my shoulder, to where the drugstore attendant stood, a dust cloth in hand. She held it to the window and stared at us.

Brynner looked down. "I have no idea who she is."

"But you—"

"Her name tag said 'Tamara.' Benton's the only school for twenty miles, and she's way too young for me."

The ease with which he lied frightened me, as did how calmly he admitted to it. "I wasn't aware there was a woman who wasn't your type."

Brynner looked old with experience, if not years. "I don't— Never mind. Follow me." He got back in the truck, waving to the lone police car sitting in the square as we pulled out of town.

The biggest thing about the Big 8 motel was the sign. Not the rooms, of which there were exactly eight, or the ice maker sitting outside, which was just a freezer with ice cube trays in it. A lone soda machine sat beneath flickering fluorescent lights, while moths danced overhead.

Brynner got out ahead of me, headed into the office. By the time I made it out of the car, he and the owner were laughing and joking.

When I stepped inside, the owner took his hat off and offered me his hand. "Welcome, ma'am. Pleasure to have you at the Big 8."

He glanced over to Brynner. "How many hours you need it for?"

Hours?

"Grace is spending the night," he sputtered. "I'm not. She'll need the weekly rate." Brynner's face turned deep red in the cheeks, flushing clean to his chest.

A look of recognition lit up the owner. "Right. Room number eight is clean and ready."

Brynner spoke before I could. "No. Put her in one. Eight has two side windows anything could crawl through, and I don't like her having to walk all the way down there."

The owner shook his head. "One's occupied till ten thirty. I could have it ready by eleven, eleven thirty if you want me to wash the sheets."

"Number eight is fine," I said, taking the key. "I can walk myself all the way there. Good night." I clopped out the door and down the broken concrete walkway until I came to room eight. The key turned easily, and despite my fears, nothing furry scurried across the floor when I turned the light on.

The tired burgundy carpet didn't have stains as much as the stains had tired burgundy carpet. I flounced on the bed and immediately rolled to the center, sagging into a mattress with a taco-shaped indentation in the middle. Field pay, I reminded myself over and over. I thought about calling the care center, but I'd been gone only one day. Not even one day.

Tomorrow, I'd earn my money and make sure if similar opportunities came up, Director Bismuth would call me first.

Outside, Brynner's truck roared to life, and headlights flashed in the window as he backed up. Tires crunched through the parking lot gravel, and then aging brakes whined. A door opened, followed by bootsteps to my door.

Would he really dare knock on my door? What exactly would he expect?

After a moment, the boots retreated, the truck door slammed, and Brynner roared off into the night. My heart slowed, until the throbbing in my ears subsided, replaced by confusion.

So I did the best thing I could, crawling into bed determined that the next day would go better. Smoother. Right.

I woke only once, disappointed but not surprised to find that the motel room had rats. Outside my window, something small scratched back and forth, gnawing something. I threw a shoe at the wall, and it skittered away. That's the last thing I knew until dawn.

9

GRACE

Dawn came early in western New Mexico. Without mountains to hide the sun, it split the plains like a giant, fusion-powered alarm clock. After a shower with depressingly little hot water, I changed into the "Bentonville" T-shirt I bought and the spare clothes Aunt Emelia lent me.

I hung my BSI field badge from my neck, just so folks would know I wasn't some floozy. I was here on official business. When I opened the motel door, the ground beneath my feet crunched. A line of white crystals crossed the door, ran under the window, and ended in a mound by the brick wall.

Salt. A line of salt across my doorway. Was this what Brynner did last night? The man lived on superstitions.

Down at the office, I roused a sleepy teen who looked irritated to be alive. "Where do you serve the continental breakfast?"

"Hold on." He yawned and opened a miniature fridge, then

set out a container of potato salad, a hard-boiled egg, and a carton of milk that sloshed like it had chunks.

I'd rather have feasted on my dirty laundry.

He pointed up the road. "There's also a diner in town."

Who knew when Brynner might see fit to rise and shine? I could at least have my glyph tables ready and maybe read a little of Osiris to get back in the groove. By daylight, Bentonville looked even smaller. If you sneezed on one side of the town, you'd get a bless-you from the other side of the tracks.

I pulled into the town square and parked, then walked through the unkempt grass to the diner. When I opened the door, the communal conversation paused as everyone catalogued the newcomer. After a moment, the buzz of a dozen conversations returned.

A Hispanic woman at least twenty years my senior pointed to the bar. "No tables."

I didn't need a bar stool for two. "What's good?"

"Nothing. He cooks everything in bacon, everything in fat." The waitress, Isabella, according to her tag, pointed with the menu to the fry cook.

"Two eggs. Whites only, not runny, fresh fruit, and coffee." I handed her the menu.

Her gaze darted to my BSI tag before moving on, then she shouted in Spanish, something that sent the fry cook into a frenzy.

"Morning, ma'am." From behind me, a black man spoke, his accent placing him from the Deep South. He slid onto the seat beside me. His shaved head gleamed, dark skin complementing the police uniform he wore. "I'm Sheriff Bishop. You must be part of the Carson field team."

"I am." The words came easily. Not a lie. I was part of it, if only a temporary part.

"Good to see a real BSI team once in a while. We get reports now and then. 'Meat-skins took my dog,' or 'Meat-skins ate the chickens in the coup.' I check them out, but most of the time it's just a coyote." He handed his menu back to the waitress without looking at it. "I'll take it all."

My plate came. I'd only ordered two things. I got three. Not one of them resembled my order. The eggs, sunny-side up, stared up with blind yellow eyes. A slab of bacon like half a pig sat to the side, with a sea of gravy slathered on top of biscuits. "This isn't what I ordered." I flagged down the waitress on her next orbit. "Ma'am? Where's my fruit?"

Sheriff Bishop laughed, a deep rumble that started in his toes. "You ordered fruit? From here? We don't do healthy, low-calorie, or low-cholesterol. Eat hard, work hard, sweat it off in the sun."

Sheriff Bishop watched me while I reluctantly dug into my meal. "You do me a favor? Like I said, mostly, we get coyotes, not meat-skins. But two nights ago, something tore up one of the Donaldsons' horses."

"Was it a wolf?"

He glanced around the restaurant before continuing. "I didn't say ate. I said tore up. I think it's all still there, though could be some guts missing. It'd do me a favor if you and Brynner looked. Coyotes I can handle."

How much I should tell him about our assignment wasn't a subject Brynner and I had discussed. So I did the safe thing. "I'll tell him, but it's his call. Could you tell me which way Brynner's house is?" I mopped up the last bit of gravy with a biscuit.

Again, he rumbled with laughter, then hit the radio on his shoulder. "James, I need you to see the nice lady here with Brynner out to his house. And take that parking ticket off her windshield, too." He showed me a smile of white ivory. "It's good to have Brynner back in town. When he wasn't tearing up graves or taking the high school girls up to the quarry, he was a good kid."

"He did that a lot?"

"The graves or the girls? Only dug up a coffin once. Only God knows how many girls he— Hey, there's James." At the diner door, a dingy white car with "Deputy" on it pulled up. I paid, left a tip just in case I needed to eat there again, and ran to my rental car.

We drove out beyond the city limits, off onto side roads, until I pulled up at a familiar ranch house. The deputy honked the horn three times, then pulled off, leaving me alone at the edge of the desert.

Bran Homer came flying out the door, watched the sheriff back up the driveway, and waved to me. "Morning. You rise like I do."

I shook his offered hand. "Not normally, but I need this job. You think today I could get to work?"

He snorted. "My Emmy just wanted to have a nice dinner with our boy before he got to work. She'll let him into the room today."

"She still angry with me about the whole religion thing at dinner?" I had my principles, but Aunt Emelia shone with such a warm kindness, the decent thing to do was attempt to get along.

Bran sat down in the swing and brushed the leaves out so I could do the same. "I think the word you want is 'confused.' Faith's such a key weapon against the meat-skins, it'd be like leaving half your bullets at home."

"I didn't mean to offend. We work to control the co-orgs every bit as much, we just do it with measurements and analysis.

So it works for everyone." I pulled the laptop from my messenger bag, opened it to the weekly briefings.

Bran nodded. "Don't you worry. If our faith depended on your belief, it wouldn't be *our* faith."

"Can I ask a question?"

"Shoot, girl. Don't mean I have to answer."

"Why do you call Brynner 'son'?"

He looked to the door first. "My Emmy and I had one beautiful daughter. She died two hours later. After that, Lara's boy filled the empty spot in our home, what with his daddy being gone on missions and Lara busy in her lab at all hours. When Lara had the accident, he came to live with us."

"What happened to Lara Carson?" I'd never seen it documented. Even Bran's word "accident" was more information than the "tell-all" books contained.

Bran rose from the swing and opened the door. "Boy doesn't like me talking about it. You ask him. Emmy might talk, or she might not, but if Brynner hasn't told you, it ain't my business."

BRYNNER

I slept in for the first time in five and a half years. The clock said 11:30; my brain asked what year. If I had nightmares, I didn't remember them. I stumbled out to the kitchen, where Aunt Emelia stood, a fry skillet in one hand and a spatula in the other.

The scent of fish fried with coconut oil filled the house.

"That smells so good." I took out a cereal bowl.

Aunt Emelia pointed the spatula at me. "Brynner Carson,

in this house, you miss breakfast, you eat at lunch. Go shower, young man. You'll be hungry enough when lunch is ready."

I was hungry already, but arguing with Emelia Homer was like playing tug-of-war with a monster truck. I'd still be arguing when lunchtime came. So I went to the bathroom, with its rusted sink and a drain that kept two inches of water in the shower at all times.

I dried off and dressed in BSI-issue fatigues. Resistant polymer, smooth so meat-skins had nothing to grapple on, tough enough to prevent road rash, and generally speaking, clothes that wouldn't get a man laid unless the circus was in town and all the clowns were sick.

When I got back into the kitchen, it hit me who was missing. "I forgot to get Grace from the motel. She'll be halfway to El Paso if she takes a wrong turn."

Aunt Emilia let out a harrumph. "Unlike *some* people, she gets to work on time. She's been translating since eight. Be a dear and tell her lunch is ready."

I lumbered down the hall to the memorial room. When I was younger, it still held a crib and changing table. When Dad died, and I wanted everything burned, Aunt Emelia took it all. Refused the BSI's offer to buy it. Refused my demands to turn it over.

I opened the door, and the smell took me back twelve years in one breath. Old leather, fountain pen, and shaving cologne. The scents of Dad. He'd come home with twelve-inch gashes, shave, shower, and then let Mom drive him to Aunt Emelia's clinic to get sewn up.

And if one minute of his life passed without him making a record of it in one of those books, I didn't know when it was.

"Morning." Grace's voice startled me from my reverie. She

sat cross-legged on the floor, wearing an orange "Bentonville" T-shirt and black sweatpants. She didn't wear a trace of makeup, letting me see every fine detail of her cheeks, which had freckles at the edges. She brushed a hair out of her face, looking at me beneath long lashes. "What?"

I looked away, caught staring. There seemed to be no safe way to appreciate Grace. If I let my eyes rove her body, she'd know me for a creep. If I drank in the details of her face, she shied away. "Lunch. My aunt cooked fish for us."

Grace rose, leaving a mound of notebooks in her wake.

"Did you already translate all of those?" My Egyptian wasn't good, but that was incredible.

Her musical laugh made me smile. "Hardly. There's no organization, so I have no idea which ones came first or last. I want to start with the last ones, if possible. How many of these did he keep?"

"All of them. Dad always had a journal. Drew maps, wrote instructions. If it was in his brain, it's here." I looked around at the stacks of boxes. "Somewhere."

Grace followed me out to the kitchen, taking a place at the end of the table.

Aunt Emelia untied her apron and hung it on the rack, then sat with us. "We'll go down to the clinic after lunch, Brynner. Get those X-rays done. Catch up on your records."

I shook my head. "Sorry, can't leave Grace alone with Dad's journals. I'll stay here just in case she needs anything. Plus, if I get any more X-rays, I might start glowing in the dark."

"I don't mind going. I could use a break to clear my head." Grace put down her fork. "If you don't mind the company."

"I do." While spending more time with Grace was my number one priority, I was *not* taking her with me to my checkup.

Embarrassing wouldn't begin to describe that. Of course, having a checkup from the woman who raised you through puberty didn't exactly fit on my list of "things I can't wait to do."

"Well, if you trust Grace with your father's journals, I'll trust her." My aunt watched me over her bifocals.

Clearly a test, one I'd normally fail. If I said no, Grace wouldn't speak to me again. If I said yes, it might be a lie. Or even worse, the truth. Because the nagging part of me I usually ignored told me Grace wasn't here because of me.

I could live with that. "I trust her."

I must have waited too long to answer. She'd read my face. Knew the conflict inside, or at least suspected it.

Emelia looked away. "Then it's settled. Grace, you are welcome to spend time on the porch swing if you need to get away. If you leave, just pull the front door closed."

I'd rather have gone back to bed after lunch. "I'm a grown man. I don't need you to drag me into the office for a checkup."

Aunt Emelia held up her palms. "Men are just bigger boys. Take care of yourself like an adult, and I'll treat you like one."

I glanced over to Grace, who didn't move fast enough to hide her smile. Not by a long shot. Then she reached over and touched my arm, her fingertips cool and smooth. "The sheriff wanted to know if you would check out a dead horse."

I didn't respond, being more focused on the chills where she'd brushed against me. When her words finally sank in, they frustrated me for many reasons, not the least of which was I didn't want to stop thinking about Grace, and her fingertips, and deep blue eyes.

Which I was staring at again. *Must focus. Focus. Not focus on Grace.* "Sorry. Let's say it turned out that it really *was* a meat-skin. I seem to recall direct orders not to expose you to anything dead. I'm not sure you should even be eating that fish." I forked another bite of my own.

Grace shrugged. "You didn't have a problem disobeying orders before."

Nothing was worth risking my operative status, or dragging Grace back into a danger zone before I got to know her very, very well. "That was the old me. I'm turning over a new leaf, at least until you are off my team."

"Excellent," said Aunt Emelia. "In that case, you'll cooperate completely."

Grace and Emelia exchanged a knowing grin. Conspiring against me together.

So I went to the clinic, rubbing my fingers over the spot on my arm where her skin had met mine.

10

GRACE

After Aunt Emelia hauled Brynner away, I went out to the porch to work. I rocked in the swing, savoring a soft breeze. How on earth would I make sense of the jumbled mess in even one of the journals, let alone all of them?

I set my sun tea on the porch rail and surveyed the yard, a mix of crushed lava rock and cactus. Red pumice ran right up to the foundation of the house—except for a gray rock line beside the foundation. A quick trip down the stairs let me look closer. The gray rock had flecks of black. On a hunch, I touched my tongue to a pebble. Salt.

The whole house was surrounded by salt.

I'd seen Brynner's line of salt outside my door and heard field operatives insist on salting the thresholds of a house before entering, but what sort of man built a house on salt rock?

I retreated to the air-conditioned sanctuary, sat down in the memorial room, and picked up another journal. The symbols, the words individually made sense. The problem was, this was a modern man, writing in a language that hadn't changed in thousands of years. The challenge lay in understanding the meaning behind the arrangements.

If I could reach into Heinrich Carson's mind, and understand why he used the symbols he did, I might be able to figure it out. I tossed aside a journal and selected another. Each time I found a starting point, scratching noises under the house distracted me. Like a rat gnawing on wood just below the floorboard. I'd finally found a section of the diaries I understood, detailing a massacre Heinrich interrupted, in which the victims offered themselves willingly. The hours slipped away while I struggled, and the late afternoon cast long shadows. The longer I sat, the less comfortable I felt.

Each creak of the house sent shivers down my spine. My mind began to invent sounds that couldn't be there. The patter of leather skin on dry wood. The scratch of sunken fingernails on wallpaper. I reached into my messenger bag and pulled out the Deliverator for comfort.

Just as I fell into a rhythm of translating, another scurry of activity startled me. In frustration, I slammed the Deliverator on the floor. The scratching stopped. Then started again, right where I'd hit the floor. I scratched once, drawing my nails across the floor.

And something answered, a long, nibbling sound. From the floorboards, a smell, like rotten lunch meat, rose. A smell I recognized from the restaurant in Seattle, sickly sweet and disgusting at the same time.

I slammed the Deliverator down again, and this time, scratched with one nail once, twice, and again.

Again something answered. *Scratch. Scratch. Scratch.*

Out in the living room, a thud made me jump. I shivered from a surge of adrenaline as much as the chill air. Half of me wanted to close my eyes. The other was more afraid of not seeing. Was the grave stench in my mind? Or was I alone with a walking corpse?

I couldn't let fear rule my life. I took the Deliverator and rose to the balls of my feet. A creak from the kitchen floor let me know I wasn't alone. Sliding the door open, I stepped out into the hall.

Something was in the house.

With me.

The wooden floor creaked as it moved, just around the corner, casting a shadow into the kitchen doorway. I wanted to call out, "Who's there?" But the co-orgs in the restaurant had responded to sound as much as movement. Any noise I made might as well include the words "Here I am! Come get me."

The more I tried to force myself to calm down, the more my hands shook. This time there wouldn't be anyone to save me. The fear threatened to flood me, paralyze me. And I made a decision: I was not going to die in the desert, without seeing my daughter again.

So I acted, stepping out into the kitchen, leveling the Deliverator, squeezing the trigger.

As the gun went off, something grabbed my hand and yanked. I flew forward, crashing into the table.

"Grace!" Brynner shouted, nearly screamed at me. "What are you doing?"

The front door slammed open and Aunt Emelia came running in. "What in hades—"

"I heard something. I thought it was—" I couldn't continue, my eyes brimming with tears. I'd let my own imagination nearly kill a man. A combination of fear and embarrassment competed to see which would leave me sobbing.

"What is with you trying to shoot me?" Brynner leaned over, looking at the hole in the far wall.

"Oh, sweetie." Aunt Emelia came over and helped me up, hugging me. "Ignore him. It's just another bullet hole. Whole house is full of them. I'll make the boy patch it up later."

"I'm so sorry. One stupid rat, and I . . ." I stopped, puzzled by the look between the two.

Brynner cocked the Deliverator and held it easily, scanning the shadows. "There are no rats in this house. Scorpions, sure. No rats."

At the mention of scorpions I panicked, trying to find my messenger bag. Rats I could live with.

He glanced to Aunt Emelia. "When did you last lay the barriers?"

"Spring. Bran and I redid them. Olive oil, amber, salt. Everything." Aunt Emelia stopped her crushing hug. "Where did you hear the rat?"

"Under the floor while I was translating. Like the sound at my door last night."

Brynner walked over to face me. "You heard something at the motel and you didn't call me?"

"I heard a rat. Did you lay the salt outside my door?"

He nodded and handed the Deliverator to Aunt Emelia. "Is the crawl space hatch in the back bedroom nailed shut?"

She shook her head.

"Good. I'm going under the house to see what it is. Put that in the gun safe?" He didn't wait, sprinting down the hall toward the bedrooms.

Aunt Emelia walked over to the kitchen and deposited the Deliverator on the counter. Then she took out a bottle of bourbon and poured a shot. "Here, you look like a mess. I'm sorry, we work to keep our boundaries up so the house is safe. One day with the boy home and there's already a damned meat-skin under the house. Probably just a spare, nothing big."

I shook my head. "Drinking on the job is strictly prohibited."

From under our feet, Brynner shouted a muffled rant of curses, then the floor shook as something slammed into it.

I took the shot glass and downed it, gagging as the burning warmth hit me. "I'm sick of hearing meat-skins and shamblers and walkers and spares. I'm good at translating, I'm not used to *this*."

She refilled it from the bottle. "Don't you worry. There isn't one field operative alive who didn't start out confused and scared. Scared is fine. It keeps you alive. Confusion we can help with, once the boy gets back."

Brynner returned, wearing cobwebs, dust, and a scowl. "There's a gap in the barriers five inches wide by the back porch. I'll get some salt and fill it in. Want to see our uninvited visitor?"

I hadn't drunk nearly enough alcohol to prepare me for what he held up. In his grasp, a severed hand writhed, fingers clawing back and forth. He waved to me with it. "Say hello to your admirer, Grace. He's not much to look at but can be handy in a pinch. I'll be back once I've disposed of him." He turned toward the kitchen and made it nearly two steps before a sharp whistle made him stop, and me take another gulp of liquid fire.

Aunt Emelia put her hands on her hips. "Boy, what have I told you about burning the dead in my good oven?"

Brynner froze, his shoulders hunched, and looked at the floor. "Not to. I'll use the grill out back. Don't worry, Grace, this one won't be making any more trouble."

I downed another glass and held it up for a refill.

By the time Brynner came into the living room, the sun had tipped downward and the bourbon had me warmer than the evening chill could touch. He'd showered and changed into a cotton shirt that stretched nicely over his frame.

The front door swung open and Bran bustled in, a pizza box in hand. "How's my favorite woman in the world?"

Emelia shook her head. "We had an incident while Grace was working. Nothing major. Be a dear and put that Deliverator away."

Bran took the gun off the table and gave me a thumbs-up. "Did you get it? Was it a big one?"

His question hung in the air unanswered. Which was answer enough.

Aunt Emelia lit the fireplace, and when it roared and popped, she plunked me down on the couch in front of it. "Boy, get your father's manuals. You have work to do."

And if it weren't for the never-ending bourbon in my hand, I'd have died of embarrassment at the thought of him schooling me. Brynner left and returned with a leather binder the size of an encyclopedia. Inside, hand-drawn sketches of co-orgs filled the pages, with a dizzying array of names.

The BSI version I received in mandatory training showed simple naked corpses. The drawings decorating Brynner's book would give me nightmares for months.

He sat beside me, making me feel like a schoolgirl studying—

or not studying, as the case had been. "The Re-Animus have plagued us since at least the Middle Kingdom of Egypt. Dad thought they were evil spirits, maybe just one, maybe a whole legion. Grandpa van Helsing swore they weren't demons, because he'd personally killed the last demon. Truth is, we don't know, but what we do know is that they live through other bodies." He flipped over a page. "This here, this is your average meat-skin. Some poor schmuck dead for a few days, grabbed by the Re-Animus just for fun. The body gets pushed around for a few hours to maybe kill a few people, and then dropped like a rock. We see these every freaking day in the field."

He turned the page, and I slumped over next to him, letting the bourbon and his warmth spread through me. He caught his breath. Nice to know I still could have that effect on someone. "This is a shambler. If the Re-Animus spends enough time in a body, it starts changing, becoming stronger, and faster. When the Re-Animus moves on, the body will keep moving. It'll do whatever comes to what's left of its mind. Not intelligent, but plenty dangerous. The police won't even shoot at them, because it might bring them running."

He leafed over a few pages. Various body parts drawn in painful detail decorated them. "Here's your friend. A Re-Animus doesn't need a whole body. It can take a spare part or two and use it, though what one would do with a severed foot, I can't really say. In Egypt I heard tell of ears and noses being animated, so go figure."

In the middle of this madness, it almost made sense. A spare part, scratching around under the floor. On and on it went. Page after page of corpses that walked, and mummies, drawings of Re-Animus that made them look like clouds of evil, pages of folk charms.

The list of things that wouldn't kill a Re-Animus would be shorter than the items Heinrich Carson said did. Salt for the foundations to keep them out, pine stakes to sap their strength, amber to poison them, alabaster to prevent them healing.

Brynner's tone said he believed it, every last bit. Why not? It worked, for him. He reached his arm around me, and the bourbon in me smiled at him. He smiled back for a moment, then frowned. "Did my aunt give you something to calm your nerves?"

I nodded. Wasn't it obvious from how I wasn't challenging any of his assertions? Or the way I gave in so easily to the urge to cuddle with him? Oh, if there were a god, I'd have him make a man for me just like Brynner, only one I could keep to myself.

Like that, the charm on his face swept away. Brynner pulled his arm back and pushed me upright. "How many nerves did you need calmed?" He took the drink from my hand and set it aside. "It's time for you to get to sleep."

BRYNNER

I thought about the first time I met a co-org. Dad brought it home in a box and locked me in the room with it and a hatchet until I took care of business. I didn't sleep for a week afterward. Grace, on the other hand, needed to sleep for a dozen hours at least.

She struggled up and off the couch, heading for the door. I snagged her hand. "Whoa, you aren't going anywhere. I'll make up the couch. Or you can have my bed and I'll sleep on the couch."

Grace rubbed one eye with her fist. "I'm going back to my

motel room. I'm not going to be another woman who got drunk and spent the night in your bed."

That stung. I didn't need or want drunk women. If a woman couldn't say she wanted me and for certain, I'd find another friend for the night. And in case she hadn't heard, work women were at least somewhat strictly off-limits.

I looked to my aunt. "Give me a hand?"

She shook her head. "You don't have any right to keep her here. If you don't want her driving and she won't stay, take her back to her motel." She didn't need to remind me to behave.

"You win." With one hand under Grace's arm and the other under her legs, I half carried, half dragged Grace to the truck. She sang most of the way home, a horrible rendition of "Friends in Low Places" that made it clear why she took up translating for a living instead of singing.

I left the truck running while I grabbed a spare key to Grace's room, then dragged her in, flopping her on the bed. One quick perimeter, closet, and under-the-bed check later, she was ready to go night-night, so far out of it that she was practically in another state.

The desert wind whipped a stubby mesquite outside, and the branches scratched the window.

Grace froze, her eyes wide.

"It's okay. Just the wind." I'd known how to tell the difference between corpses at the door and scratchy tree branches when I was ten.

"Don't leave me." Grace's voice took on the high pitch of hysteria as she took off her shirt to reveal a cream-colored bra. She wore her curves well, and if it weren't for the alcohol, it would be an offer worth taking.

"Sorry, but we both need sleep. Some other night?"

She lurched forward, seizing my arm so her fingernails cut into me. "What if it something comes? Stay. I won't tell anyone."

I closed my eyes as she continued to strip, turned away, then ran to grab a trash can. Given how much liquor she'd drunk, her stomach would stage a revolt eventually.

When I returned with the can, Grace had passed out, her arm falling off the bed. One breast peeked from under the covers, a flash of white flesh and dark nipple. I'd heard chainsaws quieter than her snoring. I left her there, locking the door behind me. I needed to hit the bar in Eaton. Find some company to take out the fire Grace lit in me.

But I couldn't drive away, any more than I could stay in her room. Taking a box of rock salt, I reapplied her barrier, then pushed through the brush, adding salt to both side windows. Grace was safe.

I could go home and sleep in a bed, but she'd asked me to stay.

God help me, I wanted to.

After returning the spare key to the office, I went back to the truck and unrolled my bamboo mat in the truck bed along with the foil blanket I kept for emergencies. With my coat pulled down over me, I closed my eyes and dozed.

Through the night, I startled awake from time to time, certain I'd heard something moving. Each time, I got out and searched the brush, and each time, climbed back into the truck without so much as a desert hare to show for it.

Grace's door stayed closed, and so I remained until the sun came up.

I woke with my cell phone ringing and a crick in my back that made it hard to breathe, rolled over, and unlocked my phone. "Brynner Carson speaking."

"Brynner, where is my translator? I've been trying to reach

her all morning." Director Bismuth's crisp New England accent shook the cobwebs from my brain.

The whole truth included several inconvenient situations for Grace. "She's asleep in her room."

She hissed into the phone, "Your aunt tells me you drove Ms. Roberts back to her motel after an incident, and that you didn't come home. What exactly were you thinking, spending the night with her? What have I told you about work women?"

I threw back my head in frustration, and a burst of pain from muscles I didn't know I had rewarded me, breaking any illusion of patience I had. "Look, I drove Grace back to keep her from driving. And turned her down when she asked me to stay."

She paused for a moment. "Lies are unbecoming of you, Brynner. You are known for many things, but restraint is not one of them. Your father would never have acted in such a manner. When are you going to live up to his legacy?"

Stunned, almost unable to answer, I whispered, "I'll try to wake her up." With my muscles aching, I rolled out of the truck bed and banged on her door so hard the windows rattled.

After a couple of minutes, Grace surfaced, withering under the dawn sunlight like a vampire. She had a bedspread wrapped around her and dark circles under her eyes. "What do you want?"

I held out the phone. "You to answer your phone. It's Director Bismuth." I didn't wait for her answer. I ran to the truck and drove, but not back to my aunt and uncle's house.

Instead, I headed to the cemetery, looking for the only person who might ever have understood how I felt.

The Bentonville cemetery stretched out into the desert, carefully clipped prickly pears and cacti providing green among the brown. I knew where I was going, waving to the caretaker, who dropped his rake and followed me.

I didn't intend to dig anyone up today. I just wanted to talk. I wasn't there when my aunt chose the tombstone, because to be there I'd have to let go of the anger I'd nursed so carefully. Coming to his funeral would have meant accepting his choices.

His grave stood out among the others, the mounds of white salt making Dad's grave like his life: a barren place where nothing else could grow.

And I couldn't find the words I wanted at first, so I stood in silence, until the unfairness of the situation bubbled out. But what came out wasn't what I went to complain about. I'd finally found a voice for the question I always wanted to ask him. "Why did you leave me there?"

Dad didn't answer any more now than all the times I asked when he was alive.

"It's not that they didn't love me. I wanted to be with you. You weren't ever going to be able to bring Mom back." I looked over at the grave next to his. "Lara Carson," read the headstone. It lied.

"I do everything you taught me. I kill anything that ought to be dead. And it won't *ever* be enough." Tears coursed down my face, making the world blurry. "I've got scars on my scars. I've broken every bone in my body twice. I'm sick of this. I'm not you. I don't know if I can do it anymore."

After a silence as long as all the conversations we'd had in the past, I turned to leave.

Aunt Emelia stood, watching me. She came every day, laying flowers by Mom's grave, and I guess Dad's.

I knew she'd heard my outburst. "I'm sorry."

The tears on her cheeks matched mine, but instead of scowling at me, she looked on me with compassion. "Don't be, boy. That's been a long time coming."

I walked toward her, when what I wanted to do was run

away the same way Dad did. "I didn't do anything with Grace. I slept in the truck. I don't know why the director—" I did know. Not like I hadn't earned her expectations.

She nodded, her face glistening. "I tried to explain to Maggie this morning."

"If she calls again, I need you to give her a message." I'd never been so certain about anything in my life.

I walked to the truck and didn't look back. "Tell her I quit."

II

GRACE

I woke with a headache like someone playing the bongo drum on my skull, and a memory of asking Brynner to stay. That would be my last foray into bourbon for at least a decade. For one moment, I panicked, incapable of remembering exactly how he'd answered my request.

If he'd stayed with me, he wouldn't have been outside, pounding on the door so hard it rattled the windows. Knowing men, he wouldn't have been angry. Smug or sleepy, but not angry.

That was it—I'd asked him to stay because the thought of one of those co-orgs clawing at the door, waiting for me to open it, made me sick to my stomach. It was one thing to see them safely trapped behind glass, razor-sharp fingernails and teeth removed.

Another entirely to be inches from one in the wild.

I should have expected the director's call, wanting to know how my first day of translation went.

After Brynner left, I'd given her a rundown of the organization issues, and my attempts to sort the journals by age. Thankfully she accepted it and let me go. Which kept me from telling her the truth.

How did it go?

Horrible.

I'd nearly shot a man, drank on the job, tried to drive drunk, and invited a coworker with a reputation into my bed. Because without a doubt, that's where I'd have had him stay. While I couldn't be certain, I had a nagging feeling I'd been planning on finding out if the stories about Brynner were true. Like I hadn't learned that lesson already.

I needed another shot at those journals. I needed this job to last at least a month. One month of field pay and the days of my phone's constant ringing would fade. Two months, and I might have a shot at catching up.

But first I needed to apologize.

For nearly shooting him. For getting completely drunk and trying to drive. If he were gracious, maybe he'd let me skip on an apology about the motel. The part of my heart I didn't like listening to insisted he would be.

When I exited the motel room, I ran into my next major issue. I'd left my car back at Brynner's house. So I walked down to the office, rousing the attendant from his sleep. "Can you give me the number for Bran and Emelia Homer? Brynner drove me home last night, and I need to get back to my car."

"That didn't take long." The attendant chuckled to himself as he jotted down a phone number and handed it to me.

Only the intervening counter kept me from kicking him in the shin. Instead, I went out to make a call. When Aunt Emelia answered, I wasn't sure what to say. "Hello? This is Grace—"

"Oh, honey. You left your car at our house. I'm out at the cemetery. I'll be over in twenty to pick you up." She hung up.

I went back to the line of salt Brynner poured out by my doorstep. The urge to kick it came in waves. I couldn't bring myself to do it. The thought of those things outside my door made me want to vomit.

So instead I sat on the concrete, wondering what sort of world this was, where people did things for each other. Certainly not one I'd lived in. My kind of people left when you needed them most, if they were ever there to begin with.

Emelia pulled up twenty minutes later on the dot, rolling down the window of her Japanese coupe so I could unlock the passenger door. "You sleep well?"

I shook my head. "I don't normally drink. Or try to shoot people. Or drive after drinking and trying to shoot people."

She waved her hand like my problems were mosquitoes to shoo away. "You aren't the first person to need a little Southern comfort after their first run-in with a meat-skin."

When we got home, Bran sat on the porch, waiting. Emelia didn't seem the least bit surprised to see him there on a weekday. She waved to me. "You best come on inside."

My fears went from vapor to rock solid. "Did something happen to Brynner? Was it because of last night? Was it because of this morning?"

"Neither. Both." Bran stood up and waved me over. "The boy's decided to take some time off. You'll need to contact the field commander and let them know."

"What do you mean, 'time off'?"

He hemmed and hawed. "Brynner told my honey he's quitting the BSI."

I'd been given a new badge, but not so much as a "Welcome to field operations" pamphlet before we left. "I don't have the phone number for field command. I'm just supposed to be getting field pay, not finding co-orgs or killing them." This couldn't be happening. Not when I was so close.

"Brynner does. We can ask when he comes back." Emelia opened the door and waved me in.

"If he comes back." Bran dusted off a briefcase. "I figured something like this was coming, the boy showing up out of nowhere. Then I saw he brought home a pretty young gal. You know you're the first one he ever brought home to meet us."

I stopped at the threshold, willing myself to not enter. To take a seat on the porch swing. And make sure they knew the truth. "He didn't bring me home to meet you. He *only* brought me here to translate the journals. We're not—anything. Director Bismuth thought you'd allow me to access them if Brynner brought me."

Bran shook his head. "I knew it was too good to be true. Boy could charm the scales off a snake and played doctor with so many girls I swore he'd set up a clinic, but bringing home a smart one? A real one? That should've been the tip-off. That boy . . ." He rose and took his briefcase off the steps, got in the car, and drove off.

I sat on the swing. Rocked. Worried. And when I couldn't worry anymore, I slid open Brynner's phone, looking for his contact list.

The picture staring back at me could have been Emelia twenty years ago. Long black hair and dainty features, she stood next to a man who looked like Brynner would in fifteen years or so. From the square jaw to narrow eyes, Brynner was his father made over again.

I looked up to find Aunt Emelia standing in the doorway.

I couldn't meet her gaze. "I'm sorry. I'll leave as soon as I contact field command. I just really needed this job."

She came out and sat down. "You seem like good people, Grace Roberts, not at all like the others they've sent. Don't go running off just yet." She took the phone from me, looking at the background photo and smiling.

"What happened to Brynner's mother?" I was already so far out on the ice it couldn't hurt to ask.

"There was only one witness. So all I can tell you is what he told us. Did you know Lara ran BSI's investigative labs?"

Ran them? I knew she'd done a stint in the armory, but I'd read no papers with her name on them. "No. I thought she believed in magic and religion. I can't imagine that mixing with science." I put my head in my hands. "I'm sorry. I'm going to go someplace else, lie down, and just forget the last few days happened."

"Oh, honey, it ain't like that. Lara believed, all right, but she liked to know as well as believe. So Heinrich finds this perfect mural, written by one of them meat-skins while the Re-Animus was in it. And she brings the whole damned mural back to her lab."

And I saw it coming, making perfect sense. "She thought it might be a spell?"

"Thought you didn't believe in magic."

I bit back the acid response that came so naturally. "Every skeptic has a level of proof. Make a believer out of me."

"Lara was trying to translate it. Understand it. My sister

swore the words were only part of the meaning, and the key was the understanding. So she kept it on a wall in their lab, trying different interpretations."

This idea of a rational Carson seemed at odds with what I'd read about his father, or seen from Brynner. Much more my style. "And?"

She paused, studying me. "One of them must have worked. Brynner said she was just gone, and in her place were the knives the boy carries, and a silver jar."

The thought that Brynner had seen—whatever it was—that happened to his mother made my heart ache. If he believed it was a result of magic, that certainly explained his reaction to my disbelief.

"I thought his dad made the blades. There's nothing like them in the BSI arsenal."

Aunt Emelia shook her head. "Heinrich believed they were sacrificial knives. Even he didn't know how they were made, only that they seemed made to kill meat-skins."

"And the jar? What was actually in it?"

She shook her head. "Heinrich guarded that jar like nothing I'd seen. I never saw him open it, but he said it was a heart."

Right there, I spotted my first problem. Canopic jars held other organs. Not the heart. Removing the heart represented ultimate death in ancient Egypt. "Where is it?"

Emelia stood and took my hand, pulling me to my feet. "I suspect that's what you were sent to find out."

I opened the phone dialing history and chose the most common number. Held my breath as it rang. When the phone picked up, no one spoke for ten, almost fifteen seconds. Then a mechanical voice buzzed. "Carson, you're in a shitload of trouble."

I swallowed, my lips suddenly dry. "This is Grace Roberts. I need to speak to field command. Brynner Carson quit this morning."

In the background, a noise like a vacuum pump continued, then the mechanized voice cut in. "We are so fucked."

The line went dead.

BRYNNER

I didn't want to go home. Couldn't go home, and not just because Grace might be there. I could blame her for the director's assumptions. Or I could accept the truth. Of the two, one of us had a history of causing trouble. I guess the shrink back in Seattle was more right than wrong. It wasn't any one thing, but the accumulation of a lifetime spent fighting an enemy that never gave up, never slept, and against whom I never seemed to win a permanent victory.

So I drove down the highway, past the high school, and up a road to a citrus farm. A dusty trail led down to the farmhouse, and by the time the truck pulled up, a man stood outside, waving to me.

"Brynner Carson," said a man with white hair and more wrinkles than skin. He walked over and took off his hat, giving me a one-armed hug. "Rory's out running irrigation, but I'll send a hand to let him know."

I missed these people. I'd spent more summer nights here than I could count. "I'll stay away from the barn this time, I swear."

He slipped his hat back on. "I'm not mad about that anymore.

Haven't been for years, if that's what kept you away. Get on in out of the heat, Mary will want to see how you've grown."

I opened the screen door, and stepped back fifty years in time. I don't think anyone ever told Mary Hughes that the fifties came and went. In her world, which I'm sure she saw in black and white, women still baked pies while men worked in the field.

And the pies smelled like a piece of heaven, blended with apple and cinnamon. Choosing Rory as a best friend had nothing to do with his mother's cooking, but it certainly hadn't hurt. His mother set down a rolling pin, which to me was a good club for killing meat-skins, and dusted off her hands.

"Brynner Carson, young man, it's about time you came back to see us."

"It's good to see you, too, Mrs. Hughes." I slid up on the bar stool.

"You come all the way to New Mexico to check out the horse killings?"

Horse killings. Not exactly my style. "I didn't. But I could take a look. Which farm?"

"The McMasters'. Rory said he ain't seen nothing like it. Poor creature just torn to parts. Where is that boy?" She hollered at the stairs, "Luce, could you keep an eye on the oven?" She washed her hands and walked out the front door.

And down the stairs came a vision and a nightmare.

Lucille Stillman, homecoming queen and my date to prom my senior year. A woman I knew so very well once. On her hip she carried a baby about nine months old. She saw me in the kitchen and stopped, her mouth open.

"Lucy Stillman." It was all I could think of to say.

"Hughes. It's Hughes now. Make yourself useful and hold

Junior." Her tone made it clear that I'd better check any pie she served me for razor blades and needles. She thrust the baby at me like he was a rabid wolverine.

The baby squirmed in my grip, fidgeting and making a square face with angry eyes. Babies, unlike knives, didn't come with padded grips. He didn't like me any better than his mother did and began to mewl like an angry cat.

Lucy looked up at me, her hands in oven mitts. "Calm him. I seem to recall you like to sing."

I seemed to recall liking almost anything a girl liked in high school. I might have attempted to serenade a couple of them. I remembered the tune Dad hummed while he worked. I bounced the baby softly and began to sing. "Hush, little baby, don't you cry, Daddy's going to stab a meat-skin in the eye, and if that meat-skin takes a bite, Daddy's going to get six stitches tonight."

The baby cooed and made burbling noises, obviously impressed with my skills as a bard.

His mother, not so much. She turned the oven off and stalked over to seize the child. "What kind of lullaby is that? Stay away from Junior, and stay away from me. I'm married now. Don't you have a rotten horse to look at?"

Once, she'd looked at me with an adoring gaze and a willing smile. That would have been before she caught me in the movie theater with her best friend. I left the kitchen, preferring the heat of the noon sun to Lucy's withering stare. Dust devils danced in the yard, and a distant line of clouds said we'd be getting a storm soon enough. It would roll through, dump a month's worth of rain, and move on. The desert would suck it up, use it to go from brown to green.

I closed my eyes, savoring the scent of rain on the wind.

The creak of wheels made me open my eyes as a golf cart rolled up, and from it came my best friend, Rory Hughes.

"Big B." He ran to me, slapping me on the back so hard my stitches hurt. "Heard about the horse. I was wondering when you big shot BSI folks would look into it. Lucy says the word is you brought someone special home to meet Aunt Emelia and Uncle Bran." Rory's dark brown hair stood up in spiky tufts on his head. He was even less related to Emelia and Bran than I was, but no one in their right mind argued with Aunt Emelia.

Rory had gained weight, a good fifty pounds, but he was as tall as me, as wide as me, and still probably capable of taking me in a wrestling match.

"I quit the BSI this morning."

Rory whistled. "Damn. You get in trouble over a woman?"

"No. I mean, yes, but that's not why I quit. Listen, I can't really go back to Emelia and Bran's. There's someone there I'd rather avoid. You think I could stay in the guesthouse?"

Rory scratched his head. "Avoiding is what you do best. But you can't stay in the guesthouse."

I nodded in acceptance. "Thanks, anyway. I know, would've been awkward, you marrying Lucy and all. I'll catch up with you over dinner sometime." I turned to leave, but Rory clamped a strong hand on my shoulder.

"Big B, I trust Luce. If you could see her face when your name comes up, you'd understand. You can't stay in the guesthouse 'cause it burned down five years ago in the Big Rock fire." Rory pointed to the barn. "I used the insurance money to finish the barn loft. If you don't mind climbing a ladder, it's yours."

"Daddy!" From the fence at the edge of a field, a girl with Rory's dark brown hair and Lucy's angled cheeks sprinted, out of breath. "I was over at the Larsons', and we went to feed her pony." Tears streamed down her face as Rory swept her up in his arms.

"It's dead. It's everywhere."

For reasons even my dad never determined, meat-skins attacked horses and other ruminants with a ferocity that made even the best-prepared operative uncomfortable. I walked back to the truck and took out my knives, sliding the sheaths onto my belt. I looked over to Rory. "Can you show me?"

12

GRACE

Brynner's phone stayed silent for exactly four minutes, thirty seconds. Then it rang with a new tone, one that blared like a warning siren. I reluctantly answered, grateful for Emelia staying by my side. "Grace Roberts speaking."

"This is Director Bismuth. Where is Brynner Carson?"

"He quit."

Her sigh worried me more than the sharp tone. "I'm aware of that. Please answer my question. Where is Brynner?"

I looked to Emelia. Given how loudly the director spoke, she'd heard. Emelia shook her head.

"We don't know. He just handed me the phone this morning and drove off. I'm at his aunt and uncle's house now, so if he comes back—"

"Is Emelia Homer present? I'd like to speak with her."

I handed the phone to Emelia. She whispered into the phone,

"He said he didn't think he could do it anymore." Emelia glanced over at me. "Give my best to Tom and the kids."

She handed me the phone back and went inside.

"Ms. Roberts. I'm sorry you are caught up in this drama. You may book a flight to Portland and take a few days off." Director Bismuth stopped, sounding almost broken.

"No." I couldn't believe I spoke the word, but I'd be damned if I didn't give it a try. "I'm not done yet. I just started in on the notebooks, and I can figure them out, I know I can."

"May I call you Grace?"

"Of course."

Director Bismuth paused to bark orders at someone. "Grace, I only wanted the heart because the Re-Animus wanted it. You haven't read sit-briefs in the last few days, have you?"

I hadn't, but she didn't give me time to answer.

"We're facing a surge of co-org activity, the likes of which are unmatched in BSI records. I have every field team in service working round the clock and have allowed more than one retiree to return. We have greater concerns than the demands of one creature."

Assuming the activity wasn't because of the heart, her priorities made sense. "So you need Brynner back to work."

"I need Brynner to be *seen* working. Like his father, the man is as much a symbol of the BSI as the emblem on your badge. When other field teams hear about him, it gives them courage. It tells them they aren't fighting a losing battle against an enemy that grows stronger every day."

I shivered in the hundred-degree heat at her implication. And now more and more made sense. "Do you arrange media coverage of his operations?"

"Of course we do."

"And his extravagant vacations?"

"It takes time to heal. Now, I refuse to accept Brynner's resignation. When, not if, he shows up, I expect him back on the job."

I thought of his stitches, done and redone when the man just couldn't rest. I left my job at the office every night. His followed him home, waiting in dark alleys and around every corner.

I couldn't imagine living like that.

The question in my mind wasn't, Why did Brynner quit? It was, How did he manage to last as long as he did? "All right, but we're going to need another field team out here. The local sheriff wanted a couple of things checked out, since there may be some co-org activity."

"Absolutely not. Even if I had spare operatives, I couldn't afford to have news of Brynner's situation leaking out to the other field teams." She paused again. "There's hardly a dot on the map where there isn't some form of co-org activity, and to be honest, Ms. Roberts, if we both agree you aren't up to handling a minor infestation, I believe it would be best for you to return to your safe office in Portland."

I couldn't go back. Not yet. "I need this job. Please, I'll figure out the journals. I will."

"I don't need the journals as much as I need that man back at work—" She paused, long enough for me to listen to the bustle of conversations in the background. "Perhaps there is something you could handle in the field. Find Brynner for me, convince him this whole quitting nonsense was just an overreaction. In return, I'll allow you to stay and continue your translation efforts for, say, three weeks. And if Brynner returns, ready to do what he does best, I'll award you three months' back pay."

I let my head rest back on the swing and stared at the porch roof. Promises I couldn't keep competed with bills I couldn't pay. "I'll do what I can." I snapped the phone shut, then rose and went inside to Aunt Emelia. "I need to talk with Brynner. How can I find him?"

She continued kneading a meatloaf. "That's not a problem. I know exactly where he'd go. I just don't trust Maggie to keep the boy's best interests in mind."

Her words might as well have speared me. Had she heard through the window? "And you trust me?"

"Oh, sweetie." She washed her hands and gave me a crooked smile. "We all have to trust someone."

I couldn't look at her as I spoke. "The director wants him back to work. Wants me to convince him to come back."

She nodded. "The boy looks like he'd do almost anything for you. Maggie will calm down. She's just surprised he quit."

"I'm shocked it took that long. How does he deal with those things every day without going insane?"

"If you're going to be around him, you need to under-stand. Brynner's not like normal men. He's a Carson. He's got his father's strength, his mother's stubbornness." She stopped mauling the meatloaf to look at me. "Like God rolled up the desert into a man. He was born to do what he does."

One phone call, one set of GPS coordinates, and a thirty-minute drive later, I pulled up at the farmhouse where Emelia insisted I'd find Brynner. The clouds overhead boiled, tinting the sky green, and the wind whipped up, blowing gravel and sand.

I knocked on the door, then banged on it, until it swung open. A tall woman with jet-black hair, a baby on her hip, and a thin smile answered. "You lost?"

"Maybe. Emelia Homer told me I'd find a friend of mine here. Brynner Carson?" I shouted to be heard over the wind.

She swung the door open, holding it while it whipped back and forth. "You're lost, all right. Come on in."

I stepped into a kitchen covered in cracked white linoleum and white Formica counters. The woman pushed the door shut, battling the winds, then turned to me. "I'm Lucille Hughes. Most folks call me Luce. That bastard ain't here right now. Him and Rory are off doing something. Just like old times."

"Luce, did I hear the door open? Are the boys back?" An older woman in her sixties came down the stairs, saw me, and froze. She looked at the BSI badge I clutched and crossed her arms. "Who do we have here?"

"Grace Roberts, ma'am." I wasn't raised to call anyone ma'am or sir, but it worked for Brynner and seemed to be normal around here. "I work with Brynner."

"She's one of his *friends*," said Luce, with more venom than a nest of cobras.

I didn't care for the way she spoke about Brynner, and leveling that stare at me almost constituted an act of war. "Coworker. Not companion."

Luce looked down at the baby on her hip and shook her head. "I'm going to put Junior down for a nap. Ms. Grace here wants to know where he is." She stomped up the stairs, like each stair was Brynner's crotch.

I couldn't hold the sigh in.

The elder Hughes hugged me. "Don't let her bother you. Luce is good in her own way. And so is—"

The door flew open, and Brynner stumbled in, soaked to the bone. Outside, hail clattered on the front porch, followed by a wall of rain like a shower curtain of gray. He grabbed the table and leaned over it, resting on his arms. "We got it."

Behind him, a man at least Brynner's height and twice his weight followed, looking like he'd gone for a swim in his clothes. "You shoulda seen him, Mom. Classic Carson. Put the meat-skin down with barely a scratch."

Barely a scratch? A river of red ran down Brynner's scalp, from a cut on his head. His shirt clung to his skin, tracing the ripple of every muscle as he breathed in and out. He raised his head, catching his breath—and saw me. "Grace? What are *you* doing here?"

I opened my mouth to answer, and the air crackled, snapping like static electricity. A split second later, a roll of thunder like a bomb shook the house, and the lights went off. Above us, the baby wailed.

I grabbed the silence like a life jacket. "I need to talk to you about the journals. Now. We can go to my car, unless you'd like to have the conversation in the rain."

Brynner put his head down on the table. "Can it wait until after dinner?"

The air snapped as lightning struck, followed by a rolling echo of thunder.

"Of course it can," said the older woman. "Grace Roberts, pull up a chair beside your man and I'll get a bowl of stew. You don't need much light to stick a spoon in your mouth." She raised her voice. "Luce, you coming to dinner?"

I stifled the urge to set her right, and instead took a seat beside Brynner, who dripped puddles onto the floor. Once the bowls were handed out, the conversation died to an absolute minimum. I can't say what the others were doing, only that I'd forgotten how good beef stew could taste.

Once Brynner and the tall man, Rory, put away three bowls each, the conversation picked up. They laughed and argued about who'd seen the co-org first and how many times Brynner stabbed it.

Luce, on the other hand, spent her time attempting to turn Brynner to stone with her gaze. If looks dug holes, Brynner would have sported a full golf course.

A lull in the rain prompted Brynner to stand up and push his bowl to the center of the table. "I'll do some dishes tomorrow morning, Mrs. Hughes. Mr. Hughes, you still looking for help?"

The old man nodded. "As I recall, farmwork don't take to you much."

Brynner shrugged. "I've never had a tiller try to strangle me. Grace, you wanted a word?"

I followed him out onto the porch. The skies still poured out like an overflowing bathtub, and the wind drove rain at an angle all the way to the door.

He pointed to the barn. "Ladder's inside. Run for the door, climb the ladder."

Without waiting, he ran. I hesitated, then sprinted through the downpour, into the dark barn.

"Up here." Brynner's voice called from the top of an iron ladder. "Come on, it's not a hayloft."

When I pushed the trapdoor at the top of the ladder, it opened to a carpeted apartment, easily the size of mine in Portland. Thick insulation made the driving rain sound like a soft patter. Through oval windows at each end, lightning strikes lit the whole apartment like camera flashes.

I rubbed a hand down the wall, feeling the wallpaper texture. "I thought wooden when you said barn. This is amazing."

Brynner grinned. "The old one burned down in an accident. I sort of set it on fire. Turn around."

"Why?"

He took off his sopping wet shirt and threw it to the side. "Because I want to change, and I don't trust you not to peek."

I let his jab go in favor of a better one. "And the younger Mrs. Hughes? Did you set her on fire, too?"

BRYNNER

The awkward just never ended with this woman. "Can we just agree that if a woman in this town looks at me angry, I did something with her at some point? Please? It will save you time and me embarrassment."

Grace almost smiled. "No. It's about the only entertainment in this town. Outside of driving up to the quarry."

I almost choked. I'd hoped that Grace wouldn't have to know about that. "Turn around for real this time."

She complied, and I got dressed faster than any of my many hotel-room escapes. Once I was decent, I lit a lantern and rummaged through my bag, looking for a shirt. "You want to talk journals."

"Among other things." Grace paced the length of the barn. "I called our field command on your phone."

Oh, what I would have given to be a fly on Dale's wall. "And how many microseconds did it take before recruiting called back? Could you hold your breath longer?"

"The director called me. She wants to recall me to Portland."

A nervous edge ran through Grace's voice, and she jumped every time thunder shook the building.

"I'm sorry. You said it yourself: You weren't cut out for fieldwork. So take your Deliverator and your badge and go be the hero of the Portland office. Most people leave the field with trophies sewn into them."

The set of Grace's jaw, the way her eyes narrowed told me her answer before she spoke. "I can't leave." She looked up, the lantern light making the shadows under her eyes dark black. I knew the look. Weeks of not sleeping. "I need this job. I need the field pay."

"Why?"

She clenched her fist and turned away. "I have a bunch of bills I need to pay, and this job will let me do it. I spoke to Director Bismuth."

Poor Grace. The director wasn't fun to deal with on a good day. I felt bad for her having to deal with the mess I'd made. "I'm sorry."

She took two steps closer, out of the lantern light. So close I could smell her perfume, and beneath it, the scent of her skin. "I need your help with the journals."

That might have been the worst thing she could have said. "Brynner, you're very attractive." Or "Brynner, I know I shouldn't." Those were phrases I knew by heart. Dad and his damned journals. "I don't read hieroglyphics the way you do. I know how to write rooster, donkey, dog, and cat. Oh, and shitty. Which is about right for my translation skills."

"I'll do the reading, thank you. But reading co-org-affected ideographs isn't just about symbols and words. At least, that's only the bottom layer. Think of it like a pyramid. The symbols, the sounds, those are the bottom. On top of that, we have sentences. On top of sentences, meaning."

She spoke in circles, losing me. Or maybe it was her eyes. I stood a better chance of staring at her breasts and remembering what she said than looking into those eyes. "You lost me."

She laughed and jumped at the same time, thanks to a thunderclap. "There are different levels to their meanings. It happens in all languages. Ask me a question I'll say no to."

I knew exactly what I wanted to ask, and exactly what she'd say. "May I kiss you, Grace Roberts?"

Whatever answer she had ready died in her throat. She blinked at me over and over, her face slack with surprise. Her voice came out a whisper. "Sure you can."

It wasn't the answer I expected, but it was absolutely the one I wanted, and I'd learned not to question a woman. And I did kiss her, a fleeting kiss, pressing my lips to hers for just a moment before I stepped away. I hadn't noticed how hot the loft was, or how loud the rain against the window sounded.

Grace turned away, walking to the window. "That was . . . sarcasm."

If by "sarcasm," she meant "electrifying," I couldn't argue.

Grace's voice trembled when she spoke. "You can't understand the real meaning without understanding the first two parts." She held her hand to her mouth, looking out into the rain. "Thank you for checking on the horse. I'm sure the Donaldsons will feel better knowing the co-org isn't going to kill another one of their livestock."

"Yeah— Wait. What?"

"I need to go." She lifted the loft door to climb down.

Outside it still looked like God turned on a faucet. It always looked like that in the desert when it rained. "Grace, you can't go out in that. Where did the sheriff want me to look?"

She slipped her feet onto the ladder. "The Donaldsons'." She pointed out the window. "And if they can go out in this, I can."

I sprinted to the window, where among lightning flashes and sheets of rain, four figures approached Rory's door. The Donaldson farm was thirty minutes in the other direction. Unless someone stuck a rocket on a corpse, it couldn't possibly have been the same one I just killed.

A co-org at the Donaldsons'. Another at the Larsons'. Whether it was a premonition, or intuition, call it what you want, I ran for the ladder, screaming over the storm, "Grace, don't go out there."

She was already gone.

13

GRACE

What was I thinking? What was he thinking? Were either of us thinking at all? He heard what I said when I answered the question. He knew what I really meant. I wiped the taste of man from my lips and stepped out into the rain. I had to get to my car. If the Hughes had company coming, an awkward situation would become downright unbearable.

I fumbled with the rental keys as the visitors walked on up the stairs. Which button triggered the lock? That one. My finger slipped, hitting the alarm button, and the beeping horn rose over the wind's wail. I unlocked and opened the door right as a bolt of lightning lit the world.

Illuminating dead faces on the Hugheses' visitors.

One by one, they lurched toward me, the flashing head-lights of my car, and the wailing siren. I dove inside, slamming the door behind me, hitting the lock as the first one smashed against the car, shaking it. Two more hit the car, pushing on the windows, stumbling into the door.

The fourth stood at a distance, then walked over, dragging its right foot. It leaned over and looked through the window, inches from my face.

With one finger, it tapped the window three times, in exactly the pattern I'd used on the floor in Aunt Emelia's house.

As it drew back its fist, I hurled myself between headrests, into the backseat. Broken glass mixed with torrential rain as the window burst open. Wrinkled fingers coated in grave dirt missed me by a hairbreadth. I leaned forward to grab the messenger bag in the front seat, and took out my Deliverator.

The co-org stuck its head through the ruined glass, swiveling to look at me. Then its mouth opened, revealing a swollen green tongue. "Where. Is. Carson?"

It spoke. I sat in stunned silence, unable to respond.

It spit out a rotten tooth. "Stupid woman. Where. Is. Carson?"

I let the Deliverator answer. I aimed low to compensate for the kick, and wound up blowing a hole through its chest. Again, I pulled the trigger, and removed half its jaw. Unlike at the restaurant in Seattle, I kept my composure, remembering how Brynner had told me every third shot would be co-org specific. Sure enough, the next bullet *burned* a hole through the co-org's stomach. Even in the rain, a cloud of black smoke burst from the hole as it staggered backward. But the smoke didn't dissipate. It funneled, like a swarm of flying insects, straight into another co-org. That one stopped pushing on the car door. Its eyes focused on me, its mouth pulled back in a grin.

So I shot the new one, too. This time, I fired with confidence, counting toward the third bullet. The first two rounds I put into its legs, knocking it down and setting the stage for the next round to kill it.

As I pulled the trigger, cold hands wrapped around my neck, yanking me backward, dragging me out of the car before I could even see where the cloud would go. I fought for breath while a weight like an elephant crushed down on me—

And let go.

The co-org behind me convulsed, a silver blade sticking out of its head. I can't say how long it took for it to die. My focus was on the cloud spewing from its wounds, twisting back to the last corpse. Unlike the others, this one looked . . . fresh. New.

I'd seen that man in the diner the day before, having breakfast.

"Carson." A different body spoke, but in exactly the same gravelly voice. "I warned you on the ship. Bring it back. Where did you hide the jar?"

Carson flipped one of his blades end over end. "In a vault in BSI headquarters. You might have heard of it. Salt dome, surrounded by an underground river. You should visit sometime."

It chuckled. "You lie. We have seen everything in the vault. It's not there." Then it stepped toward me.

Brynner countered each step, backing it away. "I've been known to lie from time to time. Then again, you want me to believe you've been inside the vault? Who else is telling tall tales?"

It leaped up onto the hood of my car, just out of his reach, and counted off on broken fingers. "A piece of the cross. A blessed blade from the Crusades. The bones of a saint. Two tons of weapons-grade plutonium. Shall I go on?"

I didn't see Brynner move; he was swinging the blade so fast the edges shone with a golden blur.

The co-org moved every bit as fast as he did. Maybe faster, dodging every blow. "You're getting slow."

Brynner sliced across it, severing a finger. Black smoke bled from it, swirling about the co-org like a whirlwind. It came at Brynner with the fury of a wounded beast. How he could react, how he could dodge or counter it, I couldn't say.

One blow landed, sending Brynner into the mud. I leaped for the car, where my Deliverator sat on the seat. When I turned around, the co-org was on Brynner.

It reached down with hands that ended in bloody red fingernails. "You're still wounded, lesser Carson. Back on the island, I believe I cut you right about—"

I fired from a kneeling position so the bullet wouldn't pass through and hit Brynner. The co-org stumbled forward, then rolled to the side and spun. My next bullet went wide, or maybe I shot straight and it just moved faster than me.

Leaving Brynner, it started back toward me. "You can die first, translator. You should have hidden in the house and read the old man's books. Now I'll wear you around like a cheap suit."

I'd been close to the co-orgs in our labs. Mindless machines, without direction or purpose. This one knew what I did, and who I was. I'd heard field team stories but not seen proof of Re-Animus intelligence. Until now.

The roar of a shotgun split the night, throwing the monster facedown into the mud. I added my own bullets, squeezing the trigger until long after the chamber clicked empty. Brynner rolled over, crawled on his knees to the co-org, and drove a blade through its body.

It exploded, smoke gushing from its mouth until the corpse stiffened and went still.

"Did I get him?" Rory chambered another shell and blasted at point-blank range. The splatter of flesh and blood covered me, red blood staining the mud. He bent over and took me by the hand, hauling me up the porch, into the kitchen.

Lucy Hughes watched from the window with terror-filled eyes. "What was that? It spoke."

"I don't know." I looked to Brynner as he came in the door.

He dripped into a chair. "That's a Re-Animus."

I tried to fit this into my view of the world, and failed. "Four of them?"

He laughed. "Just one. How many did you need?"

BRYNNER

Everyone did this. Those that lived long enough to encounter a Re-Animus did. They could talk about corpse organisms and categorize them by stage of decomposition and physiological changes. But meeting one that knew you by name blew the training courses out the window.

This one knew Grace.

And knew, if my memory was right, the contents of the innermost vaults.

I should have been more worried about the vaults.

Rory looked out the window at the easing storm. "I'm going to run the perimeter. Make sure there aren't any more out there." He started toward the door.

I shook my head. "There aren't. The clouds of evil go to the nearest host. Those dispersed. If there'd been a host within half a mile, we could've followed them."

The power flickered on, and Grace stood. "I need to make a call or two."

"To field command?"

She nodded.

An image of the war room swarming with analysts working through the night flashed through my mind. I hadn't even made it a day and I missed it. "Tell them Vault Zero is compromised. Tell them everything."

She blinked, then frowned. "You aren't going back? This is huge. Multiple witnesses confirming the Re-Animus intelligence. We've read reports, but only from one person at a time, and frankly, most field ops are . . . a little out-there. There won't be any disputing this now."

I knew what needed to happen. I had no problem doing it. "No. Congratulations. You and Dr. Egghead can discuss it at length."

I looked over to Rory. "Thanks for the offer, but I think it would be best if I moved on. Those things show up everywhere I go. I'd rather not be responsible for someone else getting killed."

Grace looked at me, a look of wild terror on her face for just a moment. The fear dissolved, replaced by determination like I'd seen in that briefing room back in Seattle. "You can't just run away. You might want to read the sit-reps. Co-orgs are showing up *everywhere*, and that just happens to include your little hometown. If nothing else, stay and defend your aunt and uncle."

Everywhere? How could that be? The Re-Animus were careful, moving with patience to effect changes over hundreds of years, according to my dad.

Grace rose from the table. "Look, you think they showed up because of you. But what if they just came on their own?"

She looked over to Rory. "I'm sorry, but you think a barrel of rock salt would have stopped all of them?"

She walked over to me. "If you want everyone to think you are brave, why not be brave? Pick a spot and defend it, like your father would have."

Cold fury raced down me. How dare she use him as a goad? "You have no idea what you are talking about. Dad would have sniffed the wind and followed the Re-Animus home, killing it in its primary host. I'm not him, and I'm done trying to be."

"Fine." She picked up the Deliverator from the table and removed the magazine, which she stuck in her bag. "As of this morning, I'm the only field operative in this area. You can run off if you want. I'll stick around and take care of whatever comes next."

What? What had gotten into her? Was it some form of temporary insanity? I grabbed the Deliverator, wrenching it from her hand with ease. "You won't last five minutes against anything but the most basic co-org. Shamblers are one thing. You can wait for them to lean up against a door and shoot them through it. You think for a moment you'd win against one with the Re-Animus still in it?"

She reached around me, grasping at my hands. "No, but that won't stop me from trying. Whatever comes, I'll be waiting. Give me my gun back."

Money. It had to be about the money. I held the gun behind my back. "This is stupid. Did the director put this in your head? You can't make money if you are dead. Your daughter will miss spending time with you more than she'll ever enjoy the BSI insurance payment."

She stepped backward like I'd struck her.

Now I handed over her gun, handle first. "The director

doesn't have any qualms about ordering people to do things that will get some of them killed. Or asking them. Tell me you won't do anything stupid."

She shook her head, the anger deflating her. "I already did." She tromped out into the night, leaving me alone in a crowded kitchen.

Rory put one hand on my shoulder, his grip nearly crushing my shoulder. "You're going after her, right?"

I shook my head. "I'll get my stuff and move on. I can sleep in the truck bed."

"You're a damned idiot, Big B. And your friend there is going to get herself killed first time you aren't around and she picks a fight with something that bullets don't touch." He went to the fridge and came back with a beer.

The mud on my only pair of spare clothes had dried to a crust. I put my head down on the table and willed myself to forget. Just like every morning in every hotel after every operation. "Why did Dad do this to me? Why is this my responsibility?"

Rory snorted and slammed down the bottle. "You're the closest thing to a brother I have, but you're a double-damned idiot. The old man is dead. You got a problem with who you are, pick a fight with God."

He looked out the window at the darkness. "Dad doesn't work the fields anymore. Arthritis, and all. But I'd do it even if he weren't here to watch me. I'd do it if I didn't get paid, cause it's in my veins. What you do, it's in yours, too."

He went back to the fridge and pulled out another bottle, but I shook my head. "I'm driving."

"Away?"

"Out to the Big 8. It's where Grace is staying."

Rory grinned like we were back in tenth grade, swapping date stories. "Now that's the Brynner I know."

The deluge had left everything covered in frost after sunset. It was so quiet I could hear the crunch of desert hares moving in the moonlight. It would be so easy to stick the keys in the truck and drive until I ran out of gas.

But I couldn't do that. Not while Grace even joked about playing a role I'd spent a lifetime training for and still sucked at. The rain would have washed away the salt outside her door.

I started up the truck and left the second-closest place to home on earth. I couldn't let Grace try to take on a Re-Animus, any more than I could just stand by and watch a civilian get killed. She could still leave this life. I couldn't.

Rory said the Brynner he knew would drive out to the Big 8, no doubt to talk my way into Grace's room. Somewhere between Greece and New Mexico, that Brynner died. Maybe I killed him. Maybe he killed himself. But he was dead, and not even a Re-Animus could bring him back.

14

GRACE

I fumed as I drove back, asking myself how exactly Brynner could blame every co-org appearance on himself. Of course the Re-Animus showed up everywhere. It probably *was* everywhere, just not usually everywhere all at once. The only logical explanation was that Brynner grew up in the shadow of Heinrich Carson.

Everything I'd read about him spoke of a man who did the impossible repeatedly, a man even the monsters feared. Skin made of iron, they said, bones that couldn't be broken. I had no idea how much of it was true, but seeing the truth about Brynner made me doubt the tales of his father.

The more I thought about it, the more wrong it felt. Heinrich Carson was dead. If his legend was the measuring stick Brynner used against himself, no wonder Brynner came up short.

He knew the Re-Animus, and it knew him. The thought of

its voice simultaneously repulsed and fascinated me. Intelligent. Cunning, with a memory and working intelligence. As fast as Brynner moved, he should have carved it like a turkey, but instead it danced just out of reach, constantly one step beyond the blades.

The BSI had to know about this.

And whatever it was, it was fixated on this "heart." What could we learn from a Re-Animus in captivity? What might the tests reveal? If that heart existed, I might—just might—know a way to get one.

I arrived at the hotel, pleased that I didn't need the GPS even once. Salt crunched underfoot as I approached the motel door.

When I swung the door open, I looked into the gaping maw of darkness and froze. The thought of something waiting just beyond the light held me in place. I could flick my hand and hit the light. Or be caught, dragged into the darkness. How did Brynner cope with this day in, day out?

I stepped backward, keeping my eyes on the motel door, opened the car, and turned on the headlights. They streamed in through the door, lighting up the sunrise painting above the bed. Nothing. I turned on the room lights and then turned off the headlights. Just for good measure, I pulled the bedspread off so I could see under the bed and opened the closet door. As a child, I lived in a constant fear of the dark. Monsters lived under my bed. Mom would come down the hall and reassure me that there were no monsters. That the BSI kept the monsters at bay.

Except the human ones, like the one that had shared my mother's bed.

I brushed away the past like cobwebs. Paranoia seemed completely reasonable after the evening's events. I couldn't relax until I had the door locked, bolted, and chained.

I dialed my home BSI office, then chose the operator. "Grace Roberts, calling for Dr. Thomas. Is he available?"

After several minutes on hold, the phone picked up, and Dr. Thomas's frail voice answered. "Ms. Roberts. My favorite field operative. How are you enjoying your assignment?"

"I talked to a Re-Animus."

He waited long enough that I thought I probably ought to expand on it. "It's intelligent, exhibits memory, recognition, possibly even emotion."

"Ms. Roberts, would you kindly stop?"

That wasn't the response I expected. After a moment, the line clicked. This time, Dr. Thomas's voice echoed. "Ms. Roberts, you are on broadcast to all BSI labs. Please continue. All lab partners will direct questions through me."

And I told them. Emphasized how the voice remained constant even after the move from one body to the next. How the smoke resembled swarming insects more than clouds of evil. How it identified my sex, my occupation, and even attempted to insult me.

And the deluge of questions that followed. Did I get a sample? No, it was trying to kill me. Did I capture it? No, it was trying to kill me. Did I have video or audio records?

No. It was trying to *kill* me.

The fact that a Re-Animus had been strangling me made it slip my mind. I started to say so, and the words died in my throat. Hadn't Brynner said exactly the same thing to me? I'd been so upset over a few ruined glyphs.

Now I had bruises on my neck to teach me the difference between theory and reality.

Finally, Dr. Thomas closed the questioning. "In light of the recent co-org activity, this is most interesting. We've heard

claims from field operatives before of intelligent action. Then
again, we've heard that virgin olive oil drives co-orgs away, and
a dozen other unprovable assertions."

He paused, and when he spoke, he spoke louder. "Ms. Roberts, on the other hand, I consider a most reliable witness.
While I wish you had captured the creature for study, I value
your life more than the opportunity for knowledge."

He picked up the phone, his voice loud and clear. "Now that
it's just you and I, I want to emphasize that last point. We'll
work with the field teams to recover a Re-Animus and study it.
I'll forward you the activity analysis from the last week as well."

"The director told me there's activity everywhere."

"She told you the truth. The Ministry of Security in the
U.K., our partners in Canada, even the Office of Normal Funeral
Conditions in China are reporting extreme co-org activity."

Outside, squealing brakes and a wash of headlights told me
I wasn't alone at the motel.

"I've gottta run. Can you give the director a message for me?"

"Certainly."

I took a deep breath, knowing I was about to make a good
decision and a bad mistake. "Tell her I'm declining her gener-
ous offer. I'll stay and finish the journals if she'll pay for it.
Heinrich Carson wrote down pretty much every thought that
came into his head, and there might be other information on
weapons or co-org nature in them as well."

"Now that would truly be fascinating. I'll relay your message, but are you aware that the BSI Analysis has a budget of our
own? Your work will be funded fully if, and only if, you actually
manage to uncover something useful. Be careful, Ms. Roberts.
As they say, don't get dead." He hung up on me as Brynner's
boots crunched through the gravel.

I stood inside the door, waiting for his knock. To say what? I'm sorry I said you could kiss me? I wasn't. What I regretted was not kissing him better, longer. It might have been a mistake, but it was one I enjoyed making.

I unlocked the door and swung it open.

Brynner crouched by the end of the concrete, brushing salt up against the wall. Mud covered him where blood didn't, dripping from that head wound he'd gotten. He looked up at me, then away.

"I thought you were leaving," I said.

He tossed the empty salt box in a trash can. "And I thought you had a death wish. Maybe we were both wrong."

If Brynner's father knew half the things about co-orgs people believe he did, I could surely find something that could be tested and applied. But only if I could decipher them, and for that, I needed help. "I'm going to work out a chronology for your dad's journals tomorrow. I'll pay you for your time. I don't have much money until payday, but it'll be easier than farmwork. I tell you an event; you tell me if it happened before or after something else."

He arched one eyebrow. "You. Pay. Me?"

"Are you not familiar with the concept? Think of it like consulting, not for the BSI. For me."

That actually drew a smile. "I don't need your money, Grace Roberts, and if I recall right, you do."

Damn him! "You may not need my money, but I need your help. The contents of that brain of yours at my command for as long as it takes to work out those journals."

He recoiled, eyeing me with suspicion. "Why are you suddenly being nice to me? I mean, I'm used to it from women who don't know me, but you—"

"Because . . ." My voice trailed off as I searched and failed to come up with a reason. It would be so much easier if I were one of the strange women. Someone who'd never met him. I could smile back at him and pretend like I had no responsibilities. "That was the old me. I'm turning over a new leaf, at least until I'm done with this assignment."

Brynner dusted salt off his hands and nodded. "If I agree, you have to stick to rules: Keep out of my way if there's a meat-skin to deal with."

"And you'll help me? Please?" I reached out to take his hand, and he stepped away.

"I'll think about it." Brynner spun on his heel and walked back to the truck.

BRYNNER

Drunk women. Desperate women. Powerless women. I admit to having low standards, but those three were deal breakers. I wanted partners who wanted me, who could enjoy the experience and return the favor.

I wanted to believe what she said, but my gut said she was dangerously close to begging me for help. I'd seen more than once how begging turned to offering. While I'd turned down Grace once, I didn't trust myself to do it a second time.

I rode my frustration most of the way to Aunt Emelia's house. There, I sat in the truck, trying to figure out how exactly I'd go about this.

The day I turned eighteen, I'd walked to the highway and hitchhiked away. Never came back. That choice set a pattern that ruled the next six years of my life. I worked to find some other emergency to chase, some reason for not returning. Saying I was wrong.

I told myself I was looking for Mom.

And ignored Dad's calls and messages until it was too late.

When I looked up, Bran stood on the porch. The man who opened his home to me. Back then, I was just too angry to accept it. Now I wasn't sure how.

I swung out of the truck and approached the stairs, painfully aware of the dried blood on my skin, the mud caking me. "If I stay here, I'm afraid I'll put you in danger. If I leave, Grace is going to get herself killed. What do I do?"

Bran looked me up and down, grimaced. "You can't come in here."

Of course not.

He pointed to the side. "You get mud on Emmy's white carpet, she'll kill you twice. Hose off in the laundry room. She's heating up dinner for you."

"But the Re-Animus—I'm scared of what it might do."

Bran came down the stairs, looking up at me to meet my gaze. "Ain't nobody gets out of life alive. You're scared because you finally found something to care about. Night, boy." He walked back inside, leaving me to find my way up the back stairs.

After thirty minutes I had most of New Mexico washed off me. Aunt Emelia met me in the hallway, a plate of fried chicken in her hand. She put one hand on my arm. "You can leave anytime you want. But don't run off."

I slept through the night, waking only when the doorbell rang, which, around here, had to be Grace. Her musical voice floated in from the kitchen, followed by my aunt's laughter.

"Brynner? Boy, get up. Grace is here." The smell of fried

eggs drifting from the kitchen made me ravenous. I stalled as long as possible, then lumbered out into the kitchen, ready for extreme awkwardness.

Aunt Emelia sat alone with enough eggs to hatch a flock of fried chicken. "Grace ate breakfast at the diner, said she had to get to work. I figure you two have a lot to do."

Not with her. "I'm going out to visit Mr. Parker. Three of those four meat-skins were recent burials. Clothes had no stains, flesh still firm on the bone." I devoured eggs while I talked. "Hadn't even started rotting proper. And the bodies weren't anywhere near done right."

Emelia's face turned the same color green as the porcelain on her stove. "It's like having your father back for breakfast."

And I let it go.

"Aunt Emelia, would you mind giving Mr. Parker a call first? Might make the visit go a little easier." I gave her my pleading eyes, which looked just like the "Come on up to my room" eyes minus the "inviting my aunt to my bedroom" angle.

She frowned. "You look a little gassy. Are you feeling okay? I'll call him in a few minutes."

"I feel fine."

She patted me on the head like I was eight. "You bringing Grace along?"

"He's not." Grace stood in the kitchen doorway. She looked over to Aunt Emelia. "I've got a mountain of journals to lay out and then start translating, but I have some questions. Did Brynner play baseball?"

My aunt nodded. "In fourth grade and fifth grade. He still holds the record for biggest brawl in Bentonville Little League."

I walked out, eager to be anywhere but there while my aunt recapped every second of my life, and got in the truck. I drove through the center of the town and out the other side, heading east. The freeway miles rolled way, until I took an exit and pulled down a side road.

The cemetery lay a mile down the road, but that wasn't where I was headed. I pulled up to a small Presbyterian church. At least, that's what I think it was originally. The old parsonage stood off to one side, along with the parking lot.

I crossed the artificial stream surrounding the church and walked up to the door. The bronze plate read "Parker's Funeral Services." Dad's body was prepared here. Mom's service was held here. I hadn't come back for Dad's.

I raised my hand to knock, and spun as the crunch of gravel betrayed someone's approach.

The clear "You might have made a mistake" sound of a shotgun shell being chambered kept me from jumping at the short man who stood behind me, a nice clear shot at my belly lined up.

"Brynner Carson. I let you in the cemetery to pay respects, since I carry the backhoe keys with me these days, but you aren't welcome here."

Mr. Parker might be one of the few fathers in town who didn't want me hurt for breaking his daughter's heart. "How's Emily?" Emily was the only girl in school who not only escaped my charms but who seemed completely immune to them.

"Moved to New York eight years ago. Married herself a nice wife; they've got a son on the way. Now get the hell off my property." He hefted the shotgun for emphasis. "This ain't rock salt."

"I'm not here to break in this time. I need to talk to you. Official BSI business." A lie, but not like he'd know. The badge didn't speak up and say I quit.

He lowered the shotgun. "I do my bodies right. All of them.

Tendons cut at each joint, jaws pinned. You got a problem with the dead, you know they weren't buried in Happy Hills. I have a log with the serial number of everyone I've processed for the last five decades, and my cousin works the computer to put them in the BSI national registry. Mine don't come back."

Of course not. The man took pride in his work, making sure the bodies were both prepared to go in the ground and fixed so they'd stay that way. That gave me an idea. "If I got you some serial numbers from the thigh tattoo on a corpse, could you tell me where they were processed?"

He walked up to me, easily a foot and a half shorter, but a man confident he had the power. "I could. But first I need to hear you say it."

I'd known this was coming all along and had rehearsed my answer. "I'm sorry I broke in. I'm sorry I stole your backhoe, and I promise, Mr. Parker. I won't dig up my mother's coffin again."

15

After thirty minutes of translating, I realized I didn't need Brynner. I needed his aunt. The woman was a walking catalogue of Brynner's life, without the risk I might kiss her.

Regular hieroglyphics could be deciphered with ease. Later glyphs often spelled out the meaning of earlier glyphs. Co-org-influenced hieroglyphics, on the other hand, combined all three sets of characters in a manner similar to Japanese. Early glyphs completely altered the entire meaning and tone of ones that came afterward. With no punctuation, the only way to make sense of it was to start at the beginning.

The other question that came to mind was, How did Heinrich Carson learn these? So I laid out the journals one by one, asking questions of Emelia as often as I could to help me pin down the order when I thought I'd ferreted out a passage.

And her patience had limits. On my twenty-first trip to the

kitchen, Emelia finally put down her paper and stared at me. "You really ought to ask Brynner."

"I tried."

"Ask nicer. Boy dotes on you something awful. Pass the sugar, sweetie."

I handed it to her, shaking my head. "Sure he does."

"Grace Roberts." She dropped her paper enough to look at me. "Was that sarcasm?"

I closed my eyes before I could roll them. "No, ma'am."

"I didn't think so. Not in this house."

Taking my laptop, I went out to the porch swing and downloaded my current mail. My connection, even with a satellite card, was so slow I could practically fly back to Seattle faster. When it finally downloaded, I opened the activity data Dr. Thomas promised me. Red dots pinpointed each co-org confirmed and killed.

The sheer amount of activity left me horrified.

Shamblers everywhere. Co-orgs popping up in places that made no sense, like the one trapped on a sandbar. How had it even gotten there? It wasn't like it could do the backstroke.

And the seaports, where co-orgs avoided moving water like the destruction it was. What were they doing along the water?

I flicked back through weeks of data.

Three weeks ago, reasonable, normal activities. The hiker grabbed here, the family dog turning up mutilated there.

Two weeks ago, and the first contact along the Atlantic coast. I rotated the Earth model and flicked back. Data from Egypt was, at best, sketchy. Those bastards in Grave Services didn't share information with us, though our best situation analysts figured they had far worse problems than we did.

As I played the data forward, an image kept forming.

When I was a little girl, my dad took me out to skip stones along the lake, as if that would make up for screaming at me the night before. The memory remained crisp in my mind, and the pattern of red on my map, more than anything, reminded me of a stone skipping across the water. One ripple leading to another.

Where had Brynner said he found the drawing? Greece. What if it wasn't a ripple? I called Dr. Thomas again, waiting for it to roll through to voice mail. Instead, after ringing over and over, he answered, his voice thick.

"This is Grace Roberts. Do you have a moment?"

"Now that I'm not sleeping? Today was my day off. You do know we're two hours behind you, right?"

I explained my theory about the ripples. "We talk about the Re-Animus like a single entity. But what if it's a pack of creatures? These don't look like a disease spreading, because they aren't. They're prey movement. Or predator movement."

Dr. Thomas waited. "Let's say this intriguing theory has merit. According to the records, Heinrich Carson was only able to kill two Re-Animus. I don't know of anyone else succeeding, ever. What would threaten a Re-Animus enough to make it flee?"

Brynner, if you asked me, would most definitely threaten one. But there was another answer, a simpler one. "A bigger Re-Animus. Stronger. More powerful. Something upsetting the normal progression and distribution. So they're all on the move. Fighting with one another. Fleeing something else."

"Hmmm. You have no proof, but a theory consistent with the data."

"Yes, sir." I swallowed, wondering how far out-there he thought I was.

Dr. Thomas sighed. "I think it's worth presenting to the director."

BRYNNER

I always did like funeral homes. In funeral homes, the bodies tended to stay put on the tables or coffins. Standard prep work involved cutting every major tendon in two places, and in high-activity areas, screwing the jaws closed. Most folks took the public safety tax credit for cremating relatives.

Mr. Parker and I drove out to the Hugheses' place and gathered up what was left of the other corpses. Of course, one of them didn't have a number, since he hadn't been dead long enough to get one. We left him for the medical examiner.

Once we got back to the home, Mr. Parker started with a standard examination. "See there? That's sloppy work," he said, pointing to the ankle of one Grace had shot. "There's a cut here, but they didn't take the time to make sure the Achilles tendon was severed." With a digital camera he documented each foot.

He slid open a refrigerated tray, revealing an elderly woman. "I take the foot off and sew it back." He lifted a toe, showing how the flesh sagged.

"Now, let's see those numbers." With a scanner, he read off the bar code. And frowned. "Done in Louisiana. Chain home, probably minimum-wage workers. I'll report these. Could you sign off on the processing report?"

He'd claim the cash credits for handling someone else's mess, too. I shook my head. "I'd love to, but I'm not here on official business. Those four showed up at the Hughes farm looking to make friends. There's a woman staying at the Big 8, Grace Roberts. Official BSI agent. She can sign, and they'll honor the credits."

He smiled at me for the first time in ten years. "Thank you, sir. According to the accident report filed with the body records, all three are victims of a carbon monoxide accident. Weren't found for a week."

Three bodies sitting around, just calling to Re-Animus like crap to flies. "Okay. That explains the color and the condition of the bodies."

"Sure, but it doesn't explain the location. See, those corpses were processed in New Orleans *yesterday*. I doubt they bought a train ticket straight here." He got up and grabbed a shearing pruner from the wall. "If you don't mind, I don't like letting them lie there intact."

With a quick clip, he severed the tendons on each leg, then at each elbow. "There we go. Now we can put them in the incinerator without getting killed."

I helped him load the first body into the crematorium, then shook his hand. "Thank you for helping me. If there's ever anything I can do to return the favor, you call me."

Mr. Parker wiped the sweat off his forehead. "There's one thing. Explain to me exactly what went through your head that day."

What was I supposed to say? I'm sorry I stole your backhoe? "I was a kid. I wasn't thinking."

He crossed his arms. "You were seventeen. Old enough to know what you were doing. You didn't knock down a single stone with the hoe."

"I didn't disturb a body. That was the point." Something I'd never been able to get across to Dad. Not while he wasn't around. Not while he was.

"No, but you disturbed a *grave*." His eyes gleamed as he spoke. "Something sacred. Special. You need to learn respect for the dead."

What happened that day had more to do with the living than the dead, but I didn't want to explain. "I'll try, sir." We shook again, and I let myself out.

I drove home. Home. A word I hadn't used for nearly a decade, so it felt foreign to think it, let alone say it. Lost in thought, I found my way up the porch and through the screen door.

And found Grace, sitting at the kitchen table. In one hand, she held a glass of sun tea. She poured another from the pitcher, and pushed it across the table to me. "Your aunt is out shopping. Said she ran out of Spam, and there wouldn't be any breakfast tomorrow without it. Sit."

So tempting. The woman, not the tea, though I longed to drink deeply of both. "I don't want to fight with you."

"Then don't. Please sit." She brushed her hair back and looked at me with what I wished were "Come with me" eyes.

I sat.

"I made progress today, but your aunt is tired of answering questions about your life, and I'm tired of bothering her. Would it kill you to take a chair in there, sit with me, and relax?" Grace wouldn't meet my gaze.

I took my offered drink, rubbing cold sweat from the cup. "No. I mean, I don't think it would kill me. But can I ask you something?"

"You just did."

I couldn't stop asking myself the question I had to ask her. "Do you like me?"

Her eyes went wide, her mouth open. But she recovered. "Sure. You're a good field operative, and I suspect that you care about people more than you let on."

"That's not what I meant. Grace, do you like *me*? Forget money and journals and jobs, and just answer the question. Because the other day, I was thinking—"

"Don't." She shook her head. "I can't. I won't."

Instincts honed from dozens of nights in hotel bars said she felt different. Why wouldn't she just answer? "Is it because of the director? I don't work for her anymore. 'No work women' doesn't apply at the Hughes farm." I glanced around. "Or the Homer house."

"Just stop. It's not the director, and it's not you. It's me."

In my experience, "It's not you, it's me" meant it was totally me. Just like "Nothing personal" usually involved something deeply personal.

She looked up at me. "I'm in a relationship."

I kept the "Oh" in my mouth but not off my face. I was so certain I knew what her response would be. I'd never considered any other possibility. I nodded in acceptance. There was no reason to pine for someone I couldn't have. Except that I wanted to pine. I wanted to pine a lot.

Grace sagged like a flat tire. "Is this the part where you storm out?"

"Will it change anything?"

"No."

I'd done enough leaving. "Will it make you like me?"

She bit her lip, her eyes crinkled up, and then shook her head.

"Okay." So this was rejection. I'd heard about it from Rory. But from the time my chest hairs turned curly, I'd found women the sweetest drug on earth, and usually so available. Except when they weren't. Like now. "Can I ask who the lucky guy is?"

Grace looked like I'd just stabbed her in the hand. "I don't want to talk about it." She took her tea and left me there at the table, savoring the bitter taste of failure that no honey could wash away.

So I went to the room where my aunt kept all the journals. How did she fit on the floor in that small a space? I picked up one book and opened it. Eyeball duck reeds. Which meant . . . I worked to remember Dad's lessons, drilling me over and over.

It meant I hadn't done hieroglyphics in ages.

I started over again, reading them as phonetics. After a good thirty minutes, I finally connected the dots, letting me pronounce the glyph. "*Reysha.*"

"*Reysha.* 'Dawn.' Could mean 'early,' or 'hope,' or 'tired.' Could mean a lot of things, depending on what was said around it." Grace stood in the doorway, her eyes red and swollen. "That's a later one. Maybe one of the last, but I was wrong."

I was used to seeing women cry around me, but not after turning me down. "Wrong about what?"

"I have to start with the early ones so I understand how he used constructs. The last ones I can't make heads or tails from. Your father had developed his own slang, his own meanings at that point. So I can read the words but not make sense out of them." She reached down, taking the book from my hand. Her fingertips grazed my palm, making me tingle all over.

"*Reysha k'ta svar eyone.* That's the easy part. He starts in mid-sentence most times, carrying on from whatever came before." She handed me the book back. "And they often end in gibberish as well."

She pushed a set of boxes aside and sat beside me, flipping through pages. She pointed to a string of symbols. "See this? This means 'son of me.' I think it's his name for you. It's everywhere in these." She pointed to several stacks. "And less in these. Not at all in these."

Talking about Dad wasn't something I wanted to do, but if it would keep Grace Roberts talking to me, I'd talk about my last medical exam. "Divide them. Those with my name and those without."

She worked through the stacks, quickly moving from book to book, eventually winding up with three piles. The smallest on her left, a medium set in the middle, and a stack three times the others on the right. "These, I'm sure, are from when you were small." She pointed to the center. "These have your name every so often, but pages and pages between them. The rest of those don't have your name at all."

I quelled my anger. It had nothing to do with Grace. "The smallest pile is before Mom died. The medium one is after her death. Everything on the right is after he left me here and ran off."

She took out a set of sticky notes, labeling each journal by color. "I know you don't want to talk about it. So answer me this, and I promise I won't ask again. Why did he leave?"

If anyone but Grace had asked me that, I wouldn't have answered. Even then, forcing out the words felt like ripping fishhooks from my skin. "He was searching for Mom."

16

GRACE

Brynner excused himself on the pretense of needing to use the restroom. I let him go because I couldn't breathe with him that close. Without a doubt there was more to his story, and for certain I could drag the truth out of him.

But what I wanted was for him to tell me. Willingly. Openly. Of course, I didn't deserve that after lying to him. Why did he ask me if I liked him? I couldn't like him. Or at least I wouldn't admit it.

But he hadn't run out when he should have. Instead, he'd sat in that dusty room, proving his skills in flirting were a thousand times more effective than his translation abilities.

With the journals divided, I could make progress by brute force if necessary. Friday was payday, and my chance to put to rest the demons calling me by name and cell phone each day.

I took one of the books and started at the beginning. *"Nfr saw tks.*" Easy enough. The phonic representations *n*, *s*, and *t* didn't match any concept. While *Nfr* might mean "sweet" or "pleasant," the subsequent glyphs didn't match in count or gender. "Thems goes blue" would be the closest English to this disaster of combinations.

The end of the book was no better. I grabbed another. "*Shm wd nfr*" made no more sense than the start. Either Heinrich Carson was horrible at writing hieroglyphics, in which case I might never decode them, or he was a genius. In which case I might never decode them.

I looked up to find Brynner watching me. "How long have you been there?"

He shrugged. "I was thinking about something."

"In the bathroom."

"Yes."

I waited for him to catch the awkward drift. "While you were using the bathroom."

"Yes. I was thinking about you."

If this was the smooth-talking man who waltzed women through his bed like a drive-through, the world's women were in worse shape than I thought. "Go on."

He sat down. "I was thinking maybe I would help you with the translation. I'll answer your questions and help you put things together."

"What do you want from me?"

He picked up a book. "Lessons. Dad taught me by writing the combination to our pantry lock in hieroglyphics. I'm hoping you have better teaching skills."

It stank of a trap. The question was, who was trapping whom? "You're sure that's what you want to ask me for?"

"Certain. Dad and I weren't on speaking terms when he

died. These are all I have left of him." He flipped to a page at random.

I wanted to tell him that part of his father sat right beside me, living and breathing. I knew he might be playing me. Using this just as a reason to be near me. Still, I understood as well as anyone the need to remember people I loved. My parents left us a trust fund, but I'd have traded every dollar for a letter from my mom, or her diaries.

I could help Brynner understand everything he had left of his father.

I opened the Universal Weighted index files and pushed the laptop toward him. "If you want to learn to read them right, you'd need to put in a few months' study on these. When you knew them by sight, we'd be ready to move to the first stage. Logograms. The duck. The crocodile. The gull. All of those mean what they look like. Then you'd learn to write them by name and know them by number."

"Number?" Brynner rubbed his chin. "Dad never mentioned numbers."

I nodded. "Universal Weight is a numbering system for glyphs. Pick a number between one and two thousand."

He watched me like I was about to perform a magic trick. "Sixteen."

"*Ayine*, a double loop, opening to the left. Transliterated as an air gap in the work. *Th'ok*." I smiled at his amazement. "How about *b'sa*, a closed *n*, indicating 'clay.' Universal Weight of thirty."

Brynner reached into a middle pile and took out a journal. He glanced back and forth between it and the screen. "*Nuswut*. An antenna, a barbecue, and a Jewish prayer hat. That's number three."

I almost choked, laughing so hard. "Wheat, *knut*, and *d'sar*. It means 'king.' But yes, its Universal Weight is three."

He flipped to the back, his frustration visible.

"You have to understand I spent *years* studying this. You spent years learning to kill things." I reached out and patted him on the shoulder.

"There's a barbecue king at the end, too." He tossed the journal aside and picked up another one. "Goldfish getting eaten by a camel." He looked up at the laugh I worked so hard to stifle. "I lost a lot of weight the first year Dad taught me."

If I were as bad at shooting as Brynner was at translating, I'd kill sixteen of the wrong people with every bullet. "That's *nwa*, the fish and the pack mule. Weight of seven, implies fortune, usually good."

He didn't respond, flipping to the back of the journal. "There's a goldfish here."

I grabbed the book from him, confirmed his brain damage didn't include basic pattern matching, then chose another book at random. "*Amun*, weight of sixteen." And on the back page, I found another *Amun* glyph. "Hand me them one at a time."

And one by one, I laid them out, matching colors and weights. Midway through them, I found it. Number one. I opened it, skipping the first ideoglyph. My mind picked apart the glyphs, discarding the conceptual meanings—those were a jumbled disaster. The logograms, too, didn't match.

My breath caught in my throat. With one hand, I reached out to grab him by the cheek, pulling him closer to look at the symbols with me. "Look. It's phonetic. He's writing phonetically. On the eighth—eighteenth of d-december, I decided that I would hua." I stopped. *Hua. Hua* what? The symbol, the

open cup. "'Master.' It's a proper glyph. I would master the—
form. Language. I would master the language of the old ones."

English. Phonetic English, mixed with ideoglyphs, demarked
with numbers so he could keep them organized. I picked up the
last journal, skipping over the weight, two hundred eighteen.

"What does it say? Does it say where the heart is?" Brynner hadn't moved, his face still next to mine.

I tried to read, and failed, both because of the jumbled
mess on the pages and the one Brynner made inside me when
he was that close. "I can't read this yet. This isn't phonetic; it's
completely conceptual, and it's using all three character sets."
I pointed to the early ones. "He's learning the language, and
quickly. By here"—I pointed to the middle set—"he's creating
constructs to represent ideas, and by the end, it might as well
be a private language."

"So it's useless."

"No, it's not." I patted him on the shoulder. I'd hit statues
less firm. "I think your aunt would say, 'Have some faith.'"

He caught the joke, smiling at me. "Always."

"I can start at the beginning and work my way forward. I'll
be able to fill in the ideographs from context, and by the time
we hit the last ones, there will be two people who speak his
language. And one of us will still be alive."

I'd be able to translate the journals. Find the heart, and
with the money I'd make, be able to stop worrying day and
night. Brynner could read his dad's writing and maybe make
peace with the demons that haunted him.

In that instant, I became aware of how close he still was, as
he spoke, his breath tickling me. "You did good, Grace."

I turned my head and kissed him, holding on for a moment
while his shock dissolved, letting go when he stopped pulling

away. Then his lips pressed against mine, softly first, then firmer. Hungrier. With one hand, I pulled him toward me, with the other, I supported myself.

He brushed my face, running his fingers along my cheek, causing me to gasp. A burning sensation lanced through my hand, and I fell back, breaking our kiss. A strangled cry of pain burst through my lips.

"What?" Brynner grabbed my hand, even though I tried to clench it into a fist.

A white dot surrounded by angry red marked my palm.

Brynner moved a box and cursed, smashing something with his fist. "I'm sorry. Brown scorpion. That's going to sting."

I gasped, clenching my fist, rocking. My fingers already puffed out, and my lips tingled. "I need my purse."

"I'll get you some baking soda to put on it. I know, it hurts like hell." Brynner moved away, and I caught him by the hair.

I gasped to spit out the words. "EpiPen. Allergic."

BRYNNER

That's exactly why I'd learned to expect something bad when good things happened to me. I ran to the living room and found her purse. Inside lay an EpiPen in a clear plastic tube. More than anything, it resembled a thick ballpoint pen that ended in a needle. I didn't stop, didn't flinch as I drove the needle into her thigh.

Her body arched, then relaxed as the epi hit her. I gathered her in my arms and carried her through the house, kicked the front door open, and nearly flattened Aunt Emelia.

"Boy, what happened?" She dropped the bag of groceries on the porch, sending tomatoes bouncing down the steps and into the yard.

"Brown scorpion. She's allergic. I used the EpiPen."

Grace lay in my arms, gasping for air.

Aunt Emelia ran for her kit and came back with a needle. "She's in anaphylactic shock. Her heart will stop if it goes on." With practiced fingers, she drew a needle and plunged it into Grace's arm, slowly drawing it out. "Get to County right now. Drive as fast as you can without killing you both. I'll call the ER and let them know."

"Come with me. If she stops breathing, you could put in a tracheotomy." I nodded to the car.

She barked at me like a drill sergeant. "Boy, you've been watching too much TV. Drive like you did as a teen, and stop arguing. Get her to the hospital before that shot wears off."

I opened the passenger door of the rental car and gently put her in. "I thought the epi would fix it."

"That attack could go on for days, depending on how sensitive she is. That dose will last thirty minutes. Maybe. If she isn't in the hospital on a drip by then, you'd need to cut down to her lungs to do any good." Aunt Emelia ran up the porch, and I tore out, driving like a tornado on wheels down the side roads and redlining the engine as I burned the miles to County.

Thirty minutes. Forty-five miles. I'd make it. I had to. I flew through Thurston so fast the cop running his speed trap didn't see me coming. Didn't stand a chance of catching me by the time he threw down his sandwich, buckled up, and pulled onto the road.

It wasn't until County Hospital loomed on the horizon that I dropped down to ninety miles per hour, then fifty, and skidded into the ambulance bay of the ER, parking signs be damned. Grace's lips had a blue tint to them that couldn't be good, and she gurgled as her chest shook.

A mob of doctors and nurses waited at the door. God only knew what Aunt Emelia told them. I followed, giving her name, her age based on the driver's license, and the BSI medical card I dug from her purse. They pushed me out. To the hallway. To the waiting room.

And I waited.

Hell isn't being attacked by dead things. Hell is hospital waiting rooms, where the clock gets dipped in cold motor oil. Each second ticked by and ticked again, and again. In the background, a newscaster showed clips of BSI field teams firing weapons, and lines of dead meat-skins.

I couldn't have cared less.

I don't know when Uncle Bran and Aunt Emelia arrived. It might have been two hundred years after they took Grace in, or maybe just an hour. Emelia wore her doctor's ID and signed in, disappearing into the warren of hallways.

I watched other cases come in. The drunk who challenged a telephone pole and lost, the cook who filleted a finger.

After hours, the door swung open, and a nurse came out to me. She strode over in comfortable sneakers and purple scrubs. "Dr. Homer says you're the fiancé."

I froze. Grace was so very private. She could kick me out later, when she wasn't in danger of dying. "Yes? Yes."

I followed her back through the ER to hospital rooms that smelled of bleach and death. There, Grace lay in a bed, covered by a thin sheet. An IV hung from her arm, and the machines surrounding her beeped in rhythm with her heart. Her face, her lips, every part of her had swelled, distorting her beauty but not hiding it.

I took her hand and sat in the folding chair beside her bed.

A doctor knocked, a young man who must have been fresh out of medical school. He sported an orange beard and a stained coat. "I'm Dr. MacArthur, attending today."

I shook his hand and waited.

"Your fiancée is extremely fortunate. Her heart stopped twice. She was stone-cold dead for almost fifteen seconds before we got her going again." He looked at her chart and adjusted one of the machines.

I enveloped one of her slim hands in my own. Even her fingers had swelled like tiny bratwursts. "What happens now?"

He held out his hands, palms up. "Now we wait. We monitor her breathing. We get her allergic reaction under control. When I'm sure she won't drop dead on the ride home, I'll let you take her."

Aunt Emelia came in behind him. "I'll take it from here, Jim."

When he left, she took out another chair and joined me. "I've seen this before. She'll be fine."

I nodded.

"Brynner, what's wrong?"

I looked back at Grace's still form. "Can she hear?"

"No." Aunt Emelia looked at the chart on Grace's bed. "Unless she's astral projecting, which she doesn't believe in, no." Aunt Emelia put one hand on my knee. "Has this one gotten to you?"

"No." I listened to the churn of emotion inside me. "Maybe. I don't know."

She nodded. "You've had other . . . friends before. What's different about her?"

I searched for a lie but couldn't find one I could stand to tell. "I don't know. When I'm with her, I want to be better than I am." There, the truth that frightened me.

Aunt Emelia rose and hugged me, squeezing my head to her like she did when I was ten. "I've seen this, too. You'll be fine, boy. Just fine."

She rose to leave, and called back to me, "You need to notify her field commander. He'll want to know, and he'll make sure her kin know." After a moment, she returned and tagged a purple band onto my arm. "That says you are family, so you can get back in."

She left me.

I paced the room, checking every few minutes to make sure Grace was still breathing. When I could put it off no longer, I rummaged through her purse to find her phone. I'd left my phone, my wallet, everything but my keys back at the house and honestly didn't remember bringing Grace's purse or her messenger bag from the rental car. Maybe Aunt Emelia had the good sense to fetch them, since I left the car parked in the ambulance bay.

Her wallet weighed nothing. A driver's license. Ten different credit cards, all with a black X in marker on them. A packet of birth control pills meticulously punched, and a smashed packet of saltine crackers, which I devoured.

At the bottom of her purse I found her phone. I took it out, and then followed the hospital signs to the designated cell area.

Dale's number came to mind, my fingers reflexively dialing, only to cancel it and dial BSI Medical. I waited for the prompts, then dialed, 9, 1, 1. A man picked up the phone within seconds. "Emergency Medical Services."

"This is Brynner Carson. Field Operative Grace Roberts

is hospitalized. County Hospital, New Mexico." I swallowed, my throat as dry as a dead cactus.

"It's an honor to speak to you, sir."

I hung up on him and dialed another number, one I hated calling. When the voice mail answered, I spoke. "Maggie, it's Brynner. I need you to find me Grace's emergency contact." After leaving the cell phone number, I hung up and began to pace.

Moments later, the phone rang. I fumbled with the touch screen to answer. "Carson speaking."

"Brynner," said the director, "what have you done?"

17

BRYNNER

The urge to scream in frustration melted like a snow cone in the desert as I thought of Grace. Her defenselessness called to me like a beacon. Instead, I explained to Director Bismuth about the scorpion. About the EpiPen, and the drive, and waiting.

And after a moment, Director Bismuth spoke. "I'm sorry. I'm truly sorry. I assumed when I heard you, that you had led her—"

"To my bed? Into another fight? I know. I don't care. I don't work for you anymore, and all I want you to do is let me call her emergency contact and let them know what happened. I owe them that much. She has a boyfriend, I think, and a daughter."

"I refused to accept your resignation."

I didn't call to fight, but that didn't mean I wouldn't. "That's because I didn't resign, I quit. You don't get a say in that. It's like saying I didn't tell you about a surprise party. Surprise."

"Brynner, we need you. I take it Ms. Roberts didn't inform you of our conversation."

"You need my father. Grace will get back to translating when she's better. My aunt will say when that is, not you. Can I call you Maggie now that we don't work together?"

"No." Her tone said she'd like to strangle me over the phone. "Ms. Roberts has a trust company listed as the benefactor on her insurance, but no emergency contact for the last four years."

The trust fund I got, but no emergency contact? That made no sense. "You sure?"

"Please, Brynner. Of course I'm sure. When she came to work, she listed a brother, but given that her file shows bereavement time for his funeral, and we have a copy of his cremation certificate, I doubt he'll be accepting our call."

So I was it for now. At least until Grace could give me the number herself. "Take care, Maggie. The TV says it's crazy out there."

"We're finding those spells everywhere now, Brynner, and not just in wells or pits or abandoned warehouses. Two days ago we found one in a cargo barge in Louisiana. A barge not even docked."

The air temperature dropped about thirty degrees in the space of six seconds, according to the goose bumps on my arms. What was it about water? About boats? "You have pictures of it?"

"Of course. I'd send them to your BSI account, but as I understand, you wish to terminate your employment." The pure pleasure in her voice infuriated me. "Am I mistaken?"

I paced the cellular area, knowing she had me pinned. "Don't—Don't do anything rash."

She left me hanging on the phone, agonizing, for several seconds. "This is certainly a reversal of circumstance. That would normally be the advice I give you, and normally, you would ignore it."

Grace's cell phone chirped, dying. Just as well, since I was fighting the urge to say some things that I could actually write in hieroglyphics. "Nothing seems normal anymore."

I hung up and returned to Grace's room.

In Grace's messenger bag, I found her laptop. Using the hospital network, I logged in to the BSI network. Thirty-five critical alerts, two hundred sit-reps, and half a dozen pleas for help littered my inbox. And one set of files I was waiting for. Downloading them took nearly an hour, but my reward was highly detailed photographs of every single inch of the inscription.

Written in blood like the others, it almost glowed against the blue cargo container walls. Why the sudden interest in water, something that would most certainly kill a co-org? Why the obsession with these inscriptions?

Drawings like that hadn't been seen for nearly twenty years. Now here they were, showing up everywhere like graffiti. But it couldn't be coincidence that a set of corpses in Louisiana took a jet-pack ride to Bentonville, and the same day a field team found this.

I believed in almost any god that would offer me an edge against the Re-Animus, and in my experience, random chances didn't usually turn out to be random.

The Re-Animus I'd driven out at the Hughes farm was the same one I'd met in Greece, despite them seeming to be territorial. So the question was, Did it come after me for revenge, or something else? Was it attempting something else on the boat when I showed up, or sent there to deliver a message to me like it claimed?

The BSI's translators couldn't keep up with all the writing our field teams found.

The one that Director Bismuth sent me didn't even have a translation. In a creaky plastic hospital chair, I hunched through the night, puzzling out words. The hours passed in shifts. Nurses changing. Doctors watching. I dozed from time to time, once Aunt Emelia went home for the night.

After the doctors came through on morning round, I returned to my efforts. The memories locked in my brain returned, of lessons forced on me in ancient Greek and Egyptian. The symbols became both familiar and foreign, haunting me with meanings I could almost remember. "Snake-barbecue-antenna, urinal-prayerhat-antenna." I paged through the listings, looking for the right glyph.

A muffled squeak from beside me caught my attention. Grace stirred and opened her eyes.

I triggered the call button over and over, then ran to the door. "She's awake!"

A new doctor ran in, an Asian American woman with short black hair. "We'll take the tube out. Grace, don't try to talk until we do."

Afterward, Grace lay sputtering on her side, sipping cold water through a straw.

I knelt beside her bed. "You scared me. That's not allowed."

"*T'war.*" Grace coughed again, and grimaced. "Snake wheat reticule. Means 'path.'"

"It can wait."

Grace struggled to sit up, triggering the bed. "Throat hurts." She called the nurse again.

After the nurse removed her IV and gave Grace another cup of water, Grace began to struggle with her hospital gown, cinching it shut in the front, then trying to drag it down over her bust. The more she fought with it, the less it covered. Finally, she shrank down under the sheet and looked up at me. "Would you mind leaving?"

If she'd shot me in the stomach, it would have hurt less. I looked away and stood up, knocking my chair over by accident.

"Brynner." She swallowed, cracked lips white and dry. "I just need to shower. By myself." She rang the call button again and repeated her request.

The nurse looked at me like I was a dead skunk. "You could use a shower, too. And have you eaten at all? I told you to go get dinner before I left last night."

I shook my head. "Takes three weeks to starve to death."

She took Grace by the arm and shoved me toward the door. "You look like you're about two weeks, five days along. Go get breakfast in the cafeteria while I help Grace feel presentable. She doesn't need you standing guard."

That wasn't why I was here. "This hospital is the third-safest place on earth. My dad oversaw the barriers himself back when Aunt Emelia practiced here. Unless a meat-skin parachutes in from the sky, it's not getting past the walls." I was here because—because it felt like the right thing to do. But if Grace wanted time alone, I could give it to her. "I'll be back as soon as I'm done eating."

GRACE

It wasn't my first time to wake up in a hospital after being stung. Not my first severe attack, either, though last time, a wasp caused it. On the other hand, this was definitely my first time to wake up with Brynner Carson staring at me like a lost puppy.

I don't know if it was the sound of his voice or the butchered translation job that woke me. If my throat didn't feel like I'd gargled battery acid, I would have done a better job of explaining why I kicked him out. It wasn't just because my gown covered less than half of what it ought to. I had no doubt Brynner had looked on finer rear ends than mine.

I felt nasty and probably smelled worse. I didn't want him near me like that. If he was going to be near me, I wanted to look my best. So with the nurse's help, I hobbled to the shower and sat in it, turning the water ever hotter.

"Just breathe the steam—it'll help with your throat. Pull that call chain when you are ready to get out." She left me in the bathroom, in the fog of the shower and my own mind.

I remembered figuring out the journals.

And kissing Brynner.

And pain, first in my hand, then in my thigh. Lights swirling overhead as someone carried me, ran with me. Dirt roads and highways passing at speeds that made the lines blend together.

When I finally turned off the water, every inch of me flushed bright pink from the heat. Brynner had told me there were scorpions in the house. But I hadn't exactly been thinking at the point where I got stung. I jerked the call chain and waited for help.

The nurse handed me a towel. "Don't you worry. Your fiancé is down in the cafeteria, signing autographs, or so I hear." She helped me over to the bed and nodded to my purse, which lay against the wall. "We brought that up with your things. I'm sorry, but they cut your clothes off in the ER."

My hands and legs felt like they weighed fifty pounds each. I could barely sit up while she slipped a top and bottom on me. "Brynner's not . . ." Not my what?

"I'm sorry," said the nurse. "We thought 'cause of the bracelet, and all. I mean, he wouldn't leave, hardly slept last night. I'll let the staff know." She knelt and slipped a pair of socks on my feet. "I think I'm going to take my morning break and go buy a man some breakfast." She walked over to primp in my mirror.

"No." The word burst out of my mouth along with a jolt of jealousy. "We—haven't been together long." Technically true, I told myself.

"I knew it. All the good ones are taken." She washed her hands and walked out.

A short time later the head nurse came in and began to brush my hair.

I glanced in the mirror. I looked better than I felt, but not good enough. "You don't happen to have any makeup, do you?"

She shook her head. "We don't, but you don't need any. You've got that natural beauty going on."

"I just want to look my best." Though I'd barely managed to admit it to myself, I couldn't help wanting to look nice. He'd asked me point-blank if I liked him.

I'd lied to him back in the house. This time, I'd tell him the truth.

"Well, you can go shopping when you're out and doll yourself up. Thank goodness it's Friday. I'm ready for the weekend."

I shook my head. "Excuse me. What day did you say it was?"

"Friday. Best day of the week. I'm not surprised you don't remember yesterday, since you were damn near dead. My cousin in the ER says your fiancé drove you here himself."

Any normal day where I woke up in the hospital after nearly dying, it would have been the fiancé remark that worried me. But for now, I needed to focus on getting to a bank by two to arrange payment. "I have to go."

I struggled to sit up and tried to throw my feet off the bed.

"If you mean 'go to the bathroom,' I'll help you. If you mean 'leave the hospital,' I'll tie you down. I've seen kittens with more fight in them." She blocked my exit from the bed, tapping her finger on the straps. "Do you think for a moment I won't do it?"

I slumped back in the bed. "I have to go."

"You aren't going nowhere today. Maybe not tomorrow. Don't get yourself on bed arrest, Ms. Grace."

Desperate times called for desperate measures. I hated what I had to do, primarily because of what might come out of the nurse's mouth while he was there, but I was out of choices. "Could you tell Brynner I'd like to speak to him?"

A few moments later, he stood in my room, towering over my bed like a mythical creature carved of muscle and bone. A quarter-inch beard covered his jaw, making him look part lumberjack.

"I need a favor. I wouldn't ask, but I don't have anyone else." My cheeks burned, and beads of sweat formed on my skin.

"Name it." He held up his arm, showing a purple band that matched mine. "Since we're practically family."

I pointed to the wall. "Get my purse." While he waited, I scribbled careful instructions on a notepad, then handed him my license and checkbook. "Routing number and contact information is on this. That goes on the slip. I need you to go to a bank and transfer from my checking to that account number."

"Don't they have apps for that sort of thing?"

"I don't trust online banking." The truth was I changed banks too often to keep up with websites and anything but my most recent account.

He nodded. "Me neither. How much do you want transferred?"

I bit my lip. "Everything in there. Please, it has to be done by two o'clock or the payment won't be in on time."

"Everything." He frowned, narrowing his eyes. "What are you—"

"Let me worry about that. I've been doing this for years. Please." I took his hand, wrapping my fingers over his scarred palms. "It's for my daughter's care center. Please."

It wasn't like I had a choice. It wasn't like he didn't. But Aunt Emelia had been right. Sometimes you had to trust someone.

He dropped my hand and stalked out of the room without a word.

18

BRYNNER

I didn't like the implications of Grace's request, not leaving money for even basic necessities. But she was an adult, and I had no say in her decisions. I took her paper and drove to a bank with every intention of doing what I was told. At least if Grace felt well enough to order me around, she had to be getting better.

Banks irritated me. Their dry, boring nature just cried out for something fun to happen, like a fire, or an earthquake. Something to brighten up those peoples' day. First, I stood in line to speak to a teller. Who told me she couldn't help. I needed to stand in line for a branch representative. Which I did.

While the tellers looked like smiling would kill them, the branch manager reminded me of a guy in a hostage situation who had someone holding a gun to his head, threatening to blow his brains out if he *stopped* smiling.

"How can I help you, Mr. . . . Carson, is it?" He shook my hand with a greasy palm.

"My friend is in the hospital and asked me to make a wire transfer for her. I've got the account details right here." I handed him the paper with Grace's numbers.

He grinned to the point where it had to hurt. "I'm sorry, but I can't let you transfer funds out of someone else's account."

"I have her signature and her license." I handed over Grace's license and her checkbook.

He shook his head. "You could have written that yourself."

"Really? How many men do you know who write like that? All bubbly? It might as well be written in glitter ink and have strawberry scratch-n-sniff on it. Do you have any idea who I am?" About then, it occurred to me that shaving so I matched my press photographs might have been a good idea.

"You're Brynner Carson. I'm such a fan of that movie they made about your dad. But that doesn't change bank policy." Somehow, he still managed to show each and every last one of his teeth through that smile. "Nothing changes bank policy. Now, shall I have security escort you out?"

He glanced to the door, where a bored rent-a-cop slouched in cheap polyester. The guard walked over, his head almost coming up to my shoulder, and put one hand on his gun. "I'll have to ask you to leave, sir."

"I just want to transfer some money. That's all I want to do."

The branch manager pointed to the door. "You asked me to commit fraud. I've asked you to leave politely. Because I'm polite."

Both of them stepped back when I stood. "Meat-skins are easier to deal with." I looked over to the guard. "If you value your fingers, you'll keep them to yourself. Pull that gun on me and you'll need an enema to reload it."

I walked out, crossing Smiley's branch off my list of places where I'd be welcome. I drove all the way back to Bentonville, to a brown brick building off Main Street, and walked into the bank president's office.

"Wilbur," I said as he hung up the phone with a look of surprise, "I need help sending money. You do wire transfers?"

A great-great-grandson of Bentonville's founder, Wilbur had looked old when I was just a boy. As an ancient man, his hair had turned silver white, and he sported eyebrows that you could take shelter under. "Brynner Carson, your aunt said you were back in town. Let me get my manager to help you. I never did learn to work the computers."

A moment later, an older man, in his fifties, with salt-and-pepper gray hair and thin wire frame glasses stepped into the office.

Wilbur stood up and pointed to me. "Chuck, you need to help Brynner with this transfer. Go on, he doesn't bite."

I followed Chuck to a side office, growing more uneasy by the minute. I recognized the man, though I couldn't put my finger on just where I'd met him. "Before we start, could you answer me a question?"

Chuck shrugged. "If Wilbur Benton says so, I could answer twenty."

"You don't have any daughters who graduated from Benton back when I went there, do you?"

He shook his head. "Both my sons were three years behind you—"

"It's all good. Just wanted to check."

I explained about the transfer, and Grace, and the scorpion, leaving out the kiss that just didn't work out, and gave him Grace's instructions. He punched numbers into a computer for a few minutes, then frowned.

"This routing number's no good. Are you sure the destination account is right?"

Could Grace have gotten the numbers wrong? "I don't know."

He pointed to a cubicle. "Use that phone, confirm the routing numbers, we'll try this again."

So I sat down in the chair. First I dialed the hospital, but the phone rang and rang, without answer. Then another idea came to me. I dialed her confirmation number and waited.

A woman answered. "Suquamish Convalescence Center, how may I direct your call?"

I almost didn't answer in time, focusing instead on where I'd called. "I'm calling on behalf of Grace Roberts. I need to speak to someone in—"

"Accounts. I hope you don't hang up the way she does."

The phone beeped, and for thirty seconds, I listened to a recorded announcer talk Medicaid benefits, and how I, too, could plan for many happy years.

When the phone clicked again, a voice like black ice spoke. "Ms. Roberts, I've been waiting for your call. Can we play a little game? I call it 'Guess the latest excuse.'"

"If you want to play with yourself, be my guest, but not while I'm on the phone." I forced myself to take deep breaths. Who knew what the history here was? "I just need to confirm an account number for wire transfer."

He coughed, cursing, and when he spoke again, his voice was deep and calm. "I'm sorry, sir, we had a misrouted call. How can I help you?"

"I told the receptionist I'm calling on behalf of Grace Roberts. Do you want this money or not? Because she's trying to transfer it to you. If you do want it, now would be a great time to give me your account number."

"Hell yes, we want it. She's always a month late and a thousand dollars short. I could throw her daughter out and use the bed for a paying customer." He relayed a set of numbers.

Grace had transposed a six and a nine in two different places. "Thank you. I'll schedule the transfer right away." I tapped my pen, willing myself to not say anything else.

And the idiot opened his mouth again. "How much is she shelling out? It better be at least half of what she owes."

"How much does Grace need?"

"Let me put it this way. Even if she paid twenty thousand right now, I'd want another twenty-five for the next six months, on account of her being completely unreliable. From now on, she pays in advance."

There was a time, when I was younger, when holding on to money mattered. When I looked at my BSI paychecks and opened my interest statements. I'd never gotten a hug from a bank note or had a savings bond watch me while I was sick with the flu. Once a year, I met with the investment banker who ran Dad's accounts, and mine when the family fortune passed to me. It made for a good nap. "What's your name?"

"Ravi Hendricks. Why? Don't go getting pissed off at me for wanting her to pay the bills. Five fucking years I've played this game with her."

Exhale desire to strangle an asshole. Inhale love and peace. "Listen to me, Ravi. Listen very carefully. You're going to receive a wire transfer shortly. You're going to smile and keep your freaking mouth shut."

"About time she found a sugar daddy."

I slammed the phone down three times on the desk, creasing the plastic, and nearly screamed when I picked it up. "If you *ever* say that again, I will show up at your front door, or maybe in your parking garage, or maybe I'll be taking a nap on your couch when you get home. Do you know what I'm going to do?"

Heads turned to stare at me across the bank while I waited for an answer that wouldn't come.

"Nothing. I'll just wait, because lately it seems that wherever I go, dead things show up and start tearing chunks out of people. I won't lay a finger on you, Ravi. But I won't stop them, either. You keep your mouth shut. You keep the money. You leave Grace alone."

I slammed the phone down again, this time in the cradle, and walked back to a very rattled branch manager. "They have poor customer service skills. Here's the correct destination number. Pull the funds from my account."

His hands trembled as he punched the numbers in.

"Is there any way she can tell where the money came from?"

He nodded. "If she noticed, your friend might ask the bank, and they'd refer her to us. We treat account information as confidential, but—"

"She'll know. She's way too smart for that. Don't do it."

"Too late." He printed out a paper and handed it to me. "That's your confirmation code. It's done. Why do you care if she knows?"

"I don't want her to think she owes me. She might get the wrong idea. It's just money." I shrugged. I knew what mattered in life, and it wasn't green paper or bank account balances.

Telling a banker "it's just money" is a great way to give them heartburn. He sputtered and shifted his eyes until I shook his hand and left the office.

The bank president, Wilbur, waited for me at the door. "I want to thank you for banking with us. Are you all set up?"

"I am. I've got to get back to County. I have a friend there." I drove back, terrified of explaining this to Grace.

GRACE

I spent two hours in a state of perpetual panic. What if Brynner didn't get the transfer done? What if they wouldn't accept it? I'd called in every favor just to get my daughter in, and worked any and every job available to keep her that way.

When Brynner walked back in the door, he must have read the worry on my face. "It's done. Here's the confirmation code."

I took the receipt from him, clenching it in my fingers. Safe for another month.

He sat down in the chair. "You look better now. How's the throat?"

Awful. Like I swallowed a box of razor blades. "Much better. I can't thank you enough. I mean it."

He looked away, obviously uncomfortable with the idea of basic gratitude. "There was a problem with your routing number."

My stomach did a 360, flopping like an angry alligator.

"Don't worry. I called the confirmation number and got the right one." He patted my hand, his tone confirming my worst nightmare.

"Who did you talk to?" *Please, don't let it be Ravi.*

He grimaced, giving me my answer before he spoke. "An asshole. Listen, Grace. About the money—"

I shook my head. "The motel is a business expense, and your aunt feeds me better than anything I could buy. You can live on ramen for months. I've done it."

Brynner looked like he'd swallowed a chili pepper, but he let it drop.

"Hand me that bag, please." I pointed to a shopping bag beside the bed, and he handed it to me. I drew out a leather-bound journal. "Your aunt brought these in for me while you were gone."

The confusion on his face made me sorry for him. He sagged into a chair, shaking his head. "My aunt said those weren't ever to leave the house. Ever."

"She said I might get bored watching soap operas on TV." I offered him the book. "Do you want them back? I'm sure they're safer with you than me."

He shook his head. "This hospital is a fortress. Aunt Emelia was going to practice here, so Dad took time off to make a few adjustments to the construction plans. The only place safer than the hospital is my aunt's house. Did you manage to read any of them?"

"I made it through the first three. Your dad switched to ideographs midway through book two and never looked back." I'd have shown him, but even reading it myself was hard enough. "Five books later, he's writing in a combination of scripts just like the Re-Animus. The man was a combination of genius and crazy."

"I hear that a lot. You seem to be doing just fine here."

I pointed to the floor. "No scorpions. Go home. Sleep. Shave. I can take care of myself for one night."

His gaze dropped to the floor; his lips turned down. I couldn't get a read on him. Angry? Disappointed? "All right. You have my number. You know those meat-skins that nearly killed us out at the farm? They were in Louisiana the day before, in a funeral home."

He was hiding something. Something he thought would upset me. He wouldn't make eye contact. "How'd they get all the way to New Mexico?"

Brynner picked up my laptop and logged on. "Here. I got these from Director Bismuth. It's a spell a team found on a cargo barge in New Orleans the same day our meat-skins went missing."

My first inclination was to argue over the term "spell," but he'd definitely talked to the director. Had he called her because of me? "You think this just magically transported them across two states? I think we're up against something intelligent, sure, and alien, but not magic."

For one moment, I thought he might yell at me. "You don't know what you are talking about. And I need some sleep. Can you translate that for me?"

I read the outer ring of glyphs, standard late-kingdom symbols. "Yeah, it's just like all the others, only still in a circle."

"Others?" Brynner stared at me.

I nodded. "Yeah. Normally I don't see them still written like this, but it's a variant of the other eight I've translated. Related to the one you found on your boat."

Brynner leaned over the hospital bed, staring into my eyes with an intensity that both frightened and thrilled me. "You've read these before. For sure?"

I tore my gaze away, looking at the screen. "Hold on. There's a standing bonus for alternate translations on all of these. I have a lot of time. Every BSI translator takes at least one shot at them. Don't you think if there were some secret to them, at least one of us would have succeeded?"

He put both hands on my cheeks, making me look at him. "Tell me you didn't read them out loud, Grace. Please."

The warmth of his hands and the rough calluses on his palms made me dizzy. "I have. Hundreds of times. I've tried every phonic combination you can imagine, and I'm one translator, in one small office." I took his hands off, holding them in mine, and looked him in the eye. "I know you think there's something special about them."

Brynner snapped open his phone, turning away. "Dale, I need you to confirm something. Grace says the spell engravings have been shared with all the BSI translators." A computerized burst of profanity erupted from the phone, followed by a noise like a fax machine. Brynner nodded. "Find out if it's true. Those are supposed to be classified."

He jabbed the phone like he wanted to stab it, and turned back to me. "I'm sorry, Grace. I just don't want to see anyone get hurt."

If he knew how many weekends I'd spent arranging glyphs into various combinations, playing a several-thousand-year-old game of Scrabble. Nothing had ever happened. Ever. "Tell me something. What would it take to convince you these are just artifacts? Like cave drawings, or engravings? What would I have to do?"

His knuckles turned white on the laptop edge; his voice came out almost a whisper. "You could give me my mother back."

I had no answer for that, only questions. "What happened

to her? Your uncle said to ask you. Your aunt told me some of it, but I don't understand. I just want to understand. Help me with that."

"You want to understand magic." The dubious look he gave me matched how I felt.

I wanted to understand Brynner. "Yes."

He shook his head. "Why did you lie to me? You told me you're in a relationship, but I tried to contact your kin. There's no one listed."

I'd known before I lied to him it would come out. Lies had a way of doing that. "It was the only thing I could think of to say."

"I asked you a simple question. Do you like me? Yes or no, you could have said either."

I choked down my pride. "I'm used to keeping people at arm's length. It's safer that way." I looked up, waiting until his eyes met mine. "Yes. The answer was—is—yes."

Brynner looked like I'd sucker punched him, his eyes completely blank. Then he slowly grinned wide enough to make a crocodile nervous. "I promised Rory I'd help him with a tractor as soon as you were better, but I'll be back tomorrow." Brynner looked like he'd swallowed a helium balloon, as he bounced out of his chair. "I'll see you later, Grace." Still smiling, he left me there.

The hours stretched out after five o'clock, becoming one long gel of nameless voices on the intercom mixed with the constant shuffle of feet outside. I lost myself in Heinrich Carson's journals. The man saw demons everywhere, monsters and magic. In an earlier age, he would have been a great shaman. A mighty king.

I finished the last of the early journals and hit a block of symbols whose pattern was familiar, but whose meaning I couldn't decipher. Based on the time, it had to have been from the year of the accident that killed Lara Carson.

I'd looked it up, trying to fill in details, but the BSI records I found contained nothing about the accident. She didn't even have a corpse number or cremation record on file, which, given her status in the BSI, wouldn't have been tolerated. We didn't allow our own to come back. Now that I'd seen the intelligence of the Re-Animus, I knew why.

The corpse of every BSI operative and analyst held secrets about what we knew, and what we didn't. So when I died, they'd burn me to ashes and scatter those. There were worse ways to go. Which made me curious. Heinrich Carson had a corpse number recorded, but no record of cremation. Why?

What I needed was to understand what Heinrich wrote about. What he felt, and thought. Stymied by the foreign concepts, I switched to the writing Brynner gave me. The longer he was gone, the guiltier I felt about sending him home. I'd begged him to do something for me, kicked him out of the room after he stayed with me, and didn't even say thanks properly.

Problem was, there's no appropriate level of thanks for "saving my life, waiting with me, and acting as my errand boy." I wouldn't find a greeting card in any store for that situation.

The outer ring of symbols on the picture I recognized as standard text from *The Book of the Dead*, just like the one I'd been summoned to Seattle for. "Open the way, show the way, the secret way," and so on. The inner ring, on the other hand, defied easy translation. "The eastern Nile delta," read one section. "The west desert edge," read another.

Down from? Up to? The paths of Osiris. If I reversed the order from the outside ring, it made a legal sentence. "From the eastern Nile delta, down the paths of Osiris, up the west desert edge." That didn't make sense, either. In Seattle, I'd had so little time to study the artifact all I could come up with was a best guess. Now I had hours to do what I loved.

The problem was, the center symbols didn't form any concept at all, just a name. Ra-Ame.

If Brynner were here, he'd read the phrases as symbolic and run with it. The paths of the dead would be mystic portals, and the other two . . . If New Orleans was the "eastern Nile," then Benton could certainly be a western desert edge.

I'd been at this too long, but couldn't sleep.

An e-mail notification popped up, and I tabbed over to it, but it wasn't for me.

Brynner had left me logged in to the BSI network, with his account, his access.

19

GRACE

Using Brynner's BSI access code violated at least a dozen BSI statutes and every rule of decency, but I wanted more than anything to understand. What happened to him that day his mother died? What exactly did she do?

It had to haunt him, and I knew better than most about painful memories. My brother hadn't exactly wanted to hug and console me after our parents died. I think he saw too much of my dad in himself and wondered if their accident was really an accident, or if Dad had followed through on his many threats.

If I understood Brynner, maybe I could reach him. He'd done so much for me, I had to. With a few taps, I switched into his e-mail, which was exactly the disaster I expected.

Dozens from his field commander. Most of them complaining about missed briefing, broken rules, or destroyed equipment.

Scores of thank-you letters, pictures of people I assume Brynner rescued, dozens, maybe hundreds of those.

Way too many from women asking why he wouldn't return their calls.

I brought up the archive access and entered "Lara Carson." This time, hundreds of records came back, confirming what I suspected: The BSI never forgot. They might have hidden, but would never delete, records.

Field reports. Lab tests. Operation evaluations. Based on what lay before me, Lara Carson might well have been one of the original field operative directors. The field reports in her name changed to lab reports at a time I assume coincided with Brynner's birth.

She'd written some of the original tests on co-org physiology modifications. Forget the old man; Brynner's mother was responsible for the more interesting aspects of BSI investigation. I didn't understand her methods. She tested variants of pine and freshness rather than studying the sap or chemical components.

Each tap brought up another document. There was a payment to Heinrich Carson from hazard insurance for Lara Carson, presumed dead. The amount on-screen left me shocked, though no amount of money would make up for losing a mother.

Next, came a work order, the complete disassembly of a BSI laboratory. Radiometry, materials analysis reports on the drywall and steel.

The accident report left me with more questions than answers. She'd been working in the lab and reported missing. A three-day search of four city blocks in Seattle and the entire BSI headquarters turned up nothing. Body unrecovered. Missing, reported dead.

"Final Disposition, Laura Carson," read the next report heading. I pulled it up. The blank screen held nothing. I reloaded the file several times to check, but it refused to open.

The final entry read "Interview H. Carson, and minor, session six." The video, grainy black and white, showed one of our debriefing rooms. A middle-aged woman sat with her back to the camera, shuffling through papers. She turned and looked at the camera. "Bring them in." Maggie Bismuth. Now director of the BSI.

A door opened off-camera, the hinges whining, and a deep voice with a heavy German accent spoke. Moments later, a hulking man sat down at the table. If it weren't for the date on the video, I'd have sworn I was looking at Brynner. Beside him sat a young boy, maybe ten, with wild black locks and his father's chin. It had to be less than a week after the accident, based on the date.

"Let's begin again, shall we?" Maggie pushed a can of soda across the table toward young Brynner. "Tell me what you noticed first."

Brynner didn't look up. Didn't touch the offered soda, until his father prompted him in German.

Then Brynner raised watering eyes to the camera. "The wall was gone."

The director leaned back in her chair, her eyes narrowed. "Gone, as in destroyed? Like your accident in the armory last year?"

He looked up at his dad, his eyes wild. "No. It was just gone, all of it."

She nodded. "And your mother?"

He whispered so softly they'd put subtitles on the video. "She went into the cave."

"Vault Zero?" Heinrich Carson's voice sounded like a bear growling.

Brynner shook his head. "The cave where the wall used to be. With the statues in it." He looked back to his father. "Can we go?"

Heinrich put a hand on his son's shoulder, as if he could will Brynner to continue.

Director Bismuth bent over and brought out a box. "And where did she get these?"

She opened the lid, revealing a set of daggers. I'd seen them before, in Brynner's hands.

"You said they disintegrated," said Heinrich Carson, swiping the blades in a motion that made it clear he'd spent years honing his skill with knives. "You lied to me."

Maggie sat back in the chair. "Those are BSI artifacts recovered from an incident site. Neither your property nor your business. Brynner, where did your mother get them?"

"From the body on the table." Tears ran down Brynner's cheeks, and he shrank toward his father.

Maggie leaned forward. "You've done so well. I just need you to stay with me a little longer. When your mother went back into the cave, where did she go?"

Brynner shook his head, his eyes wide with fear, his lips pursed together.

"I wouldn't ask if it didn't matter. Where exactly did she get this?" She picked up a black velvet bag and undid the drawstring. Inside rested a silver jar the size of a bowling pin, a symbol of Horus carved on the lid.

Heinrich Carson shot to his feet. "You said it was safe in the vault. Not to be removed. Do you have any idea what danger this represents? What the Re-Animus will do to get it back?" He seized it, the iron set of his jaw daring her to take it back.

She waved her hand. "Security, restrain Mr. Carson."

The door burst open, but Heinrich Carson was waiting, expecting the guards. The first one flew past the camera, crashing into the wall beside the director. Another screamed and fell, never entering my field of view. The last slammed into the window so hard the camera flashed with static.

"Stay here, son. I'll be back once this is secured." Heinrich Carson strode out of the room, the jar under his arm.

After a moment, Maggie Bismuth stood and set her chair back up. She scooted toward Brynner, reaching out to cup his chin so he'd look at her. "Young man, what happened to your mother?"

He whispered, the subtitle reading "She didn't see them coming for her." He dissolved into tears. His hands over his ears.

Maggie Bismuth stood and looked toward the camera. "We're done. Find Carson and recover the jar if you can without being killed. Someone get in here and clean up this mess."

I paused the video, my gaze locked on the boy. There weren't words for the pain I felt for him. I wanted, more than anything, to call him, hug him. Wished that someone had done that for him. I'd never look at the director the same way again.

I wiped tears from my eyes, then reversed the video frame by frame, reading the glyphs off the jar. One by one, I pieced them together until it made a name I recognized and a phrase that brought more questions than answers: *Ra-Ame, daughter of the pharaoh. Her heart, for eternal death.*

The hospital phone rang, startling me so badly I threw the laptop off my bed. It landed in a crash of sparks, the screen broken. I picked up the phone, my hands shaking. "Hello?"

"Grace." Brynner's voice slurred like he'd just woken from a deep slumber. "I'm sorry to wake you, but I screwed up. Do you have your laptop?"

A bolt of fear lit me up from head to toe. It lay just out of reach beside my bed. "I—I had it on my bed. It was right here."

He cursed. "Someone probably stole it while you were sleeping. It's my fault for leaving myself logged in."

"Let's not jump to conclusions. What makes you think it's stolen?" I struggled to keep my tone normal as I asked.

"BSI network security reported an intrusion a half hour ago. Someone tripped a file marker on a high-clearance server."

"I don't understand."

"All the secure files have a few in them that trip alarms when opened. Anyone with access knows better than to load them. I left your laptop connected as me. I'm so sorry. They're going to do a remote shutdown and just catalogue everything that got pulled. We'll get you a new one, but any pictures or documents you had on it are toast."

My hands shook now even harder. My voice caught in my throat. "I didn't have anything personal there."

"Go back to sleep. I'll report the theft. God knows they expect this kind of crap from me. Night, Grace." He hung up, leaving me asking myself why I'd lied a third time to him in one day.

I got out of bed and picked up the remains of my computer, which, despite the crack in the screen, still somewhat worked. I held down the power until it clicked off, then dumped it in the waste container outside the door.

As I lay back in my bed, the adrenaline drained from me, making it near impossible to keep my eyes open. Then my phone chirped. A new e-mail message, high priority.

I unlocked the phone and read the mail. I read it again, to be sure. It came from Director Bismuth, sent just seconds ago. The body contained a list of files, dates and times, along with my laptop name.

The last line sent chills through me.

"We need to talk."

20

BRYNNER

I slept in until one and ate a dozen-egg omelet when I got up, compliments of the best chef in the world, my aunt. She granted me a onetime exception to her "no breakfast after noon" rule on account of how much time I'd spent in the hospital. Overnight, I'd had an epiphany, so long as "epiphany" meant I really wanted to talk to Grace.

My aunt made a call to the hospital and then reported back to me. "They're releasing Grace today. You *will* be there to pick her up, right?"

Like she needed to remind me. "Aunt Emelia, would you please not help me? I've been wining and dining women since I was fourteen."

She smacked a spatula down an inch from my hands. "Sharing a beer with a girl behind the hot dog stand does not count, Brynner Carson."

It had worked out fairly well for me. But that brought up another question I'd been dying to ask once I wasn't near comatose from lack of sleep. "She has Dad's journals. At the hospital."

Aunt Emelia nodded. "Of course she does. I brought them to her."

"You wouldn't let the BSI near them, wouldn't even mail them to me, and you give them to *her*? How much did the BSI offer to pay you, and how many times?"

She sat down beside me. "I wasn't ever interested in the money."

I took her hand, remembering so many meals like this. "Then why? Why did you want the journals?"

"I thought one day you might need them. I hoped you'd come back, if only to get them. I don't care about the journals. Your dad is gone. My sister is gone. And for so long, you were, too."

"I'm here now."

When she spoke, her voice cracked. "I don't have that jar you're looking for. I don't have anything to drag you back once you leave."

"I'm not going anywhere." I put an arm around her. In my memories, she seemed so tall and intimidating. Sitting next to me, I couldn't help noticing how frail and small the years had made her.

She looked up at me, her eyes both stern and sad. "You're a Carson, like your father. I don't know why God made you that way, but I'm glad he did. You'll leave. You'll have to. Maybe it'll be a meat-skin attacking a school. Or in a nursing home, like last year, but sooner or later, you'll do what you do."

She knew how the drive to find and kill the Re-Animus filled me. I hugged her so tight I almost cracked her ribs. "Then I'll be back."

After breakfast, I showered, shaved, and dressed in my finest gray BSI field suit. Ladies love a man in uniform. I picked up a bouquet of flowers, then grabbed a box of chocolate-covered scorpions chosen more for the box than the content. Can't say that ladies loved chocolate-covered scorpions, but they seemed fitting.

When I arrived at the hospital, I entered through the emergency room. A naked Indian man stood in the center of the lobby, mumbling to himself. He grabbed me as I walked past. "Do you want to know a secret? I'm going to live forever, and you are going to die soon."

I'd have punched him, but my hands were full of flowers and chocolates. I called to the nurse, "This guy's going to have one heck of a sunburn if he goes outside."

"Oh, dear lord. Is that the med student from last month?" said the triage nurse. "Someone page Psych. And buzz Brynner through."

When the door opened for me, the naked man sprinted through, shrieking and waving his hands. Last I saw, he had three orderlies and a nurse chasing him.

I jogged to Grace's room.

Which was empty.

"They moved her upstairs this morning. Fourth floor, room 418." The nurse in the doorway looked at me, bemused.

I ran up the stairs rather than wait for the elevator, and nearly ran over Grace in the hallway. She wore a white blouse with yellow buttons and tan pants that showed off her figure. I hadn't seen her in them before, because anything that looked that good on her wouldn't be forgettable. "Grace—"

When she looked up at me, my tongue caught in my throat. I shoved the flowers at her. "These are for you. And these."

"Chocolate scorpions. I'm just getting out of this place."

She handed the box to the nurse and took a carnation from the bouquet, which she slipped into my uniform collar like a boutonniere. "I love carnations. You like the outfit? The head nurse in maternity is the same size I am and lent me clothes so I wouldn't have to wear a gown back to the motel."

I snagged the box and handed it back to her. "Love the outfit, and you are going to love this. Trust me."

The nurse she'd been talking to laughed. "Grace, Dr. Fielding is covering for our psychiatrist today. He'll be right back to discharge you once he's done with an emergency."

Sure he would be. Just as soon as my immortal friend had a nice soft bed and a handful of antipsychotics. "I'll wait with Grace."

Grace held up a bag full of journals. "I didn't sleep much last night, and they woke me up at morning rounds. I made it through to . . . recent years."

It would have hurt to say it before, but listening to Grace, nothing hurt. "The ones I'm not in."

She nodded. "You or your mother. There're three sequences I can't make out that appear everywhere, but by that point he was pretty much inventing ways to express ideas. There's no easy way to say 'regret,' for instance, so he writes it as 'the sad yesterday.' We thought there were lots of these, but most of them only cover a month or two."

"I don't really want to talk about my dad today. Have you reported to the director about your progress? She's going to be delighted."

Grace looked like a rainstorm on a sunny day; the worry that passed across her face cast her blue eyes downward. "Not yet."

"Did you have time for my translation before your laptop got stolen?"

Again, worry shaded her beautiful smile. I cursed myself for bringing it up. They'd probably take it out of her check.

She finally looked at me. "Yes, I did, but I lost my notes with the laptop. The inscription referenced Ra-Ame. Last time you brought her up, I argued. This time, I want to hear what you think about her."

Though the name confirmed my fears, I held myself calm for Grace. And as for Grace believing in Ra-Ame, I'd sooner believe Grace wanted me to cut her liver out. "You've met a Re-Animus. Remember how smart it was? How fast it was?"

"I remember." The blood drained from her face, and Grace glanced quickly to the door.

"Ra-Ame is basically their god. Dad thought she might have been one of the first, or maybe just the oldest left. So when her name comes up, we pay attention." When her name came up, I usually didn't sleep for a few days.

Grace nodded. "And you believe this, too?"

How could I answer? I put one hand on her shoulder, careful to make sure it came across right. "I'm as sure of it as I am anything. You've heard the Re-Animus talk about her."

"I've heard adults talk about the Easter bunny and honest lawyers. On the other hand, the Easter bunny hasn't tried to kill me. Her name comes up in your dad's journals quite a bit. I can't quite decipher the surrounding text, but I'll get there."

Which reminded me of the other thing about Ra-Ame. "If you find anything about her, it has to be reported to Director Bismuth immediately."

Grace sighed, her shoulders dropping. "I'll call Director Bismuth tonight."

With a rumbling like a thousand thunderclaps, the world exploded beneath us.

GRACE

The building shook, and a roar like a fighter jet broke all the windows, throwing me to the ground. Outside the windows, black smoke billowed. Brynner got to his feet first, sprinting to a broken window to look down. "Are you okay? Building's on fire. Let's get you out of here."

"I'll live." I ran to my room, grabbed the bag with Heinrich's journals, and followed him down a stairwell. Screams and shouts of chaos filled the dark, until Brynner kicked a door open, letting blinding sun in. "Get out." With strong hands he forced me out, guiding a stream of patients behind him.

To the south, the front of the building lay in smoking ruins. I choked on the acrid black smoke and the reek of natural gas.

"Get them away from the doors, send them as far out into the field as possible." Brynner squinted, looking out into the field. Bodies lay scattered like leaves blown by the wind.

Bodies that now moved, rising to their feet. They pivoted toward the exit door, and lurched forward, barely moving. These weren't like the ones at the farm. Their motions seemed dull, their gaze unfocused.

"You deal with these. They'll be easy kills for the time being. I'm going to go take care of the ones inside."

I looked over to him. "I thought you said co-orgs couldn't get past the barriers in this place."

Brynner shook his head. "Barriers can be blown up, if one managed to get inside. After that blast, I doubt any of the barriers are intact."

The corpses stumbled in our direction, slack mouths open wide. Brynner drew his daggers and sprinted for them, burying the daggers in one after the other, but the wisps of smoke that came up looked more like steam than the clouds of darkness from the ones I'd seen before. He ran back to me, reaching into the bag. "Take this."

He handed me the box of chocolate-covered scorpions.

Which felt quite heavy. I threw the box top off and found a Deliverator inside.

"They're all special rounds." Brynner took my hand for a moment, looking straight into my eyes. "Make sure if you point it at someone, they're already dead. Otherwise, you'll have to shoot twice. Once to kill them, once to keep them that way."

As he pushed into the stream of frightened people leaving the building, I shouted, "Where are you going?"

"The nursery is on the second floor." He pointed to the field. "Guide the evacuation, move everyone away from the building, and keep them safe. I'm going to make sure the nurses can get everyone out." He disappeared, using sheer strength to swim upstream in the frantic crowd.

"Move," I yelled, forcing myself to stand tall and act braver than I felt. "Move in a line, no shoving, no pushing. Proceed to the far end of the parking lot as fast as you safely can."

After what seemed like an eternity, the gush of people in the emergency exit slowed, and my first nurse appeared, holding two babies in a sling and one in each arm. I grabbed her for a moment. "How many more are up there?"

She looked at me, her eyes wide. "They're everywhere."

"Babies. How many more babies?" I looked into her eyes, willing her to answer.

"Six. The other nurse will bring them. If she's not—" A second explosion rocked the building. The nurse shrieked, throwing herself to the ground. "There's oxygen tanks in there."

I watched her rise and run for the field. When I turned back to the stairwell, a nightmare waited.

A bloated, burnt corpse staggered out of the stairwell, one side charred to ash.

If I'd watched that nurse two seconds longer, I might have died. I stumbled backward, then set my stance and brought the gun to bear, lining up for a chest shot.

It stopped, wavering back and forth, then opened its mouth, splitting the skin on its cheek. "Grace Roberts. Come with me. Bring the books." This voice was different. A different Re-Animus.

I shot it and kicked the body out of the way. Hearing my name spoken by co-orgs would have left me stunned if it weren't for more pressing matters. Even if the nurses got the other babies out, what about the patients in the cancer ward?

Of course, if the Re-Animus was truly interested in me, the safest thing to do might be to flee, drawing the dead away from the hospital. What had I said to Brynner about running away?

I had a field team badge. Received field operative pay, and had a teammate missing inside the building. I ran for the remains of the emergency entrance. Where the security door stood, a naked man wandered, dazed.

He flailed at me, but I avoided him and ran for the nearest stairs. In the hallway, one of the nurses who treated me stumbled out, a metal rod driven through her chest. "Grace Roberts, come back," said the same voice through her lips. A different voice than the one on the farm. I couldn't bring myself to shoot her, even though I knew she was gone.

I dashed up the stairs to the second floor, where the fire

sprinklers doused everything, keeping the flames at the end. Every crib lay empty, but from the sounds of crashing metal and breaking glass, I wasn't alone.

I didn't flinch as I shot the doctor who was missing most of his face and arm, not even when he mouthed my name. Beyond the neonatal ward, a crowd of corpses pressed in, hands outstretched.

In the middle of them stood Brynner, his daggers flying, leaping from side to side, on top of dead co-orgs. I picked two on the outside and shot them.

They stopped, letting Brynner tear into the nearest ones, and the crowd turned toward me. In one voice, they spoke. "Grace Roberts."

"Get out of here," yelled Brynner. "Get out and stay out."

I shot two more as they stumbled toward me. "Did you notice I have a fan club?"

"Not funny. Stay in the sun, shoot anything that approaches you. Please." Brynner stabbed another one, and spun one away from me.

The sound of crying in a room down the hall caught my attention, and I shot the three co-orgs in my way to run to the door. In the bed, a woman lay, hooked up to IVs and monitors. Her ashen face said she didn't have long to live, but no one deserved to die like this.

I pulled out the IVs, ripped off her monitors, and flopped her into a wheelchair. We rolled through flames to where Brynner stood, knifing the last co-org from the pile.

I pointed to the main stairwell I'd come in by. "The one we used is on fire. I'm going out the main entrance with her."

He nodded. "I'm going to start at the top and sweep the

floors." He ran for the east stairwell, running up into smoke, avoiding the flames below.

I pushed her to the main stairs. If I lost control of the wheelchair, she'd break her neck on the way down. I slipped one arm under her and lifted. "You need to hold on to me. Can you do that?"

My patient looked up and nodded, her eyes sunken deep. "I can do it."

With my one arm under her and the other holding my Deliverator, we limped down the stairs. Every few steps I looked back to make sure nothing came after us from behind. When we reached the ruined emergency room, I practically dragged her through the twisted doors, where an orderly ran to help me.

"Grace Roberts." The Re-Animus voice sounded close enough to touch.

I spun and aimed.

The naked man from earlier looked at me with wild eyes, a pair of dead women flanking him. "Come with me. I open the way to the woman and the books; he gave me eternal life."

I kicked him in the crotch, and both of the corpses behind him collapsed at the same time, holding testicles they didn't have. Still half dragging the woman, I limped toward the door. When we stepped out of the building, I couldn't help feeling better. Just outside the doors, I set her down and took a deep breath.

Someone yanked my head backward, dragging me by the hair, back into the emergency room. I grabbed the wrist dragging me and kicked my way onto my feet, then drove myself forward, head butting the man right in the stomach. He fell backward, his arms lying limp to show slashed wrists, which still oozed blood. While he lay there, I took stock of my assailant, a thin Indian man with dark brown skin and not a stitch of clothing. Black smoke writhed on his wrist wounds, entering his body and surging out like a wave.

His eyes opened again. "You cannot leave. You are my price. My pathway." He clutched his hands to his head. "Destroy the barriers first, then embrace death, and let the darkness take me.

"Surrender, Grace Roberts. She may let you keep your miserable life. If you serve Ra-Ame well, she will grant you entrance to the next." He staggered toward me, using his arms and legs like an animal.

Ra-Ame. Godess of the Re-Animus. He spoke of her like someone real. I lined up for a shot at his head. The Deliverator clicked but didn't bark.

I ran back toward the stairs, climbing with leg muscles that burned hotter than the fire licking the carpet edges. At the second floor I stopped. Neonatal. The down arrow said "Emergency." The up arrow, "Labs and Isolation." I ran up.

Through labs filled with smoke I sprinted until I reached a long hallway of double-pane glass doors.

I threw emergency breakers as I ran, tripping a set of alarms that joined the chorus and searching each of the glass pods for what I needed. When I looked up, the naked man was standing in the doorway, a group of corpses in his wake.

When he spoke, they all did. "Grace Roberts, I give you my final offer. Surrender or the Sin Eater will give you the death that does not end."

"Make me." I threw the Deliverator at him, striking a corpse beside him.

He recoiled, rubbing his face, then sprinted for me.

I held still, waiting, counting as he came barreling down the hallway, and at the last moment, I threw myself at his ankles.

One knee caught me in the ribs as I fell, knocking the air out of me with a resounding cracking sound I felt rather than heard.

I collapsed as he pitched forward, striking the double-pane glass and careening to the side. Behind him, each of the corpses lay motionless. I forced myself up and shoved him, rolling him over and over.

His hand grasped my foot as I stepped back across the threshold.

I kicked, tearing it loose as I stumbled backwards, then slammed the door and locked the seal with him trapped inside.

The monster rose to his knees and pounded on the glass, screaming. After a moment, he slumped over, and a funnel of darkness exploded from his mouth. The dark swarm darted from edge to edge until it covered his body again, sinking in like ants retreating from the light.

I'd thrown the isolation barriers on the unit before I lured him in. No air exchange. A microbe tight seal and glass that would stop an elephant.

His body stirred again, and the Re-Animus pounded on the glass, convulsing, cursing, trapped.

Every corpse in the building began to wail, a phrase that sent pangs of fear through me.

"Save me, my maker."

21

BRYNNER

The meat-skins called for Grace. Why? What had she done? These dead didn't behave right. They stumbled through the hospital halls worse than a shambler, searching for something or nothing, I couldn't tell which. I knifed a few more and cleared the way for a group of nurses and patients to make it to the far stairwell.

This whole attack made no sense. The Re-Animus driving these creatures lacked skill or grace. The mindless monsters gave me no challenge, presented little threat. Once I escorted the nurses out, I jogged out to the crowds, scanning for Grace.

I spotted the woman Grace had been helping and ran to her. I knelt beside the cot she lay on. "Where is Grace? The woman helping you?"

She looked up at me with bloodshot eyes. "The naked man grabbed her."

I cursed myself for not taking time to tackle him earlier and sprinted for the hospital. I'd introduce Captain Crazy to a new world of pain if he hurt Grace. Meat-skins crowded the hallways, mumbling Grace's name. They didn't react at all as I stabbed them. The sound of tearing flesh and a gurgling scream drew me to the emergency room entrance, where the fire alarm system failed to contain a rapidly spreading fire.

There, a black man the height of an NBA player rammed a piece of rebar through a meat-skin, slamming the meat-skin into the wall, where flames licked at it. He shouted at it as it collapsed, "My patience is at an end. Get out of my way."

His strength made me look like a weak puppy.

The man followed up with a blow across the meat-skin's head, then pinned it against the wall.

Given the ebony skin, dark green uniform, and bright red beret, he was probably an operative on loan from Sudan. Whoever he was, I could take lessons from him on how to deal with co-orgs without a set of ceremonial daggers. Hell, this man made ceremonial rebar look deadly.

"That's quite a trick," I said, crossing the remains of the waiting room.

His head whipped around like a snake, and only the fact that I was several feet away kept me from getting a rebar beatdown. He drove the rebar into the meat-skin at his feet and put his hands together in a mocking bow. "Well, if it isn't the lesser Carson. Our paths just keep crossing."

A Re-Animus appeared to be fighting with itself, which was reason enough for confusion, but I knew that voice. The smug tone. The Re-Animus from the boat, and the farm. "You picked a bad day for a fight. I'm feeling better." I circled, keeping myself between it and the stairwell to the second floor.

If Grace was upstairs, I would make sure the Re-Animus wasn't.

It moved faster than the eye could see, becoming a blur as it withdrew the rebar from the dead co-org and hurled it at me.

I moved on instinct, not awareness, and the jagged metal grazed my side instead of piercing my abdomen. Before the Re-Animus could throw anything else, I leaped toward it, closing in to where my knives could carve dead flesh.

It curved its back like the word "spine" meant nothing, smoothly avoiding my blows. But that had never been the point in the first place. I dodged a blow meant for my kidneys, dropped one of my knives, and snagged a fire extinguisher from the wall.

"The barriers in this place cost me dearly to bypass. I had to make a deal. My apprentice took care of your father's protections." The Re-Animus danced back and forth, just out of range, gloating. And though he'd sworn I couldn't get him to reveal anything, overconfidence could fell even the strongest warrior.

"You blew up a hospital to get at me? And since when did the living make deals with the dead?"

It shook its head. "I wanted the woman and the books, my spawn wanted to live forever. He kept his end of the bargain, and I mine. As for the bodies, the new ones need fresh meat to practice with. So crude and weak."

Understanding finally flooded me. A Re-Animus wasn't some evil spirit like Dad thought. It started out as a human, someone who managed to retain their identity through death. That at least explained their nature, because I'd met men who would have matched Grandpa's demons ounce for ounce when it came to evil. And new ones could be made.

This one had spawned a new Re-Animus just to get to Grace.

Used a living body to bypass the wards, and a traitorous mind to destroy the barriers. I couldn't let the disgust and shock I felt over the thought of people willingly joining the Re-Animus show. "If your spawn is as lousy as you are, Grace will kill him by herself." I triggered the extinguisher, blasting a stream of sulfur foam at the Re-Animus.

All of its skill and speed couldn't stop the Re-Animus from getting totally coated. Even the dead couldn't see through the foam. It flailed, and tripped, losing traction in the slimy mess.

"Carson, I will tear your eyes out and offer them to Ra-Ame when she arrives." The Re-Animus rolled over and crouched, his hands held out before him like feelers.

I threw a chunk of rubble to one side. When it hit, the Re-Animus swiped in the direction of the sound. I sliced three fingers from one of its hands, then leaped away as it lunged to the side. "Well, you won't be giving me the finger with that hand. Who's slow and injured now?" The amber would kill it, given time.

I should have kept my mouth shut. It swiveled its head, then locked on to my voice like a bat. I dove forward, letting it pass over me, and sliced its Achilles tendon.

Not even a meat-skin could stand with that kind of injury. It collapsed to the ground. When it spoke, the voice echoed from dozens of mouths around me. "Spawn. Get out of these bodies or lend me your strength."

Nothing happened.

"What's the matter? Every dead body here already occupied?" I leaped on the wounded meat-skin like a lion on a bacon-flavored zebra, driving my daggers into its back again and again. When I was sure it wouldn't be moving, I'd drag it out the front door, into the sun, and there'd be one less Re-Animus when the desert sun cleaned up. A wail like the cries of every soul in hell came from all around me, interrupting my frenzy. I remembered Grace, alone with another Re-Animus.

"Master. Help me kill the woman," the corpses around me wailed in unison.

Cursing, I drove a dagger through the Re-Animus's skull, looking away as black fumes exploded from the mouth. When it was gone, I ran for the stairs, picking up my other blade as I went. Aimless meat-skins stood, without even the sense to rend and tear as I made my way through them.

The sign at the top of the hallway said "Isolation Rooms." The meat-skins gathered before a glass door in the wall, pounding on the door, stumbling into it over and over.

After disposing of the last, I knocked on the glass. The hallways beyond held rows and rows of identical examination rooms, each with their own door.

Grace peeked out from one of them, then ran to the door. She triggered the release, letting me into the secure area, then sealed it behind us. "You took your sweet time." Her eyes twinkled under long lashes, betraying the smile that spread across her face.

I put away my knives. "Got delayed. The Re-Animus that tried to kill you at the farm is now down one body, and a body it spent some time and effort on. Unfortunately, it's still alive."

She took my hand, not fazed at all by the blood coating me, and dragged me to the last isolation room.

On the other side of the isolation door, the naked man I'd seen earlier knelt, pounding on the glass and shouting muffled obscenities. His wrists were slit from his palms to his elbows, and the same black fumes that came from a dead meat-skin leaked from his wounds.

"Let me out. Sin Eater, save me." His eyes locked on to me,

and fear swept across his face. He hurled himself away from the door, huddling in the far corner.

I couldn't speak. Couldn't breathe. This wasn't a mindless corpse. Or a lesser body, picked up by the Re-Animus and thrown away when it was no longer useful.

Grace put her arm around my waist. "So what if one of them got away? One of them didn't."

GRACE

For the first time since taking a field assignment, I felt like the equal, perhaps even better, of Brynner Carson. A Re-Animus captured. Controlled. The look of shock on his face as I relayed my story made me think I might have jealousy problems.

"Well? Did I do good?" I waited for him to say something. Anything.

He swept me up in a hug that nearly crushed me, lifting me so my feet hung a good two inches off the ground. "You are amazing. More amazing. Amazinger. You're going to be more famous than me. Wait until the director hears about this."

He reached into his pocket and took out a cracked cell phone. "This is Carson. Send everything. Army. Marines. We caught one." He looked down at me. "Grace caught one."

We sat together in the ruins of County Hospital. Brynner killed the occasional co-org when it stumbled from the shadows to pass time. Waves of police arrived within minutes, then army troops established a perimeter, followed by defenses on the room.

"What's with the troops? What exactly are you expecting?" I asked Brynner as another troop of machine gunners set up.

He shook his head. "We have no idea. Mom—Mom always said capturing one would be the key. Dad said it would be an act of war."

Someone hadn't been paying attention around here today. "You want to tell me we aren't already in a war?"

He sat beside me, his shoulder brushing mine. "I want to believe this is good, but every time something good happens in my life, it's followed by something worse."

"You need a better life." I leaned up against him, thinking I needed one, too. Maybe I finally had what I needed to make one.

Around midnight, the first BSI support landed, followed by a film crew. While Brynner talked security and showed them where he'd expect attacks, I encountered a new type of terror: an interview.

I expected debriefing. I expected conference calls and lab tests. Instead, a mostly plastic newscaster ushered me to a hastily set up interview booth, where I struggled to form coherent sentences in response to questions that didn't make any sense.

I mean, they made sense, but they weren't the questions that *mattered*. Who cared how I felt about capturing a Re-Animus? What mattered was what we could learn from it. Where I was from, how old I was, was I single? I think it was the last question that made me tear the microphone off and storm away.

I found Brynner doing his own version of the microphone torture, and he'd obviously had more practice. He smiled at the camera, not a fake smile, the same one he used around his aunt's table. And denied any involvement in the capture.

"We were fortunate to have the services of a crack BSI analyst on this operation." He paused a moment. "If we could have a dozen Grace Roberts and a couple of me, we'd put an end to the Re-Animus threat once and for all."

When the interview concluded, he brushed off the adoring women and stalked away to check on the Re-Animus. I followed, amazed that these people deferred to me as much as him. "Brynner."

He turned and saw me, his face troubled. "Grace."

I grabbed his arm. "If there were a dozen of me, I'd want at least a dozen of you. Maybe a few spares in case I wear one out."

He faced the Re-Animus, which screamed mutedly behind its sealed pod. "There's only one of you and me. Dad was right. This is the first battle in a war."

The doorway behind us opened, a gasp of air tainted by smoke drifting in. "Well, if it isn't my two favorite field operatives." Director Bismuth walked forward, flanked by a pair of bodyguards the height and weight of Brynner, though not, in my opinion, as handsome.

Brynner tipped his head. "Maggie."

She frowned. Not nearly enough, more like a calculated amount of distaste. "You know your father insisted on calling me that. I suppose I won't be able to convince you otherwise." She looked over to me. "I recall telling you this was a safe assignment. Perhaps I'll need to review the meaning of the word safe."

She bent over, looking through the glass like she was watching a zoo exhibit. "Your mother would have loved to see this day, Brynner. Lara dreamed of capturing a Re-Animus for study. She'd be proud of you."

"She'd be proud of Grace." He smiled at me in a way that had to hurt.

The director looked around. "I understand you had contact with a second Re-Animus. Is there a reason you haven't pursued it while it is wounded?"

Brynner looked back to me. "I—I thought I'd stick around here. Make sure the one we captured was safe. I'm not that eager to pick a fight I might not win." He walked over and put his arm around me.

Director Bismuth frowned at him, then her eyes darted to me. "Are you sure we are safe here?"

Brynner looked around, then let me go. "I'll go check the perimeter again. Truth is, I've got a bad feeling I can't shake."

He walked out, waving to her bodyguards.

Director Bismuth paced to the end of the secure corridor and hit the seal, locking us in. "Ms. Roberts."

I knew this was coming. "What do you want?"

"We need to come to a bit of an understanding. I believe that today you've done the human race a supreme service. Capturing a Re-Animus will yield information we've needed for years." She paced down the hall toward me.

"I wasn't alone."

"Indeed. Which brings me to my second point. You are going to do another service." She stood two inches from me. "Are you in a relationship with Brynner?"

"That's none of your business." My feelings confused even me. I wasn't about to share them with her.

She kept her eyes fixed on me. "Judging from how you are blushing, that means no. Fine. Do you understand what you've done?"

My cheeks burned hotter by the second. "I captured a specimen of the controlling parasite behind the co-orgs."

She nodded. "Do you have any idea how intelligent they are?"

I had a better idea than she did. I nodded.

"Without a doubt, the attacks will double. Triple. Multiply by ten thousandfold. I'm preparing for a war. I have an army. I have a general, and either you are going to help keep my general focused or I will be forced to regard you as a distraction."

Her cold, calculating nature didn't even remotely surprise me.

"What do you want? If you're suggesting what I think you're suggesting, I'm going to be looking for a new job, and you're going to be looking for your front teeth." I was no one's whore, and my body was mine to do with as I pleased.

She crossed her arms, appraising me again. "That is, of course, your decision. When we return to BSI headquarters, you'll make it clear to Brynner that you are neither available nor interested. Let him find some waitress to soothe his soul, and return to us a man unattached to anyone or anything but the BSI." She unsealed the door.

I gritted my teeth and held on to my pants to keep from punching her. "You are so far over the line I'm not sure if you even know where it was. You can't tell me who I can have relationships with or who I can't."

She gave me the same cool smile. "I can. You'll do exactly as I tell you. First, there's the matter of the network access. The camera on your laptop captured several photographs of you while you browsed our database. How would Brynner feel if he knew you'd viewed those files? That video? You know how dearly he guards his secrets."

"Bitch." I spat the word, knowing she was right.

Director Bismuth laughed. "I prefer the term 'focused.' In case you are imagining throwing yourself on his mercy, I'd recommend you check your bank account. I've honored our agreement and rewarded you for convincing Brynner to return to his post."

I gasped in shock, then hissed, "I turned you down."

She opened the door and motioned me out. "Ms. Roberts, is Brynner aware of your financial situation?" She paused long enough to drink the fury that boiled within me like a fine wine. "If I show him a printout of the deposit, who do you think he'll believe? Myself, I would expect that a desperate woman pretended to be attracted to him. For money. How do you think he'll feel about that?"

22

BRYNNER

I paced beyond the perimeter we'd set up around the hospital, listening and waiting for an attack as the sun set. After dark, surely the Re-Animus would return, unless I'd wounded it so badly it couldn't. Though a Re-Animus could survive sunlight while in a host body and didn't need the shadows, they had perfect night vision and often exploited our blindness for ambushes. The night air carried the scent of danger, making every inch of my body hum with adrenaline. My fellow field operatives wanted to trade cheers and celebrate, but I knew better.

What did it say about me that I couldn't enjoy their celebration? All I could think about was how many people died at the hospital. How many innocent people died because Grace got stung by a scorpion? How many more would die when the Re-Animus knew, if they didn't already, that we had one of them?

And for certain, we faced a "they." Dad went through theories, that there was only one, or that there were hundreds, but for sure I'd seen one that knew me, and one "spawn" that knew nothing. We'd see what Grace and her lab analyst friends could learn from the captured Re-Animus.

And what about Grace? I saw her during her interview, thrust into a spotlight that might not ever go away. The BSI would make sure it ran on every news station in America, and would distribute copies to the world, once it was edited. Dubbed. Smoothed.

Would our public relations portray her as a warrior, like me? Or a strategic genius, a mastermind?

Whichever was most likely to keep the recruiting classes full.

"Brynner." Director Bismuth.

I'd been hoping for Grace's voice. I pointed to the spotlights back at the hospital. "You shouldn't be out here. Stay behind the firing line, and stay in the light."

She stood beside me, shivering as she looked out into the darkness. "I'm safe with you. That's what you do, keep people safe."

"A couple hundred families would disagree."

"There will be casualties in this war. Sacrifices, both horrible and acceptable."

The desert had nothing on her tone for cold. This was why she ran the BSI, and I knew it, accepted it. "Aunt Maggie" probably viewed me much like the vehicle fleets. So many years and miles left, and so much damage. "What do you plan to do with Grace? I saw the news crew."

She caught her breath, her entire body tensing. "Ms. Roberts will be the new face of BSI Analysis, should she decide to remain with us. In my opinion, she's earned the full reward for capturing a Re-Animus, and with that sort of money, she might not feel required to work."

The reward money didn't matter to me. I had enough money left over from Dad's estate. A few million more wouldn't matter. "So she'd be squarely outside the 'no work women' rule, right?"

"I remember Heinrich before Lara's accident, Brynner. A jovial man, given to pranks and games of chance. Afterward, he was a paragon of destruction. Nature's perfect predator for the Re-Animus. But most of all, I remember that he blamed himself for what happened to her."

She put a hand on my arm. "Heinrich never forgave himself for putting Lara in harm's way. How will you feel *when*— not if—something happens to Grace? Ask yourself: Where would she be safest? In your presence? Or on an island, far, far from you?"

I jerked my arm away. "Leave. Go back inside, and don't come out here again. It's not safe."

She left me.

When I was sure she'd gone, I wandered in the cacti, listening for the sounds of dead feet in the sand. As the moon began to rise, I heard footsteps from the direction of the hospital. Silver moonlight illuminated the face I'd been waiting for. The peace and acceptance with my decision almost dulled the pain. I walked back to meet her so she wouldn't trip into a cactus. "You should go home and get some sleep."

She jumped at the sound of my voice. "I wanted to check on you."

"I hear congratulations are in order. Your money problems are over." I stood near enough to smell her. Close enough to touch.

Like a desert hare under a hawk, she went rigid. Dear god, had she not found out yet? "You could put your daughter in a better home now. Hell, you could afford a private nurse for her round the clock. Didn't Director Bismuth talk to you?"

Her wide eyes brimmed with tears in the moonlight. "She talked to me, all right. I want you to take me back to the motel."

One last time, I hooked my arm in hers, savoring her warmth and the way she pressed my arm into the side swell of her breast. Together, we walked to the Black Beast. The explosion had blown out both side windows but left the windshield no more cracked than before.

Grace didn't say a word the whole way back, staring out into the night like she expected to see something beyond sand and cactus. It wasn't until we pulled up at the motel that she looked at me. She'd been crying again.

"Your daughter's going to be fine now. No more worrying about money, or eating ramen." I reached out a hand, and she opened the truck door and sprinted to her room. She didn't even stop to check inside before she went in.

It was easier this way, to let her go. It felt like the coward's decision. Facing a horde of the dead was easy. Tearing myself away from her, on the other hand, nearly killed me.

I drove out of the parking lot, cursing myself the whole way. Maybe if I imagined her as a nurse, or a waitress, or the woman who came to sell me life insurance that one time and left after a very intimate physical exam, I could work up the courage to talk to her.

I'd almost made it home when I remembered the salt. I forgot to salt her doorway. And given what had happened, I'd probably need to add olive oil inside the salt ring for extra protection.

GRACE

I meant what I told Brynner: Take me back to the motel. I meant what I didn't tell him: Stay with me. It wasn't like this was the first time I'd let my heart make bad choices. Ones I knew would lead to pain. Though Director Bismuth had also made a mistake by threatening me—one I'd be sure to impress on her.

When we got back to BSI Headquarters, he would be Brynner Carson, star monster killer, and I would be Grace Roberts, the woman who ignited a cold war. In Bentonville, he was just Brynner, and I was a woman who liked what I saw, and more important, what I didn't see.

Letting him drive away hurt. I told myself it wasn't as bad as keeping him there would have been.

I was wrong.

Then the squeal of worn brakes and the flash of headlights made me catch my breath. The engine died, letting me hear his bootsteps approach. This time, I didn't wait. I opened the door, catching him pouring out a line of salt.

He blushed like I'd caught him peeking in my window. "I'm sorry. It just makes me feel better."

I reached out a hand, brushing his chest. He held his breath, his muscles tense under my fingertips. I pressed firmly, not pushing him away, but making it clear this wasn't an accident, and stepped closer, so close I could whisper. "You want to stay?"

"I can't." He tensed like I'd attacked him instead of complimented him.

I winced at the thought of what the director might have said. "Why?"

His breath came out in a hiss, his body shuddering as I flexed my fingers lightly on his chest. "I just can't."

I whispered in his ear. "I'm not asking you to marry me. I'm an adult. You're an adult."

He wrapped his arms around me, nearly crushing me, and I pulled him inside, throwing the door closed. His lips, rough and warm, pressed against mine. And broke away, too soon. "I don't have any condoms. I'll—"

I put one finger on his mouth, tracing the lines of his lips. "I went to the gift shop before you came to pick me up." I kissed away any answer he had.

He ran fingers through my hair while his tongue probed mine.

"Here," I said, pulling his hands onto me to rove.

And he did, unbuttoning my shirt with ease and letting his thumbs trace my nipples until they stood erect.

I broke off the kiss to pull my shirt up and his off, finally free to let my hands slide over the road map of scars on his skin. I'd known I wanted this at some level for longer than I cared to admit.

He fought to keep control, and I to make him lose it. I wrapped my hands around Brynner, grinding my hips against him, then ran my hands down his sides. Each time he bent to kiss me, I pulled him back toward the bed, until we tumbled onto it, a tangle of passion.

With my fingernails, I pressed deeply into his back as he unzipped my pants. This was going to be better than I'd imagined, and worth any consequences.

Brynner froze.

His whole body went as stiff as parts of him had been moments before. I nuzzled his neck, kissing lightly, reaching for his lips.

And he rolled off me. Then the world turned upside down as he flipped the bed, rolling me off and onto the floor.

I landed on my stomach, the wind knocked out of me. Trapped under the blanket, I fought my way free to find Brynner pinning down something.

An arm.

A brown-skinned arm with black hair, covered in tattoos. Brynner knelt on top of it, pinning it with his knee.

Under the bed, a perfect circle of hieroglyphics lay traced in blood.

Brynner lifted the arm into the air like a baseball bat. It wiggled and twisted, making a rude gesture. He carried it into the bathroom, then the shower door creaked and slammed. Brynner came back. "It's trapped. Can you tell me what that says? Is it a spell?"

The only thing I hated worse than scorpions were reanimated body parts, but I forced myself to concentrate. "It's something. This section here, it's a location. A pathway. This other one here is a door, and this—" I stopped.

Brynner's eyes hadn't risen above my shoulders during the whole discussion. He was under a spell, all right. One I broke by hooking my bra back together. "You want me to start again?"

He paused, his eyes still on my breasts.

Nothing ruins a romantic moment like a severed body part attacking you. "Explaining. You want me to explain?"

Brynner backed away, sweat on the side of his face. "Yeah." He stared at the floor. "Explain."

"Outer ring is the same as always. Crap about the paths, the way, the usual." I zipped my pants and snapped the button. "This one is different. 'Western desert' we've seen before, but *s'kr't'n*—that's 'city,' and that's 'sunlight.' The city of midnight sun. New York?"

"You almost sound like you believe in this stuff." He wouldn't look at me now, his gaze fixed to the hieroglyphics.

"I believe, all right. I believe they mean something, and when we understand what that something is, we'll know more about how the Re-Animus think. How they plan. The other four are simple. This one's 'Death that follows—'"

"Finds. The Death that finds." Brynner nodded. "We've got lots of pictures of that one." He looked up, all the way from the tips of my toes to my eyes. "That's the name they used for Dad."

One of these days I was going to have to teach him the limits of his knowledge. "No, that would be the crane followed by the arch and sun. This one says 'Death that follows.' That's not your dad. It's their name for *you*. You have a *name* among the Re-Animus."

Brynner knelt by the edge of the circle. "And? What's the last one? Beauty? Goodness? Light?"

I smiled at him. "You're getting better. Did you stay up late studying?"

"No." He picked up his shirt and dabbed blood off where the hand had clawed him. "Call it a lucky guess. If that one's me, I figured the other ones would mean 'Grace.' You have a name, too."

Somehow, it didn't come across as a compliment. The Re-Animus were infinitely patient, cunning beyond measure. It wasn't a question of if I'd encounter them but when and where.

I grabbed one edge of the bed and turned it right side up. Brynner caught the far side as it fell, and looked at me across it. It might as well have been six miles wide. I struggled to regain the moment we'd almost had before it slipped out of reach. "So. You, uh, want to . . ."

Brynner fidgeted, then shook his head. "Maggie was right. Things like this are just going to keep happening." He picked up his cell phone from the bedcovers and dialed a number. The phone rang for ages before a woman answered. Brynner turned away and spoke. "It's me. We should move the Re-Animus as soon as possible."

23

BRYNNER

One hour. Was that too much to ask? That I'd have one hour with Grace? One hour to make a mistake I'd treasure and regret for the rest of my life? I drove back to the hospital, leaving Grace safe with the field team sent to secure the motel.

Through the night and early morning, vehicles continued to arrive at the hospital. Armored trucks with belt-fed machine guns. Amphibious vehicles and a bridge layer, just in case. By midafternoon, we had the largest secure caravan in history ready to roll out. I walked through ranks of BSI operatives to check again on the tractor-trailer hauling the containment pod. BSI eggheads had come up with a way to encase the whole damned room in quick-set concrete, then load it onto a heavy trailer with tires as tall as I was. The crane they'd used to remove it didn't leave much of the hospital standing.

Aunt Emelia arrived in my uncle's sedan an hour before

dawn, and, as usual, she insisted on checking every scratch, every stitch, and every bruise on me while we sat in a field hospital tent.

I buttoned up my shirt and slipped a light Kevlar vest on with Aunt Emelia's help. "You and Uncle Bran need to be extra careful now."

"Honey cleaned the shotguns last night, and today he's going to dust off the flamethrower. We'll be fine once you're gone, boy. This plate looks damaged. Are you using borrowed armor?" She didn't look up from the vest.

I bent over so I could look her in the eye. "I'm serious. A meat-skin snuck into Grace's room and was waiting. How did Mom deal with them coming after Dad?"

Aunt Emelia fussed with my jacket, her eyes unfocused. "Lara was a force to be reckoned with before she met your father. Top of her class in marksmanship, and had certifications in heavy weaponry and demolitions. I think she enjoyed the occasional attack."

"Mom? Mom was *not* a killer."

"Brynner." Aunt Emelia narrowed her eyes at me. "This isn't about your mother. This is about Grace, isn't it?"

I nodded. "She's not like me. I don't want anything to happen—" My voice broke off.

"I understand. You're more like your father than you realize, son. It will be all right. You'll find a way to make it all right." She reached up and hugged me.

From the tent door, Director Bismuth's voice broke the moment. "Operative Carson, are we on schedule?" She nodded to my aunt in acknowledgement.

"Got it, Maggie. I'll ride with the cargo. We have advance teams every fifteen miles ahead and behind, air cover and backup from the armed forces. You have a plan for what happens when we get to Seattle?"

"Brynner, have faith. We've been planning for this day longer than you have been alive. Everything from the capsule we are transporting to the enclosure waiting was built for this moment." She pointed to the truck. "We roll out now, ahead of schedule, and drive on through. No stopping, sleep in shifts, and no communication outside the convoy."

I glanced around. We weren't supposed to leave for another hour, but if the Re-Animus had spies inside the BSI, they wouldn't be expecting it, either. I still needed to find Grace. We needed to talk. The heat inside me said we needed to do more than talk, but Grace would never be safe with me around.

A horn blast jerked me from my reverie. The semi driver blared his horn once more while police cleared the roads. I ran for the cab instead of looking for Grace. She'd be safe in an armored personnel carrier. I'd find her in Seattle, drive to Portland if that's where she was working, and explain.

From the semi, I looked back to where Aunt Emelia waved, a smile on her face. She cupped her hands and shouted, "Give 'em hell, boy."

The convoy shuddered as hundreds of engines roared to life, and we crept away. The miles rolled away beneath me, taking me away from the place I hadn't wanted to come back to. Now I could hardly stand to leave.

After half a mile, the semi finally reached its top speed of fifty miles per hour, which wasn't bad given the load of concrete and steel strapped to it, but would make our trip that much longer. The field radio crackled constantly as police radioed sections of the highway clear. Eventually I crawled into the sleeper cab. Through the rear window, I could keep an eye on the containment pod strapped to our trailer.

The gentle rolling motion lulled me into a dreamless sleep.

A crash jolted me awake. The truck veered from side to side, the trailer lashing behind us. I slid out of the sleeper, into the cab, to where the driver sat, his knuckles tight on the wheel.

Across the windshield, a crack like a spiderweb spread, painted red by a smear of blood.

"What happened?"

He didn't dare look away. "Goose. Hit the window, damn near broke it out."

A thunk on the roof, followed by a burst of feathers exploding from the radiator told me we had serious trouble. I thumbed the radio. "Carson speaking, all convoy members listen up. We're getting hit by birds here. I need a shield vehicle to nose up with us."

Seconds passed while another bird splattered, and our windshield turned to flecks of gray glass. An army transport truck pulled alongside, then cut over, riding just feet from our bumper. With a snowplow front and a reinforced shield, we could bash enough blackbirds to bake a pie and not even slow down.

The radio crackled. "We have a problem up front. Advance troops are reporting the road is blocked by cattle. Dead cattle."

"Barbecue them," said Director Bismuth. "Nothing stops this train, nothing slows it down. Let the undead bastards know we have their number."

Minutes later, we passed the first field ops. Armed with flamethrowers and snowplows, they'd cleared the road for us to continue. The smell of charred beef made my mouth water.

"All vehicles except primary, switch to radio channel two. Primary, hold channel one." Director Bismuth's voice came in clear.

Why? Why switch everyone else in the convoy to a separate radio frequency? "This is Carson. You want to fill me in on what is happening?"

She answered. "Brynner, stay with your cargo. Let the army handle this."

I rolled down the window and stood up, poking my head out of the cab. Ahead of us, walking corpses covered the fields. The responsible disposal law hadn't been in force more than twenty years. Anyone burying the dead earlier than that wouldn't have taken the proper precautions. Then again, the rotted condition of these bodies left most of them barely mobile.

Like the mummies of ancient legend, they might cough on you or crumble all over your uniform, but they didn't make good hosts for the Re-Animus. The army would cut them down like weeds, even without special ammunition.

A cloud of darkness overhead gave me a split second of warning. I dodged just as a rain of sparrows exploded on the roof. They would have split my head open if I were any slower.

The radio beeped, static voices on pattern two bleeding over. Vehicles pulled to the side, letting us pass.

Then came the director's voice. "Carson, remain calm. We're heading into a hot zone; I'm splitting the convoy. Support personnel will divert east and meet up in Seattle. All armored vehicles form up around primary transport."

That meant Grace. She belonged here, with me. But for certain we'd only seen the beginning. The director was right—the farther away Grace was, the better. The safer.

As we rolled northward, the sky turned the color of old asphalt, and raindrops splattered on our windshield, washing blood away.

I thumbed the radio switch. "Watch out. No sun means the Re-Animus won't get a sunburn."

"Acknowledged," the director answered. She rode in an armored truck at the head of the caravan. "We'll be—" In the background, someone barked a warning, muffled by the radio. The director shouted in answer. "Fire. Fire on it now. I have authority from the president himself."

"What the hell's going on?" I hit the signal button again and again. In the clouds above, a dark shadow loomed. A jumbo jet, dropping lower and lower, growing closer by the second. The roar of the engines rose until it shook the windows.

An explosion as bright as the noon sun blinded me, imprinting on my eyes the image of the jet disintegrating. Fighter jets roared over so close I could have touched them.

And the sky began to rain bodies. Horrible, blackened lumps that rolled before our escort, hands waving feebly. One of them bounced off the cab, appearing in the side-view mirror.

I called in. "This is Carson. What happened?"

"That was flight 549 to Colorado. Passengers reported some sort of gas released in the cabin. We're guessing cyanide. Two hundred and thirteen—" The dispatcher who answered stifled a sob.

The shock of what I'd witnessed left me speechless, flinching as bags and debris continued to rain down. The wreckage didn't constitute a real threat, unless— I snapped off my seat belt. "Carson here. I have to check on the cargo."

"Negative. We aren't stopping."

"Who said we were?" I clipped the radio to my belt and opened the cab door. Immediately behind the cab, I was protected from the wind. More important, I could get a clean view of the flatbed cargo trailer.

Two mutilated corpses clung to the trailer, gnawing on the straps holding the container. I drew my daggers and crawled along to knife the first one and throw it off. The other worked the ratchet, pulling the strap loose.

I kicked it, sending it sailing into the path of the transport next door, then fought the winch. They were designed to be run on flat ground, where the driver could get leverage. I braced myself against the container and heaved, drawing the strap down one click at a time until it secured.

Then, holding on to the edge of the container, I edged my way along it to check out the back end.

As I stepped around the edge, someone hit me. Punched me, to be exact, right in the cheek, then shoved me so that I almost flew off the side.

"Lesser Carson, I thought I might find you here." The Re-Animus I'd nearly killed at the hospital. It wore a flight attendant now. Only half her face moved. The other half had a look of terror frozen forever on it.

I caught its fist as it punched at me again, and swung around onto the trailer, locking its arm. "Get off my truck."

It wrenched the arm, breaking it at the shoulder, and hit me in the stomach and then the throat. "You have no idea who I've awakened, Carson. Now she's coming. I wanted to give her heart back as an offering, but I'll settle for yours."

It knelt over me while I struggled to breathe, and pulled one of my own daggers from its sheath. My throat swelled from the punch, but I fought to remain conscious and keep the dagger from killing me as the Re-Animus forced it down.

GRACE

I volunteered to drive a group of three med techs and myself. I'd waited by the field hospital and armory for Brynner, certain he would come and find me. We had unfinished business. Words unspoken, and flesh—I couldn't think about that. Not right now.

So I drove, my eyes on the pavement and the speedometer. Then came the birds, mostly small ones, crashing into the windshields, dead eyes bulging until I flipped the wipers on in a mess of blood and feathers. I turned on the air conditioner for a split second, long enough for the stench of dead birds to permeate the car.

Brynner's voice crackled on the radio, his worry broadcasting clear through the speakers. After a few minutes longer, Director Bismuth came on. "All support personnel divert and head toward Denver. Reorganize and meet up in Seattle. Do not attempt to rejoin the convoy."

I kept in line.

"Where are you taking us?" The nurse to my right pointed as the others fell into the right lane to split off.

I checked my fuel tank. "I'm part of Brynner Carson's field team. I'm going with them."

"Not with us, you aren't. Pull off. Let us out." The chorus of shouts made me want to slam on the brakes and kick them out right there. Instead I pulled off onto the grade alongside the personnel buses.

An administrative officer ran up and pointed down the line. "Give me your numbers and get on; once I'm clear on heads, we're rolling out."

While my passengers bailed out, I shook my head. "I'm a field op, heading back to the convoy."

He squinted at me, then his eyes widened in recognition. "It says here . . . You aren't on my list. You want to take a rental into that?"

"I'm part of Brynner Carson's field team. Field teams stick

together." I patted my messenger bag, which held the Deliver-ator and ten spare magazines. "Always."

The awe in his eyes said he hadn't seen what it was like to face a co-org up close and personal, where it could choke or stab or tear. He held up a hand and trotted back to the bus, and came back with a clamp-on purple light. "Keep it on, or the rear guards will blow you off the road. Godspeed, Ms. Roberts."

If there were a god, why would he create something like the Re-Animus? I nodded and cut across the highway, heading back up the exit ramp. I'd never driven over sixty-five miles per hour in my life but I took my commitments seriously.

With my BSI warning lights flashing, I blew past the police trailing us and into line behind the last field operative SUVs. In the sky high above, a fireball like a second sun blossomed for just a moment, lighting the low-lying clouds.

Debris began to fall, clattering like hail on the roof. A carry-on bag bounced off the road, cartwheeling over my hood.

"Tail vehicle, you have missed directions." Director Bis-muth's voice cut in over the two-way radio. "Fall back and rejoin support personnel."

"Negative. I'm a field operative rejoining my team." Would she recognize my voice?

Then another voice came in. "Command, Carson is exit-ing the truck. Repeat, he's left the truck. We're not scheduled for a rolling refuel yet."

I floored the accelerator, weaving between the army trans-ports until Brynner's cargo semi came into view. A figure crouched behind where the pod stood strapped to the trailer. That's when I saw Brynner.

He edged his way around the cargo pod and fought with the woman—the co-org—on the back of the trailer. Brynner had to be losing. Every blow he took seemed to hit me as well. I picked up the Deliverator but couldn't get a clean shot through the windshield.

Not that I trusted my aim. I could just as easily put a bullet through Brynner. The co-org had one of Brynner's daggers, and as he raised it to stab Brynner, I hit the accelerator and jerked the wheel, hitting the rear corner of the trailer.

The trailer swung out, throwing the co-org to the side. Brynner rolled with it, wrenching the dagger away and driving it into the monster's shoulder.

It slipped off the edge, flying back onto my hood, then smashed its head through the passenger side of my windshield.

For one moment, it looked at me, recognition dawning in its eyes. I shot it at point-blank range, blasting a hole right through its head. Black smoke poured from its mouth, swirling away in the wind.

The empty corpse slipped away, bouncing off the pavement in the rearview mirror. Brynner rose to his feet at the edge of the flatbed trailer, stooped over from the wind. He smiled at me and gave me two thumbs up. Then, fighting the wind, he scrambled around the edge of the containment pod and disappeared from my view.

Through fields and farms and over mountains we rolled. I pulled off three times for gas and restrooms, joining half a dozen other field ops to eat a meal on the run. I have no idea how Brynner ate. He probably didn't.

The hours wore on me, without anyone to give me a break. I finally picked up the radio. "At the next fueling point, could I get someone to swap me out?"

After long minutes, a man answered. "Pick up your relief driver at mile marker twenty."

I counted off the miles until at last twenty came up. Beside the road, a young woman stood, roughly my age. Her long black hair she wrapped in a scarf that covered her head, while her dark brown skin spoke of years in the sun. Tangled leather bracelets covered her arms from wrist to elbow, decorated with coins and trinkets.

I rolled down the window. "Afternoon."

She walked around the car and opened my door. "You are Grace Roberts? I am Al-ibna Al-habeeba."

She stopped and smiled as I scrunched up my face, trying to process the right pronunciation.

"Americans. Would Alifyahmeenyah be easier to pronounce?"

While I could read ancient hieroglyphics, that didn't mean I could speak Arabic in the slightest. "I'll do my best, and if you correct me, I'll get it right."

She shook her head, then dug in her pocket to produce a worn passport. "The man who made my passport gave me an easier name—ah, here it is. 'Amy Roost.' No, 'Rust'? This you can pronounce."

"I could learn the other two if you prefer, but yes. You're not from around here."

Amy shook her head vigorously. "You know of Grave Services in Egypt? I am on loan to the BSI to help secure the old one."

Whoa. Egypt had worse problems than we'd dreamed of. The Grave Services personnel were famous. Some would say infamous for brutal efficiency. They kept to themselves and had a reputation for being surly. A reputation that didn't match the woman before me.

"Can you drive? If so, do you mind driving?" I stood, my arms stretching.

Amy laughed. "I would love to drive, Grace Roberts. I

learned many years ago, but in my home country, men question what women are capable of."

"You'll fit right in here, then." I handed her the keys and walked around to the passenger side. There, I sank into the seat. "Can you pronounce your real name for me again?"

"Al-ibna Al-habeeba. Do not insult me by mispronouncing it."

Her nasal consonants and accent made it near impossible to replicate. "Amy it is. What do you do for Grave Services?"

She shook her head. "We do not speak of such things openly. Grave Services returns the dead to their rest. By force if necessary."

At six feet, maybe 160 pounds, she didn't look like a warrior.

"I have trained since I was a child for this role, Grace Roberts. I am told you read the old language as well as our best experts. And you captured the old one yourself."

Grave Services also had a well-deserved reputation for spying on everyone and trusting no one. I wondered who told her about me, and exactly what they told her, but exhaustion made it near impossible to think. "Old one. You mean a Re-Animus?"

"Yes, Grace Roberts. That is what I meant. Such a strange name you use, for those who have survived the centuries untouched." She turned on the radio, dialing it to a channel with a foreign beat and an echo that sounded of barren lands and foreign shores. Lulled by the hum of the road, I fell asleep until after midnight, when Amy and I switched off.

One thing I had to give her: She knew how to keep her peace, watching the road signs and pronouncing the names under her breath, but while I drove, she leaned back in her seat, her eyes almost closed. After a few abortive attempts at conversation, I resigned myself to silence.

We settled into a pattern, pulling off at times to exchange places or fuel up, and then rejoining the convoy, which proceeded down the highways at its ponderous pace. The following day, Amy took over next to a pile of burning corpses stacked as high as the "Welcome to Oregon" sign, and having driven most of the night, I settled down into a restless sleep, staying that way until someone shook me awake.

Amy looked down at me, then back to the road. "Grace Roberts, we have arrived."

BSI Seattle. Visible off Interstate 5, the BSI building loomed over its surroundings, a tower of granite and glass. We exited onto city side streets, passed the building, then stopped, caught in the afternoon traffic jam. Up ahead, dozens of guards swarmed the tractor-trailer while a forklift unloaded the containment pod and then backed down the ramp into the BSI parking garage.

When the traffic cleared, we followed, turning down the ramps to the lowest levels of the garage, where a set of guards armed with multi-round ammunition waited.

"Out of the car," they ordered, and we complied.

Brynner came looming out of the shadows, his hair wild, his eyes sunken. "Grace. Thank God you're okay."

"Okay?" I pushed him back. "Okay? I'm better than okay. In case you didn't notice, I was the one saving you back there. Otherwise, you'd be on a slab getting ready for a date with the crematorium."

"I noticed. That was quick thinking. Who's the friend?" He smiled at me, then turned to Amy, who bloomed under his gaze like a desert flower.

I answered for her. "Amy Rust, Grave Services. You can ask her to pronounce her real name later."

She dipped her head and then flashed him a smile.

The shock on Brynner's face matched mine when I'd heard she worked for Grave Services. He took both her hands in his. "Thank you so much for agreeing to help. My dad said Grave Services were the best in the world. Period. You combat rated?"

She nodded. "I believe on your system, you would say I am a seven point nine. And you?"

Brynner whistled, looking her over again. "Not seven point nine. Come on. They're transferring it now." He put one hand on my arm.

Amy watched and offered him hers. "Is this an American custom? I like it."

"No," I said through gritted teeth, and brushed his hand off.

Brynner took a step back. "Follow me." We walked to a pair of double doors, where guards checked our IDs again, then to an elevator that lowered us farther and farther into the ground.

The door opened to the sound of roaring water. To the right of the doorway, a waterfall fell, boiling beneath our feet, inches below the metal railing. Brynner pointed high up. "Artificial falls, artificial river, complete Re-Animus protection. It starts over two hundred feet up."

"Is it safe?" Amy cowered at the back of the elevator.

"The bridge is two-inch steel mesh. Unless you are a Re-Animus or a piece of suede, it's not dangerous at all." He offered her his hand, and they walked across the river to a wide band of white. "And this is . . ."

Amy kicked at the powder. "Pure salt. Bad for the skin, but not—"

"—dangerous." Brynner nodded, letting her go.

Amy took one step onto the salt and collapsed, screaming.

24

BRYNNER

I recoiled, slid my daggers out, and stepped so I stood between Grace and Amy.

Amy rolled over and stood up, laughing as she walked toward us. "You two are so much fun." She sprinkled salt on her tongue. "Your father looked at everyone from my country with suspicion. I thought I might enjoy a laugh at your expense."

Dad was a paranoid bastard, primarily because the world was out to get him. "That's a really good way to get yourself knifed. How about we go with shaving cream balloons or fart cushions for jokes from now on?"

"You would not stand a chance of harming me, Brynner Carson."

Her smug assurance had gotten more than one co-org sent back to the grave. "Right. Let's go." I looked to Grace, who radiated annoyance. Surely she didn't think I was interested in

Amy, did she? We crossed the white salt sand to an arched door. Beyond it stood a stained glass tunnel, with beams of brilliant white light bursting up at intervals.

I used my best museum curator voice. "Welcome to the hall of symbols. The lights above and below replicate all shades and variants of sunlight. The walls feature every symbol from every religion known to man." I pointed off to the side, imitating the way Director Bismuth had when she showed me. "That's the only Moai statue ever removed from Easter Island."

"Jesus Christ," said Grace.

"In every flavor, color, and depiction imaginable." I pointed out my favorites, African American Jesus, a man who looked like he grew up in the Mediterranean, and Catholic Jesus, who obviously had a skin condition and a fear of the light.

Amy traced the walls, studying each symbol. "Genius."

"Dad was a little crazy, and it helped. The big guns are right here." At the end of the tunnel, we hit a right-angle turn that led to the sealed containment pod, now locked into concrete by metal rods. I patted a set of searchlights, each as large across as I was tall. "These were tested against samples of Re-Animus we recovered from meat-skins. They'll toast it, even inside the skin."

Grace pushed past me to look at them. "Then it should be on, all the time, facing the hall of symbols."

"Not a bad idea, but they tell me it uses more electricity than a small city, and might catch fire if we have it on for more than thirty minutes." I moved to stand near her, and she moved away, approaching the glass barrier that held the Re-Animus. Double walls of glass combined with ozone electric air filters kept it contained.

"Let me go," it screamed. "She's coming for me. I have to get away."

Grace pressed her hand to the glass. "Who?"

"Ra-Ame, the pharaoh's daughter, scion of the darkness, our mistress and queen."

Amy swore under her breath. "How dare you speak that name? It is a name that brings only agony to those who say it. The words themselves are cursed."

"Ra-Ame." Grace spoke softly, clearly. "Ra-Ame. Ra-Ame. I don't believe in curses. Or spells. What I do believe is that in the next few months, we'll learn enough about how the Re-Animus work that if she shows up, we'll put her in a box right next to this little guy. They can be buddies."

Amy shook her head in disbelief.

I rushed to intervene. "All right, ladies, I think that's enough show-and-tell. How about we head on up to the cafeteria, and Amy can fill us in on what they do differently where she comes from?" I could stay between them, play referee.

"Brynner Carson, report to dispatch, emergency. Director Bismuth, report to dispatch, emergency." A woman's voice on the intercom gave me an escape plan.

I would have run to the elevator, but I had to wait for Amy and Grace, and they took their sweet time, trading jabs with each other.

Director Bismuth met me when we exited the elevator, spreading her arms. "I specifically said you were not to be called, Brynner. You are to report to Medical. Ms. Roberts, I need your translation skills."

Her tone said she was hiding something; what, I couldn't say. I'd spent years learning to read people, especially women, but the cues I learned to focus on didn't really help in this case. "What's going on?"

"Medical, Mr. Carson. Right now." She tried to look imposing, and failed.

"You didn't say please."

A troop of field operatives burst around the corner, nearly running into me. The commander saluted me. "Sir, we don't know what to do. There's a security situation out front. I thought you'd want to handle this personally."

"What?" I glanced to the director. Her eyes were glassy. "What is it?" I pushed the director aside, walked down the hall, and exited the building. In front of the building, the BSI logo graced a ten-foot copper disk set in stone.

Around the outside lay a circle of hieroglyphs, in fresh blood.

"Grace?" I turned back to the entrance, to see she'd followed me out.

Grace knelt, scanning the hieroglyphics. When she looked up, her eyes stared through me, vacant.

"Don't be afraid. I'm right here. What does it say?"

She looked past me, to Director Bismuth. "Where?"

Director Bismuth ignored the question. "Brynner, report to Medical to complete your evaluation immediately."

"This is the seal, the intent." Amy stepped up, pointing with a nimble toe. "It says, 'Vengeance is mine, I will repay a thousand times.'" She knelt, pointing to the glyphs in the upper quadrant. "'Let his name be erased.'" She moved on, quarter by quarter. "'Wipe his blood from the earth.' 'Let death hunt those who love him.' 'Death that Follows.'"

Grace looked around wildly, her eyes brimming with tears. "Where are they?"

And a wave of terror eclipsed me, one I hadn't known for nearly two decades. I flipped out my cell phone and dialed. It rang and rang.

I dropped the phone and ran to the commander who'd come for me. "Show me."

"We dropped them with standard rounds, then used type twenty-two symbols. Found the ID on the man and figured you'd want to know." He moved a line of guards to the side, and I fell to my knees.

My aunt and uncle lay on the sidewalk, their bodies broken. And I could no longer think.

GRACE

I knew the moment I read the outer ring what it meant. Knew right then who the messengers had been. I wanted to take care of Brynner, but what words were there to say? It didn't escape me that I, and the only person left I cared for, might be next.

Aunt Emelia's face was distended, purple where she'd choked to death. Bran's neck twisted at an impossible angle. Bullet holes covered them, and blood drained from the fingertips they'd used to write the glyphs.

Amy stepped up and looked at the bodies. "They still carry traces of the old one." She knelt and held one eye open. It blinked close, then opened again. "We must finish what has begun."

From the black sheaths on her hips, she drew out curved blades that fit across her fingers, like brass knuckles with blades. I moved to shield Brynner's view. If he wasn't mad with grief already, seeing someone slice their bodies would push him to the edge of reason. Who knew if he'd come back?

I held him, though he stood so tall his chin rested on my shoulder, while the recovery specialists removed the bodies. Amy had cut the tendons so their limbs flopped lose.

When crowds gathered, I led him inside, like a six-foot-six, 250-pound child.

Director Bismuth caught my shoulder as we headed in. "I'll have medical take Brynner to one of the furnished apartments on the twenty-fifth floor." She consulted with an administrative assistant. "Number 253 is open." She looked back to me. "It would be better if he spent the night alone."

In what world? In what possible world would someone want to grieve alone? Or did she want to remind me of her not-so-subtle threat?

The doctors who surrounded Brynner left me at the elevator, and I fought to keep grief of my own from drowning me. Aunt Emelia had taken me in, welcomed me, even after she knew why I'd come. Only the fear that my daughter might be next kept me focused. I walked to the dispatcher. "I was wondering where I could stay in the area. Do you have a recommendation?"

She scanned my badge, and held up a hand. "Security says you aren't to leave the building. Stay right here." After a moment on the phone, she motioned to a side conference room.

I waited there until a young woman, barely old enough to drink, entered the room. She smoothed her black slacks and jacket, then entered the room. "Ms. Roberts?"

"Call me Grace. All the people who call me 'Ms.' I don't like."

"It's such an honor to meet you." She blushed. "Could I get your autograph?"

I sat down, completely flustered. "Why?"

"You're the woman who captured a Re-Animus. The president spoke on TV earlier about the operation. Is it true you did it single-handedly?" She waited raptly.

Yes might encourage her to do something that would get her killed. No was a lie. "I'm part of a field team. We do everything together."

She frowned and checked her tablet. "That's odd. I don't see you having field status. It says here you're chief of operations in BSI Analysis. Must be a mistake."

No mistake. A promotion. And a message. "I need to know what hotel I can stay at. Something a step up from a Big 8."

Asking where I could butcher a cat would have gotten a better response. She glanced around as if looking for backup, then shook her head. "You'll have to share an apartment, but we wouldn't dream of you being out on the streets. It's not safe out there."

"And it's safe for you?"

She shook her head. "They aren't finding *my* face painted in blood, or finding my name scribbled at the sight of massacres. I have an ex-boyfriend in field ops. He says yesterday a corpse *spoke* to him. Said two words. Your name."

She handed me a plastic key like a hotel door card. My badge holder had a slot for it. I hadn't known they kept apartments, though now it made sense. Finding a room wasn't my number one priority. "I need to talk to someone from Personal Resources. About a private matter."

"Are you pregnant? I can get a test to confirm if you are worried, and you'll want to see Dr. Iridian on twenty. She's real nice."

"I am not pregnant, not that it's any business of yours. Get me a Personal Resources representative. I'll wait here until you do."

She shook her head and left.

The minutes crawled by, becoming half hours, and then hours. And the man I'd wanted to see when I came down came in, the green button on his chest identifying him as Personal Resources. I'd never understood why the department existed.

The employee introduction video drilled us over and over: You went to Personal Resources anytime you needed help.

In private conversations, every new employee learned what wasn't in the video. Personal Resources could get you anything you wanted. Want to get high? They could arrange that. Need companionship for the night? They knew who could be trusted. Legal, illegal, personal, or mental, the men and women with a green dot could get it all, do it all.

Now that I'd seen the Re-Animus, I knew why Personal Resources existed. To keep BSI employees from going someplace else, where the Re-Animus might provide everything, in return for favors.

"I assure you nothing said in here will leave this room," he said, the best introduction a Personal Resources manager could ever offer. "I'm Jarvis Harrington, and I'd be pleased to assist you, Ms. Roberts. Is this in regards to a sexual harassment incident with Mr. Carson?"

I shook my head.

"Would you like to discuss the matter with a confidential counselor? Again, I will sooner die and not be cremated than reveal the nature of your problem." He spoke the truth. It was Personal Resources who put me in touch with my daughter's care facility in the first place, finding a way to make it almost work on my meager salary.

"I have a lot of money. That's what people tell me. And no, I don't need financial counseling. I need you to make arrangements for me. My daughter's in an invalid care facility in Portland. You can get the name from the records."

"Records?" He raised an eyebrow.

"My last visit to Personal Resources."

He shook his head. "To maintain your absolute confidence,

I'm certain we don't keep such records. Certainly not in computers. Perhaps in the head of the person who assisted you, but I've worked hard to make my memory not what it used to be."

I wrote down the number. And the name. "I want to know my daughter will be somewhere absolutely safe. I want to make sure no one else knows where she is. That number is a woman I trust to care for her."

He tucked the paper into his vest pocket and nodded. "I'll take care of this immediately. It was a pleasure serving you. Please understand that if we see each other in passing—"

"You don't know me. I owe you."

He shook his head, and left without answer.

I took the elevator up to my apartment. Three floors below Brynner's, and probably nowhere near as swank. Though tonight, he wouldn't know or care about the plush carpet or silk sheets.

I wanted to go upstairs and knock until he let me in, and lay beside him, sharing a grief I knew personally. When a drunken bar fight claimed my brother, I spent three days in the psychiatric ward at Western State.

I held my badge up to the door lock, and it clicked. Inside, black travel bags lay scattered across a brown couch. A halfhearted kitchenette, two bedrooms the size of postage stamps, and a shared shower so very much in use.

With relief, I noted the sports bra hanging from the bathroom doorknob. For a moment, I'd wondered if they bunked me with a man. The doorbell rang, a gentle chime. I turned to open it.

Brynner stood outside. His eyes red and swollen, his skin pale. He trembled like he might have a fever. "I need to talk to you, Grace."

25

GRACE

I glanced back to the shower door. "I'm not really alone, but—"

"It's okay. We don't have to be alone. I know you and I . . ." His voice trailed off, and he shook his head. "I thought maybe you and I . . ." Again he stopped, slumped up against the door frame. "You saw my aunt and uncle."

I nodded.

"They never did anything to anyone. They wound up dead. Worse than dead, because of me."

As he finished the sentence, I held back my urge to vomit. I'd been worried that he'd say "because of you." Which was true, since I'd captured the Re-Animus. "How do you feel?"

He shook his head. "I don't feel anything. It's like everything is a thousand feet away, and I'm watching it from outside my body. That's wrong, right?"

I nodded, deeply familiar with that feeling. I couldn't bring myself to tell him that what came next would be worse.

"We had fun, didn't we?" He barely looked at me, his eyes red.

The tone of regret in his voice made me worry. Not for my safety, but his own. "More than fun." I stepped closer, inches from his face.

"Stay away from me, Grace. If I have nothing, those god-damned Re-Animus can't take it from me." He put out a hand to shove me away, but I pulled him to me.

And kissed him, once more, his lips salty with tears, his body shaking with pain that no stitches could heal. For a moment, I thought he might melt into me, yielding. But he stepped back. Then his gaze locked past me.

"Brynner?" asked a woman with a familiar accent. Amy. She stood at the bathroom door, with a towel wrapped around her waist and her arms crossed over her chest. Water dripped from the tangled bracelets on her wrists. "I did not know you would stop by. I would have dressed." With that, she stepped back into the bathroom.

"I'm leaving." Brynner looked back at me. "Good-bye, Grace."

When he'd gone, I shut the door, and slid to the floor with my back up against it.

Amy came back out, dressed in black silk pajamas. "I am pleased to have company. Are we sharing this apartment?"

I put my head down on my knees. "For as long as I'm here. I want to see a few of the tests, but I think it's time I found a new job."

Amy sat on the kitchen floor across from me, her legs crossed. "I do not think that is wise. You would be taken within days, perhaps hours if the night was dark."

I looked up at her, meeting her stare. "Why does everyone think the Re-Animus care about *me*?"

"Few have slain an old one, Grace Roberts, and lived to tell the tale. Never has an old one been taken against its will. You have brought fear to them."

I wanted them to feel fear. "Good. And you think I'm safe here?"

Amy pushed herself to her feet and walked the perimeter of the living room. "This building is like no other. Even the old one who sent a message dared not come himself. Only Ra-Ame, or perhaps her soldiers, could enter it."

"So I'm safe."

"No." Amy began to laugh. "You will learn soon enough, the old ones are vengeful of wrongs committed against them. Their wrath follows for generations, for even the slightest offense."

Generations. That would include my daughter, but only if they could find her. If it was her life, or that of every Re-Animus on earth, I had no qualms about my choice. "I'd love to see them try. We captured one, Brynner nearly killed another, and if another one wants to volunteer for my lab, well, I can use samples. Are you thinking one stronger than the one Brynner fought at the hospital?"

"No. Those committed to Grave Services do not leave our home for such a trifling matter." Amy's voice fell to near a whisper. "For taking an old one, you will surely stand in judgment before Ra-Ame herself, Grace Roberts. In the old land, the seers hear whispers in the shadows, saying she is awake. Salt and water, sunlight and holy symbols, legends say these mean nothing to her. But against the lesser old ones, you are safe."

Amy underestimated me. Underestimated BSI Analysis. But

I loved my freedom. "So I'm stuck here in the same building as Brynner." The thought of an army of the dead waiting for me didn't bother me as much as one man. "I can't stop thinking about him."

She pointed a finger at me. "Then speak no more of his name tonight. Instead, you will tell me something else you are passionate about. Trade one passion for another."

I shook my head. "I'm tired. Even with you driving, I'm tired. And by the way, talking to a man while wearing a towel? In American culture, that says something—I don't know—I guess it's different in Egypt."

Amy's lips split in a smug smile. "No. The language of a woman's body remains the same. Did you expect modesty?"

"A little. I'd heard Egypt is somewhat reserved."

She laughed. "I am not a Muslim, Grace Roberts. I wore a hijab because in my home, men expect such things. I had hoped to taste American life, and American men. Did I appear coy and surprised?"

With a pain in my heart I wanted to lie about, I pointed up the stairs. "You nailed it. And as for men, there's one more on the market as of a few minutes ago." Was he ever off the market? I didn't know, but couldn't lay claim to him anymore.

"Where I come from, we would say he is not a man. His kind live to hunt the old ones, like the demons of long ago. No man can hunt monsters so long without becoming one."

Where I came from, we said please and thank you to people who risked flesh and bone for others. "He's the 'monster' who has saved more lives than anyone else I know, including mine. And demons . . ." I glared at her. "You don't even want to get me started."

Amy's eyes lit up. "Yes! Tell me what you know of demons. And tell me what lies you Americans say about these 'Re-Animus.'"

"I'm not in a good mood."

She nodded and walked to the cabinets, where she found a coffeepot. "That means you will be honest. Where I was raised, we say polite speech is the garden path to lies. Let there be no lies between us, Grace Roberts."

"Demons. Don't exist, end of story." I rose and walked to the table. "Re-Animus. Well, let's start with the fact that they aren't some sort of evil spirit. How's that for something to argue?"

"You would understand why I believe otherwise?" She arched her eyebrow at me without a hint of defensiveness.

"Sure. You're just like Brynner. Doesn't make you right. I think the closest analogy we have is a pack animal." I caught her question coming and held up my hands. "I'm not talking intelligence. They're incredibly intelligent. I'm talking nature. Territorial. Defensive. The longer they're around, the bigger their territory seems to grow, and they don't tolerate each other."

She didn't respond until the coffeemaker spewed black bile into the carafe, then she served me a cup. "It is a fascinating theory, Grace Roberts. I do not think correct, but fascinating. Explain more."

We talked, through the evening, late into the night, or early into the morning. Amy's answers came from "legend," or "the Koran," "the Torah," and worse. Her passion for mythology and folk solutions left me nearly yelling at times. And yet, her eager curiosity mirrored my own. When at last I looked up at the clock and declared it time for bed, Amy bowed and wished me a restful sleep.

When I woke, Amy was gone. A call to the commissary got me five sets of drab but at least fitting clothing delivered. I didn't think I looked good in beige, but functional beat fashionable any day. One more call to security fetched a courier to deliver all but one of Heinrich Carson's journals to Vault Zero. I still owed the BSI a translation, though I didn't want to read about the man, because I didn't want to think about his son.

Once I'd gotten dressed, I found my way to BSI laboratories, and Dr. Thomas.

"Grace," he said, "I heard I was taking on a partner, like it or not. I'm so glad it is you."

"I don't know the first thing about real lab work, but I can learn anything." I looked at the cubicles lined up along the walls. "I'll take the one on the end if it's open. I have a stack of journals taller than I am to get through."

He took my arm and dragged me toward the elevator, one faltering step at a time. "Oh, no. You'll need to put that aside, since you and I have much more important work to do. We're going to unlock the secrets of the Re-Animus."

He led me to the Vault Zero elevator, which, to my surprise, opened for my badge. I rode down with Dr. Thomas. When the elevator door opened, we stepped out on the ground level of the containment zone. Just past the salt barrier, they'd brought in lights and desks, centrifuges and mainframes. An entire lab, in the most secure vault ever built.

Dr. Thomas pointed the way. "Tell me something, Ms. Roberts. Can you find a better way to kill the dead?"

26

BRYNNER

I'd intended to avoid Grace for the first couple of weeks when we got to Seattle. It wasn't hard, since I spent most of the first few days curled up in a ball on the living room floor. I wasn't alone in my apartment; I had grief to keep me company.

Grief never left. Grace never came. Sure, I'd told her to stay away, but when had she ever listened to me before?

When I could no longer lie on the floor, I found empty actions to fill the hours. Working out in the gym until I was barred from using the punching bags. Sparring with people until there weren't any partners willing to get in the ring.

After nearly two weeks, Director Bismuth dropped by to tell me they'd decided to honor my aunt and uncle with a full BSI funeral ceremony. Cremation, as was standard, followed by dispersal of the ashes into living water. A far better fate than most bodies possessed by a Re-Animus, burnt to ashes and then mixed into concrete.

The day of the funeral, I dressed as my dad did. Gray BSI battle fatigues and a trench coat he wore rain or shine, cold or sun. I met Director Bismuth at her office and paced to the elevator with her. When the elevator stopped, and Grace and Amy got on, I wished I'd taken the stairs. We rode in uncomfortable silence to the bottom floor.

And as we transferred to the secure elevator, Grace spoke. "I just want to honor their memory."

I nodded, wishing I could let myself hold her.

When the elevator opened, we stepped out onto the walkway behind the director. Amy took my arm, leaning against me. The roar of falling water made me glad I knew the ceremony words by heart, though I never dreamed I'd hear them for my aunt and uncle.

I spoke the pronouncement from memory. "For service to mankind." Though I fought to remain focused, I couldn't hold back the memories that flooded my mind like the raging torrent of water under foot. Flashes of Aunt Emelia standing on the porch that day my dad drove me there.

"For sacrifice of life." The sound of laughter around that table, on days when I wasn't taking my anger out on them.

I opened my mouth, but my voice wouldn't come.

Grace spoke from behind me, her voice trembling. "Rest in honor. Rest in peace."

Director Bismuth took the metal urns and handed them to me. My hands shook as I emptied them into the water gushing beneath our feet, white ash lost in the churning foam in seconds. They were gone. My last ties to the world I grew up in. What could I do now?

"Brynner, words cannot convey my regret." Director Bismuth. "I'm ready to stand beside you. With all the forces the BSI can muster."

I shook my head. "I don't want an army. Just a team of people I can trust." Dad would have known where to go, where he'd find the creature responsible. Dad just knew, which is why we figured the Re-Animus called him Death that Finds.

Director Bismuth shouted to be heard above the water. "It doesn't matter what you want. You'll need one anyway. In the last two weeks we've received one of these every day." She drew out her cell phone and showed me a block of hieroglyphics.

I glanced at it, then showed it to Grace. "A demand for Ra-Ame's heart?"

Grace nodded, her lips drawn tight. "And yours." Tears still shone on her cheeks, slick wet tracks that ran down to the point of her chin.

I walked to her, wanting to take her in my hands, knowing I couldn't. "I need you to do something for me. Complete your translation. Find where Dad hid the heart." I looked over my shoulder. "Director Bismuth, when we know where the heart is, I'll be going after it. In the meantime, I'm going to take a trip. I'm going to Las Vegas."

Director Bismuth's mouth fell open, then turned down in a square frown that resembled a snarl.

Amy pumped her fist in the air, shouting, "Vegas, baby!"

"A word, Mr. Carson." The director motioned me down the hall, but I wasn't about to budge.

Being someone's tin soldier wasn't a life I wanted, for however long my life lasted. "You think I'm off to gamble? Get drunk? Go whoring? Think again. I'm going to Vegas to do something my father only did twice."

As I said the words, it locked into place. My mission. My purpose. "I'm going to kill a Re-Animus."

"You kid." Amy looked at me with disbelief, but I'd never been more serious in my life.

Grace put a hand on my arm. "How do you know there's one in Las Vegas?"

"I've had two weeks to lie on the floor and ask myself what I could have done differently. Two weeks to think about every single thing the Re-Animus has ever said to me. When I met it on the boat, it slipped up."

I had a rapt audience now. "It couldn't resist taunting me. Called itself the Sin Eater who walks the new temple." I brought out my phone and pulled up a picture of a hotel in Vegas. "A pyramid. A new temple. In the city of sin."

"Always, the old ones are undone by their talking." Amy rubbed her hands together. "It has surely earned a final death. If you will allow, I would offer you my assistance."

Grace looked over to Director Bismuth. "Tell him how stupid this is."

Whatever problem Grace had with the director, those two would just as soon kill each other as trade looks. Dad told me that when Mom and Aunt Emelia fought, he stayed out of it.

The director narrowed her eyes and shook her head. "No. Brynner has shown a tendency to quit when challenged. This time, I might not have—"

"Stop." Grace looked over to me. "Come with me. The rest of you, I don't care if you leave, but you aren't welcome in my lab." She led me across the bridge and through the salt, to where an array of machines, tables, and boards stood. "Give us time. Hold off for a few months, and we'll make so much more progress."

She pointed to a machine the size of a coffin. "That used to

manufacture industrial diamonds. We've modified it to produce these." Grace held out a box of bolts.

"Stainless steel?"

"Pure iron. It disrupts their control. And pressed onto the
bolt, at roughly sixteen thousand pounds of pressure . . ." She
motioned for me to smell it.

"Sap? Amber?"

"Artificial Amber. Field ops have been using pine stakes to
kill co-orgs for decades, but now we know why they work, and
why your daggers are so deadly. Odds are they were ceremonial daggers dipped in sap, used to kill Re-Animus."

"That is wisdom, Grace Roberts." Amy stepped up behind
me, having apparently invited herself along. "I believe those
knives are sacred instruments, created by the old ones themselves."

Grace gave Amy a look that would have stopped a rhino at
fifty paces. "You think the Re-Animus created these? To use
on themselves?"

"Exactly. Who would know how to harm the old ones? Who
would have more need to dispose of them?"

I didn't actually care who made the daggers, so long as I
got to use them. "I bet it really cheeses them off when I turn
their own weapons against them."

Amy picked up one of the bolts and turned it over in her
palm. "A weapon fulfills its purpose, regardless of who wields
it. You should know that better than most, Brynner Carson."

Grace snapped her fingers for attention. "We're working on
getting a press form that will let us do blades. Imagine if every
BSI operative carried a few dozen of Brynner's blades. But that's
not the fun part." Grace motioned us on, to the second part of
the lab.

"We've learned more in two weeks than the previous two thousand years. For instance, what changes a med student from Minnesota into the world's newest Re-Animus? We're not certain yet, but he rambles constantly, and we theorize it has something to do with him being still alive when a microscopic amount of the Re-Animus invaded him. Instead of it winding up in control, he did."

"You unearth darkest magic," said Amy.

Grace shook her head. "Just science. We're having ethical debates about whether or not allowing terminally ill patients to test our theory is acceptable. Sometime in the next couple months, we may manufacture a Re-Animus."

I swore under my breath. Did she not realize how bad an idea this was?

Grace looked to me before continuing. "We're working on making them, and on breaking them. With time to test, we not only know what drives out the Re-Animus, we understand why." She pointed to a graph. "This is a graph of serotonin and dopamine levels in a normal human."

Waving to another graph with a lower set of lines, Grace continued. "This is from a fresh corpse animated by our friend in the box. He can't help it. We put a corpse in the box next door, open the air valve, and in a few minutes it's on its feet. This"—she pointed to a spike on the graph—"is the endocrine system in the host body. Which shouldn't need to function, but we think the Re-Animus can't control what parts of the host operate and what don't."

"So what's the blip?" I compared the two, finding nothing that made sense.

"That would be a dopamine spike, which preceded Re-Animus control breaking down. Three and a half seconds later, the Re-Animus evacuated its host. Those religious symbols you've been passing around make a hell of a lot more sense now."

This was way too easy. "You can't tell me you've adopted religion now. That you believe."

"Oh, I believe." She shot a smile to Amy, who shook her head. "I believe that this corpse belonged to someone who believed. Christian, in particular. We've known religious worship causes dopamine and serotonin spikes in the brain for ages. It turns out . . ."

She opened a drawer and took out a syringe. "We can manufacture instant religion for most individuals. It's not as effective as a real response, but in a few months, every agent will carry dart guns that shoot these."

"There will not be a few months." Amy looked at the ground, her voice low. "The old ones have tolerated humanity for ages, but this is your atomic bomb of weapons. When you unleash it, there will be no reason for them to hold back. And what will happen when the old ones learn of how your medicines work? They will find a way to suppress it. To remove their weakness."

Grace crossed her arms. "I'll find more weaknesses. Salt. Like most things that harm them, salt disrupts electrical signals. We're fairly sure lightning would work, too. Stun guns don't. We tried."

I pointed to the waterfall. "And running water?"

"Deionized water does exactly jack to them. Again, it's about disrupting their control. The Re-Animus control network is horribly weak in most bodies. Even the most minor electrical pulses obliterate it. But give it enough time in a host, and it starts making cellular changes, getting stronger. Kicking it out isn't so easy then."

I picked up a box of her amber-coated bolts. "So this time, when we go up against that thing, we'll be ready?"

Grace nodded. "Give me a few months, and I promise it's going down for good. People tell me I started a war. Now we're going to finish one."

I was done waiting for the Re-Animus to attack. Done waiting for them to commit atrocities. "I'm not waiting on the sidelines anymore. Always being one body too late to a city, one rampage behind. Those victims are someone's family."

Grace bit her lip and looked away. I waited for her to give an answer until I was sure she didn't have one, then patted her on the shoulder and left. I had to prepare for a war of my own.

GRACE

By the time I'd managed to find my tongue, Brynner was gone and I was cursing myself for not speaking sooner. I wished I felt as brave as I sounded. The truth was far less certain. Oh, we'd made incredible advances in understanding the Re-Animus problem, analyzing its control methods, and isolating weakness, but what we didn't know bothered me more than what we did.

I had teams of experts at my command. So while brain chemistry wasn't my forte, I could snap my finger and get someone to explain the chart to me until I could explain it to someone else. As Dr. Thomas put it, what I really brought to the table was a desire to *know* and a refusal to accept anything I couldn't prove. I demanded explanations.

By night, I continued to puzzle my way through Heinrich's journals. As I gained insight to the man, I wavered between calling him genius and maniac. If half the recorded kills were true, the man put every standing BSI unit to shame—before there

even was a BSI. Tidbits of knowledge from the journals only led
to more questions. Why did eucalyptus sap burn co-orgs? What
fueled their aversion to a brown and tan zebra pattern?

Though I swore I'd be finding a new job before, my new
position in the lab made work something I loved getting up
for. Over time, I'd meticulously documented every supersti-
tious trick the field operatives used, and then attempted to re-
produce them, identifying which ones didn't work, and why. Why
was it that the dopamine injections didn't work on all corpses?
Why was it that sunlight, real sunlight, killed an unhosted
Re-Animus every time, but artificial light only injured it?

I could find out. Or order someone to find out, or pay someone to find out, but I needed time. Time I wasn't going to get. I'd
been afraid Brynner might do this since that horrible day his aunt
and uncle died, and now no one, not even the director, seemed
bent on stopping him. But that didn't mean I couldn't try.

I went to Brynner's apartment and knocked on the door. I
would convince him to abandon his ridiculous plan, one way
or another.

Amy answered the door.

At least she was mostly dressed, and that's the best thing I
could say about her. Her skin glistened, and she dumped a bottle
of water over her head. "Grace Roberts, come in." She opened
the door for me. "Brynner has offered to teach me his way with
blades, and I to teach him *tan za'r*. It is the art of movement."

Brynner didn't look up, his face a mask of focused fury.
He dipped a stick in a tin of red paint, and they squared off in
the living room. Brynner had pushed every piece of furniture
into the kitchen.

If I believed in God, I'd say he made those two to comple-
ment each other. Brynner brought strength and speed, but Amy,

she wielded *nothing* like it was a weapon. Wherever he swiped, she was one inch beyond his reach.

They moved faster than thought, a dance like a mongoose and a snake, weaving back and forth. In one sweep, she stepped inside his arm, forced him to drop the stick. She caught it in midair, spinning out of his grasp, the stick now held like a blade.

And raked it up along his chest, leaving a trail of red paint from his crotch to his chin. "That is how you will die, Brynner Carson. If you do not learn to move along with your enemy, you will die in the sand. Why do you hold back?"

Brynner's hands curled into fists. "So I don't accidentally kill you. If I'm fighting a meat-skin, I don't need to think, my body knows what to do. When I'm sparring, I have to measure everything. If I ram that stick through your ear, it may sting a bit."

"You don't stand a chance against me." Amy brushed the sponge edge along his chin for emphasis and walked away. "Grace Roberts, I would like your help tonight, if you do not mind." She walked out without waiting for an answer.

Brynner watched her leave with a smile that faded as quickly as it came.

"You need a cigarette? A cold shower?" I didn't mean to allow my annoyance to show. It was just that what I'd witnessed felt . . . intimate. An exchange of passion instead of bodily fluids.

"It's not like that." Brynner picked up a water sponge and wiped the paint off, only making him look more smeared. "She's incredible. Almost better than me."

Almost, my ass. If I had to bet, this would be one place I'd bet against Brynner every time. "She's out of your league. I bet you aren't used to hearing that."

"She's not. I can't let myself fight her the way I would a Re-Animus. But she is really good. What's with the look?"

"You're being a goddamned idiot. If I believed in a god. Or hell. Any god that can afford a heating bill for hell but not feed starving people isn't a god I want to follow. What makes you think there's a Re-Animus in Vegas?"

Brynner wiped sweat from his face with a towel. "You did."

I did what?

He pulled a couch back from the kitchen and sat on the arm. "Look, I don't agree with you about the Re-Animus being parasites, but you were right about other things. Come here. I want to show you something." Brynner stood and walked to his bedroom door.

"I don't think—"

"It's my office." He glanced to a set of double doors. "That's the bedroom. Jesus, Grace, when did things get so awkward?"

I shoved him to the side and walked into the sparse office. "How about when you told me to stay away from you? Does that ring any bells?" I studied the full-wall monitor, a Mercator map lit in shades of red.

"I was—wasn't—thinking. You want me to tell you how you were right or not? Dad said women love being right. And that Mom was usually right."

He touched a point on the monitor, and it zoomed in on the States. "I'm not good with these graphs, but it turns out we have a lot of people working at BSI who are. These are maps of every report, confirmed or not, of Re-Animus activity. Thirty-five years' worth of data."

Some states flared dark red. Nearly crimson along the East Coast.

"Here's Bentonville. Notice anything odd?"

I did. I should have seen it sooner. "Almost nothing. What was it the director said? Not exactly a hotbed of activity."

Brynner put his finger down on an area in the south. "What she didn't say was that Dad killed his first Re-Animus right here. An old one. A strong one, though nothing like the Sin Eater. There's been no activity for nearly thirty years since. You told Amy they behave like territorial animals."

"How do you know that?"

"We've been training for the last week. She's the only one crazy enough to still get in the ring with me. I almost beat her the other day. The point is, you were right. Now look at Vegas. If it weren't for the casinos' financing private patrols, that place would be a ghost town. No one in their right mind would live there."

I reached out, tentatively touching the dot, and the map moved. Up close, Vegas was covered in co-org sightings, minor attacks, major deaths. "You think killing this one will make a difference? Or is this about revenge?"

"Grace, the Sin Eater is old, and powerful. I've met it in Europe twice, once on a *boat*. We kill it, we take out a major force among the Re-Animus. And I can do it. I almost had it at the hospital."

I shook my head. "If you recall right, it nearly killed you at the farm, and if I hadn't been there to save you on the truck—"

"You were."

"That's not the point. You have no idea where in Vegas that thing is. You have no way to contact it, and even if you could, you'd be picking a fight you might lose permanently."

He put one hand on my shoulder. "I won't. Because I'm not going alone. I'm taking Amy with me. I'd like to take you. You're part of my team."

I couldn't respond for a number of reasons, not the least of which was his touch on my shoulder. "What happened to 'I need to keep you safe'?"

Brynner dropped his hand and turned away. "The last few weeks have been the worst of my life. At first, I thought I needed to push everyone away." He shook his head. "You'd think I would know better. It didn't work for Dad. You don't have to go, but I'd feel better if I knew you were with me." When he turned around again, he took both my hands. "I'm not waiting another week. Probably not another day. What do you say? Go with me? Be part of my field team?"

27

BRYNNER

Grace bit her lip, looking down. "No."

I blinked, resisting the urge to shake my head. "'No' what?"

She looked up at me, her eyes on fire. "No, I won't go with you to Las Vegas. I won't help you throw your life away when a few months might make all the difference. How do you plan to find a Re-Animus, if it's even there?"

Now, that part I'd actually given some thought to. "That one hates me like you wouldn't believe. It would do anything to kill me. So I'll show up in Vegas. Give a few interviews. Go to casinos, and then, I'm going to head out into the streets, back alleys, and just wander. I don't have to find it. It will come for me."

Grace went from angry to flat-out furious in one blink. "You are insane." She pushed me, her palms firm against my chest. At least she tried to push me, and it was the thought that counted. Plus, I liked her touch, even when her goal was to anger me.

I tried Dad's way of making women happier. "You have a better plan that doesn't involve waiting? I'm not proud. You come up with a better one, I'll run with it. Otherwise, I'm going with this one."

"Oh, I have a better plan, all right." She shouldered her way around me and slammed the apartment door on the way out. I'd offered to take her with me. What more did she want? Maybe if I told Grace it was the thought of *her* that kept me from falling into a rage haze, she'd listen.

My cell phone rang, and I ran to pick it up, hoping it might be Grace.

"Carson speaking."

"Brynner," said Director Bismuth, "may I see you in my office, immediately?" Her tone said it wasn't a request.

When I reached Director Bismuth's office, I found Grace sitting in one chair and the director sitting at her desk. She pointed to the open chair. "If you don't mind?"

I sat.

The director looked at me over her glasses. "Ms. Roberts has concerns about your operation in Vegas."

"That's exactly why I wanted her to come with me. I don't listen to Dale, but Grace makes a good voice of reason." I didn't look at Grace but chose my words with care. I was already in a hole with her. "What do you think?"

The director's gaze locked onto Grace. "Ms. Roberts no longer has field operative status, so I believe that's out of the question. She's clearly expressed her desire to not go."

"That's not what I said." Grace looked over to me, her jaw set. "I told her I didn't want you getting killed for nothing."

"Nothing?" Director Bismuth cocked her head. "The death of a Re-Animus, particularly a powerful, high-ranking one, would go far to ease the public mind. Perhaps you haven't been paying attention, but we've had four hundred times the number of co-org incidents in the last two weeks. I could hardly call this nothing."

I sat forward, willing Grace to look at me. "It'll cause a power vacuum. Upset the balance of power among them, leaving them open for us to find more of them and kill them." Why wouldn't she look at me?

She finally did, her tone cold as the steel in my blades. "And if you die, it's a coup for them." She looked to the director. "Didn't you say he was your general? Don't you usually keep generals somewhere safe?"

"I recall telling you a number of things, Ms. Roberts. Brynner is not my slave, nor yours. If he chooses to take a risk with such high reward, it is not my place or yours to interfere." With every word, she seemed to nail Grace to the wall.

I could fix this. "I'm done waiting for the Re-Animus to hurt innocent people. I'm ready for them to be afraid. Afraid every day of their miserable existence that today might be Brynner-Carson Day. The day I show up and end them."

I reached out to pat her hand. "You knew my aunt and uncle. I thought you might want to get revenge as well."

She stood up and turned to the door. "Not nearly as much as I want you alive."

Her answer left me completely stunned. "Then come with me and keep an eye on the co-org activity reports. I'll let you decide if the situation looks too dangerous. You say the word, I'll scrub the mission and we can fly back to Seattle. Together."

"Ms. Roberts." The director spoke like a death sentence. "I appreciate your concern for Mr. Carson's safety, but this is none of your business."

Grace shot back, "You don't get to say that." Her voice trembled. Her body trembled, and I rose to envelop her in my arms, wanting to calm her.

I had my nose buried in Grace's hair when the director spoke. "You know how much I appreciate what you've done for us, Ms. Roberts. You've captured a Re-Animus. Made amazing discoveries I'm sure you will improve upon. Most important, you returned Brynner to us when we thought he was gone forever."

Grace's body went rigid, where seconds before she clung to me. I let go for a moment. The words didn't make sense. I put my hands on her cheeks and looked into her eyes. "What is she talking about?"

Director Bismuth spoke louder, almost shouting. "When you quit, in New Mexico, I honestly had no way to encourage your return. Ms. Roberts approached me and offered to convince you. For a fee, of course."

I let go of Grace and stepped back, trying to read her emotions, but the only thing I saw was terror. She'd been caught. "Grace. What . . . is this?"

The director continued, as if reading the morning news. "We're grateful to Ms. Roberts for her service. And Ms. Roberts, I was going to wait until tomorrow, but I met with the board of directors, and we agree that your unauthorized access of Brynner's personal files merits no further action. We'll amend your personnel record appropriately."

"What files?" I closed my eyes, taking deep breaths. The world seemed to spin around me.

The director's chair squeaked, and her voice moved as she spoke, coming near. "When Ms. Roberts was in the hospital. You used her laptop, and afterward, she used it as well. Mostly reports on your mother's accident. Your personal e-mail. Your field notes. Oh, and the video of our interview regarding your mother's disappearance."

Grace didn't have to confirm it. The look of shock and fear told me everything I needed to know. Almost everything. "Why? Why didn't you just *ask*?"

Grace's eyes brimmed with tears. "I was afraid you would say no."

Like I could have refused her anything. Even worse, she'd lied to me. "You had no right. None."

She didn't answer, just stood there, her mouth hanging open.

I looked to the director. "I'll leave as soon as possible."

With a nod to the door, I spoke to Grace. "Get out. Now."

28

GRACE

My feet wouldn't move, and my mouth had picked an inconvenient time to stop cooperating. I stood in the director's office and tried to think of something to say, anything that would explain to Brynner why I'd watched that video.

"If you aren't leaving, I am." He stalked out of the office, and a moment later the elevator ding told me he'd gone.

"Why?" I found my tongue and wanted to leap on Director Bismuth and take out my frustration on her.

She sat down and began organizing papers. "I warned you not to interfere with my general. The choice was completely yours. You can't blame me for your decisions. I hear that you made a call to Personal Resources. While their matters are confidential, I could most certainly find out why, if I put my considerable resources to it."

I'd never call Personal Resources again. Ever.

Director Bismuth tapped the screen on her tablet and studied it before continuing. "You may think I have no leverage to keep you cooperative now. You would be wrong."

I took out my phone and unlocked it. "And if I call Brynner right now, you lose your leverage."

My blood ran cold as she leaned forward in her chair. "It would be a shame if the location of your daughter's facility leaked out. You are safe here. No Re-Animus can lay a claw upon you. Not everyone is so fortunate."

"Bitch." I fought the urge to fling a stapler at her. Or myself.

She didn't even flinch. "I'm making decisions in the interest of humanity. You are deciding with your crotch. Which of us is the bitch?"

I'd wear that title with pride, if it meant making the right decisions. "What use is a dead general?" Unless—"Not a general. A martyr. Do you want him dead?"

"Don't be ridiculous. Our recruiting classes have swollen to six times the normal size in the last week. Your face, young lady, is driving more qualified applicants than his. You are dismissed, Ms. Roberts."

I was dismissed. Like so much garbage, waved away. I picked up my phone and held it up for her. "I wasn't calling anyone. This is a voice memo app. If anything happens to my daughter, I'll make sure this gets leaked on the Internet. You want to risk that?"

"Clever." She nodded to the phone. "I might have expected as much from you. My ability to hold my tongue is contingent on yours, then." She looked down at the desk, making a point of ignoring me until I left.

More than anything, I wanted to go straight to Brynner and thrust the phone in his face, making him listen. The risks were simply too high. While I could afford to house Esther almost anywhere, if her location leaked out, she would be in danger, and I couldn't move her again so soon. It put too much strain on her fragile body, so that was out of the question. I wandered aimlessly, finding my way back to the apartment more by accident than design.

Inside, Amy waited, sitting cross-legged on a chair.

"Grace Roberts, what is wrong?"

And I told her. Everything. About the files, and the motel. And the video. Just as I started to describe the director's threat about my daughter, Amy held up her hand, her head cocked to the side in rapt attention. "The jar, is it the heart the old ones desire?"

I nodded. "I'm certain. The inscription said, 'Ra-Ame, daughter of the pharaoh. Her heart, for eternal death.'"

"That matches what I know of it. What happened to it?"

I went into my room and brought out volume forty-two of Heinrich's journals, which remained my light reading at night. "The answer is somewhere in here. Have a go at it."

Amy flipped one open and began to read, her mouth forming familiar sounds. I couldn't help smiling, even though my own heart might as well have been torn out and placed in a jar. She struggled further and further, finally slamming the book down. "Garbage. This is garbage, madness. I knew children who wrote the old language better."

"Then you're going to love one of these." I handed her one of the final journals.

After three pages, she looked up. "You can read this?"

"It's an acquired skill. I'll show you how I did it, if you want. You have to get inside Heinrich Carson's head. Understand how he thought. He's using the same style as the Re-Animus, but with his own vocabulary."

Amy pushed the book back to me. "I could never learn this way of writing the old language. You must do this. When you know where it is, it must be recovered."

"Does it matter?"

"The old ones love to drive bargains. In exchange for her heart, Ra-Ame might let Brynner live. In exchange for her heart, Ra-Ame might forgive your trespass, your theft of knowledge." She tapped the journal. "If you want to save that man, this is the key. You are the key."

I'd pissed off everyone else today. Why not Amy? "Can I ask you something?"

"Anything, Grace Roberts. I am not required to answer, so you may ask."

"Why are you here? You said you came to help guard the Re-Animus, but you were in the support convoy." It'd been bugging me off and on for days.

Amy gave me a knowing smile. "Are the men in this country accepting of women's claims? Or do they believe that perhaps I would make a better nurse than butcher of the dead?"

"I'm so sorry. Men are pigs. Most of them."

Amy took a blade out of her sheath and ran it along the bangles on her wrist. "And to answer your question, I had to see this Brynner Carson myself. His name is whispered, revered, feared. So many legends about this man 'Carson.'"

"That would be Heinrich Carson." I grabbed my laptop from the table and brought up a picture of the elder Carson, then handed it to her. "Another question?"

Amy held up both hands with palms out, waiting.

"You're Egyptian. You probably know the history better than I do. I thought Canopic jars never held the heart. It always stayed with the body. The inscription says 'for eternal death.' Why was Ra-Ame's removed? Was it a punishment?"

Amy's face clouded over, and she scrunched it up in thought. "An insightful question. I will not say I know the answer. Would you accept one of your theories?"

At that point, I'd accept a crayon drawing. "Anything. I'm coming up blank here."

"In the old days, people believed the heart was the seat of the *Ib*. You would say 'soul,' but to them, it was the key to the afterlife. I have heard it said that she requested it be separated. Perhaps removing it was her way of seeking eternal death. A death from which there could be no return."

An immortal creature that desired death. "I'm guessing she didn't find it."

"No, Grace Roberts. I do not believe she did."

"And this Ra-Ame, you believe she exists?" I knew the answer. Amy probably believed in the Easter bunny and the tooth fairy, too, but there weren't undead creatures worshipping them.

Amy looked me in the eyes, her face calm. "You do not believe in anything, Grace Roberts, so I cannot give you an answer that makes sense. Does it matter if Ra-Ame is real? If the old ones revere her, and offer her sacrifices, and act on her behalf, is she not real?"

"Yes, it matters. If she's fake, or dead, or doesn't exist anymore, we've got a war on our hands, but one we can win."

Amy nodded. "And if she is real?"

"Based on what I've seen the Re-Animus do, if Ra-Ame is its god, and she's real, we're completely screwed. What if Brynner goes to kill that thing and it calls on her?"

Amy went to the kitchen to put on the coffeepot. "Why

would the old one dare call upon her name? Consider what it has said. It has created a spawn without her permission, allowed it to be captured, and failed to recover her heart, kill Brynner Carson, or free the spawn."

I hadn't thought about it quite like that, but then again, as an atheist, I tended to leave quibbling about nonexistent deities to other people. Except that this one might be more existent than I felt comfortable admitting.

"If I were the old one, I would never speak Ra-Ame's name, for fear she might hear and find me." Amy smiled at me.

A knock on the door broke my reverie, and with great reluctance I answered.

A BSI dispatcher stood on the other side, a field duffel bag at his feet, a weapons case in hand. "Amy Rust? You're going on assignment immediately. Report to dispatch in five." He turned to walk away and added, "Don't get dead."

Amy went back to her room and brought out another duffel. "Are you going?"

"I can't. The director kicked me off his field team, and I doubt Brynner would want me there, either." I wouldn't dare mention her threat to my daughter.

Amy dropped the bag at my feet. "I did not ask those things. I asked if you are going. If you want to go, come with me. If you do not, I will see you when we are both dead, or sooner if we succeed."

"I can't. Don't get dead."

"Then do not." She picked up the bag at the door and walked out. "Do not get dead here, either."

The elevator doors had barely closed before I dumped Heinrich's journals into the bag, hefted it onto my shoulder, and ran for the stairs. After ten flights down I hit the button

just as the elevator arrived. The door slid open and Amy nodded to me, stepping to the side. "It is good when women do
what they want, and not what they are told."

"Then I'm being very good right now."

Then I hit the basement button. "I'm taking five minutes
to get ready."

"You may not have it."

I looked over to her with a grin. "I didn't ask if I had it, did I?"

"I will not let them leave without you." She got off at the
ground floor, sauntering toward the dispatch desk, looking
better than I would have after hours of makeover.

At the basement, I switched to the secure elevator, holding
my breath until the guards let me pass. I nearly ran over Dr.
Thomas on the way out, carrying a gym bag filled with weapons and my spare clothes. "Grace, where are you going? And
why are you carrying that?"

I could have lied, but he'd allowed me to work with him.
"Field trials. Unauthorized field trials."

He laughed, shaking and holding on to his cane. "My
favorite kind. You'll make full notes on what does and does not
work, if you survive, right?"

"Right."

"Well then, I wish you luck, and may you not wind up on a
slab in the crematorium." He went back to admiring the waterfall, and I ran to my makeshift lab. Bolts and blades, three dozen
syringes of my dopamine-serotonin mixture, and a handheld
solar flare light went into my bag.

When the elevator door opened to the lobby, Amy stood
alone, her arms folded.

"You said you wouldn't let him leave without me."

"You said you needed five minutes. It is seven and one half."

After a moment, she laughed. "I told Brynner I am having woman's problems, that I would meet him there. He could not stop asking questions fast enough."

I pushed open the door, nodding to the building guards. "You're scary, you know that?"

Amy followed, carrying her bag like a feather. "I know, Grace Roberts."

And as we drove to the private airport, the flaws in my plan became more and more evident. "You know, I don't think he'll be able to miss me on the plane."

"I do not think he would be able to miss you anywhere. His eyes wander you like a desert, whenever he thinks you are not looking." The casual way in which she said it made me wonder what else I'd missed about him.

I pulled up at the private airport, showing my badge to the guard, who thankfully verified that we were BSI, but nothing else. When I rolled up beside the sleek private jet, Amy got out first. "Give me ten seconds, then follow me up the stairs," she said.

"Got it." I hurried after her, waiting at the flight door as Amy entered, throwing her bag into the first seat.

"Brynner." She strode toward him. Amy wrapped her arms around him, spinning him around and kissing him on the lips.

I stared in shock as he flailed for a moment, then ceased.

He pushed her back and wiped his mouth. "Amy, I—I don't think that's exactly how you want to greet me."

Amy fixed me with a stare, nodding her head toward the seats.

I threw myself into the first seat, hoping he hadn't followed her gaze.

Amy spoke with mock innocence. "It is a sign of affection. Did you not enjoy it?"

"No." Brynner's frustration came through loud and clear,

though he'd taken a long time to push her away. "You going to be okay to fly with your . . . problems?"

I could almost hear Amy's eyes rolling in her head. "I am not dying, Brynner Carson."

"Good. We're ready." Brynner called to the pilot. I put my head over and lay still while the pilot bolted the door, and while we taxied to take off, I listened each time the radio crackled for someone to announce I was missing from BSI headquarters.

The drone of the engines lulled me to sleep. I stirred when we touched down, bounced out of a dream in which no one had died gruesome deaths or told awful lies or made mistakes.

When the front door slammed open, I jolted fully awake. Brynner stood over me, his arms crossed, a look like a thunderstorm on his face. Behind him, the exit door hung open, revealing inky sky.

"What the hell are you doing here?"

29

BRYNNER

Grace lying about my network access: not okay. Accessing private videos of one of the most painful days of my life: definitely not okay. Stowing away on an airplane to Vegas, where I meant to find and kill a deadly monster?

No way in hell okay.

When I asked her to come, I'd planned to take an entire tech support crew, including a set of personal guards assigned only to Grace. Guards I'd left back in Seattle when I thought Grace refused.

"I asked her to come." Amy picked up her bag and blew me a kiss as she walked down the stairs. "Are you two ready?"

"Are you trying to get her killed?" An ugly thought occurred to me. "Wait, was she on board when you—greeted me?"

Grace whacked me in the chest as she got off. "I most certainly was. You say hello to all the ladies like that?"

How did this go from being about her stowing away to Amy kissing me? I yelled down the ramp. "Did I miss something again?"

Grace waited at the bottom. "Yes. Someone was probably kissing you."

"It wasn't me this time," said Amy.

I grabbed the pilot as he exited. "You can fly this thing back, right?" I'd give Grace the opportunity for another in-flight nap. At least she'd be safer in the air.

"We aren't going anywhere." The pilot brushed my hand off. "We've got to refuel, and we're last in line. Probably be three or four hours."

I couldn't leave Grace sitting in a plane on a runway, a perfect target for a mob rush of pitifully weak corpses. I stomped down the stairs and glared at Grace. "Do you have any idea what sort of danger you've put yourself in? What were you thinking?"

Grace spun around like a whirlwind, stepping to within an inch of me before poking her finger in my chest. "I was thinking that maybe you might be a little less cavalier with your life if you were thinking about someone else. I'm not afraid of a fight. Women have always been warriors, all the way back to ancient Egypt." She looked over to Amy. "Right?"

Amy nodded. "Some of the most deadly. If only you knew how Grave Services deals with the dead, you would be grateful she fights by your side. When the restless dead come like waves at sea, it is the women who take up their knives and do battle."

It was goddamned mutiny.

A little show of force might be in order. "I know more about Grave Services than you think. Like, for instance, that their elderly or ill field ops have a habit of setting themselves on fire to prevent the Re-Animus taking them over at the moment of death."

Amy crossed her arms and looked away. "It is an act of defiance, to deny the enemy any foothold. Besides, only a fool thinks they will escape life alive."

I glanced at Grace. Amy had a point, but I'd made my peace with the inevitable by embracing the pleasures of life as often as I could. Warm sun, cool water, and the touch of a woman. When I died, I'd take those memories with me to whatever waited and count myself lucky to have known them.

"Fine, she can come," I said to Amy. "You're on point now. Grace, you're my shadow until we find this thing, then you hang back. I don't want to have to rescue you."

Grace's mouth fell open, and she flushed bright red. "You did *not* just say that." She unzipped her bag and held up her Deliverator. "You're carrying a pair of steak knives. I've got a Deliverator full of co-org ammo, a crossbow full of syringes, and a handheld sun. Go find yourself another damsel to rescue."

That was not at all the tone I expected from her. Amy laughed at me as I carried my bags to the car.

The outskirts of Vegas, dark and dusty, whizzed by as I drove us to the strip. I didn't brief the others on my plan, because, in truth, my plan ended at "find the pyramid, hang out near it, and wait for something bad to happen."

Grace pulled a tablet out of her purse. "You want to avoid the main strip, head for the card houses on the north end. There's nightly co-org activity there, and you need to see and be seen, but you don't want to have it out with the Re-Animus at night."

Like I didn't know that. Well, I didn't know about the

meat-skins coming out to play, but I did know I couldn't kill it, not permanently, without the sun. "I'm not. We'll piss it off tonight. Kill a few of its hosts, make it angry enough to try something stupid during the day."

Following Grace's directions, we drove to a nastier, lower-class area of town—exactly my sort of place. The cheap neon here flickered, and even the working girls shied away from the dark, gathering in the pools of light at street corners like rats on an island.

"Look," said Amy, pointing into the darkness. "There."

I looked, but couldn't see anything. "Does Amy stand for 'bat' in Egyptian?"

"Amy means 'better than you at everything,'" she replied. "There's one there. Get to it before the private patrols."

I turned, trusting Amy's eyesight and cursing myself for not having a good comeback ready. In the distant headlight beams, a woman stumbled, the telltale gait of a shambler. "This one's no good. I need to find one the Re-Animus is actually possessing. We can just run this one down. Grace, want to try one of your darts?"

"Listen." Amy leaned forward and put her mouth near my ear. "For an old one this powerful, it is many places at once. Kill its vessel slowly. Make sure it has time to understand and recognize you."

I slowed the car and unlocked the doors. "How will I know when the Re-Animus recognizes me?"

Amy undid the door and stepped out before I'd even come to a stop. "You will know. Grace Roberts, take the wheel and be ready. You do not know where or when it will come, or what it may look like."

Grace climbed over the seat, still scowling.

I opened the door and ejected. "You are a piece of work, you know that, Grace? Do you even feel bad about lying to me?"

"I'm still pissed at you for that 'rescue' comment."

I gave her my stern look. "Not even a little bad?"

For a moment, she softened. "If I say yes, will you back out of this?"

I shook my head.

Grace pursed her lips, her eyes closed. "Then go tease that tiger. Don't get dead and I'll apologize."

I slammed the door, attracting the co-org's attention. "Why do I feel like I'm the one who screwed up here?"

Amy laughed from the shadows. "Because you're a man. Four thousand years of history say you either did or will so soon it doesn't matter. Move. Take the host before it gets away."

Get away, not bloody likely. I hefted the spikes I'd gotten from the armory, fresh yellow pine, sticky to the touch, sharpened to a point. The daggers would work better, but I didn't want better. The shambling monster picked up speed, running toward me. Sprinting.

For one brief moment, it occurred to me just how bad of an idea this might have been. If the shamblers on the Sin Eater's home turf sprinted, what would a body it cared for and spent time building up act like? I let it swing at me and rolled with the punch, not even trying to dodge.

And came up backhanding the spike into it.

It stumbled. Knelt, and rose, no longer moving like an Olympic sprinter.

"Hey, meat-skin. I carved a turkey in better shape than you." I whipped out a blade and took off one finger.

It froze, head going slack. For the length of a heartbeat, I thought I might have killed it. Then the head snapped up, the eyes pitch-black. "Brynner Carson."

"Say good night." I slammed the dagger into its head, looking away as the Re-Animus exploded like the smoke from a carpet fire. The corpse fell to the ground, dead, and I let it. "I think I got his attention. Amy? You out there?"

She called from a side alley, where she stood among a pile of dead meat-skins. "Did you manage to kill that one yet? I found these and did not want to bother you."

Sweet Jesus, if I could do that . . . No, I could never do that. "Like I said. I got his attention, I think."

From around us came wails of rage and anger, unearthly voices with inhuman tongues.

"Yes, Brynner Carson." Amy pointed to the shadows, where dozens of shapes converged. "I think you have."

30

GRACE

I sat in the car fuming over Brynner's question. Did I feel bad? I didn't feel bad. I felt *awful*. What a stupid question. If he weren't on a mission to get himself killed, I'd be working on a way to make it up to him. Whatever it was, I wasn't about to jump into bed with him just to say I was sorry. I had a perfectly good voice for that.

I'd pulled the car down the block and turned around, figuring Brynner could handle one little co-org by itself. I turned off the lights and cut the ignition, peering through the tinted glass. Under the streetlamp, Brynner had the co-org staked. Then he knifed the thing, killing it again.

Part of me hoped he got the message through to the Re-Animus. The rest of me hoped he didn't. I rolled down the window to call him, but before I could speak, the night found its voice.

The cacophony of wails that rose around me sounded like

someone had set a pet shop full of parrots on fire. The wailing grew louder, louder, and fell silent.

Which bothered me as much as the noise.

A whisper of cloth against the car sent a bolt of fear through me. And another one, from the other side. Then the car shook, and just outside my window, a corpse moved past.

I didn't breathe. I didn't blink. I couldn't trigger the door locks, or they'd know the parked car wasn't empty. Once I drew attention to myself, how long would it take the Re-Animus to ram a brick through the windshield? Or someone's spare head?

And the crowd continued, ringing Brynner in. He stood in the middle, under a streetlight that cast his gray BSI uniform in purple and orange light.

"Brynner Carson." The crowd of co-orgs spoke as one, that same guttural voice I'd heard back at the farm. "You come to my home. You kill a perfectly good body. You mock me."

Brynner turned from side to side, a blade in each hand, and shouted back. "Of course I mock you. Your choice of any face, and these are the best you can come up with? You know, I didn't come here to fight. I came here to gamble, but that one was so ugly I thought I'd do you a favor."

As a group, the corpses howled in rage, then stumbled forward, crushing one another in a desperate attempt to get at him. Since the game was on, I opened the car door and let fly with the dopamine-syringe crossbow.

Shooting a crossbow takes practice I'd only had against paper targets. In the real world, against a live target, I gauged and re-gauged my shot. I aimed for the chest, and nailed my first one in the calf. It fell over, a tornado of black gushing from its mouth. Which is where my second toy came in handy. The pocket sun put out a ten-million-candle-power beam of

light for about thirty seconds at a time. Any longer and it
would melt the plastic case, and probably my hand.

I hit the cloud with a beam from my pocket sun, and it
caught fire in a burst of purple light. In half a second I had the
attention of half the crowd. Where Brynner was, I couldn't
say, and didn't really have time to worry about. I shot the first
five with the crossbow, then pulled out the Deliverator in one
hand, the pocket sun in the other.

Shoot and shine, shoot and shine, this is why I'd been
ticked at Brynner's comment. I didn't need a rescue. If I was
on a pedestal, it was so I could get a better shot. The sooner he
figured that out, the better.

I didn't mind the idea that a man would want to treat me
like that. That part was sweet, but not as sweet as the respect
he'd give me for standing on my own.

The co-orgs kept coming, and the pocket sun smelled like
I'd baked a plastic pie. I dropped it to lock another magazine
into the Deliverator, and the lens shattered. Darkness swirled
around me, killing my ability to see more than a few inches.

"Grace Roberts. I owe you agony for what you did to my
spawn."

I shot the corpse speaking in the mouth, but another one,
just two steps behind it, continued.

"If I tear your heart out and offer it to Ra-Ame, she may
have mercy on me. For yours and the man's, she will most certainly be pleased."

At five yards out, they stank, a deep, earthy smell like mush-
rooms and rotten fish combined. I turned to run to the car, only
to find more corpses blocking the way, their mouths open in
crazed grins. Panic made locking in another magazine impossible as the dead closed in on me.

A lithe figure wrapped in the night landed just outside the ring, slicing a co-org's head open. With five fluid strokes, she carved the next five, her blade moving like a surgeon's scalpel and an artist's paintbrush in one. "I thought you did not need rescuing." Amy leaped past me like a ballet dancer with a knife.

"We girls have to stick together." I ran to the car, jumped in, and started it. It was time to do a little rescuing of my own. Headlights on, throttle full down, I aimed right for the pack of co-orgs surrounding Brynner.

At the last moment, I cut the wheel, plowing through a pile of them and sending more flying. From point-blank range, I used the Deliverator to blow holes the size of dinner plates in everything dead.

"You could have killed me," Brynner screamed at me as he sliced another co-org.

I reloaded the crossbow. "If I *wanted* to kill you, I would have run you over. I'm trying to apologize."

"You lie to me. You go behind my back, invade my privacy, and make up for it by killing a bunch of meat-skins?" With each word, he rammed one in the head.

I'd heard the best apologies fit the person. "Nothing says I'm sorry like a pile of dead corpses."

Every corpse for fifty feet dropped to the ground, lifeless. Not because I'd shot them. Even the ones I hadn't gotten a chance to ventilate fell, gushing black smoke into the night.

"It is time to be going." Amy ran past Brynner, slid across the hood, and pushed me into the passenger seat.

I fumbled, reloading my Deliverator. "Was that too easy?"

"There was nothing easy about that." Brynner slammed the rear door, the car shifting from his weight. "Amy, where were you?"

Amy backed the car up. "I took the big group. I thought you two could handle the little group. Less flirting, more killing would make it easier." She floored the accelerator, tearing down the street, through stoplights so close I saw several other people's lives flash before my eyes.

"Slow down, you're going to get us all killed." I glanced over my shoulder.

And regretted it.

Behind the car, maybe fifteen feet back, a misshapen form sprinted, moving faster than human speed. It ran on all fours, a ghastly head appearing and disappearing. We ran lights, straight through intersections, anything to put more space between us. With easy leaps, it cleared the traffic we dodged by milliseconds.

Brynner followed my gaze out the window. "What is that?"

"You came to his home and challenged him. He has brought his best body, and we have hours until the sun." Amy swerved as the Re-Animus leaped into the air, its claws swiping down inches from our bumper.

Brynner kicked out the rearview window, shattering the glass.

"What the hell are you doing?" I twisted around in the seat to stare at him.

"Giving myself a clear shot. Give me your Deliverator."

I handed it to him.

He waited, not even breathing, for the Re-Animus to jump. As it flew toward us, Brynner fired in bursts, squeezing off shots.

The beast fell inches short, its claws tearing gashes in the trunk. It disappeared in our taillights as Amy kept accelerating. We drove for miles upon miles, until the moon rose and at last we could look down the long highway and know it no longer followed. Blue moonlight lit the desert like an alien planet.

Amy pulled over to let the car cool down, and I got out to throw up.

I looked for Brynner and found him standing by the trunk, watching down the highway. "I'd say you got its attention. Now how are we supposed to kill that?"

31

BRYNNER
—————

Dad hadn't mentioned anything like that. Ever. He'd fought a Re-Animus in places no other man had gone and lived to tell the tale, but never once mentioned something like that monstrosity. Now that I'd upset it, I'd have to do something. I looked to Amy, who had swung out of the driver's seat to scan the horizon. "Amy, you have any suggestions?"

She held one hand to her chin, thinking for a moment. "Run far away. Never stop running. Pray you die before it finds you."

"I'm going to take that as a no. Grace?"

She still knelt by the back of the car, one hand holding her golden ponytail back, the other across her stomach. She shook her head. "Atomic bomb? Maybe? What the hell was that?"

Amy came over and put her arm on Grace's back. "That is a Re-Animus who has had time to prepare his body. First they look human. Then, over time, they look like that."

Grace looked up. "And after that?"

"Grace Roberts, if you prayed, I would say pray you never find out."

Grace had been right. A fool's errand, a suicide mission. Why hadn't I listened? "I say we call home and wait for reinforcements. I'm sorry I brought you both out here. I was wrong."

"Can I get a recording of that?" Grace held out her cell phone. "I want to set it as my ringtone."

"The time for running is past. You must kill it tomorrow." Amy walked over and grabbed me by the chin, pulling my gaze downward. "You cannot wait. Tonight it will call for reinforcements of its own. Though the old ones are suspicious, they will eventually be persuaded." She cursed in Arabic. "By itself, the old one may be vulnerable. Give it more than a day and it will be unstoppable."

When the sun rose, we headed back into town. Amy drove, and she followed a route she seemed to know, until we pulled into a motel that made the Big 8 in Bentonville look high-class. I swore as we passed the corner where I'd nearly been killed. "We need to sleep, but we can't do it here. This is suicide."

Amy got out and grabbed her equipment from the trunk. "It is the only place it will not look. Anywhere else in the city, it will have eyes and ears, but all of the eyes here are gouged out. All the ears"—she motioned to her head—"cut off. You sleep, I will keep watch."

The three of us rented a single motel room, the motel owner's lecherous stare telling me he so desperately wished he could watch what went on in our room.

I slept with Grace.

That is, I slept beside Grace, so close I could smell her deodorant and brush her hair. Amy sat near the window, her legs propped up, her head down. Every so often, a fly would buzz against the window and her head would snap up like a croco-dile's.

When I woke after four hours, I felt ready.

Ready to die.

Grace woke when I rolled off the bed, took her entire uni-form set into the shower and emerged with the energetic look of someone who hatched a plan on how not to die. "Amy, let's say you wanted to get ahold of a Re-Animus. What would you do?"

Amy shrugged. "One that has been here this long? I would pick up a phone. It will have ears listening everywhere."

Grace handed me her tablet. "I need to know if they've torn down the Rainbow's End Casino yet. I wanted to go there, but last year I heard they were closing."

I took it and tapped in a few search terms. "How about sharing your genius with the rest of us? Your brilliant plan?"

Grace shook her head. "I don't have a brilliant plan. I have parts of a suicide run, and that's about it."

"You are going to die anyway. Let us hear it." Amy sat on the edge of the worn bed, her arms folded.

"I have no intention of dying here. Or at the casino, but if we have a hope, we've got to get moving. I need high sun." She zipped up her bag and grabbed it. "We're heading to the local BSI station first. Rearm. Reload. Then the nearest pool supply."

"I will drive," said Amy. She handed Grace one of Dad's journals. "You have another mission."

As we drove through Vegas to the BSI outpost, I caught sight of the headline "Rampage kills 108 on strip." TVs in windows showed news footage of last night, casino patrols gunning down hundreds of meat-skins, terrified gamblers taking their chances in the dark rather than hiding in overrun card halls.

"What have I done?"

Amy laughed, a short, choppy harrumph. "Your eyes are opened, too late."

Oh, they were open. We pulled up at the BSI outpost, and the place looked like a war zone. Built to Department of Defense standards, the low concrete roof with narrow windows and wide support pillars would survive anything short of the apocalypse.

Apparently the apocalypse happened the night before.

Every bit of glass lay in glittering shards. Dead meat-skins lay heaped up around the building, and most telling, smoke stains showed where the local command had activated emergency flamethrowers.

I knocked on the heavy steel door. "Brynner Carson. Open up."

After a moment's scrambling, the heavy doors rolled away, and I walked out of a war zone and into a field hospital. The wounded lay everywhere, and blood painted the black and white tiles. Frightened faces lifted to see me, like I was some sort of savior.

"Mr. Carson." A gray-clad BSI officer saluted me. Had to be ex-military, since I'd grown up in the BSI and the only salute I used was my middle finger. "Thank you for coming. We sent out the SOS, but with what's going on in New York and L.A., honestly, I thought we'd die here."

I glanced to Grace, an unspoken conversation. I couldn't ask, "What exactly happened?"

"Situation report," snapped Grace. "I want all your intelligence, news feeds, and every report. You have ten minutes. Brynner will secure the building and set up defenses. You take me to your war room."

The commander turned to her and nodded, the paced off with Grace at his heels.

I glanced to Amy. "You want to help me, umm, secure this place?"

"What is the point?" Amy pointed with one hand to the bent steel beams and cracked concrete. "This is no longer a fortress; it is a tomb. Any who choose to stay here are embracing death." She tapped the shattered glass, hanging on only by the steel mesh within it. "If this is the damage wrought in a single night, then when evening comes, the old one will tear this place from the ground."

She spoke aloud what I thought, what everyone inside had to be thinking. But sometimes the key to pulling off the impossible was believing you could. "That's why we're not going to give it the chance." I went outside and swept the dead meat-skins into piles, knifing a few that still feebly moved. By the time I returned, Grace waited in the front. She carried an ammo bag under her shoulder and kept her face emotionless.

She turned to the field commander and the small squad of walking wounded who followed. "We've come with weaponry so advanced BSI Analysis hasn't even approved its use outside of emergencies. You will stay and hold this position, because every co-org attacking you isn't attacking some civilian. We are going to hunt this thing down and kill it." She looked over to me.

And left me completely unprepared for a speech. "Well? You heard the lady. Lock down and hold until after we're done. Don't get dead."

I spun on my heel and nodded to Amy. "Let's move."

Grace joined me as we walked down the corridor and out into the sun. "Who's in charge here?"

She gave me a smug smile. "I am. Let's get to the hardware store, head on over, and set up. We only get one shot at this."

Two stops later I pulled up at the chain-link fence barring entry to the Rainbow's End Casino. A grand, sweeping staircase led to an enclosed glass entrance. Black tarps covered the once-majestic glass, shielding it from the sun.

I used a pair of bolt cutters on the gate, then the front doors as well, letting loose chain clink to the chipped concrete.

"This is it." Grace opened the door and stepped inside. "Perfect."

The Rainbow's End opened to a lobby that spread longer than a football field. To one side, the check-in counters stood; to the far right, wide-open areas where once slot machines spun, stealing money. In the center of the casino, on the second story, stood a two-story pool with solid glass walls.

Once, you would have been able to watch swimmers dive deep into the water, frolicking on imported beach sand, while below the casino ran. The pool still held water, a foul green sludge.

Grace walked in with a bag of salt over one shoulder. "Okay. Get the water on, get the lights on. Amy, don't let anything surprise us."

It took nearly two hours, even with a water main the size of a fire hydrant gushing water, to refill the pool. Grace ferried the salt we'd brought in, dumping it herself.

Grace called me to the stairs, and Amy followed like a curious cat.

"The pool only has about fifteen feet of water in it, but it'll have to do. Brynner, you're going to wait at the top of the stairs for it." She pointed down the staircase, then turned to look at the pool behind me. "When it comes in, say something stupid to get its attention."

Her brilliant plan sounded less brilliant by the moment. "That thing will steamroll me."

"I'm counting on it. Roll with it, let the motion carry you into the pool. That's saltier than a strip of bacon, and the pump has it churning. Amy, I want you on the roof. Pull back the tarps when it enters the water so we can hit it with sunlight." She scanned the glass ceiling. "And don't fall."

"We're going to get killed."

Grace nodded. "Possibly." She turned and ran down the stairs to the front door.

I called after her, "Where do you think you are going?"

"I'm going to make a call. Stay put, be ready." Grace didn't look back.

GRACE

It sounded like a bad plan. It was a bad plan. It was also the only thing I could think of. Nothing short of the ocean could kill a monster like that, and I was short one ocean. So many things could go wrong I didn't even want to count them. But it started with a phone call. Two blocks from the casino, I found a convenience store and paid the owner twenty dollars for a two-minute call on the store's phone, punching in the numbers from memory.

When the receptionist answered, I knew what to say. "Field Operative Grace Roberts for Director Bismuth. She'll take my call. It is an emergency."

Seconds later, the phone clicked off hold.

"Grace Roberts, where are you?" Director Bismuth's worried tone tickled me to my toes.

"Vegas, with Brynner and Amy. We're holed up in a shut-down casino. I don't think we can kill this Re-Animus, so around five we're going to get out of here and back."

"Not until you finish what you've started. Do you have any idea what has happened in New York? Or Los Angeles? Or Dallas?"

I was running on borrowed time. "You know, waiting until five sounds stupid. We'll leave ASAP." I hung up the phone and sprinted for the casino.

Brynner met me at the front gate, and I shoved him, which was like pushing a garbage truck. "You were supposed to be inside. In position."

"I was worried about you." He ran on ahead, easy since he hadn't sprinted two blocks already.

Inside, I moved up the center staircase, around the pool, and out onto the wide balcony leading to the old hotel rooms. From there I'd have a clean shot across the lobby.

"Grace?" Brynner called out to me, his voice echoing. "When it gets here, no matter what happens—"

I couldn't think about what might happen without my stomach knotting like a boa constrictor. "Got it. I'll rescue you again. Your dad give you any tips on how to kill a Re-Animus?"

Brynner turned away, kicking at the sand by the pool edge. After long seconds, he answered. "Dad said there were three keys to killing one. First, you had to have a plan. Second, you had to understand that no matter how good your plan was, something would go wrong."

I waited, listening to the gurgle and splash of water in the pool. Brynner stretched, jogging in place.

"I can count to three, you know. What was the third key?"

"You couldn't let yourself care if you lived or died." He

looked up at me, his gaze drilling straight through me. "I can't quite get to that one yet."

Before I could answer, Amy's shadow skittered across the floor. High above, she leaped along the steel support beams. How she'd gotten on the roof, I didn't know or want to know. If Grave Services needed hundreds of people like her, Egypt must be a complete hellhole.

I checked the time again, and again. What if it hadn't heard? What if it didn't come until dark?

The ceiling exploded in a rain of glass.

Brynner leaped over the staircase, diving under a craps table to escape the deadly hail. Through the gaping hole, the Re-Animus came, landing in the sand beside the pool, cracking the concrete. "Brynner Carson. Running away again."

I crouched and fired a syringe in an arc that ended right at the monster's chest.

It looked down at the syringe sticking out of it and crushed the plastic with a gnarled hand. "Woman. Be patient, I will deal with you in time." It stood at least eight feet tall, with chalky white skin and a skull the size of a football helmet. Heavy bone ridges covered its head. It flexed arms that ended in claws like a tyrannosaur's teeth.

A shadow on the floor distracted me for a moment. Amy dangled from a girder, kicking her feet to climb back on. She'd have to take care of herself. I swapped out the syringes for one of my artificial amber bolts and fired again.

And smiled as the monster staggered, black smoke catching fire under the sun.

"Still think you'll wear my skin around? Have some more." I fired again and again, sinking bolts into it.

It came for me, leaping onto one of the support columns and climbing like a monkey.

"Run!" yelled Brynner, climbing out from under the table. He shook bits of glass from his hair and took out his blades. "Hey, ugly. Pick on someone your own size."

I ran down the hall into the hotel portion of the casino as it crested the rail.

Behind me, the Re-Animus roared, "There is no one my size."

I turned corners as fast as they came, letting it slide on the marble floors, knowing in a foot race it would be on me in seconds.

At the next hallway, I ducked into a stairwell, ran up to the second floor, and ran for the lobby.

Behind me, the stairwell door wrenched off the hinges as the Re-Animus howled in rage.

I ducked into a conference room, out the other side, down a row of open hotel rooms. Two of them I slammed shut, then ducked into an empty one across the hall, hiding behind the door.

It came, each step shaking the floor.

The scent of the grave came before it, empty earth, vinegar, and rotten meat. With each step, its skin crackled like glass crushed underfoot. "Grace Roberts. Come out and I will take you to Ra-Ame as an offering."

It dragged one claw along the wall. "I can hear your heart beating. Like Ra-Ame's, still alive. I woke her when you took my spawn. Whispered your name into her tomb. The old Carson is dead, and she has nothing to fear. She is coming."

A crushing explosion sent clouds of wallboard dust billowing into the room, choking me.

"Come to me," it snarled, smashing another wall.

Like smoke, the dust filled the air. I covered my mouth, breathing through my sleeve, but couldn't stifle the gagging cough.

The hallway fell silent. Then rubble cracked as it moved, standing in the doorway. It rumbled, a low laugh that echoed in the darkness. "Come now, sweet flesh."

I knew in that moment how I would die. In a condemned building, in the desert, sixteen hundred miles from my daughter. I clutched the Deliverator, held my breath, and prepared to step out.

I would die, but die fighting.

"Hey, ugly." Brynner!

His voice came from down the hall. "What'd I tell you about picking on someone your own size?"

It shuffled, turning toward him, and sprinted down the hall.

I stepped out, but Brynner stood right behind it, and I might hit him.

Brynner crouched at the end of the balcony, his daggers drawn. As the monster leaped at him, Brynner hopped onto the balcony edge, his arms outstretched. "Come to Papa."

It sailed over the edge with him.

32

BRYNNER

It had taken precious minutes to find Grace, or rather, to find the Re-Animus tearing its way through a line of hotel rooms. I followed Grace's plan. Somewhat. It came after me, six hundred pounds of ugly and mean.

I leaped onto the balcony railing. Below, green water churned like a maelstrom. I didn't like swimming even as a kid. I liked diving even less. Especially diving into water that had a heaping helping of broken glass.

Diving with a monster at my feet ranked even worse, but the alternative involved getting shaved by a barber with six-inch-long claws. I threw myself over the railing a roach's breath ahead of it and plummeted to the water below.

In a crash of bubbles, I swam for the surface and grabbed a deep breath before a claw grabbed me by the ankle and ripped me under. The salt water wasn't killing it. Oh, sure, black fumes leaked out, further tainting the water, but it wasn't going to die before it killed me. It stood on the bottom of the pool and swung a shard of glass like a sword at me.

Only the water saved my life, slowing it down just enough for me to dodge.

Above me, the water churned as another body jumped in. With Amy, I'd stand a chance.

Then a tendril of long blond hair swirled into view.

Grace?

She held her Deliverator in one hand and lined up to shoot, aiming way too low.

The explosion from her gun hit me like a fist, the bullet splitting the water, sailing harmlessly past the Re-Animus. And into the glass wall of the swimming pool, right at the bottom edge.

Cracks blossomed like a desert flower, then exploded outward. Pool water spun into a tornado. The Re-Animus let me go, and with burning lungs I broke the surface, caught in a whirlpool. The whirlpool raged around me, throwing me into Grace and then the wall. I grabbed on to the wall with one hand and caught Grace's hair with the other, holding us safe.

Beneath us, the Re-Animus writhed, smoke dissolving in the water, then caught fire in the midday sun. It fell to the ground flailing, then rose, unsteady on feet the size of mailboxes. I let go of the wall, leaving Grace lying against it, and stepped between her and the Re-Animus, drawing my daggers.

The pool water had drained, leaving only a few soggy inches to splash in as we closed the distance in the ruined swimming hole.

In a flash, it was on me, swinging claws like swords.

In that split second, Amy's words came back to me. I'd die in the desert if I didn't learn to move *with* my enemy. So I danced with it, not my normal method, lunging from blow to blow, but waiting for it to strike and extending my blades as I dodged.

Around the pool we fought, broken glass underfoot. With every cut, it grew slower. Dropping its arms, it hurled itself shoulder first at me, slamming me into the wall. Its voice gurgled from the pool water in its lungs. "We die together, lesser Carson."

"You first." I rammed a blade into its heart.

The blade snapped off clean at the handle.

The Re-Animus gushed from its corpse, the smoke catching fire under harsh sun, and even still, it struggled to rise. "I will be avenged. Ra-Ame knows you have her heart. She will bring her armies to reclaim it. Your world will burn."

I knelt over it, putting my knee on a chest that felt like rock. "Look at me while you die. I'm Brynner Carson. I'm the death that follows."

Its eyes burned with hate. "Do you want to know how your family died? It was easy. I shook a child until the woman came out. I bent the woman until the man joined her."

I punched it on the chest, driving the embedded blade farther in, and leaving my knuckles a bloody mess, but the rage inside me burned hotter than the desert at noon. "You will never kill another person."

Grace limped over and pulled out her Deliverator. With care, she lined up and squeezed off a shot into its leg, paused, and moved up, putting a bullet hole every few inches.

It writhed, each shot leaving it weaker. "She's coming for you. Ra-Ame is coming."

Grace put her Deliverator to its head. "When she gets here, we'll kill her, too."

The gun roared, and with a gush of darkness, the Re-Animus died a second, final death. With Grace's help, I crawled through the hole in the swimming pool wall, stepping out of the pool into a flooded casino, and staggered toward the entrance.

The front door opened, and a woman walked in, the brilliant daylight casting her into shadow. I shielded my eyes. "Amy?"

"Hold." The woman's voice rippled with strange power, a familiar voice. With each step, gold jewelry shimmered on every inch of her body. "Listen. I am a message from Ra-Ame. You have killed one of her children, imprisoned another, and stolen knowledge. Your blood desecrated her tomb and stole something precious."

Her voice worked a spell over me, a voice that echoed in my memories, dreams, and nightmares.

She stepped closer. "Her armies wait at the door, but there is still time. Deliver her heart, and that of a Carson, and she will return to her slumber."

She took one more step, and the light from the overhead windows hit her. "Death that Follows, do you understand?"

I finally did. "I do. Mom."

"This is but a host for Ra-Ame. Daughter of the pharaoh, child of darkness, the willing sacrifice. This body walked the paths of the dead, desecrated my tomb, and stole from me."

Her cold, calm logic only made me angrier, but, looking on the face I'd wanted to see for years, I couldn't act. "You killed her."

She stepped closer. Woven cotton wrappings covered her body beneath the jewelry. "My guardians know only to kill. It is an instinct, like scratching an itch or slapping a mosquito. When she no longer needed this body, I took it. Preserved it, maintained it. It is special to you, is it not?"

It was, and that made me hate Ra-Ame that much more. "My mother is dead. You aren't her. I saw you kill her."

"Had I awakened sooner, I would have offered her a choice. Those who see the final sign are rare, and those that understand, even more so." One more step, and I could touch her. I wanted to, so badly it brought tears to my eyes.

She looked up at me with eyes that no longer focused. "You have one week to return her heart. Bring it, and that of your father, to the place she will show you. You could have ended this so many years ago. Do not fail to do so now."

"Or you kill me." I'd gotten used to things threatening me.

She pressed a cold hand to my cheek and shook her head. "Your own life does not matter to you, son of this body." She looked to Grace. "I will take hers."

GRACE

The only thing keeping me from giving it more holes than a golf course was that Brynner stood so close. He stood, completely frozen. For once, I think I understood why. If my brother's corpse had come to me, speaking in his voice, I'd have had a hard time acting.

Of course my brother wouldn't. I took the three-hundred-dollar credit for cremation as the only good thing to come from his death, though it was gone in an instant.

I leveled the Deliverator at her and spoke as I took the safety off. "You can try to kill me. I've proven more resistant than you might think."

Faster than I could see, faster than I could move or think,

she threw Brynner to the side and lashed out, grabbing me with a finger in my ear and a thumb in my mouth. She lifted me so I stood on tiptoes, and whispered, "I have walked in your shadow, and you did not see me. I have opened the door to your apartment, watched you sleep, and you did not wake."

She shuddered and dropped me, her eyes bulging from her head. The point of Brynner's dagger stuck out of her chest, curiously blood free. He wrapped his arm around her neck, stabbing her over and over, until she collapsed, a funnel of darkness evaporating in the light.

"Brynner." I reached for him, and he shied away. "I'm going to call for medics. Will you be okay here?"

He sat down on the stairs and put his head in his hands, not trying to hide the tears that fell. "No. I don't think I'll ever be okay."

I ran out the door and stopped, shocked.

Corpses littered the front of the casino, gutted like fish. Amy knelt at the far edge of the parking lot, surrounded by a mound of slaughtered bodies. I cupped my hands and shouted, "Amy!" I ran toward her as she rose to one knee. "Are you okay?"

She looked up at me, panting. "Even I have limits to my strength, though I will never admit that to a man. Grace Roberts, you have survived. You were successful?"

I shook my head. "We won, but I don't know if it counts. Could've used your help."

She pointed to a misshapen corpse. "The old one brought friends. Many friends, and I cannot be everywhere."

"Keep an eye on Brynner. I have to call a medic." I ran to the same convenience store as before, and dialed BSI Emergencies. "This is Grace Roberts. We're in the Rainbow's End Casino. The Re-Animus is dead. We need medical help."

The dispatcher answered, her voice warm and confident. "Stay put, we're on the way."

I waited nearly an hour in the dusky, still air, beside a man who neither moved nor spoke. Sirens wailed like wolves in the distance. Then flashing lights lit up the front of the hotel. But the first people through the door weren't paramedics or police.

It was a camera crew. News reporters, soundmen, and garish lights that flooded the place so brightly the noon desert would have seemed dark. The endless questions. The constant narrative. The monster was dead, right? So everyone was safe, right?

The only one to escape the reporters was Amy. When I asked her to pose for a group photo, she spat on the ground. "In the old country, the faces of warriors are a secret. Not even the old ones know who is a hunter and who is prey. You and your television, spreading your name and your face for all the world to see."

And then came the BSI Analysis group, taking first the Re-Animus, and later, Brynner's mother. Still he sat, motionless. Only when the news crew had packed their gear and the analysts left did I try to move him.

"The BSI outpost commander called a few minutes ago. They're dealing with a few hundred shamblers, but nothing major. You did it. Killed a Re-Animus. In its home." I sat beside him, taking his arm.

When he finally answered, his voice came out like a whisper. "I broke a blade on it."

"I know. The skin on that thing was like flexible concrete."

"I broke the other one on—her." He dropped a handle, letting it bounce down the stairs to where Amy stood.

"The old ones are not so vulnerable to such weapons when

they have changed their bodies. This was a special blade. One of a set." She spun the handle in her fingers, then pointed to the grip. "Do you see these markings? They were used to separate the soul from the body. Where did you get them?"

Brynner rose and walked past. "My mom found them."

Amy shook her head. "Such artifacts are prized and protected. Where would an American find such things?"

"Her tomb. Ra-Ame's tomb."

Amy handed him back the handle, then clasped his hand. "Then her claim is true. Your mother disturbed the grave. Stole the daggers that kept Ra-Ame in her slumber. And took the heart."

Brynner shot to his feet, looming over her. "She's dead. What does it matter now?"

I moved between them, pushing the two apart. "Stop. Just stop. We're all tired, and hurt. Let's just table this discussion for now. We need to go find a better place to sleep and get some rest."

"We'll sleep on the plane. I'm flying back to Seattle tonight on the cargo transport with the Re-Animus body." Brynner threw the blade handle on the floor and walked out. I followed him.

Somewhere between the military landing strip and Seattle, I lost myself in Heinrich Carson's journals, once more wrapping my mind around the arcane set of symbols he used for everything. When Brynner said we'd been delayed to let a storm pass, I waved him away. Faster and faster I read, until I reached for the last journal, that last page.

And threw it across the hold, cursing in rage. "Wasted." I stormed past the co-org casket to throw a bag of books at Brynner. "All that time wasted. It's not in there."

Amy took my hand, trying to pull me to sit beside her. "Calm yourself, Grace Roberts. Start from the start."

"The heart. I don't know where he hid it. I read everything. Everything."

Brynner shook his head. "He used to leave me thirty-minute voice mail messages. It's the only thing he talked about the last few times. He never let it out of his sight. I just don't believe it."

"Believe it. Heinrich Carson took the location of the heart to the grave with him." I sat down between the two of them, so frustrated I could barely keep myself from screaming.

Amy looked at Brynner, her brow furrowed. "Could it be buried with him? His tomb is, how to say? Unique."

"I don't think so. Uncle Bran said he didn't have it with him when he came home for the last couple weeks. We'll know in a few days for sure, when we dig him up."

"Are you feeling okay?" I reached to feel of his head, and he let me brush his skin. "Tell me you didn't say what I think you did."

"Dad wasn't given a BSI standard burial, because he wanted to be cremated with Mom. After she—died, he left me with my aunt and uncle and went everywhere, searching for Ra-Ame's tomb. Trying to recover her body." He walked down the cargo hold to where the second casket lay, and I followed.

He stood over the casket like a soldier keeping watch. "I'm going to take her home and put her to rest as soon as we're done in Seattle."

Which reminded me of the other thing that had been bothering me. "I've got unfinished business in the lab and with the director."

Brynner's eyebrows raised, and he tilted his head, looking at me askance. "You can throw any words you want her way, but if you try to punch her, I'll have to carry you out."

"I'll let her decide how we play it. Frankly, I could have it out with her over the phone. I'm going back to the lab to finish what I started." The more I thought about it, the more certain I became. "How to kill a Re-Animus without a fifty-thousand-gallon pool."

Amy spoke over my shoulder, almost giving me a heart attack. "Flashlights and syringes will not aid you against Ra-Ame, if she keeps her word. Did you not see the old one?"

For once, it was my turn to be smug. "I did. I think what it calls strength, I call weakness. If that's what an old Re-Animus looks like, I'm going to build a weapon to kill them all."

Brynner and Amy competed for "best surprised/shocked look." Amy found her voice first. "Grace Roberts, how do you plan to do this?"

33

BRYNNER

I prodded Grace for at least the hundredth time since we started our landing pattern to touch down in Seattle. "How?"

Just like before, she shook her head. "I have to run a set of tests first."

The midnight streets let us through without delay, but we'd barely made it to BSI headquarters when she disappeared into the lab, following the guards transferring the Re-Animus corpse.

And I had debriefings and re-briefings until I couldn't keep my eyes open. The last meeting was with Director Bismuth. I arrived to find Amy and Grace waiting.

Director Bismuth stood at the head of the table, her arms behind her back. "I will not lie to you. I did not expect success on your mission. While I have utmost faith in you, Brynner, only one other man has killed a Re-Animus and survived to brag."

Amy snorted and shook her head, but kept her mouth shut.

Director Bismuth glared at her for a moment before continuing. "After we broadcast news of your victory, teams in Los Angeles and Dallas banded together to fight the Re-Animus rampaging in their area using similar methods."

"And?" I waited.

"The Dallas office has one trapped in a bomb shelter. At dawn they'll blow off the roof and gun it down. The one in Los Angeles fled its primary host under fire from saltwater pressure washers."

"So it is war you want." Amy shook her head. "And the heart? What of Ra-Ame's demand?"

Director Bismuth's eyes lit up with anger. "They prey upon us, treating us like cattle, and now we have the power to fight back. We will hunt them like dogs and kill them where they hide."

Amy shot to her feet, leaning over the table. "Ra-Ame is coming. Ask Brynner Carson if you do not believe me, and if legends are true, she brings with her an army the likes of which you cannot imagine." She pounded the table, causing all of us to jump. "I have seen one with my own eyes. Salt water and sunlight will not stop these creatures any more than it will her."

"Stopped the one in Vegas cold," said Grace, her tone dangerously close to a challenge.

Amy spun to face her. "Grace Roberts, that one was young. Not more than two centuries, at most. Ra-Ame has seen four ages come and go. Legends say she has gathered her army that long. Monsters with skin like stone, eyes like eagles, and claws like dragon's teeth."

"I'm not going to wish her away. I'm going to shatter her, and anything else that comes with her." Grace took a hunk of white rock out of her purse and set it on the table. "This is a piece of the skin from the one we killed earlier. It's flexible when stretched, hard as stone when hit. We'll be making armor based on the design soon enough."

I nodded. "That sounds fantastic."

Grace laughed. "If you like that, you're going to *love* this. This 'skin like stone'? That's how we kill them. They're vulnerable to sonic shock. The key is going to be finding which frequencies and patterns. It won't be a steady tone—their skin stretches and moves as they do."

She took a small vial from her purse and dumped it on the table, leaving a pile of white sand. "This was a second chunk of skin that I cut from the Vegas Re-Animus with a diamond saw, then subjected to shock waves. It took me four hours to find the right frequency, but once I did, you can see how much good 'skin like stone' did."

Amy put her head in her hands. "Call Grave Services. Beg them to tell you everything about Ra-Ame. Would it not be wiser to return her heart and let her return to slumber?"

Director Bismuth laughed. "If I had it, I'd give it to her, all right. Use it as the bait for a trap. These things may be immortal, but that doesn't mean they can't die. Brynner, where do you strike next?"

I cleared my throat. "I don't. I'm taking my mom's body home once it's cremated, and mingling her ashes with my dad's."

She shook her head. "I need you fighting. Ra-Ame may have legendary monsters, but you are our legend. You are my general. Humanity's general."

The vial in Grace's fist shattered, and her fingers welled with blood in half a dozen places. She gasped in pain but kept her eyes locked on the director. "You don't treat him like a general."

"Unless you have the heart of Ra-Ame to offer me, you are

dismissed, Ms. Roberts." Director Bismuth looked to Amy and me. "I ask you to reconsider. We've found evidence of a weaker Re-Animus in Detroit."

Grace ran her fingers along the table, creating a smear of blood. "You said we started a war back in Bentonville."

"Your point?"

"Why weren't there guards with Brynner's aunt and uncle? You knew what we'd done. You knew there'd be reprisal. You knew damn well the Re-Animus could find his aunt and uncle." Grace rose, her fist clenched. "You said there would be sacrifices. Acceptable ones. Horrible ones. Which ones were they?"

And with those words, it became true to me. Obvious to me. How could I not have seen this, or known it? I met the director's gaze, realizing for the first time she had to look up to speak to me. "Why didn't you post guards at their house?"

"I was preparing for a war. I didn't have spare field operatives to wait—"

I rose. "Protective custody. You couldn't move them? Help them run? Give them a warning? Do you *know* what you've cost me?"

Grace put one hand on me, and Amy took my other arm. I hadn't realized I was shaking so badly. Then Grace turned to me. "That's not all. She encouraged you to go after the one in Vegas. Hoping you'd be so full of rage you wouldn't think straight. When I called for a medic, who did they send? A media team."

Amy spat on the table. "Even the old ones have more compassion."

The director picked up her phone. "One more word, Ms. Roberts, and I will have you detained under National Security Directive 5.2.8, section C."

"Stow it. Brynner, you should hear a voice memo I recorded between the director and me. Yes, she offered me money if I got you to come back, but I turned her down. That would be when she threatened—" Grace's phone chirped three times in a singsong pattern. She fumbled for it and stared at the screen before looking up with teary eyes. Her voice came out so soft the air conditioner drowned it out. "I have to go."

"To your quarters, Ms. Roberts. Brynner, you should get some sleep. I'll pick a new target for you tomorrow, when you are rested and healed." The director waited, phone in hand. "Are we clear?"

"*I have to go. Now.*" Grace grabbed her purse and ran for the door.

Which remained shut, no matter how Grace turned the knob.

Director Bismuth rose, keeping one hand on the emergency lockdown button under her desk. "Grace Roberts, by order of the Bureau of Special Investigation, I place you under arrest. You will go nowhere without a level-zero clearance escort. Return to your quarters, or I will have you held in jail. The jail is outside this building, remarkably insecure."

While I had questions I would force the director to answer, I also had priorities, and first among those was keeping Grace from committing a murder. I lunged forward, intercepting Grace's charge and picking her up. Maggie unlocked the door under my withering stare, and I carried Grace out to the elevator with Amy following behind. Once I pressed the call button, I set Grace on her feet. "Calm down, and tell me everything."

She shook her head. "I have to go now. Right now. *Right now.*" Tears ran down her cheeks.

Grace just didn't understand. "The only way you're getting

out of this building is if I go with you. I was born with level-zero clearance."

Amy stood in the corner of the elevator, muttering to herself. "You should not go out. The old ones have eyes and ears everywhere, and they will most certainly kill you both to earn Ra-Ame's favor."

That was the last thing we needed. "Killing us would do that?"

"If they believe it will, does the truth matter?" She put a finger on my chest, over my heart. "You are the son of the woman who stole her heart, the son of the man who hid it, and the slayer of an old one." She turned to Grace. "You stole a spawn and learned from it terrible knowledge. They will kill you both as a matter of course." Amy cut a strip from her top, leaving just enough fabric to not get arrested for indecency. She wrapped Grace's hand and tied the cloth off, then offered the rest as a handkerchief to Grace.

Grace put her arm around Amy. "We'll be safe."

Amy shook her head as the elevator door opened to her floor and she stepped out. "I do not think you will be safe anywhere."

We rode down to the bottom floor, where I showed my badge and escorted Grace out of the building to the motor pool. With the keys to a coupe in my pocket, we headed to the parking garage, where Grace stopped.

"Brynner, I need you to do something for me."

"Anything."

Grace wiped the tears from her eyes. "I need you to stay here and let me handle this alone."

"Not gonna happen. I've got a better outlook than Amy,

but she's right—it's not safe out there. Not by a long shot. And the Re-Animus might hate you more than me."

"Please." She put a hand on me, running it up my side.

And I took it off. "You don't look like you should be driving. Where do you want to go?"

Grace bit her lip. "Portland."

I could lose my job for taking her out of the building. Get thrown in the brig again. But Grace was a woman of reason, and she had to have one. "What's in Portland that's worth risking a trip?"

She hung her head and turned away. "My daughter. That text was from her caregiver. My daughter's in the hospital."

34

GRACE

"Let's get going. Portland's a long drive." Brynner ushered me to the car and got in. If he had comments, or questions, he kept them to himself. I was asking so much of him, to take me out of the building, violating the director's orders. I had to get to my daughter. Whatever consequences came next, I'd deal with.

On the highway, Brynner lit up the flashing light and floored the accelerator, reaching Portland in record time. The morning traffic snarled streets, which made Brynner glance about nervously, as if he expected the dead to attempt a carjacking. We took to side roads, winding our way around the city until we reached the children's hospital. Finally, we pulled up into the parking lot, and Brynner got out with me.

I tried to block him. "You can wait in the car if you want. You don't have to do this."

"Grace, I want to go with you." He tenderly took my hand, avoiding the slices where the glass cut me.

And then I saw the truck. A battered, banana-yellow truck with rust spots and a bashed front fender. I knew the truck, recognized it, since I was the one who bashed in the fender five years ago. "Will you do something else for me?"

He tossed his head from side to side, hmming to himself. "Well, let's see. You nearly killed me with the car, but I'm almost certain you saved me in the pool. I guess I could float you this one."

"There's a reason I wanted to do this alone. I try not to think about this part of my life, and I didn't want you—or anyone else—to see it. I need you to keep your mouth shut. Don't get goaded into saying or doing things we'll both regret."

He put both hands in his pockets and whistled as he walked along behind me into the hospital. At the desk I showed my ID and waited. After minutes or years, a nurse walked out. She glanced at her tablet, then called, "Ms. Aker?"

I held up my hand, trying to ignore how Brynner's eyes narrowed. "It's actually Roberts now."

She shrugged and waved toward the door. "Follow me." I did, with Brynner hulking behind me, his mouth closed in a tight frown.

There, in the intensive care unit, lay my little girl, Esther. Beside her bed, an older Hispanic woman slept on a roll-out cot. I shook her gently. "Juanita?"

She sat up, looking to Esther, and then back to me. "Ms. Grace, I was so worried. I checked her lungs every day, and yesterday, I was thinking she needed sun, so I rolled her outside."

"Juanita, you didn't cause her to get pneumonia by rolling

her out in the sun." Juanita had cared for Esther in the old home. My only request to Personal Resources was that she continue in that duty. I looked around the empty room. "Where is he? I saw the truck."

She held her fist up, imitating a phone. "Outside, making calls. I did not want him in, but the nurses said he is on the papers."

Another mistake I'd correct shortly.

"Brynner, this is my daughter, Esther Rose." I took his hand and pulled him to the bedside. "I told you I was in a relationship. With her."

He studied her face, his eyes glancing up to look at me from time to time. "Hello, Esther Rose." He looked up at the wall of machines. "What . . . what happened to her?"

"Her brain didn't develop during gestation." I stroked her face as I spoke. "Doctors told me she wouldn't live to be six months old. Or one year. Or three. But she's a fighter."

He sat down in the chair beside the bed. "The credit cards—"

"You try paying for a full-time nurse on an analyst's hours. I wasn't even getting salary. The life insurance from Mom and Dad, my trust fund, you have no idea how much it costs." I tried not to let bitterness creep into my voice.

Brynner sighed. "The worst costs aren't the ones in the checkbook, are they? You didn't have to do this alone."

"That's what I told her six years ago. Turns out Grace likes to do things alone," said a man in the doorway.

That's how an awful, beyond awful, day went from bad to worse. Trevor Aker.

He walked in, offering Brynner his hand. "Grace, why don't you introduce me to your friend?"

I bit my lip to avoid a fight. "Brynner, this is Trevor Aker. He was Esther's father."

He let that same sneer that always followed him spread across his face. "Funny, you say 'was,' but look who they called."

"I'll fix the paperwork to prevent that from happening again. You can go. I had your parental rights terminated." I kept my voice calm.

"Don't make me out to be the bad guy, Grace. You're good at that. The lone woman, carrying such a heavy load." He looked at Brynner. "She'll tell you I left her. She won't tell you the doctors wanted her to take Esther off life support at two days. And at a week. And a month."

The same fights as before. The same discussions. I couldn't help myself as I shouted back, "Look at her. Look at my daughter and tell me that's right."

He did. "I'm looking, Grace. I guess I just don't see the same thing. You chose this. You chose this over me. So work your job. Get another ten credit cards and file bankruptcy, but I would have been with you while you grieved."

I hissed at him. "Like you've been with me the last six years? You'd support me the way you supported me the last six years? I'd rather be alone. Get out."

Trever took a step toward me, and Brynner's chair creaked as he shifted his weight. "You didn't want me around. I told you I couldn't handle this. Never living, never dying, this isn't life. This is just you making yourself feel better, because you don't have the guts or the courage to make hard decisions."

Brynner stood, drawing himself to full height, looking down at Trevor. "Courage isn't walking into a building with a thing that will tear your arms off. It's going to work every single day at a job that kills you, just to take care of someone."

Trevor crossed his arms. "Bullshit. She just wants to make up for things she regrets."

"I don't regret my daughter. I regret you." I stood and pointed to the door. "Get the hell out, Trevor."

Trevor walked to the doorway and then looked back at Brynner. "You want to know the secret to getting Grace into bed? Smile at her. Lie and tell her she's pretty, and then take her out to a fast-food restaurant. It worked for me every Friday night for two years straight."

BRYNNER

I'd broken men beefier than Trevor Akers the way I wanted to break him right then. How easily he spewed bile at Grace made me sick. Unlike dealing with a Re-Animus, I didn't need any special blades or syringes or lightbulbs for what I had in mind. My fists would do just fine.

I looked over to Grace, whose cheeks flushed bright red, her eyes brimming with tears. "Can I hit him? Please?"

"No. He'd love that. Don't give him the satisfaction." She closed her eyes, and tears streaked her cheeks.

"I'd love it, too." I looked down at the thin, worthless man, trying to figure out how to say what I felt without my fists. "You don't deserve Grace. I don't *deserve* her. If she figures out a way to stop the storm that's coming, it won't be because of you. It will be because of that little girl. You'll still live in this world because of her."

For just one moment, I think he considered a snappy reply, and I had five fingers' worth of comeback just waiting. Grace would get over being angry, and it wouldn't be my first assault charge. He met my gaze for a moment, then shrank from the room like a shadow and walked away.

I thought things might be better once he left us. If anything, they were more awkward. Grace kept staring at me every time I turned around, and the look on her face wasn't one of the two I was familiar with. "Woman about to sleep with you" and "woman not going to sleep with you" were all I'd needed to recognize for so many years.

She confused me. Bewildered me.

Juanita excused herself to the senoritas' room, leaving Grace and me with a silence that could give birth to a thousand conversations, none of them comfortable.

"Go ahead." She spoke to me but kept her eyes on Esther Rose.

And I didn't know what to ask. If there was something to ask. "Akers or Roberts? Which one is your name?"

"Roberts. I was only Mrs. Grace Akers for a year. He could be sweet. Funny, and charming. It wasn't all sad."

"Why don't you just tell people about Esther?"

She stroked her daughter's cheek again. "It was easier to let people believe what they wanted to. 'Woman has credit problems' is easy. 'Woman can't let go of daughter who will never know her name' isn't. People understand what they want to understand."

A tall man with a gray beard and mustache knocked on the door, introducing himself as the attending doctor, and I left Grace and him to discuss pneumonia treatment options, recovery, therapy. Down at the nurses station, they gathered, watching the television.

"Evening, ladies." I couldn't summon my super-charm voice. "Anything new?"

One of them pointed to the screen, and I stepped forward to see it.

The BSI headquarters leaked smoke from dozens of windows, most of which were broken out. One nurse looked back at me. "There's been another attack."

I ran to Grace's room. "Grace, I have to get back to Seattle."

She rose, looking to the doctor. "Do the full antibiotic course." Then she exchanged a hug with Juanita. "I love you. Thank you for loving my baby."

"Grace, you don't have to go. I'll handle this, you stay here. Keep Esther Rose safe." I took my keys and my jacket, and in the moment it took me to do so, Grace was at my side.

She took my hand. "I am going to keep her safe, by doing my job. Field teams stick together."

We ran to the car together, turned on the emergency lights, and flew up the freeway toward Seattle, but were hours away even at top speed.

I thought Grace had gone to sleep, but she looked over at me and whispered, "I'm sorry."

"For what?"

"Everything. Nothing. I just am. Pull over at the next rest stop." She pointed to the exit sign, and I cut across all six lanes to zip into the commercial truck lane. Couples in minivans chased kids and pets through the tall grass, while distant cars whizzed by.

I crossed my arms and leaned back my seat. "I'll wait here. Bathrooms are over there."

She undid her seat belt, and then slid over, her weight resting on my chest. Her head laid up against my shoulder, then she pressed her lips to mine for far too short a kiss. "I'm not used to being vulnerable. But I feel like I can be with you. Ask me anything. I'll say yes."

I wrapped my arms around her, as though with pure muscle I could will her to be safe. Desire warred within me. To kiss her lips again, and once more trace her curves. I kissed her again, running my tongue over her lips, and meshing my hands in her hair. "Grace?"

"Yes?" she whispered.

Vulnerable. I liked to think I didn't know what that felt like. My nightmares told me different. Regardless of what the world saw when they looked at me, I couldn't forget the truth I'd kept to myself. Though every fiber of my being sung out not to, I spoke. "Do you want to know what really happened the day my mother died?"

35

GRACE

"Do you want to know what happened?" That was *not* the question I expected from Brynner. I pushed myself away from him but let my hips stay firmly where they were to emphasize what he'd given up. Damn it, I did want to know. "Yes."

He closed his eyes for a moment. "Could you get off me? I can't really think with you like that."

Which was the point.

Brynner rolled down the window, sweating, and sat his seat up. "I'll talk while I drive."

When we'd resumed our mad dash down the freeway, he finally spoke. "Mom ran the lab. Dad killed the monsters. That's how I grew up. Dad taught me to whittle pine stakes at age seven. I shot my first meat-skin when I was eight."

Giving an eight-year-old a gun was near criminal, in my opinion.

"If I wasn't hunting with Dad, I was with Mom while she

worked in the lab. She was certain she could figure out the secret to some drawings Dad found. Hieroglyphic drawings. Like what I found on the boat."

I nodded. "Or under the motel bed." He glanced over at me, his eyes momentarily focused on my breasts. "Eyes up."

Brynner shook his head. "Sorry. I'm sorry—"

"Don't be. Just don't be driving over a hundred miles per hour next time. Go on."

He slowed down, his body alternately tensing and relaxing. "She had one of the drawings hung on the lab wall, and she'd spend her lunch breaks showing me how to fight with knives or trying to decipher it."

"And one day, at lunch, when I looked up to show her the hooked stake I'd carved, the wall of the lab was gone. Not destroyed. Gone. Like it was never there. The wall just opened up into a tomb. Except that no one would build a lab into a tomb like that."

"How did you know it was a tomb? Torches?"

"You don't believe me." The hurt in his voice, or the acceptance, I couldn't tell which was worse.

"I believe you believe. That's the best I can do."

"You can believe what you want to. There were two stone slabs, and light filtering in from overhead. Torches have to be maintained. Torches burn. I don't think anyone had been there for centuries. Everything was covered in dust."

I willed myself not to comment. To listen, if only to support Brynner. "And your mom?"

"She thought it was some sort of illusion, until she stepped out of the lab and into the tomb. Then she saw the blades."

I thought of the broken knives. Sacrificial blades, Amy had called them. "Your blades?"

He nodded. "One slab held silver jars. The other, a young woman's body, with half a dozen blades sticking out. She wasn't rotted at all. Her skin was dusty white. Mom took one knife out, and then another."

"How did she die?"

Tears rolled down his face, and he wiped them away. "She brought the knives back and put them on her desk. Kept tapping them like she thought they'd disappear. And ran back to grab a jar."

"The heart."

He nodded. "The moment she touched it, they moved. The guardians. I thought they were statues. Terra-cotta warriors with gold spears, but they moved like cats, gliding through the tomb."

I waited, my hands squeezing the armrest for what had to come.

"She didn't see them. She looked at me, and down at the spear sticking through her. She threw the jar to me."

I put one hand on his, wanting to console him.

"You saw the video. You know what the BSI knows. But there's more." Brynner's voice wavered.

"After a moment, her head slumped over. And then she looked up at me and spoke. But it wasn't Mom's voice."

"Ra-Ame. What did she say?"

Brynner didn't answer for so long I thought he wouldn't. "She said to bring it back. She said she'd let my mother go. That we could be together. And I don't know how to explain it, but the air rippled in waves."

"What did you do?"

"I couldn't move. I wanted to. I wanted to bring Mom back.

But I was afraid. A moment later, the spell just faded away. The wall was back. Mom was gone. I never told anyone Ra-Ame spoke to me."

I believe in a lot of things. Good dentists. Honorable politicians, but magic spells that opened portals pushed the limits of what I could accept. Saying so directly would alienate a man I had no intention of pushing away. "You were a boy."

"I wanted to help her. I could have."

Spells and other questions aside, guilt was a topic I knew all about. "Could have done what? Against those things? You would have died, too. You were afraid."

"I won't be next time. Whether I find Ra-Ame, or she comes for me, next time I won't hold back, Grace. I'm not a little boy. I'm a man, and it's time the Re-Animus learned to fear me the way others fear them." His fingers tightened on the steering wheel until I feared he might break it.

I thought of what Aunt Emelia had said about Brynner. That he wasn't like other men. "Like God rolled up the desert into a man." Brynner would never rest. Never forget. Never forgive, himself or the Re-Animus, for what happened.

He didn't speak again until we reached Seattle. We left the car parked ten blocks back and walked on foot, pushing our way through crowds and police lines until finally we reached the building.

The smoke on TV hadn't done it justice. Or the lines of field ops in battle armor forming a ring around the building. These men stood ready to defend, but against what? Who? They had the haunted look of a force already beaten.

The ring faced BSI headquarters.

As Brynner passed, the men saluted him, letting out a rousing cheer. Though a shadow of worry flashed across his face, he snapped to attention. "Situation Report."

"Sir, we were attacked four hours ago. The attacker broke through the building defenses, destroying defending units."

Brynner looked to the building. "Attacker? As in one?"

"Yes, sir." The field commander's voice quavered. "I've never seen anything like it."

"You saw the one I killed in Vegas, right?" Brynner put his hand on the man's shoulder.

He nodded. "Bigger. Much bigger. Not human. Guns didn't work. Neither did the lab guy's weapons. Not even the pressure washers hurt it."

I stepped up and spoke, looking him in the eye. "You're sure there's only one?"

"God help us if there were more. We're forming a line to try to protect civilians, but we're not going to be able to stop it. Doesn't mean we won't try."

Brynner nodded. "It's inside, isn't it?" He looked up at the building, then spoke with new urgency. "Where is Amy Rust? Egyption, Grave Services?"

The field commander's gaze fell to the ground. "I can't rightly say. Last time I saw, she was fighting with it on the sixth floor. We got a lot people out safe thanks to her."

High above, a chunk of the wall exploded, and from the sky, something plummeted to the ground like an asteroid. It crashed through the roof of a bus and smashed out the bottom, making a hole in the asphalt that spewed water where it broke a water main.

"There." I pointed above, to the edge of the hole. Clinging to a bent girder was the lithe figure of Amy Rust. She dangled, kicking and scrambling to pull herself up.

"Go," shouted Brynner, and we ran into the building.

BRYNNER

Without my blades or any form of weaponry, I wasn't keen on challenging the Re-Animus host that had decided to level our headquarters. At the moment, a much more mundane but persistent and deadly enemy threatened Amy: gravity.

I ran upstairs. Then walked upstairs and finally limped upstairs. If I had to, I'd crawl up the stairs until I reached the floor where Amy hung. When I finally arrived, two things occurred to me:

First, I was amazed that the building hadn't collapsed. The interior walls had creature-sized holes punched from one end to another.

Second, the sheer number of spent bullets confirmed exactly what the field commander said. If that thing could be killed by anything short of terminal kinetic energy poisoning, I didn't know what it would be.

The outer wall on the east side lay in shreds, the supporting girders blown out where the creature exited.

"Amy? Amy?" I leaned out the edge, looking to the distant street below.

From above, the metal creaked. "Brynner Carson. I did not expect you to come." She leaned over, perched on the edge of a girder.

Like we would leave her. "Well, I wanted to leave you, but Grace wouldn't hear of it. Give me your hand."

She swung down, kicking back and forth, and leaped for me.

With all of my body weight, I snagged her wrist and hauled her inside, collapsing onto the carpet. "You're heavier than you look." The second time in five hours I'd had a woman on top of me and all my clothes on.

She put a hand on my chest, rising to her knees. "You will die alone if this is your charm, Brynner Carson."

"Amy?" Grace walked across the floor toward us. "Brynner?" She put her hands on her hips, frowning.

"I got her." I scrambled to my feet.

She glared at me. "I can see that. What exactly happened here?"

Amy rolled her head and shoulders, stretching. "The creature could not be stopped, so I lured it out the window."

"And then?" Grace still fumed, like she'd caught me naked with a waitress or three.

"He got me. Relax, Grace Roberts, I am not interested in taking your man, any more than you are." Amy sauntered past her toward the stairs.

"What does *that* mean?" Grace's tone told me I'd be better off shutting my mouth and staying out of it.

"If you wanted the man, you would be sharing a bed with him now instead of making moon faces at him. You are here and not there." She walked down the stairs, leaving Grace to fume at me.

I walked toward Grace, my palms held out. "I wasn't—"

"Can it. You've done enough *talking* for one day."

I caught her wrist. I'd gotten myself in trouble more times than I could count by saying yes, but this was the first time I'd earned a woman's wrath for revealing secrets I hid from everyone else. "About earlier—"

She punched me in the ribs, hard. "I said—"

"Grace. I've never known a woman like you. And I've known a lot of women." I cringed. Not smooth.

She looked up at me with tears in her eyes. "Your taste for

'women's flesh,' as Amy puts it, is legendary. Except for me. Is it because I was married? It that your problem?"

Amy needed help with her English. "No one knows what I told you. No one. Not even Dad." I picked my words with care this time. "Do I want to make love to you? God, yes. But not in a car, not beside the road at a rest stop."

I gently placed my hand between her breasts, so her heart beat under my fingertips. "I've had enough of flesh. I want more than just sex. I don't want it from Amy."

The last time I saw a dazed look like that on a woman, she had severe blood loss. Grace teared up and wavered like she might collapse. After a moment, she leaned forward and kissed me on the neck, then rested her forehead on my collarbone.

I whispered, "That's it? I give you that speech and I get a kiss on the neck? What was that?"

She put her arms around me and spoke into my ear. "More."

I'd thought there'd be more to the "more." Still, a destroyed building. A dead monster, black smoke everywhere. That had to be one of the most romantic moments of my life. Which is why when the helicopter circled the building and landed, I wasn't amused.

"That would be the director." I pushed Grace away, savoring her smooth skin. "Standard rules for any disaster, the director will evacuate immediately." I walked to the stairs to start climbing, and Grace grabbed my hand.

"Let her come to us."

And when she finally came down the stairs, I made sure Grace and I were as occupied as two adults could be with their clothes on. Which wasn't nearly occupied enough.

"Attention," she snapped. "Carson Brynner. At attention."

I let go of Grace. "I'm sorry. My attention was focused elsewhere."

She stood before me, radiating useless intimidation. "Have you secured the rest of the building? What is the status of the facilities? What about casualties? This is not how a general behaves."

"I was securing the rest of my field team. Who, incidentally, dealt with the creature. You know, I do need to go find Amy." I took Grace's hand to leave.

"You mean the creature that got away? And the field team that failed to contain or kill it?"

I spun, dropping Grace's hand. "What?"

The director clucked her tongue. "What were you up to that you could not spend thirty seconds to kill it once and for all? The creature rose from the asphalt ten minutes ago and fled, leaving a trail of carnage in its wake. If you were not otherwise engaged, you might have saved lives."

She turned to Grace. "And is it true?"

"What?" Grace stepped back.

"The captured Re-Animus escaped."

36

GRACE

Escaped? It couldn't be. Not after what it took to capture it. Not after what it cost to transport it. Not for what we could learn from it. With Brynner close behind, I ran down flights of stairs, passing Amy in the lobby. In the basement, the secure elevator doors stood open, hanging from their hinges like twisted taffy.

Brynner leaned out, looking down. "What's left of the car is at the bottom." He swung into the shaft and grabbed a ladder rung, then started climbing down. On the third try, I caught the rung and followed.

At the bottom, I climbed down through the roof of the elevator car and crawled out into the vault.

The artificial waterfall had stopped, and the bridge over it hung in tatters. We hopped into the knee-deep artificial river channel and waded across, where wide tracks through the salt traced the creature's path. Just beyond the salt, my entire lab lay in ruins, including a smoldering pile that had to be the Sin Eater's remains.

I sprinted down the hall of symbols, to where the Re-Animus cell was. I stopped, blinded. The holding pod lay smashed open. Inside, its body lay, basking in the light of two sun spotlights.

It hadn't escaped.

It was dead.

"Grace." A feeble voice from the shadows caught my attention.

One of the desks lay crumpled like a tin can, trapping the withered body of Dr. Thomas. "Our weapons didn't work, I'm sorry to say."

Brynner knelt, seizing the entire desk, and struggled to lift it.

"Don't," Dr. Thomas practically shouted. "Leave it alone."

I knelt, taking the hand that wasn't trapped and squeezing. "Hold on, I'll get the medics."

"It's too late for that, Grace." Dr. Thomas shook his head. "In fact, I don't believe my heart has beaten in at least half an hour."

I dropped his hand, noting how cold his skin was, and how his eyes hadn't blinked the whole time. "You—"

"Yes. The monster didn't bother once he smashed the desk on me, but when he killed our test subject, a portion of the Re-Animus entered me."

I shook my head. This wasn't how things were supposed to be. "I'll find a cure. A way to drive it out." Turning to Brynner, I pulled on him. "The hall of symbols."

Dr. Thomas coughed or laughed, I couldn't tell which. "Grace, I never believed in anything, any more than you do. That won't work. And I've injected myself twice with our serum. As the minutes go by, I'm only getting stronger."

"I'll save you." I almost whispered the words, wanting to believe them true.

"Grace." Dr. Thomas waited until I looked at him, a weak smile on his lips. "I have no desire to become the BSI's newest test subject, trapped for eternity in a glass cell. And my thoughts are changing. I'm hearing voices, whispers of other minds. Minds that want me to tear you to pieces. Would you be so kind as to lend me your Deliverator?"

"No." Brynner shook his head. "I can't hand you a weapon—"

I tried to pull my Deliverator out, but my hands shook, and my eyes blurred with tears. Brynner took it from me.

"Please, I beg of you, end this while I can still decide." Dr. Thomas looked over to me. "Don't give up, Grace. Keep asking questions and pursuing answers. Curiosity is our most powerful weapon."

He closed his eyes, his free hand clenched into a fist. "I'm ready."

Brynner pulled me toward him, and fired, over and over. The gunshots echoed through Vault Zero.

"Grace Roberts, are you safe?" Amy's voice from my lab called me back from the cloud of regret and fear. "Were you attacked by the old one?"

Brynner rose, leaving me on the floor. "It's dead. Not escaped."

Amy trotted down the hall. "Ra-Ame's foot soldiers were not known for mercy."

Brynner winced. "What did you call that thing?"

"A foot soldier. A single member of her army, sent to do her bidding. If the legends are true, her forces number in the thousands." Amy beckoned to me, and I went.

"We can't kill one of them, let alone a thousand." Brynner paced nervously.

Amy nodded. "At last, you understand. Grace Roberts, would you mind translating this?"

I finally saw what she pointed at. On one side of the lab, the creature had worked a circle of glyphs that looked like all the others. I mouthed the words, working through the symbols. "The paths of the dead, the way, the hidden, Ra-Ame—"

Brynner shouted, "Stop!" He paced toward me. "Never out loud. Never speak them out loud."

Amy stepped between us. "Brynner Carson, the scribes of Grave Services have read them every way imaginable. It is said if one cannot see the fifth sign, these inscriptions are harmless." Amy pointed to the quadrants. "Four quadrants. Five signs."

I knelt and traced them. "There aren't five concepts here. Four, just like in all the others."

Amy shrugged. "I can only tell you what is said. And what of this?" She pointed to the other area, where a normal block of hieroglyphics written in blood lay.

I read the symbols. And again, and a third time to be sure. "It's from Ra-Ame. Her demands."

Brynner stood beside me. "She already killed the Re-Animus and destroyed the Sin Eater's body. What more does she want? Her heart?"

I nodded. "And yours."

He shrugged.

"And mine."

Brynner stiffened, his eyes narrowing. "Why? I understand hers. And mine." He looked to Amy. "Grave Services has put up with these things longer than we have. What do you think?"

Amy pursed her lips. "I do not know what you expect of me, Brynner Carson. Do you expect me to tell you the mind of Ra-Ame? You will be disappointed." Then she caught my eye. "Grace knows things that she will not be permitted to know and live. Though the old ones are destroyed, their secrets live here." Amy pointed to my head.

"I'm not giving up." I stood up a chair and pushed a desk over. "I won't go easily." I looked to Brynner. "Interview everyone; reconstruct its actions. I want to know its exact path through the building."

He nodded, his face somber. "And that helps how?"

"She knew where the Re-Animus was. Look at the other doors on the way here. Are any of them broken? She knew how to disable the waterfall. At the casino, she said she'd watched me sleep. We have a traitor in the BSI."

Brynner nodded. "I'll get on it. Amy, would you mind helping me keep things straight?"

"Gladly. It will not matter if Ra-Ame's army arrives." She followed him out.

And though I struggled to force my mind to the task at hand, pressing amber bolts, my thoughts drifted to the artifact at my feet. Again and again, I divided the circle into its component symbols, then their ideas.

Whoever created it definitely had a theme in mind. Opening the way, the hidden paths, reveal, and of course, Ra-Ame. But there wasn't a fifth symbol. I had to be losing my mind to even think it was possible.

But Brynner and Amy seemed so certain. If he lied to me in the car, it was because he believed it himself. Did madmen know they were mad? Would the deluded recognize their delusion? I emptied my mind and filled my hands running the press, coating each bolt with a hot, burnt glaze.

These were no weapons to kill a monster.

Those sacrificial blades, on the other hand, were a weapon worthy of a warrior. As the hours went on, and I filled syringes, my eyes grew bleary. Yet the drawing called to me.

There had to be an answer. Something had happened to Brynner's mother. Even Director Bismuth believed these drawings held significance. But what the connection was escaped me.

I never liked doing translation.

It wasn't for lack of skill. It was that in almost all cases, it was impossible to be certain. At some level, it always came down to interpretation. To assignment and testing of the meaning. What I wanted more than anything was to be certain.

And just for a moment, when I looked at the artifact, I caught a glimpse. A ghostly afterimage, not formed by the lines of the other glyphs, but by the negative spaces between them.

Not a proper symbol. More of a suggestion.

The minutes turned to hours as I grasped at images just beyond sight. I thought of dead eyes, staring. Never blinking. Like them, I stared with weary eyes until the images floated before me. And when I closed my eyes, it hung in the air, imprinted before me. This glyph had no equivalent in true hieroglyphs, and yet the meaning burned its way into my mind. The words came unbidden, in the ancient language, a language not fit for human tongues.

Open the way, the paths of the dead, to Ra-Ame . . . The last sign was "exist"? "Arrive"? *Be.* The fifth sign wasn't a word, it was a concept, one of existence.

When I opened my eyes, the west half of my lab was gone. My hands and feet felt leaden, like I'd fallen asleep at the lab bench.

I picked up a wrench and tossed it a few feet past where the salt floor became bare rock. It bounced into darkness.

I knew right then I'd lost my mind. Fallen asleep at the

machine. Or maybe snuggled up to Brynner in his car, having a nightmare. But my mind wouldn't stop. The two stone slabs. One with five silver jars, each overturned. The other slab stood empty. I took a step inside and touched the ground. The dirt beneath my fingers felt real. Smelled real.

A scorpion skittered by, out of the tomb and into my lab.

It was very real.

I glanced up, looking at the stone figures at the corners. Tall wooden spears in their hands, with iron points.

Brynner had said they didn't move until his mother touched the jar.

I thought of the knives. Four more of them lay on the second slab. Four knives to replace two lost. I ran for the slab, picking each up by its tapered handle. I kept my eyes on the guardians, who stood still as stone.

When I glanced over my shoulder, the lab wavered, like an image of the sky in a pond.

While my head was turned, a noise like the whisper of rat's feet came to me. I leaped, onto the second slab, into the air. I landed on my lab desk, knocking the air out of me and sending blades clattering.

Rolling over, I looked back to the tomb. And saw nothing. The lab stretched out like it had before.

The symbols on the ground had changed from red to burnt black, crumbling.

I gathered the blades from across my lab. Four perfect, amber-coated blades, with a streak of white where alabaster inset the blade.

They were real.

Which meant I was crazy.

I slipped them into an equipment box, slung the box over

my shoulder, and carefully climbed up the elevator shaft to the lobby. After a few minutes of wandering, I found Brynner. "I need to talk."

"Grace." Brynner's furrowed brow and crossed arms made me hesitate. "You were right. One of our clerks pressed a second card key for your room. Got paid a few hundred thousand for it." He stopped, scanning my face. "What's wrong?"

I began to shake as I fought to reconcile what I *knew* to be true and what I could deal with. "I think I need help."

"Medic!" He stood and shouted, waving over a field medic from the line. I clung to Brynner when the medic asked him to leave.

The medic took out a penlight and looked into my eyes. "Can you tell me what's wrong?"

I held up the box. "I'm having a mental breakdown."

The medic pushed it aside. "Lady, given what you've done in the last month, you can have five and no one will blink." He nodded to the box. "You didn't"—he looked to Brynner—"cut anything, did you?"

Brynner took the box from me, prying my fingers from it, and clicked it open. His eyes grew round, and he shook his head. "Where?"

I closed my eyes and gritted my teeth, willing this to make sense. "I saw the fifth sign. I read the fifth sign. I saw her tomb. I. Saw. It." And when I opened my eyes, he still held a silver blade with yellow edges. I lunged at Brynner, grabbing him by the collar and giving voice to the terror inside.

"She isn't there. *She is coming.*"

37

BRYNNER

I'd seen men do worse over less. I turned the blades over in my hands again and again. Perfect matches of the ones I'd broken. Ancient weapons designed to keep a Re-Animus dead. Once I was sure the medic had Grace sedated, I made a beeline to Amy, who lounged in the sun outside.

"I need you to stay with Grace. She's sedated, and she's not well." I handed her a medical bracelet that matched the one I'd put on Grace.

Amy swung out of the lawn chair on the sidewalk, her face unreadable. "What has happened?"

"Grace came after me, started screaming that Ra-Ame was coming."

"It is good that Grace Roberts recognizes this." Amy folded her hands together, nodding.

"You know better than that. She doesn't believe anything

unless she can prove it. But she doesn't just believe it. She *knows* it. And it's driving her crazy."

"How? I could spend a thousand summers and not convince her of what is."

The thought made me sick, but the proof lay strapped to my sides. I drew a blade slowly out. "She said she saw the fifth sign. She gave me this."

Amy cursed in Arabic, staring at it. "It is the sister of those your mother stole. There can be no doubt. Grace Roberts has walked the paths of the dead to Ra-Ame's tomb."

"That's what I am afraid of. Grace said the slab was empty. And that Ra-Ame is coming. Can you stay with Grace? I don't want her to wake up and wander. Her view of the world just took a mighty hit."

Amy patted me on the back. "You will go to her lab and make certain nothing else returned?"

"Yes."

"Then I will wait with Grace Roberts. She will have questions when she wakes, so many questions. I will not let her invoke the paths of the dead again. The guardians of Ra-Ame's tomb should have slain her. It is a dark miracle she did not die there, as your mother did."

And every fiber in my body screamed. "How did you know that?"

Either she didn't realize how close I was to cutting her down as the Re-Animus spy, or she didn't care. "Brynner Carson, your father lied on passports and searched the empty lands for a tomb. He carried with him relics no man would be allowed to remove. How could I not know?"

"I'm sorry. It's getting to me. Aren't you the least bit afraid I might have stabbed you?"

Amy shook her head. "You move slowly. You show no skill. One day, if you focus, train and meditate all your life, you will never be my equal."

The Grave Services folks had serious issues with standards. "Thanks. I'll be back as soon as I can."

"Take care, Brynner Carson. If legends are true, her guardians are deadly beyond measure." She moved, as graceful as a house cat, the crowd parting before her like magic.

I spent the next few hours in Vault Zero, cataloguing everything. Nothing escaped my study. The burnt writing on the floor. The scorpion, so far from home in rainy, wet Seattle. The amber-pressed bolts, which bore only passing resemblance to my ceremonial blades.

I felt guilty just carrying them, even though they fit my hands perfectly. I told myself they were mine.

Given to me by Grace, at a cost so high I shuddered to consider it. I'd seen the guardians move. I knew how quickly they struck. Why had Grace gone in there? She should have run. Should have gotten me, or Amy, or anyone else.

Instead—instead she was herself. Of course she'd gone into the tomb. If Grace was right—and when was she not?—Ra-Ame's body no longer lay on the slab. Which meant, in my book, she was up, moving around, and probably very cranky after a four-thousand-year nap.

I checked the Re-Animus containment pod again. Six-inch steel smashed like it was butter. How could I hope to stand against one of those things, let alone a thousand? After rechecking everything, I climbed back out and went to the director's office to report, using the one working elevator.

Director Bismuth sat in her chair, the only furniture in her office that hadn't been smashed or thrown out the window.

She looked up from the sheaf of reports in her hand. "Mr. Carson, have you found the creature?"

Her very tone demanded a response, bred into me from my earliest days. "We did not."

"And the state of the lab?"

"Destroyed. The Re-Animus corpse is torched; the one we captured was killed. Vault Zero is no longer secure, and I'm not sure it can be repaired. We're forming secure lines and have glazers repairing windows. The building superstructure is repairable."

She nodded. "And I understand we've received a new demand?"

"Yes, ma'am. The Heart of Ra-Ame and two others, in return for peace."

Director Bismuth threw the papers on the floor. "I don't want peace in which the Re-Animus survive. But tell me how I can fight these things. I'm starting to wonder how many of her demands I can meet."

Amy was right. The Re-Animus weren't the only monsters. "Grace Roberts may be your only hope if Ra-Ame doesn't keep her word. Did you think about that? What if you gave Ra-Ame everything, and everything wasn't enough?"

Her eyes narrowed as she contemplated my words. "You've put me in a difficult situation. Your mother and I went to college together. Your father and I were good friends. And yet, times change. What would your father do if his death could save a million lives? What would he do for just one?"

"Keep Grace out of this. I made a call to Grave Services; they're rechecking every place my dad had a dig permit and a bunch more he didn't but might have snuck off to. If we find the heart, I'll take it to Ra-Ame myself." I left her in her office. She didn't look up as I left.

I went back to the medical room, where Amy sat cross-legged, whittling a pine stake with one of her curved blades.

"Is Grace awake?"

"No. You people sleep more than the dead."

If I had an ounce of Amy's energy, I could kill every meat-skin in America and run a marathon. "And you don't sleep at all."

"I will sleep when I am dead. If you are tired, rest. I want to feel the night air again." Amy rose and walked out of the room.

I took a spare blanket from the emergency supply box and slipped onto Grace's cot, wrapping my arms around her. She sighed, pushing herself against me, and slipped back into sleep. It seemed I blinked, and in that moment, Grace was awake, looking around, and up at me.

"I had a bad dream."

I squeezed her. "You unlocked the paths of the dead. Traveled to Ra-Ame's tomb. Do you believe in magic now?"

She shook her head. "I don't know what it is, but I can find out. Maybe some sort of space fold? When we can control it, we can use it to go anywhere."

Grace would be okay. Magic could fit into her world, so long as it was described with quantums and electrons and gravity and folds.

"Why did you risk going into that tomb?"

She shivered despite the warmth of our skin and the heavy blanket covering us. "The blades. I needed to replace your blades. The guardians—"

I jerked myself up. "You could have been killed."

"But I wasn't. And I got out with them. You have four now. Four times the danger. Four times the death."

I wanted to scream but forced a whisper. "I don't want new

weapons, Grace. I want you. My dad lost his wife. I lost my mother."

Grace shuddered, tears coming to her eyes, but I didn't stop. Wouldn't stop until she understood. "Dad lost the person he loved the most, and all he had in return were two knives and a silver can. I spent ten years hating him for dragging it with him everywhere. Like it was the most precious thing on earth."

I pressed my forehead to the back of her head. "But God help me, I understand him now. It was all he had left of her. And if you died, these blades would be all I would have to remember you. The only thing left that you touched. You can't hold a blade at night to stay warm, or kiss a blade and have it kiss back. Dad held on to the heart not because of Ra-Ame. Because of Mom. All he had was an empty coffin and a jar—"

I jerked upright, throwing off the covers. "Can you move?"

"You normally sleep with a girl and then run out?" Grace ignored my fuming and stretched. "I'm woozy, but I'll be fine. Where's the fire?"

"Get a bag of weapons. Find Amy. I'm going to go get my mom's ashes." I rose from the cot, then knelt to kiss her. "I know where the heart is."

GRACE

I can't say which made me happier. Brynner's declaration that he knew where that cursed heart was or that he valued me more than an irreplaceable weapon. My limbs didn't move well, but eventually I managed to stumble out of the door and out of the building.

Far beyond the safe line of the BSI headquarters, Amy stood in a throng of people going to and from work. When I caught up with her, she smiled at me. "I like it here. Reminds me of home, where the streets were always crowded."

"I hear you had to take turns babysitting me."

She shrugged. "Many men cannot handle when the world changes. But I knew you would be well, Grace Roberts. Is it true? Did you discover the fifth sign?"

My voice caught in my throat. "It is. And I can show you how to see it, too. It's hidden in plain sight. The lab might be gone. The bodies might be gone, but we have archives of everything."

Amy regarded me with a dark stare. "This is what got your heart added to Ra-Ame's demands."

"She can have it when she takes it from me. Until then, I'm going to fight. Brynner thinks he knows where the heart is."

Amy nodded. "Yes, finally, the location is revealed. It is in Director Bismuth's possession. She will turn it over to Ra-Ame tomorrow."

I glanced back to BSI headquarters. "What? The director has it?"

"So she claims. Director Bismuth has asked me to guard the heart until tomorrow. Ra-Ame will claim it then." Amy furrowed her eyebrows. "You can believe in magic but not that Ra-Ame would do so?"

"It's not magic. Just because I don't know what it is yet or how to control it doesn't make it magic. I'll set up studies with the other artifacts. Now that I know how to trigger them, we'll learn to build them. Control them." I turned back to Amy. "I don't think the director has the heart."

"Ra-Ame will not forgive a lie from anyone, not even the

director of the BSI." Amy took my elbow, walking me back to the building. "It is not safe for you out here, Grace Roberts. Many of the old ones know your name."

They'd know more than that, if I had my way. They'd know the joys of eternal death. "And it's safe for you?"

We stepped past the BSI firing line and Amy pulled her hair back, adjusting her ponytail. "Did you know Grave Services gives each member a funeral when they are sworn in? It is so they understand they are already dead. There is nothing to fear."

"So you won't come with us?"

"No. Brynner Carson did not know where the heart was before. I have seen the truth in his eyes. He does not know now, I think. And this director, she may lie or tell the truth. Only time will tell." We walked through the lobby, where crews worked to replace the elevator.

"Then I need to ask a favor." I didn't really want to ask. It wasn't mythology. It was research, I told myself. "Would you mind taking an hour or so and telling me everything you know about Ra-Ame?"

Amy laughed, a grin on her face. "I have made a believer out of you? Amazing, Grace Roberts. It is a true miracle." When the door opened to our apartment floor, she waved me down the hall.

"I didn't say I believed in magic. I'm just open to understanding the possibilities. Legends. Stories. I want to hear them. There might be answers in them, hints of the truth."

"Then sit, Grace Roberts. And listen. Children's stories. Madmen's tales. I will tell you what they say, and you must decide what you believe."

Our apartment floor had escaped the creature's rampage,

though it stank of plastic smoke, so I opened the window, letting in the summer sun, and sat in a rocking chair across from the couch. "Make a believer out of me, Amy."

"As if such a thing could be done." She handed me a cup of coffee and sat on the couch. "So listen to the stories of Ra-Ame. I can tell you only what is known by men, and only guessed at, but Ra-Ame was born in the Middle Kingdom. You would say four thousand years ago. We would say four ages. She was not the most beautiful of Hotep's daughters, nor his favorite, and for her father's attention she worked without fail.

"Legends say she taught the crocodiles to weave baskets for her and gave a mountain of baskets to her father, but he said, 'What do I need with baskets? I have no fish to put in them.'

"Then she charmed the river fish, so they jumped from the Nile into the baskets, and brought her father to see. And her father scoffed, and said, 'What are fish and baskets, if I have no salt to cure them?'

"Finally, Ra-Ame whispered to the scorpions, and they brought a mountain of salt. 'I have done well, Father. Here are a thousand baskets and ten thousand salted fish.'

"When he looked upon all she had done, he finally loved her for a time. Then a plague came. The people said a sorcerer brought it. And some said it was a curse from the sun, or the earth itself. It blew in clouds like the desert sand, dark like the storms of spring.

"And where it passed, the dead rose and attacked.

"Hotep went to his wise men, and asked them to divine how to drive away the plague.

"They answered, saying only a royal sacrifice would appease it.

"And the pharaoh took Ra-Ame, and chained her in the Valley of Dust, where the kings go to die.

"When darkness came, he kissed her cheeks and slit her wrists. And the plague came upon her, finding her. Dwelling in her. Seeking her very soul.

"At sunrise, when the priests came to deliver her body, she greeted them. Her heart did not beat. Her lungs knew no breath save to speak, and her blood mixed with the sand. And they worshipped her, the willing sacrifice.

"As children became old men, and old men became dust, the people began to fear Ra-Ame. A new pharaoh rose, one who envied her. So he ordered a tomb constructed and six knives made. And in her tomb, he drove the knives through her body and ordered her soul destroyed.

"Ra-Ame swore with her final words that if she ever rose, the world would burn.

"When the priests took out her organs, they found only black sand. And from that, they knew she was cursed. The heart was only a lump of black diamond that shifted and moved. So they tore the heart from her chest, sealing her cursed soul in the jar.

"Ra-Ame slept but did not die.

"Sheepherders said that at night, her spirit roamed the dark, whispering, and retreated to her tomb at dawn. And she captured those who died under the darkness, stealing their bodies to guard her own. Ra-Ame was dead, and yet she lived on.

"One night she took a man who fell in the desert, holding his heart. But he did not come to her. He left and sailed away, taking a piece of her with him.

"The legends repeat many times. A scorned woman who stabbed herself, but awoke. The cattle man bitten by an asp. Some she took as her guards, and those that still had will left to become her children. The plague's children became the old ones.

"And Ra-Ame slept and dreamed of revenge on the kingdom. Over time, she gathered an army, kept underground, underwater. The spears of men did not break their hide, nor the salty seas leave them empty. But when Ra-Ame looked out on the world, it had changed. The old men were gone. New men, in new places roamed."

Amy stopped and leaned forward. "Then a woman walked the secret paths her children used and stole her heart. And without the ceremonial knives, her spirit returned to her body. That is what I believe."

I sat for several minutes, digesting the details of Amy's story before I finally spoke. "If I believed in souls, I'd buy that. Let me tell you my version: Someone did something horrible to a woman. She became a host for a parasite that grew stronger with time, and occasionally this parasite reproduced, spreading itself across the world." I sipped my now-cold coffee. "It's every bit as plausible as yours."

Amy regarded me like a toddler. "And these paths of the dead? Do you have an explanation for them?"

"Not yet. Give me time. And thank you. I don't know what the answers are yet, but at least I have better questions. And I'll figure out an explanation for their obsession with water." Even now, it bothered me that I hadn't been able to derive a pattern.

"Water? What of it?" Amy cocked an eyebrow at me, her head turned to the side.

"We have evidence the Re-Animus in Vegas was writing artifacts over water. On a boat, on a barge. On a restaurant over a pier."

I waited as Amy crossed her arms, her eyes closed in thought. "I will tell you nothing for certain, but perhaps a legend explains this."

"Go on."

"Ra-Ame grew tired of her children waking her constantly, always demanding her favor. So the legend says she laid down a rule of blood. If her children could not open the paths above water, they would be destroyed the moment they set foot in her tomb. Only the most powerful of the old ones would dare try. But I suppose you have another theory for that as well."

"I'll figure one out. Take care of yourself, Amy." I gave her a hug and ran for the elevator. At the armory, I grabbed a fresh set of Deliverators and a bag with Brynner's name on it, promising I'd deliver it myself. When I got to the lobby, Brynner stood, conversing with an Indian man wearing a white doctor's coat. As I walked up, he nodded to me.

Brynner kept one hand on the doctor's shoulder. "You wanted to know how I felt. I felt hurt. Wounded. Alone." He looked past the doctor to me. "I'm still hurt. I'm not healed, and I'm so sad at times it almost kills me. But I'm not alone." He turned around, cutting off the conversation, and took my hand. "You took your sweet time. Where's Amy?"

"It's just us. Now let's go get that heart."

38

BRYNNER

I expected trouble on the way to the airport. I expected trouble when we boarded the plane. It wasn't really until we were in the air at cruising altitude that I felt like maybe we'd avoided disaster. Grace and I leaned back in our first-class seats and sipped our first-class wine, and I tried to calm the feeling of impending disaster in my chest.

Beside me, Grace tapped on her tablet, reading papers on immunology, physiology, and other -ologies. It wasn't that I couldn't learn to understand them. It was just that I knew my role in life. Grace would never be able to cut the artery of a monster in one swipe while blinding another and killing a third. I didn't mind.

Under the seat in front of me rested the urn with my mother's ashes.

When we touched down, I stood armed and waiting for an attack that never came while Grace got the rental car.

She pulled up, and I tossed our equipment in the rear. "Head to the Bentonville cemetery," I said, sliding into the passenger-side seat.

Grace drove like a snail. We were being passed by stationary objects. Then she looked over with that "Brynner, it's time we talked" look.

"Don't tell me our relationship won't work. We barely have one." I took her hand. "Please."

She rolled her eyes. "I was going to tell you why Amy didn't come. Director Bismuth asked her to stay in Seattle and guard Ra-Ame's heart."

I'd have said I was shocked, but nothing that woman did surprised me anymore. "Bismuth is lying." Then again, maybe she'd known the location all along or had it in her possession. "She told me she'd use it as bait if the BSI had it."

Grace stared out the window, lost in thought. "If they knew where it was, why send me to translate Heinrich's journals?"

"They didn't. I'm certain I know where it is. Absolutely certain." And I was. The only question in my mind was why I didn't realize it sooner.

We pulled up at the Bentonville Funeral Home, and I got out, with Grace at my side.

She grabbed my arm. "You want to tell me what you're doing?"

"I'm keeping us from getting shot." I knocked on the door and waited.

When Mr. Parker answered, he looked at me with awe. "I saw you on the news."

"We recovered my mom's body. I thought this time I'd ask for help." I held out the box with her ashes.

Mr. Parker went inside and came out with his hat on. "Go on up and wait. I'll bring the backhoe. Which one are we digging up?"

"Both."

We drove to the cemetery entrance and walked the rolling hills. I looked over to Grace, who waited patiently. "The last time I saw Dad, I was still angry with him. He wanted me to come to Mom's grave and talk. He said he needed to tell me things.

"And I told him that Mom wasn't there. That he wasn't there. Mom was dead and he might as well be. He just carried that goddamned jar with him everywhere."

We crossed the stream that ran from the top of Dad's tomb. "I snuck out and stole Mr. Parker's backhoe. Dug up the coffin and threw it open. I just wanted to make him admit she wasn't there. That standing and talking to a headstone didn't help."

Grace put her hand on my back. "And the heart was in her coffin?"

"No. It was empty. I called Dad and he drove to the cemetery. I made him look. The next morning I went out to the highway and caught a ride. Hitchhiked to New York and caught a boat to Europe, where the BSI let me float as a remote operative."

She knelt at Dad's grave, tracing the stone. "And you never came home to avoid charges."

"There were no charges. Dad buried the coffin with Mr. Parker's help. Sheriff Bishop made sure the report just listed 'vandals.' They never told anyone else what happened. And I didn't come home when Dad got sick. Or when he died."

I stood before Dad's headstone. "I finally understand. It

was all he had left of her. That's why he held on to it. It's why it was the only thing he wrote about."

Grace shook her head. "I've read all the journals. He only mentioned the heart twice."

I'd snuck his journal more times than I could count on the rare holidays when he came to visit. And I knew enough hieroglyphics to recognize my own name, Son of Me. "So what did he write about?"

"You. He kept track of your assignments. Your injuries. Your commendations. I think he worried about you constantly."

The diesel engine of a backhoe signaled Mr. Parker's arrival, rolling up the road and over to Dad's grave. He killed the engine and shouted, "You sure this is safe?"

I nodded. "Mostly. You pull the coffin out, I'll take it from there."

Grace stood with me, keeping watch over open plains as Mr. Parker worked. In time, he stopped using the large bucket and switched to a hooked harness. The harness clinked as he locked it onto the coffin. With gentle care, he raised the hoe arm, lifting out Dad's coffin, setting it in the grass. Mr. Parker leaped from the backhoe and scrambled down the hill as fast as he could hobble.

Grace watched him leave. "Where is he going?"

"Same place you are. Get moving. Dad's ashes are in the coffin."

She paused. "I read his report. He wasn't processed or cremated."

"Not in the traditional way, no. Dad figured the meat-skins would want to come after him." I laughed, remembering his wild eyes as he made plans. "Those locks will only open under full sunlight. His ashes are in the coffin, along with six hundred pounds of plastic explosives, rigged to go off when the lid opens. Dad figured if a Re-Animus dug him up to get at the body, he'd pay for it."

Grace ran down the hill.

I knelt by Dad's coffin, finding the trigger locks that would disarm the counter, and pressing each three times.

Holding my breath, I threw the lid open.

Inside, packed in a mound of gray and wires nestled a box like the one I'd brought from Seattle. Grace came back up the hill, and I took the other box from her.

She waited as I walked, mixing handfuls of each together, and spreading them across half a mile of the desert my mom had loved so much.

Now they were part of it for eternity.

By the time I came back, Mr. Parker had uncovered Mom's coffin as well. With the desert sun streaming down, I forced the lid open. Nestled in the white lining lay a silver urn, wide as a bowling pin, with the mask of Horus on top.

"Here." I picked it up and handed it to Grace. "The heart of Ra-Ame."

GRACE

Her heart. Not some legend. Not a myth. The actual heart of Ra-Ame lay in my hands. And beneath my fingertips, it shifted, as though a rat scurried inside. "Brynner! Is it supposed to move?"

He nodded. "It does that. Try sleeping with it under your pillow sometime."

"I don't like your version of the tooth fairy."

"Really?" Brynner smiled at me. "The tooth fairy always left me high-caliber ammo. I loved losing teeth." He shut Heinrich's coffin and turned to Mr. Parker. "I removed the detonators. There's no reason to keep them anymore. You can turn off the stream, too."

"I'll see that things are set right here. I was right worried about you when I heard about Seattle." Mr. Parker got up in the seat of the backhoe and started the engine.

Brynner stopped. "What about Seattle?"

He killed the engine, frowning. "The BSI building in Seattle collapsed. An hour and a half before you got here. I thought you knew."

It must have been right after we touched down.

I hit the network connect on my tablet and logged in to the secure net. "The buildings. The labs."

Brynner looked over my shoulder at the news feed of smoking rubble. "Amy. I hope she got out." He whipped out his cell phone, dialing. It rang over and over, clicked and rang again. "This is Brynner Carson. Put me through to whoever's in charge."

The phone buzzed, a woman's voice speaking.

He shook his head. "Security code is Radio Glow Orange. I'm not dead."

Why did they think he was?

He pressed the speakerphone, holding a finger to his lips while looking at me.

The phone beeped, then a robotic voice spoke. "Attending: Brynner Carson, BSI field operative."

An equally robotic voice answered. "Carson, you son of a bitch, you alive?"

"Pays to work remote, Dale. What happened?"

A keyboard clicked in the background. "BSI headquarters

went down in dust. The director made it out with a handful of the staff."

Brynner looked down at the ground. "We had a Grave Services operative in the building. Amy Rust. Egyption, tall, brown, beautiful."

"Did you sleep with her?"

Brynner almost threw the phone into the dirt. "Goddamn it, did she make it out?"

After a moment, Dale answered. "That means no. I'm checking survivor registries." A computer chirped and whirred. "We only have BSI personnel on the registry. I'll check with Grave Services and see if she's reported in. HQ is gone, Carson, and it was Ra-Ame. The queen of them all."

I snatched the phone, practically shouting, "What does she look like?"

"Furry." The keyboard clicked furiously. "Fuzzy. Damn autocorrect. Cameras all crapped themselves near her, but she's a woman. When she knocked out the west support column, you can see the outline of her tits. Sending video and stills now."

"Send them to Grace," said Brynner.

When the pictures clicked up on my tablet, I thumbed through them. Both his assertions were correct. The camera stills had vertical lines, like they'd been hit by an EMP. And the outline was definitely feminine. I clicked over to the video.

Taken by the security cameras, it showed a line of operatives with gas pressure washers. Their pulsing jets converged on a moving figure who stood rock-still in the middle of the room. The operatives advanced, keeping her pinned.

The mist obscured what happened next, but a man's body came flying and knocked the camera off-kilter, pointing it to the floor. What it did capture was the torn corpses that flew past, rolling on the carpet.

Brynner looked away, keeping his eyes off the tablet. "How'd she pass the wards?"

Dale gasped for breath several times, then answered. "If you believe the reports, she entered the building on the twentieth floor and headed straight for the director's office. We've got incoming reports on co-org activity from everywhere. People are shitting themselves." From the other end, the keyboard clicked once more. "I'm going to drop off and engage with field units that will listen to what I tell them."

Brynner took the phone from me. "I've got the heart. For real. I'm going to try to negotiate a return."

"You found it." The sound from the phone was like an army of rabbits gnawing through a plastic plate, which I guessed passed for laughter. "You've got to be kidding, you son of a bitch. Way to go. Should I tell Director Bismuth when we establish contact?"

I cut in over him. "No. This is her fault from the ground up. We're going to try to find a way to communicate with Ra-Ame. Meet her some place out here, make the trade."

Brynner mouthed, "We are?"

I nodded.

"You're the chick who saved Brynner's ass in the hotel?"

I laughed at Brynner's pained expression. "I'm the woman who's going to save yours. Don't get dead, ass hat."

I clicked the phone off and took my own, ignoring Brynner's questioning gaze. "I spent weeks with Amy."

"Me too." He crossed his arms, waiting.

"Not as her roommate." I waved the phone. "I have her number."

I dialed the number, waiting. If Amy lay crushed in the rubble of the BSI building, I'd never hear her voice. Again and again it rang. And then cut off.

"She's not—"

The phone rang. "Amy?"

Through the static and fuzz, she spoke. "Grace Roberts, for the sake of everyone, tell me you found the heart."

Brynner leaned over. "What if we say no?"

"Tell Brynner Carson that if the answer is no, everyone will die."

39

BRYNNER

Everyone would die. A scenario I usually worked to avoid. The jar in Grace's hands might be the key to escaping, though a nagging worry at the back of my mind said it might not include me. No matter. "I've got it. Grace is holding the jar right now, and we're going to try to contact Ra-Ame to arrange an exchange."

"Any ideas on how to do that?" asked Grace.

"Grace Roberts, is this phone encrypted?" Amy's tone made the hair on my skin stand up.

"No." Grace closed her eyes and leaned her head back, her fist clenched.

"You would be safe to assume she either knows already, or will within minutes. The old ones have ears to spare. Do not let the jar from your sight, Brynner Carson. I will join you as soon as possible." Amy muttered in Arabic, a curse, judging from the tone.

I didn't want to know, but I also had to ask. "Did you see Ra-Ame?"

"I have looked upon her."

"And survived? How?" Grace couldn't hide the shock in her voice.

Amy chuffed like a cat. "Only a fool stands against Ra-Ame."

"That's a polite way of saying she ran," I added. "You know, you are better than me at everything. Including running away. And I'm glad. We've got one more day until the deadline."

"I will be there as soon as possible. Wait for me. If you have truly spoken with the pharaoh's daughter, and Ra-Ame knows you hold her heart, she will forbid the other old ones to interfere. Perhaps we can still reach an agreement." Amy hung up the phone without saying another word.

Grace sat down on the grass next to the backhoe. "She doesn't exactly have the world's sunniest disposition."

"I'm not sure there's anything to be cheery about. You saw the footage. She took out a support column with her hands." I closed my eyes, trying to imagine Dad speaking. What would he do? Even if I knew, could I do what he would?

Dad would know just because of who he was. I stood and took Grace's hand, helping her up. "Come on." We walked back to the car and basked in the cold of the air conditioner. "We have two days."

"One. A day begins on the evening of the day before, in the old way of counting. One day. At evening tomorrow, she'll come for the heart."

I put the car in gear and drove. "If we're going to die, I'm going to die happy. Grace Roberts, have you ever had *cabrito*?"

She mouthed the word. "Goat little?"

"Young. Steamed in a fire pit. I know exactly how I want to spend the last night of my life." I smiled at her, because it was true.

She laughed. "A cheap motel and hours of passionate sex?"

"Me?" I said with mock offense. "No. I'm going to take you out on your dream date. A proper date. A perfect date. With no one to tell you they went to high school with me. No waitresses I slept with. Just you and me, pretending that we're not facing the mother of the undead."

"Why don't we just settle for a nice dinner someplace quiet—"

I held up my hand. "I said perfect. I have a long history of perfect first dates."

Grace wiped her bangs out her eyes. "You're cocky, you know that?"

"Confidence. Well-earned confidence. I never have anything but perfect dates."

Grace frowned at me. "In that case, you are already doing it wrong. Start over." Grace crossed her arms and waited. "Well? Are you going to ask?"

"I just did."

"No, you told me what you wanted to do. You didn't ask me what I wanted to do." She nodded. "Go on."

Squelching the aggravation inside me, I summoned my most charming tone. "Grace Roberts, would your perfect date be eating dinner at an authentic goat roast with me?"

She grinned like a little girl. "No. Not at all."

"What?" I swerved, nearly hitting a car, then pulled over. "You weren't supposed to say *no*."

Grace batted blue eyes at me. "You asked. Ask again."

"Grace—"

"Do the voice!" She didn't even bother trying to hide her glee.

Fine. Forcing myself to smile like a man-eating skeleton, I looked up at her. "Grace Roberts, what would you like to do tonight?"

She thought for a moment. "I want to ride on a boat."

Every word that came to mind, I could write in hieroglyphics. "We're in the middle of the desert."

"You asked."

Not that it had ever occurred to me she might say no. "What are you doing? I thought you were just going to say 'a nice dinner' or something."

"This is payback. For all the women you sweet-talked with a line or batted those eyes or flexed one of your gorgeous pecs at, and they just melted into your bed. Sweet, sweet payback." She put her head back on her seat, giggling. "Just admit that not even the legendary Brynner Carson can fix everything, and we can go eat Bambi."

"Bambi," I said through gritted teeth, "was a deer. Which are also tasty." Fine. She wanted a boat ride in the middle of the desert? I'd give her one.

We drove nearly two hours to the reservoir, stopping only for Grace to grab a change of clothes in a department store, while I ran to a bank to withdraw money. It turns out "I'd like to rent your boat for the night, here's thirty thousand dollars" will get you a nice boat, a cabin cruiser with bunks for eight. Such a ship belonged on the sea.

Once I'd gotten us pushed out from the dock, onto the lake, Grace tapped me on the shoulder. "You forgot to ask about dinner."

"Come again?" I hadn't forgotten. I just didn't eat on boats because if I ate dinner, I'd lose my dinner.

She stood up on tiptoes and whispered in my ear, "I want cannelloni. On the boat."

I just about pulled my hair out. "Couldn't you have told me that before we got in the water?"

"You didn't ask. This is for every woman you ever ordered for without letting her check the menu." Grace patted me on the back and took a seat in her deck chair. She'd changed into a sleeveless top and white shorts, with a wide brim straw hat.

"Those women *liked* what I ordered them. I never had one complaint, ever." Finding an Italian place where I could bribe the delivery guy to meet me at the dock took another hour and a half. As I finished the order, a terrible fear came over me. "Grace."

She took off her sun hat and turned to look. "Yes?"

"What kind of wine do you like?"

Her mouth dropped open in a perfect O. "Chardonnay, please. You're learning."

I was. And I wasn't done yet. "Grace."

When she twisted those sleek white shoulders to look at me, I seriously considered tossing her off the boat, innocent look and all. "Yes?"

"Dessert?"

She put a hand to her chin, thinking. "Cheesecake, please. With chocolate drizzle."

Never let it be said a Carson couldn't learn his lesson.

She ate on the deck, then we cruised the reservoir for hours so Grace could lean out at the bow and feel the wind on her face. When the moon rose, I dragged a couple of mattresses up on deck to lie on and look at the stars.

And I wondered how I'd missed this in life. Why I only found this here, now. But at least it was real. After midnight, I rose and went downstairs to get a blanket for Grace. When I turned from the bed, she was standing on the stairs. "You forgot something."

I sighed, counting the steps to the deck. Yeah, I could carry her up and toss her in the water in ten seconds flat. The Virgin Mary herself wouldn't blame me at that point. In fact, she might give me a hand with Grace's feet. "What is it? Just tell me."

She stepped down the last step and pressed her body close. "Make love to me."

"But—"

She covered my lips with hers, then took a breath. "Less talk. More sex."

I dropped the blanket I'd been holding, folded my arms around her, one hand at the base of her back, the other caressing the line of her chin, and kissed her.

One kiss, or many, it began and ended, stopped and started in between breaths, until Grace turned her head, and tickled my earlobe with her tongue. She held on to my hips, keeping me close enough to feel each shift of her body as she rocked against me.

I buried my nose in her hair, breathing in the scent of sweat and perfume, deodorant and desire, and cautiously placed a hand on her breast, rubbing the side swell from the top of her shoulder and circling her nipple.

And she shuddered, her body going rigid against me for just a moment. And then her hand slipped lower, tugging at my pants until the zipper came loose. The urge to press against her overwhelmed me, as she slipped her hands against my skin, cold fingers grasping me.

"Careful," I gasped, but she didn't back off, kissing the sides of my mouth, pressing against my shoulders.

With both hands, I ran my thumbs down the center of her back, pushing gently into her muscles, massaging her so with each pass of my hand, she pushed against me. And she let go, pulling up her shirt, wriggling so my hands slipped into her pants.

I knelt, drawing down her pants, and then tracing a line up from the ball of her foot to the inside of her thigh while she stripped off her bra.

Her breasts, plump, with dark nipples, hung free, and I rose to kiss each, stepping out of my pants, and tripping as I hopped out of my underwear.

Grace caught me, or grabbed me and fell, landing on top of me. Her palms pressed me down as she rocked back and forth until my hips ached with desire, and her name was the only word I could summon to ask.

She answered, settling onto me, her back arching up, and away as she moved, each motion a burst of pleasure. And I slipped a hand between us, massaging her until her breath came in ragged gasps, and she jerked, shuddering, and cried out, neither name nor word. Only pleasure.

Grace pulled me over, her skin slick with sweat. She moaned softly as I moved, faster and faster, her hands pulling me against her until at last I came, a wave of pleasure wracking me.

She held me close until eventually I fell away, rolling off her to lie spent on the covers. I shivered and steamed simultaneously, unable to move until moments faded into minutes.

I drowsed, resting against her, but when I opened my eyes, Grace lay propped up on one elbow, looking down at me. Her nipples, now soft, barely protruded from her breast, but the way her hand lay on my hip, claiming me, made me desire her once more.

Grace smiled at me. "What are you thinking about?"

"I was thinking how beautiful you are." I leaned up and kissed her. "You?"

She moved her hand ever so slightly, stroking my thigh. "I was just wondering why Ra-Ame didn't summon her army and raze everything. Why she wouldn't just send them to get the heart."

She read the shock on my face and added, "Also, I was thinking about how amazing that was."

I knew Grace. She'd been honest the first time. "Sure you were. You were thinking about how to fight her. How to kill her."

"Well," she said, leaning down to kiss me again, "make me think of something else."

And I did.

40

GRACE

I woke before Brynner, going for a swim to wash myself clean. He deserved sleep; I'd kept him occupied until he nearly collapsed from exhaustion. And at least some of his bravado was well deserved. If only I'd been less obstinate, I could have enjoyed that so much sooner.

But what woke me was the very thing I accidentally told Brynner. And to be fair, "that was amazing" did cross my mind, once I reached the point of being able to think at all. But what crossed my mind almost immediately afterward was that heart.

If Ra-Ame had an army of creatures capable of destroying most of the world, why not just destroy the world and spend the rest of eternity scouring the rock for her heart? Why the insistence that we hand it over? And by the time I climbed back up on the boat, I had the beginnings of an answer.

"Grace?" Brynner called to me from inside.

I walked down the stairs, reveling in how his gaze raked my body. He couldn't possibly—

"You look beautiful." Brynner rose, stretching. White lines crisscrossed his body, scars on scars everywhere.

I slipped on my panties and walked over to run my fingers over the scars carved like Chinese characters into his skin. "What happened to you?"

"It's the Carson way. Dad always taught me not to run. Deal with the meat-skins up close and personal." He picked up his belt and the dagger sheaths. "Carsons don't use guns."

There was no easy way to go about this. "We can't give Ra-Ame the heart."

Brynner nodded and went back to getting dressed.

"Aren't you the least bit curious why?"

He pulled on a shirt, stretching it across his chest, and shook his head. "Grace, you're, like, I don't know, fifty times smarter than I am. You tell me giving back the heart is a bad idea, I'll buy it. My gut says if Dad knew what we were up against, he'd destroy it first, negotiate later."

"This isn't based on a gut feeling." I didn't do gut feelings.

He nodded. "Of course not. And I trust you."

Which aggravated me. I'd thought all night about possible scenarios and reasons and kept coming back to one real likelihood. "She hasn't summoned her armies because she *can't*. Think about it—why didn't she bring them to kill your dad and take it? The heart, I think it's the key to her reclaiming all her power. You give it to her, and she'll have the ability to call them."

"And if I don't?" He looked at me. "You saw what happened to the headquarters. How am I supposed to kill something capable of that?"

I didn't like this Brynner. His best asset was unshakable confidence in his own abilities. Confidence we'd so desperately need to pull this off. I slipped up next to him, wrapping one hand around a knife handle and pulling it from the sheath. "These." I turned them over again and again. "They were driven through her skin, Amy told me. So she's not invulnerable to them. They kept her so injured she couldn't move, until your mom took two out."

He gazed down at me, his eyes locked on either the knife or my breasts, then nodded. "Call Amy. I'm going to drive out as far into the desert as possible. If Ra-Ame wants the heart, she can come get it from me there, where there are fewer people to get hurt."

"To get it from *us* there." I put one hand over his. "Us."

"Grace—"

I pushed him backward, slapping his chest. "Don't. Don't you even think about some speech about how it's okay for you to die and me to live. You and your hero complex. You are not Heinrich Carson or Jesus Christ. You don't have to die for everything to turn out right."

If I'd slapped his face, I couldn't have hit him harder. And if it saved his life, I'd do it again. "You need the heart, but only so you can draw her to you. And when she comes, I'll be with you. Waiting. You might need me to rescue you."

My phone rang. I read the number off the display, and answered. "Amy, where are you?"

"Grace Roberts, that is the question I would ask you. I am sorry it took me so long."

"Are you talking and driving? We've got a plan—we're heading into the desert to make the exchange. If Ra-Ame wants the heart, she'll come and get it there."

"I do not think a change of location will matter, but I will be with you until the end."

I relayed the directions Brynner gave me, while he fired up the boat and motored back to the dock. And then we headed into town, collecting water bottles, a sun shelter, and enough equipment to fill the backseat.

The last stop we made was at the closest BSI outpost. When Brynner strode into the hall, decked in his BSI uniform, the local field commander just about choked. "Sir!" He rose, saluting Brynner.

"I need to find a shambler, and I need it soon. Do you have any reports?" Brynner leaned over the desk, dwarfing the saluting men.

"Sir, I'm sorry, but we used saltwater pressure washers on a band last night. You could sort through what's left." He turned to me. "You need a sample for tests, ma'am?"

I nodded. "New communication system."

We followed him out to a pickup truck, where dozens of corpses lay waiting to be burnt. He pointed to them. "Some of them were still blinking last night."

Brynner climbed into the truck and began rolling over bodies. At last, he grabbed one by the legs and dragged it out. He knelt over it, staring into the dead face. "Ra-Ame, can you hear me?"

Seconds ticked by with no response, until Brynner rose. "Let me get another."

"No." I pointed to the co-org, whose vacant eyes now stared at Brynner. Its mouth moved, but no voice came. The lips moved again, and I gave voice to the words. "I can see you, Death that Follows."

Brynner nodded and rummaged in the back of the truck.

"Good." Then he drew out a fire ax and came back. He put one foot on the shambler's chest and hefted the ax. "Time to make you more portable."

BRYNNER

I made it quick, but not quick enough for Grace. I'm glad we hadn't eaten breakfast yet. And when I brought the head back to the car, she made that "You aren't going to put that in the car with me" face. Which I'd never seen before but had no problem recognizing.

"No?" I held it up like Medusa's head.

"No."

So I tied it to the grill of the car, where it made one hell of a hood ornament. And we drove, following a route roughly similar to what I'd told Amy. Mostly. Truth was, I didn't really know where I was going, only that it had to be farther away. If a turn looked emptier, more desolate, I took it.

Until at last we hit a dead end.

I got out and looked around. "There." A rocky outcropping rose from the desert. "We'll be able to see her coming from ten miles away."

Grace nodded, collecting the bag with the heart, heading to the outcropping.

After we'd set up the tent shelter, and the water jugs, I took out three lawn chairs and dragged them to the top of the hill. "You want to sit and talk, keep your feet up." I pointed to the ground. "Brown scorpions everywhere. They don't bother most folks, but I'd hate for you to miss the fun."

Grace yanked her feet up, wrapping her arms around her knees and staring at the ground. "Got it." She didn't sound like a woman facing her death. "I never dreamed it would come to this."

"I'm glad you're with me." Most people didn't dream that the most ancient of an evil race would be meeting them in the desert. I'd had that dream a couple of times in the last few days. I stripped down, taking out my new armor, the bag Grace grabbed from the armory back at headquarters. Unlike my old armor, this fit me like a glove, ventilated so I didn't roast, with woven Kevlar mesh almost everywhere. "You like?"

"I love." She rose, looking at the lines. Then frowned. "What about here?" She tickled me under the arm.

I squirmed under her touch. "There and the back of the knees. I have to be able to bend. Now for the finishing touches." I took out the last part of my ensemble. Actually, my father's ensemble. A BSI gray trench coat he'd worn year-round.

"Dad kept this thing stocked with more weapons than the whole armory." I shook it out and slipped it on. "How do I look?"

Grace's lip puckered under. "You look great." She unzipped her equipment bag and dumped it out. "You'd look even better with a couple of these." Deliverators lay in a heap at my feat, along with a pile of spare magazines. "And these." She kicked a crossbow toward me.

"I'll leave those to you. I like things that cut. It's how I was raised. How I learned."

She ran one hand down my chest. "You can learn new ways. I taught you last night."

Oh, had she ever. So very well, but this was different. I slipped the jar into one of the inner pockets, then studied the array of additional blades. "What do you think? Those are better for blocking, but honestly, if she hits me, I'm probably dead." While I waited for Grace to decide, I put relics from every single religion Dad visited into different pockets. I'd jingle like a street pimp but had to be ready for anything. Ancient Sumerian or Rastafarian, I had it all.

"I don't think so. Again, if Ra-Ame could knock down buildings all the time, she'd be doing it."

I strung a Russian orthodox cross around my neck and slipped it in between the armor. Dad said the cross had saved him on a number of occasions, and I could use every ounce of help possible.

At last, I sat down in my chair and leaned back to doze in the heat.

"How can you do that?"

I patted the back of the chair. "There's a lever here. It lets me lean back."

Grace sighed. "No. How can you be so relaxed? Don't you know what's about to happen?"

I sat up, the chair creaking under my weight. "Grace, do you know why you were born? Do you know why you exist? I do. I don't know what my dad did to whatever god he did it to, but this is what he was born for. What I was born to do."

"I'm sorry, I just don't believe that." She scooted her chair closer. "Let's say we succeed. What then? If this is all you live for, what happens when Ra-Ame is gone? When the Re-Animus can be killed by anyone with the right weapons?"

I closed my eyes, searching for an answer I'd never given a moment's thought. "I don't know. But I do know someone who is scary smart. I might ask her for help finding something else to do." I opened my eyes, and she'd cracked a wry grin. "My purpose is to kill Ra-Ame."

She put her hand in mine. "Are you scared?"

"Terrified. Not of dying. Amy's right. Everyone dies at some point. I'm terrified of failing. Truth is, I don't know what Dad would have done. We never talked about this."

Grace squeezed my fingers. "There's more to you than your dad. Last night, I called the Ministry of Death, Grave Services, anyone who would listen and explained everything. Mailed half a dozen copies of my files. And left a message thanking them for Amy's help. We'd be dead without her. I asked them to send her a commendation."

I imagined Amy giving a dour expression as she received her medal, or shrugging. "I'd pay to see that." I must have dozed, because when I looked up, the sun hung straight overhead.

A car engine rumbled in the distance, while Grace shook me. "She's here."

GRACE

Amy's car came flying along the road, a white rental coupe with both windows down. She skidded to a halt beside our car and got out, dressed like a tourist. She wore bangle bracelets and a tank top that showed her curves without straining to hold them, and brown khaki shorts.

She jogged up the path to the rocks, kicking off her sandals to stand in the bare dirt. "Am I too late?"

Brynner nodded. "She came a few minutes ago. Just missed her." He offered her a hand, and she stepped away, giving me a hug.

"You are a funny dead man, Brynner Carson."

"That's the Amy I know and love. We sort of gave Ra-Ame a homing beacon." He pointed to the head on our car. "If it's noon, she'll be here any minute."

Amy surveyed the desert, holding her hand over her eyes. "She may already be watching. You do not know the eldest of the old ones, or what she can do."

I looked to Brynner, and he nodded in agreement. "We're not going to hand over the heart."

Amy looked up in alarm. "You stand no chance. Did you not see what happened in Seattle?"

"I saw." I took her arm, guiding her to the shelter. "But I have a theory." I explained what I thought about Ra-Ame's army. About her abilities. And finally, about the heart. "So, I'm guessing the worst thing on earth would be for her to get it. I don't know what she can do with it that she can't without it, but I'm not going to find out."

Amy took her chair and imitated Brynner, leaning back. "So many theories, Grace Roberts. And you know you will die if you are wrong?"

"I know I'm going to die either way. What I don't know is when exactly she's going to bless us with her appearance."

Amy laughed, a deep laugh from the bottom of her belly. "If the legends are true, you will know."

The clock ticked closer and closer to noon, and Brynner began to pace. Finally, he came over. "I have to—umm—use the little boys' room, and I think I'm going to grab a bigger knife, just in case. Keep an eye out. Shout if you see anything."

"Don't sit on a cactus." I sat up and looked out across the desert.

Amy waved her hat after he left. "That man stinks of sex. Did he satisfy you, or should I cut off his testicles?"

Which explained exactly why Amy was still single. "I'd like them left attached. And no comment, but I'd like to think the satisfaction was mutual." I sat in the chair beside her, taking Brynner's spot. "Why are you here?"

"They say Ra-Ame was beautiful. Perhaps I want to see for myself. But many things are said of her. Willing sacrifice. Who is willing to die? We will know the truth soon enough."

I looked down the hill after Brynner but kept my mouth shut. Too willing. "You want a gun? I offered one to Brynner, for all the good it did. I figure Ra-Ame's vulnerable, or she would have torn through the firing line in Seattle just to make a point."

Amy patted her knives in response. "Why are you here?"

"Because of Brynner. And my daughter."

Amy's mouth fell open. "You have a child? I did not know."

"She's in a care home. It's hard to explain." It was easy to explain Esther's condition. What was hard was explaining my inability to face the truth. "She's . . . sick."

"Your daughter was well hidden, if even the old ones did not know or suspect."

My phone beeped. And again. And then again. I walked over and unlocked it, reading the messages.

"What is it, Grace Roberts?" Amy crossed her arms, one eyebrow raised.

I turned away. "Re-Animus attack in Chicago. Hundreds dead."

I spun, lunging for the pile of guns, and went flying, crashing through the chairs, landing in the dirt. Behind me, Amy stood, kicking the guns away. She chuckled to herself. "Grace Roberts, what is wrong?"

"I called Grave Services last night. Told them what a great

teammate Amy Rust was. How much we liked her. How much I owed her." I rose, wincing from the sharp pain in my ribs, and tossed her the phone, with the message that had just come in still on-screen. "There is no Amy Rust. And I should have realized before, *Ame*. Ra-Ame."

Amy nodded her head. "Always with the theories. But this one, this one is right."

"You showed up right after we captured the spawn. The Re-Animus said he crept into your tomb and woke you. That he whispered my name. And you knew my name before I told you." I shuffled around the sun shade, looking for a weapon.

"You are special, Grace Roberts. Your eyes see the fifth sign. The paths of the dead are open to you. And your mind, it sees our weaknesses. So though I have come to reclaim my heart, I will offer you a different choice." She took out one of her curved blades, slicing away the bangles on her wrist, to show ancient wounds.

"I died, Grace Roberts, but here we are. And you, too, may join me. Did you not say you would die? I will give you a piece of myself, and you will remain. I will keep you safe while you grow strong. You know the new ways."

She had to be kidding. "There is no way that will ever happen."

"That is always your decision. Perhaps when the Death that Follows is gone, you will feel different. Perhaps if we visited your daughter, you would feel different. I could speak through her, if you wish."

Blinded by rage, I leaped at her, winding up in the dirt again. And inches from my face, a scorpion crawled. I scrambled away from it, backing into Ra-Ame.

"What is this, Grace Roberts? Why does your heart pound?" She walked past, hips swaying, and picked up the scorpion.

"Where I was raised these were pets and food. That was so long ago." She tossed it away into the brush.

Ra-Ame reached over and touched my cheek, making me shiver. "I have never lied to you, Grace Roberts. I told you I came to see that man for myself. And I meant in my heart to kill him that first night. But I met someone. A woman my equal. I had forgotten, through the ages, what it meant to laugh and discuss."

My hands trembled as I spoke. "Let Brynner go, and take me. I'll cooperate if you do." I bowed my head before her.

"You would not believe me, Grace Roberts, but I have consulted many oracles in the last year, heard many prophecies. I must possess the heart of a Carson to survive another age." Ra-Ame spun a knife on the tips of her fingers.

"There are no oracles."

"I said you would not believe. For a time, I thought it meant I must have his body. But prophecies are like the old language. There are many ways to read them. I will do both. I will tear his heart from his chest, and still keep it safe for the ages."

"Then you'll fail. You can't have both." Her insanity exceeded words.

Ra-Ame grinned at me. "I believe I can, Grace Roberts." She whistled. "Brynner Carson. Ra-Ame is here."

He came crashing through the brush, pulling his trench coat around him and looking around like a wild animal hunting prey. His eyes met mine, and he reached into his trench coat.

In a blur I couldn't see as much as feel, Ra-Ame pointed a Deliverator at me. "Do not move, Death that Follows. Obey my instructions, and only you will die here. Disobey, and I will kill her, then you."

I shook my head. That wasn't going to be part of the plan.

She waved the gun in my direction. "First, give my heart to Grace Roberts."

Brynner drew it out of the trench coat and tossed it underhand to me. The jar clinked as I caught it, then shifted as the heart moved.

Ra-Ame stepped between Brynner and me. "And now the blades. Be careful or I will carve off her lovely nose."

He pulled two blades from his belt and threw them into the sand, a hairbreadth from her toes.

"Kneel before me, Death that Follows." She looked back to me. "Open the jar, Grace Roberts. Give me my heart. Do not fear, the sun will not harm it."

I knelt in the sand and pried the lid open. Though I couldn't remove the top, from inside, a musty odor like burnt mushroom wafted.

Ra-Ame hefted the Deliverator. "Guns. These are no weapons for a warrior." She threw the Deliverator into the brush and drew her blades. "You thought to harm me, Brynner Carson. To wage war against me and my children. But you are not fit. You move like an ox. You have no skill. And now you will die in the desert, just as I told you."

Brynner rose. "If I'm going to die, I'm going out fighting." He raised his head, reaching back inside the trench coat.

Four knives. I'd brought him four.

Ra-Ame laughed and curled her fingers in, beckoning to him. "You are worthless, lesser Carson. Your father, I would have killed from a distance. A man of skill. A warrior my equal. He would have recognized me so long ago. You are not your father."

Brynner hung his head, struck by her words. "So everyone

keeps telling me." He drew out his hands, holding twin Deliverators. And shot her twice. "Dad would have insisted on knives." He followed up, putting a bullet through one eye. "Dad would have gone toe to toe with you."

He fired again, blasting into her kneecaps, and then over and over until both guns ran dry. "I'm not my father."

Then he reached into his jacket and withdrew a single blade.

Ra-Ame collapsed forward, her limbs moving weakly, but the holes in her did not bleed.

As he knelt to drive it through her skull, Ra-Ame convulsed. The brown skin covering her boiled like water, peeling off. Beneath it lay a ghostly, pallid carapace. She rolled, dodging his killing blow, and leaped for me.

Blind, white eyes stared at me as she came, screaming.

I ran.

I sprinted for the rocks we'd camped by, still pulling at the jar.

The moment the lid came off, a bulbous, wet mass pushed itself out onto the sand.

Brynner tackled Ra-Ame from behind, buying me precious seconds.

The heart unfolded, moving and oozing from side to side. It writhed in the sun like a monstrous black maggot or a tiny infant, letting out a high-pitched squeal.

Ra-Ame's head jerked up at that sound, her face contorted in rage. With a kick like a draft horse, she sent Brynner flying and charged toward me. I swung the jar like a club, hitting her in the head, causing the jar to rattle. Rattle?

Brynner tackled her, rolling in a pile of flailing blades. He shouted without looking at me, "Kill the heart, Grace."

I turned over the jar, and a dagger slipped out into my palm.

Four daggers. Two in the sand. One his hand . . . and one in mine.

I flipped it over and drove it down through the heart.

It lurched to the side and lashed a slimy tentacle up at me, wrapping around my wrist. It twisted, revealing a parrot-like beak underneath, with razor edges, and let out a new squeal. Not terror. Rage.

In the blink of an eye it was on me, clicking its jaws as it forced itself toward my throat. I fell backward, blocking its bite with my arm. The beak sank into my arm, sending a river of pain through me.

Before me, Ra-Ame and Brynner faced off.

If before Brynner and Ra-Ame fought like a mongoose and snake, now it was like watching a shadow fight with the light, or bolts of lightning entwined.

Ra-Ame twisted, spun, leaped. And her blades returned to her, dripping with Brynner's blood from half a dozen slices. Brynner stepped back, red stains spreading through cuts in the trench coat.

When Ra-Ame spoke, her voice rattled like bones in a coffin. "Run away, lesser Carson. You do not know the art of movement."

"No." Brynner slipped the tattered trench coat off and tossed it on the ground. "Al-ibna Al-habeeba." His pronunciation of her name matched hers perfectly.

Ra-Ame hissed, "I did not know you spoke that language."

"There's a lot of things you don't know about me. Dad taught me the secret to killing a Re-Animus." Brynner shifted from side to side, like a boxer in the ring.

The laugh, if I could call it that, that came from Ra-Ame's throat would haunt my dreams for years. "I heard. You must not care if you live or die. You do not look like a man who doesn't care, Death that Follows."

"You want to know a secret? Dad was *wrong*. The secret isn't not caring about yourself." He danced backward, just out of range, as she flicked her blades out toward him. Brynner shook his head. "The secret is finding what or who you'd die for." If I'd blinked, I would have missed his movement. Surging forward like a sandstorm, he leaped on her. They bent and turned, twisting, blades flashing in the desert sun. Faster than I could move, faster than I could think.

I'd never seen a man fight that way. Wouldn't have believed it possible, if it weren't for my own eyes, for the human body to move with such precision or skill. And the mesmerizing dance of blades nearly cost me my life. Ra-Ame's heart had lashed out with a tentacle, drawing itself toward my throat.

I forced the dagger between us, letting the heart impale itself. It squealed again, recoiling, and dropped to the ground.

For one second, Ra-Ame looked away, back to me.

In that instant, Brynner stepped in to her, slamming a blade into her stomach, then tearing it away. As he turned back, he sliced her elbow tendon and the one under her shoulder.

Black smoke gushed like a river from the gash in Ra-Ame's stomach.

I stomped on the heart and drove my dagger straight through it, pinning it to the sand below, and held it as the heart convulsed, bursting into black flames beneath my foot.

Ra-Ame ignored Brynner, lunging toward me, but he sliced her leg as she passed. She fell, lurching sideways into a rock. Her blind gaze never left me as she flailed her arms, throwing rocks and sand, nearly blinding me. And a stinging bolt of pain in my neck said she'd found her mark. I fell to the side, my hands on my neck, but no blood gushed. No wounds hung open.

She rolled over to hiss at Brynner like a cobra.

The world spun around me as I clasped my neck.

Brynner knelt over her and drove the dagger through her chest with the weight of his body.

Ra-Ame convulsed underneath him, dying a final death. One of her hands lay empty. In the other, she clasped the body of a common brown scorpion.

Too late, I recognized the choking panic in my throat. My breathing turned to whispering gasps, and my limbs convulsed. I fell over, unable to even shut my eyes against the sun, as a wall of darkness exploded from Ra-Ame.

And came down on me.

I never knew death. Only the burning feeling as the blackness worked its way into my eyes and my nose, under my fingernails.

"Grace." The look of horror on Brynner's face told me he'd seen what happened.

Held hostage in my own body, I rose. When my lips moved, it was not my voice that spoke. "You have taken something precious from me. And so I take from you. Grace Roberts will never know death. Your spirits will be forever separated. Or you will kill me, and her with me. Can you live like that, Death that Follows?"

Brynner dropped the blades, holding his palms up. "Let her go. Let her go, and you can kill me."

My lips curled into a smile. "I can do that at will already,

Death that Follows. And this body is beautiful, no? Such a shame about the scorpions. But I have learned many secrets. It is so simple to change how these shells behave." Like a wave of fresh water over me, I shivered, and my lips stopped swelling. My lungs stopped whistling with each breath. "There, it is done. I will never surrender her."

My body kicked the bag of weapons, spun, and came up holding a pine spear. "Kill me if you can."

I fought it, pushing against its will, which lay across me like an iron blanket. Brynner dodged my feet and hands, which now moved with deadly precision, wielding a spear so fluidly it made my mind dizzy, if not my body.

Brynner cycled through relics, dodging my thrusts, not moving with the speed and power I knew his toned body held. Because of me. Because he didn't want to hurt me. And that was the reason Ra-Ame had chosen me in the first place.

The heart of a Carson. I had it. And she had me.

He threw a cross, and a vial of holy water, and a sprig of pot, but I'd never been a Rastafarian. And that was the other reason she chose me. I never believed in anything, so there were no marks upon my psyche, no weapons that could drive her out.

Her spear flashed, overextending, and he caught her/me, pulling us to him. "Fight her. Fight her off."

And I did, pounding on the mental wall while I watched my own body relax against him. My lips opened. "It's working." What? "The orthodox cross. My parents took me . . ." My mouth lied to him instead of screaming a warning.

He reached for the chain around his neck, fumbling with the armor that kept it in place.

For one moment, his eyes left me.

In that second, my hand slipped downward. And drove the spruce shaft into him, right at the shoulder joint where we both knew he was vulnerable.

"Fool." My body kicked him over, while he clutched at his arm, trying to quell the bleeding. "Now you will be the first new sacrifice."

Brynner rolled onto his back, his eyes staring up at me in shock. In acceptance. He mouthed the words I'd always wanted to hear. Never from him, I told myself. Or only from him. "I love you."

My body froze, like a battering ram of ice had just clubbed Ra-Ame. I surged against her, feeling for the first time her pressure lift. How had he done it?

Not he.

We.

Because while I didn't pray to the cross, or kneel at a stone, or avoid bacon, there was one thing I *did* believe in. Love. "Again." My lips moved of my own accord, then my jaw bit down, filling my mouth with blood as I warred with the pharaoh's daughter.

He rose to one knee. "I love you, Grace."

And he *did*. I knew it the way I knew the sun rose in the East. I believed in it the way I believe in gravity and taxes. He had to. No other power could change a disaster like Brynner Carson into a man I—I loved. It had come upon me unawares, in disguise, but in plain sight. Like Ra-Ame herself.

The knowledge, the sheer elation poured through me, making me tingle from the tips of my toes to the top of my head. I was loved. Completely. Totally.

Black smoke poured from my mouth, tasting like I'd eaten roadkill for breakfast. With a final wail, Ra-Ame poured out of me into the light, scalded from within by the love that coursed from my heart, and burnt to ashes by the merciless sun.

Long after the last of the smoke left, I lay drained in the sand. Brynner's face, a pale gray, drove me to rise and drag myself to my purse.

One emergency call. A helicopter flight. Two units of blood and three dozen stitches later, the doctors came to me and said I wouldn't live the rest of my life alone. And I waited by his bedside, for him to wake.

41

BRYNNER

I woke to find Grace asleep by my hospital bed, and enough tubes and wires run into me to make Dale envious. I wanted to wake her, but each time I looked at her, the words died in my throat. I couldn't ever tell Grace how close I came to dying. How I heard my father calling me, welcoming me to the halls of the dead.

But I couldn't go. Not alone. Not without Grace. She'd never believe me if I told her. I loved her anyway. When I brushed the hair out of her eyes, they flickered open, and Grace threw herself onto me, doing her best to bust my stitches.

It was completely worth it. If I'd known that's how she would greet me, I would have gotten stabbed by an insane monster sooner.

We left the hospital together and hopped a plane to Portland as soon as the doctors let me. And for weeks, I didn't answer the phone, or the door. I testified by phone during Director Bismuth's court martial trial, then called Dale to let him know I really was quitting the BSI.

It wasn't that the dead didn't still need killing.

It was that I'd had enough death to make me appreciate life and the woman I wanted to live it with.

The morning Grace made me breakfast, I knew something was up. I never did work up the courage to tell her that she'd mistakenly used salt instead of sugar in the French toast, or that the crunchy bits in the omelet were eggshells, not bacon bits.

She led me to the spare bedroom, her warm hands over my eyes, her body pressed against my back. "Look."

On the spare bed, my armor and equipment lay, polished, repaired, replaced. I turned to her, wrapping one arm under hers and running my hand down her cheek. "I don't understand. I quit."

"In Chicago, there are reports of a co-org terrorizing one office tower in particular. No others. And only at night. The field team there is stumped." Grace kissed me. "How about being a freelance contractor for the BSI?"

Grace knew me, knew that while I loved curling up with her at the lake, I craved the hunt, the rescue. "I don't want to leave you."

"Don't be silly." Grace pushed away from me and opened the closet door. There, a second suit of armor. Lightweight, thin, built for speed and agility. "I'm going with you. You might need rescuing."

So we packed up our weapons and headed up to catch a

charter flight to Chicago. The weapons manifest had six new types of ammo Grace had created in her workshop, a sonic gun we thought might tear the armor off a Re-Animus, and an anti-depressant formula that put a smile on a stone statue.

What it didn't list was the love I honed every day with Grace, and every night when she lay in my arms. With the blades on my hips and Grace at my side, the dead didn't stand a chance.

J. C. Nelson, the author of the Grimm Agency novels, including *Wish Bound*, *Armageddon Rules*, and *Free Agent*, is a software developer and ex-beekeeper residing in the Pacific Northwest with family and a few chickens. Visit the author online at authorjcnelson.com.